Falkirk Council Library Services

This book is due for return on or before the last date indicated on the label. Renewals may be obtained on application.

Bo'ness 01506 778520	Falkirk 503605	Grangemouth 504690
Bonnybridge 503295	Mobile 506800	Larbert 503590
Denny 504242		Slamannan 851373

Home Library Service
Falkirk Library Basement
Hope Street, Falkirk
FK1 5AU
01324 506800

STAGESTRUCK

STAGESTRUCK

Peter Lovesey

WINDSOR
PARAGON

First published 2011
by Sphere
This Large Print edition published 2011
by AudioGO Ltd
by arrangement with
Little, Brown Book Group

Hardcover ISBN: 978 1 445 85836 4
Softcover ISBN: 978 1 445 85837 1

British Library Cataloguing in Publication Data available

Printed and bound in Great Britain by
MPG Books Group Limited

A NOTE FROM THE AUTHOR

This is a work of fiction. I have a deep affection for the Theatre Royal, Bath, which I hope is conveyed in these pages. The characters—with the possible exception of the grey lady—live only in my imagination and the shocking, scandalous and gruesome events have nothing to do with the true history of this great theatre, its management, staff and performers. Liberties were also taken in depicting the layout backstage, which I was privileged to visit on one of the regular tours.

Many sources have been consulted. In particular I wish to express my indebtedness to *The Theatre Royal at Bath* by William Lowndes (Redcliffe, Bristol, 1982) and *Past, Present, Future, A Recent History of the Theatre Royal Bath, 1979–2005* by Anna O'Callaghan (Bath, 2005), and to the files of the *Bath Chronicle* and its theatre correspondent, Christopher Hansford. Anyone wishing for an accurate account of the theatre should consult these experts, not me. For an insight into the Garrick's Head, nothing can beat a personal visit, but I also recommend *Bath Pubs* by Kirsten Elliott and Andrew Swift (Akeman Press, 2003).

Peter Lovesey
www.peterlovesey.com

CHAPTER ONE

'People keep asking me if I'm nervous.'

'Really?'

This week's star attraction gave a broad smile. 'Believe me, anyone who's played live to a million screaming fans on Copacabana Beach isn't going to lose sleep over this.'

'Right.'

'As if a first night in an itsy-bitsy provincial theatre is going to make Clarion Calhoun wet her pants.'

But the face told a different story. The woman waiting to apply the make-up watched the confidence vanish with the smile and spotted the tell-tale flexing of the muscles at the edge of the mouth. Clarion was outside her comfort zone. Acting was a different skill from pop singing. Because of her inexperience, she was getting special treatment from the Theatre Royal. Almost all professional actors do their own make-up. This one couldn't be trusted to create a simple nineteen-thirties look with nothing more technical than a Cupid's bow and kohl-lined eyes.

She was getting the nursemaiding in spades. 'You'll be a knockout. They love you, anyway. A lot of the actors who come through here have it all to prove. You've got it made.'

'My fan base, you mean?' Clarion looked better already. 'Every ticket sold, they tell me.'

'Right through the week. The management are over the moon.'

The dresser unscrewed a new jar of cold cream

1

and picked up a sponge. 'Your day make-up is gorgeous, but it won't be seen under the lights. Do you want to remove it yourself?'

'Go ahead. I'll think about my lines.'

Clarion meant the lines in the script, not her face. A few more of those were revealed as the cleanser did its work. She was past thirty and her days as a rock star were numbered. Time to revamp her career. She was playing Sally Bowles in a new production of *I Am a Camera*. With her name on the billing, it was almost guaranteed a transfer to London later in the year.

A thin layer of moisturiser went on.

'Remind me of your name,' Clarion said. A touch of humanity. They'd met before the dress rehearsal, but frequently the leads treated everyone backstage like furniture.

'Denise.'

'So, Denise, how long have you been doing this?'

'Working in theatre? Most of my adult life.'

'Here in Bath?'

'No, I've moved around. If I can be personal, your skin is marvellous.'

'It should be, all the money I spend on treatments. Is that the colour you're going to use on me?'

'The foundation.'

'I don't want to look as orange as that.'

'Trust me. You won't.'

'What is it—greasepaint?'

'Glycerine-based cream. It's going to feel dry. That's why I used a base of moisturiser.'

'I may sound like a beginner, but this isn't the first play I've been in. I was drama trained before I

2

got into the music scene or I wouldn't have taken this on. I always promised myself I'd get back on the stage.'

Denise passed no comment as she smoothed on the foundation, working it down the neck and as far as the cape.

'Do you want to put some on my front? I wear that really low gown in the second half and a little extra shadow in the right place would be all to the good.'

'Later. I'll finish your face first.' She did the shadowing and highlighting. Then she used a plump rouge mop to brush on some powder.

'May I see the result?' Clarion asked.

'Not yet, if you don't mind. Eyes and lips make all the difference.'

In another ten minutes Clarion was handed the mirror.

'Hey! Transformation. Sally Bowles.' She switched to her stage voice. 'How do you do, Sally? I'm terribly glad to meet you.'

*   *   *

There was also some nervousness in the audience. Towards the back of the stalls, Hedley Shearman was fingering his lips, trying not to bite his nails. The casting of Clarion Calhoun wasn't his doing. He gloried in the title of theatre director, yet the decision had been made over his head, by the board of trustees. Until now, he'd always had final approval of the casting, and it had more than once earned him certain favours. No such chance with this megastar, who treated him no better than a call boy. Each time she looked at him he was

3

conscious of his lack of height and his bald spot.

Clarion's name guaranteed bums on seats and a standing ovation from her fans, but Shearman dreaded the critics' verdict. He cared passionately about the Theatre Royal—almost as passionately as he cared about sex. In two hundred years all the great actors from Macready to Gielgud had graced this stage. This woman was expected to get by on that dubious asset known as celebrity. True, she was a singer playing a singer, but this was entirely an acting role. She'd learned her lines, and that was the best you could say for her. Speaking them with conviction was a difficulty that had become obvious in rehearsal.

He only hoped her glamour would dazzle the critics. A week with every seat sold, including matinees, was the pay-off, whatever they wrote.

The lights were dimmed and the excited buzz of voices stopped, replaced by a scratchy phonograph tune that nicely evoked Berlin in the thirties. The curtain rose on Fräulein Schneider's rooming house, tawdry, of its time and place: tall, tiled stove, pendulum clock, washstand, bed partly concealed by a curtain, Medici prints, wicker flower-stand, three-fold screen, sofa and chairs. The set designer was a professional, thank God, and so was the head of lighting. The single shaft of light on Isherwood focused attention for the speech that set the tone for the entire play. Preston Barnes, the actor playing Isherwood, had learned his craft at Stratford. Could he compensate for Clarion's wooden delivery? The irony was that *she* was supposed to be animated, while Preston cultivated the passivity of the camera.

The opening minutes couldn't have been

4

bettered. Preston's soliloquy was exquisitely done and so was the dialogue with the landlady. Yet Shearman couldn't ignore the fact that everything was just building up to the entrance of the real star.

Immense anticipation.

And there she was.

A burst of applause from her fans.

Give Clarion her due. She moved with poise. She had the figure, the strut, the sexuality of a nightclub singer, all the attributes of a Sally Bowles. Until she opened her mouth.

Shearman slid even lower in his seat, trying to tell himself his involvement made him hypercritical and no one else would notice. It could be worse—couldn't it? At least she was delivering the lines.

Others in the audience were shifting in their seats. Someone in the row ahead leaned to his companion and whispered in her ear. The restlessness was infectious. Movement from an audience so early in a play is unusual.

On stage, Clarion pulled a face.

Her mouth widened and brought creases to her cheeks. Her eyebrows popped up and ridges spread across her forehead.

Shearman sat up again.

Nothing in the script called for her to grimace like that. Sally Bowles was supposed to be in command, outspoken, a girl about town, out to impress, demanding whisky and soda when coffee was offered. Instead she was baring her teeth, staring towards the wings as if she needed help.

Stage fright?

You don't expect it on the professional stage, not in such extreme form. Her eyes bulged and she

5

was taking deep breaths.

Preston Barnes as Isherwood had spoken a line and Clarion needed to respond. She didn't. A voice from the wings tried to prompt her, but she appeared dumbstruck. Gasps were heard from the audience. Few things are more destructive to drama than an actor drying.

Barnes improvised a line to cover the silence. It brought no response from Clarion.

She put her hands to her face and clawed at her cheeks. Her make-up would be ruined, but that didn't seem to be a concern.

She was way out of character now. Nothing the other actors could do would rescue the scene. There was a bigger drama on stage.

And now Clarion screamed.

This wasn't a theatrical scream. It was piercing, gut-wrenching, horrible. The sound echoed through the theatre, shocking everyone in it, from backstage to the box office.

Someone had the good sense to lower the curtain.

Even the house lights coming on didn't bring relief. Behind the curtain more convulsive shrieks could be heard.

*　　　*　　　*

By the time Hedley Shearman got backstage, Clarion had been helped to her dressing room. Doubled forward in an armchair, she was still crying out as if in severe pain, the sound muffled by a towel pressed to her face. The room was full of people wanting to help and uncertain what to do. A St John Ambulance man was talking to

Clarion, but she was too distressed to answer. The man turned to Shearman and said, 'We should get her to hospital.'

To his credit the little theatre director rose to the challenge, saying he'd drive her to the Royal United himself. Aware of his other responsibility, to the shocked audience still out front, he asked if the understudy was ready to go on. He was told she was already getting into one of the Sally Bowles dresses and could be on stage inside five minutes. An announcement would be made to the audience that Clarion was unwell and unable to continue, but the play would resume shortly.

No one understood what was wrong. The entire theatre was awash with theories. An extreme form of stage fright? Food poisoning? Mental breakdown? Drugs? An allergic reaction?

Clarion's dresser Denise did her best to comfort the star in the back seat of the Jaguar as Shearman drove at speed to the hospital.

There, still clutching the towel to her face, Clarion was met by the triage team and rushed inside to be assessed.

*   *   *

Not long after, a doctor invited Shearman and Denise into a side room.

'She appears to have come into contact with some irritant that inflamed her skin. There's considerable damage to the face and neck. Did her role in the play call for anything unusual to touch her?'

Shearman shook his head. 'Nothing I'm aware of.'

7

'I'm thinking of special effects. Smoke, dry ice, any sort of vapour produced mechanically?'

'Absolutely not.'

'Do you know if she recently used a cosmetic that was new to her? Stage make-up, perhaps?'

Shearman, alarmed, turned to Denise. She reddened and shrugged. 'She didn't do her own make-up. I looked after her.'

'You never know with skin,' Shearman said, to close that avenue. 'What's all right for one person can produce a reaction in someone else.'

'We don't think it's allergic,' the doctor said. 'We'll get a dermatologist to look at her, but our first assessment is that these are acid burns.'

'*Acid?*' Shearman said, horrified. 'There's no acid in stage make-up.'

Denise, saucer-eyed, shook her head.

'I'm telling you what we found,' the doctor said. 'She may have to be transferred to the burns unit at Frenchay.'

'I can't understand this. It makes no sense at all.'

'It's not our job to make sense of it,' the doctor said. 'We deal with the injuries that are presented to us. All we want to find out is the likely source of the damage so that we give the right treatment.'

*   *   *

CLARION'S AGONY ON STAGE ran next morning's tabloid headline. The theatre was besieged by reporters, distressed fans and, it has to be said, ticket-holders wanting refunds. Upstairs in his office, Hedley Shearman was urgently conferring with Francis Melmot, the chairman of the theatre trust. Silver-haired and silver-tongued, Melmot, at

8

six foot eight, towered over the stumpy theatre manager.

'The latest is that she's being treated at Frenchay Hospital, where they have a burns unit,' Shearman said. 'The skin damage is severe, I'm sorry to say, and could be permanent.'

'Hedley, this is irredeemably dire,' Melmot said. 'How could it have possibly have happened?'

In the privacy of his office Shearman could be frank. 'The obvious explanation is that her skin reacted adversely to the make-up. The burning is all on her face, neck and upper body, the areas that were made up. She rubbed some of the stuff off with a towel and they're having that analysed.'

'You've spoken to the make-up person, of course?'

'Denise Pearsall.'

'She's a dresser, isn't she?'

'Yes, but she was specially assigned to do the whole thing, costume, make-up, confidence-giving. If you remember, you said Clarion must be feather-bedded.'

'Oh, I'm responsible, am I?'

'Denise is in shock. Can't think how it happened. She used her own make-up on Clarion. She's been with us for years, as you know.'

'What was it—theatrical make-up?'

'The same stuff they all use. Tried and tested, used in theatres up and down the country.'

'But was it new?'

'Well, yes. It's not good practice to use something that's been in contact with another actor.'

'So it's possible it was a bad batch—the fault of the manufacturer?' For Melmot, this was all about

9

apportioning blame.

'I find that hard to believe. The hospital were talking of acid burns. Acid isn't used in cosmetics. I can understand something being wrong with the mix, only not enough to cause such a violent reaction. Denise is devastated.'

'If this disaster is down to her, I'm not surprised,' Melmot said.

Shearman didn't like the way this was heading. 'I didn't say it was Denise's fault. She's a trusted member of the team.'

'Someone is responsible. You say she's devastated. I'm devastated, too. We could find ourselves being sued for a small fortune. A large fortune if Clarion is permanently scarred. She's a mega earner and no doubt she had contracts lined up for months ahead.'

'It's too early to talk of legal action.'

'It isn't. This could bring us down, Hedley. I'm bound to report to the trustees.'

'They'll have read the papers like the rest of us.'

'I must still inform them properly.'

Shearman's world was imploding. He had status in this theatre, the best job he'd ever had. Sensing he was about to be unfairly blamed, he surprised himself with the force of his anger. 'I'd like the board to know I was bulldozed into this. I didn't like the idea of engaging the bloody woman. She's no actor. Certain people insisted she was box office. It couldn't go wrong, they said, but it has, spectacularly.'

Melmot chose to ignore the outburst. 'When the make-up woman—'

'The dresser.'

'When she saw Clarion in the dressing room

10

before the show, was she in any discomfort?'

'No—and she was fine while she was waiting to go on. The first signs of anything going wrong were on stage.'

'How long after she was made up?'

'Twenty minutes, at least. If there was going to be a reaction, why was it delayed? I'm mystified.'

'Have you impounded the make-up?'

Shearman clapped his hand to his head. 'God, you're right. I must see to that. I'll speak to Denise. We'll confiscate everything that was used last night and lock it in the safe.'

His phone beeped. He snatched it up and said without waiting to hear who was on, 'I told you I'm in a meeting.'

The switchboard girl said, 'The police are downstairs, sir.'

'The police? That's all we need.'

Melmot was already moving to the door. 'I must leave you to it, old man. Urgent calls to make.'

CHAPTER TWO

Hedley Shearman's job was all about telling others what to do. He prided himself on his social skills. He told the police in a calm, considerate way that they weren't needed.

The senior of the two uniformed officers, a sergeant whose bearing suggested he was nothing less than a chief constable, said, 'It's not your call, sir.'

'What does that mean?'

'We don't work for you.'

11

'I'm aware of that, but this is my theatre. I'm the director here.'

The sergeant said to his female colleague, 'He's the director here. We're in the right place, then.'

It sounded like sarcasm. Already under strain, Shearman said with more force than the first time, 'But you're not needed.'

'Like London's Noble Fire Brigade?'

'What?'

'Belloc.'

'I beg your pardon.'

The sergeant chanted, '"Until Matilda's Aunt succeeded in showing them they were not needed."'

'I'm a busy man.'

'Then permit me to introduce Constable Reed. Reed can write at speed, so Reed is needed. Oh yes, there is a need for Reed.'

The young policewoman looked at Shearman and winked, as if asking him to make allowance. To confirm that this was for real, she had opened a notebook and was writing in it.

'And I'm Sergeant Dawkins,' the ponderous introduction continued, 'in pursuit of the truth, and as the poet said, "Beauty is truth, truth beauty, that is all ye know on earth, and all ye need to know." So I'm needed also. Dawkins and Reed, addressing the need. We're here about the occurrence last night.'

Out of all the verbiage one word struck home, and to Shearman's ear it carried dangerous overtones. 'Occurrence?'

Sergeant Dawkins said, 'In your theatre, on your stage.' Then he had the cheek to reach into one of the model stage sets on Shearman's bookcase and

12

touch the figure of an actor, tipping it over, face down.

Shearman was incensed. He wanted to tell this smart-arse to go to hell, but you don't say that to a policeman. 'You didn't have to do that. I know what you're talking about and I wouldn't call it an occurrence.'

'What would you call it, then?'

'I don't know. It didn't amount to anything.'

'An incident?'

'Nothing like that. One of the cast was taken ill, that's all.'

'Occurrence.' Dawkins made a horizontal gesture with his right hand like a cricket umpire signalling. Then he repeated the movement six inches higher. 'Incident.' Then higher again. 'Offence. Occurrence, incident, offence.'

'It's not an *offence*, for God's sake. Anyway, we're dealing with it ourselves.'

'I bet you are.'

Blatant insolence. If this man had been on the theatre staff he wouldn't have lasted a moment longer. 'It's the responsible thing to do,' Shearman said.

'Dealing with it?'

'Of course. That's my job.'

'And we investigate. That's our job.'

'But I didn't send for you.'

Sergeant Dawkins parted his lips in a grin that revealed sharp canines. 'If we waited to be invited, we wouldn't get out at all.'

Shearman felt as if he'd strayed into a play by Samuel Beckett. 'So on whose authority are you here?'

'Take your pick.'

13

He hesitated, wary of a trap. 'My pick of what?'

'Avon and Somerset Police. The Home Office. Her gracious Majesty.'

Either the man was a crank, or he was trying to wind Shearman up for a purpose. 'Who, precisely, sent you?'

'Are you thinking we came of our own volition? Are you thinking of us as ambulance chasers?'

Shearman gave up. The whole conversation was surreal.

'Rest assured,' Dawkins said. 'We're not ambulance chasers. We're at the receiving end.'

'There's no point in this. I don't follow what you're saying.'

'We don't follow either.'

'Follow what?'

'Ambulances.'

'It wasn't me who mentioned ambulances.'

'We follow up. Follow up occurrences. Or incidents. Or offences. When an occurrence is deemed to be an offence you really do have something to be concerned about. Any unexplained injury of a serious nature that shows up in A & E gets referred to us and we follow up. Were you present at the occurrence yourself?'

That word again. Shearman's mind was made up. He refused to submit to interrogation by these two. They had to be challenged here and now. 'This has gone far enough. I intend to speak to your senior officer.'

Dawkins was unmoved. 'You'll be wasting your time and ours, sir. There's a chain of command and it's cast-iron solid, from the chief constable all the way down to PC Reed. We're ordinary coppers doing our job and our superiors back us every

14

interview of the way. So let's get down to question and answer, shall we? Did you see what happened last night?'

A straight question, and no mention of an occurrence. Perhaps it signalled a change of approach. Reluctantly, Shearman gave Dawkins the benefit of the doubt. The wise option might be to get this over quickly and send them on their way. 'I'm always in the audience on first nights.'

Constable Reed continued making notes, her hand moving at prodigious speed.

'You don't have to write all this down.'

'You're a witness,' she said. 'You just confirmed it, sir.'

'But nothing of a criminal nature took place.'

As if Shearman had just sprung the trap, Sergeant Dawkins said, 'Who mentioned crime? Not one of us. A crime is an offence.'

Constable Reed seemed to be putting every word in her notebook.

Shearman made a huge effort to be reasonable. 'Look, everyone here is extremely concerned about what happened and I'm going to carry out a rigorous enquiry.'

'So are we,' Dawkins said. 'Rigorous and vigorous. And so are the press by the looks of it. Have you seen all the newshounds downstairs?'

'That means nothing. It's a matter of public interest when a celebrity of Miss Calhoun's stature is unable to go on. Nobody's broken the law.'

'We don't know that, do we—or do we?' the sergeant said, his eyebrows arching. 'She's in hospital with burns.'

'You don't have to tell me,' Shearman said. 'I drove her to A & E myself. In the theatre we're a

15

family. We look after our own, and, believe me, we're taking this seriously, but I want to spare Clarion the added distress of a police investigation. Surely you understand that?'

Constable Reed looked up from her notes. 'You're speaking rather fast. Would you mind repeating the bit after "taking this seriously"?'

Unable to contain his annoyance any longer, Shearman said, 'There's nothing worth writing down. All of this is pointless. Please leave by the side door rather than the front, where the press are.'

'Not before we've finished,' Dawkins said. 'If this ever comes to court, we'll all be obliged to PC Reed for taking notes.'

The reminder of the process of law subdued Shearman again. 'What else do you need to know?'

'When were you first aware that Miss Calhoun was in trouble?'

'That's self-evident. When she missed her line and started screaming.'

'Did you see her before the show?'

'Personally, no. I was meeting some VIPs. Others who saw her said she was in good spirits.'

'Spirits may have been her undoing.'

'Just what are you hinting at?'

'Spirits of this or spirits of that. You never know what chemicals they use in the cosmetics industry. Did she do her own make-up?'

'No. She's not experienced in the theatre, so we provided a dresser for her, and that's who looked after her.'

'The make-up?'

'Yes.'

'A dresser dresses,' Dawkins said. 'I know about

16

dressers. Constable Reed thinks a dresser is an item of furniture for displaying crockery, but this isn't my first time in a theatre and I know dressers don't do make-up.'

'You'd better revise your ideas,' Shearman said. 'This dresser was specially asked to assist Clarion.'

'With her make-up? When was it applied?'

'Some time before curtain up. I wasn't there.'

'Have you spoken to this dresser?'

'Yes, I have.'

'I expect she has a name.'

'I'd rather not say. I don't attach blame to anyone.'

'Blame?' Dawkins picked up on the word as if Shearman had condemned himself. 'Are we starting to play the blame game?'

'I said I'm not blaming anyone.'

'All the same, we need the name.'

He told a white lie. 'It escapes me.'

Dawkins wasn't willing to let it pass. 'You said you were a family. You must know her.'

This interrogation had become a minefield. 'Do you have any conception how many are employed in a theatre? Too many to know all the names.'

'How do you address this member of your family?' Dawkins gave the toothy smile again. 'We may look like plodding policepersons, but we are not incapable of discovering the identity of the dresser who looked after the female lead.'

Shearman sighed and gave in. 'Denise Pearsall.'

'Would you kindly spell that for PC Reed?'

He did so.

'And is Ms Denise Pearsall available for interview?'

'I can't tell you.'

17

'But as the director you can arrange it.'

'Now?' Shearman reached for the phone. He'd given up the struggle. Passing these two on to Denise would come as a massive relief.

Dawkins lifted a finger and moved it like a windscreen wiper. 'Not until we've finished with you. Was Clarion Calhoun the popular choice for this play?'

Reluctantly Shearman removed his hand from the phone. 'It depends what you mean. Her fans were ecstatic. We sold every ticket in advance.'

'Let us be frank. The lady is not famous for being an actress,' Dawkins said as if he knew about casting. 'How did the rest of the cast feel about performing with a pop singer?'

'I'm not aware of any hurt feelings. She's pre-eminent in her field.'

'As a singer. Does she sing in the play?'

Shearman gave an impatient sigh. 'This isn't *Cabaret*, for God's sake, it's *I Am a Camera*. Clarion plays a nightclub performer and all she sings are a couple of lines in the third act.'

'She has to do some acting, then?'

Explaining the basics was wearisome to Shearman. He said with sarcasm these plodding policepersons wouldn't appreciate, 'Quite a lot of acting.'

'So you're telling me no one had any reason to dislike her?'

This was heading into dangerous territory. 'What are you suggesting—that she was injured deliberately? That would be outrageous. We're a theatre. We work as a team to produce a top quality production, the cast, the backstage crew, the front-of-house, the director. We're too damned busy to go in for petty feuds.'

'So it's a team? Just now you were calling it a family.'

'Same thing.'

Dawkins shook his head slowly. 'Not so, if I may be so bold.'

This sergeant had the trick of making courtesies sound like insults. Shearman stared back and said nothing.

'There are regulars like yourself and the scene-shifters and Denise the dresser, am I right? I can see how you think of them as family. And then you've got the actors who get replaced each time you put on a new play. With respect, they're not family. They're a team.'

'If you're trying to say it's a case of them and us, you're wrong. We all have a common interest in the show succeeding.'

'Getting back to my question about whether anyone disliked Miss Clarion Calhoun, did you pick up any untoward vibrations?'

'*Vibrations?*'

'Bad vibes?' Constable Reed translated for him.

They both looked to Shearman for a response.

'No, and I don't care for this line of questioning. Whatever went wrong last night, it was not deliberate.'

'How do you know?' Dawkins asked.

'Couldn't have been.'

'Why?'

'Because I'm in charge and it's my job to know the people here, call them a family, or a team, or whatever you choose. No one in this theatre would stoop to the sort of mindless attack you seem to be suggesting and I must insist you say not another

19

word about it. If the press get a sniff there'll be hell to pay.'

'The press are not slow, Mr Shearman. They've sniffed and got the scent and are in full cry.'

'What do you mean by that?'

'They'll be writing tomorrow's headlines as we speak.'

'They'll have it wrong, then.'

'Which is why we need to find out what really happened. I suggest you exit stage left and cue the dresser.'

*   *   *

The two police officers met Denise Pearsall over coffee in the Egg café, at the far end of the theatre block. The name of the place had nothing to do with the menu. It was taken from the shape of the children's theatre it adjoined. The café was much used by mothers and toddlers and should have been a relaxing setting, but Denise was too strung out to touch her coffee. Probably in her forties, she was red-haired and pretty, with brown eyes dilated by fear. Or guilt. She stared in horror at PC Reed, waiting with pen poised, and then Dawkins. The first thing she said was, 'Have we met before?'

'Not to my uncertain knowledge,' the sergeant said in his stilted style. 'Have you *seen* me before? Very likely. I'm easy to spot in my uniform and I'm often around the streets of Bath. Have I seen you before? If I had, you would be known to the police, and you don't want that. Are you going to tell us about last night?'

'I've worked here for six years and never experienced anything so awful as this,' she said,

20

plucking at her neck, 'and I can't blame anyone else. I did Clarion's make-up myself. Most actors do their own, but she hasn't worked in the theatre for years, if at all. She was the female lead, she needed help and I was asked to give it.'

'Was she the only one you worked on?'

She nodded. 'The others are perfectly capable of doing their own make-up. My responsibilities begin and end with Clarion. I'll deliver some costumes to other dressing rooms because I work for the wardrobe department, but I was asked to take care of her personally.'

'Who by?'

'Mr Melmot, the chairman. Of course, the director of the play talked to me about the look he wanted for her.'

'Who is the director?'

'Sandy Block-Swell. He wasn't there last night.'

'The director missing?'

'Not missing. He watched the dress rehearsal and took a plane to America.'

'To escape the critics?'

'No, he said he was well satisfied. He's a busy man. He has a film to direct in Hollywood.'

PC Reed looked up from her notebook. 'Would you say the name again?'

'Block-Swell, with a hyphen between the "k" and the "s".'

Dawkins said, 'A hyphen in one's name is transforming. I could call myself Sergeant Daw-Kins and it has a certain ring to it. You could be Ms Pear-Sall. Imposing. No such refinement for someone with the name of Reed. You said he talked to you about the look. What is the look?'

'The thirties. For the women, Cupid's bows,

dark eyes and the green fingernails for Sally. The men are clean-shaven and part their hair in the centre. Nothing too difficult. Sandy made the decisions. The leading men, Preston and Mark, as Christopher and Fritz, are very experienced and so is the woman playing Fräulein Schneider. Then there are Clive and Natalia and Mrs Watson, all well capable of looking after themselves.'

'One moment, madam,' Sergeant Dawkins said.

She was startled. 'What's the matter?'

'These names are meaningless to Constable Reed and me. We haven't seen the play.'

'I'm so sorry.' Denise turned bright red. 'There are three male roles and four female. I was explaining why I worked on Sally.'

'Who is this Sally?'

'Sally Bowles, the character played by Clarion.'

'Understood,' Dawkins said with a force that made Denise jerk back in her chair. 'Sally is Clarion, or should I say Clarion is Sally?'

'Yes.'

'For simplicity . . .' He paused, insisting on a response.

'Yes?'

'For simplicity, let's use their real names.'

As if she was catching this policeman's pedantry, Denise said, 'I doubt if her real name is Clarion. She's a show person, like Madonna.'

'Or Beyoncé,' PC Reed said to Dawkins, taking the baton and happy to run with it. 'Duffy, Lady Gaga, Little Boots.'

'Clarion will do,' Dawkins said. 'I don't need to know her real name.'

PC Reed said, 'But you just said let's use—'

'Enough.' He stopped her, and turned back to

22

Denise. 'What did you use for make-up—greasepaint?'

'No, that's hardly ever used in the modern theatre. It's too heavy and oily. The basic foundation, moisturiser, cream liners, rouge and blusher, powder and the usual liners for eyes and lips. Professional brands made from the best materials. They shouldn't produce a reaction, certainly nothing like what happened last night.'

'Shouldn't, wouldn't or couldn't,' Dawkins said, and he seemed to be talking to himself.

Denise looked ready to burst into tears. It wouldn't take much more of this abrasive questioning. In fact she was doing more than her interrogator to bring a semblance of structure to the interview. 'Well, if an actor suffers from acne it can get inflamed, but Clarion had a healthy complexion.'

PC Reed looked up from her notes. 'Some people have sensitive skin.'

'Allergies, yes,' Denise said, 'but she'd have known. She'd have told me, wouldn't she?' Uncertainty clouded her face and her hand clutched at her throat again. 'Besides, we had the dress rehearsal on Sunday and she was perfectly all right.'

'Dress rehearsal?' Dawkins said.

'Sunday afternoon.'

'With all the warpaint on?'

She looked pained again, but didn't take issue. 'That's what makes this so hard to understand. If there was going to be a reaction it should have happened then.'

'Except . . .'

'What?'

23

'If you used something different last night.'

'I didn't. All the pots and sticks were freshly opened, but exactly the same brand. We've used it for years in this theatre and never had any problems.'

'It was Clarion who had the problem,' Dawkins said.

'That's what I meant.' She sank her face into her hands and sobbed. 'Oh dear, I feel dreadful about it.'

*   *   *

The damage to Clarion's face was referred the same day to the head of Bath's CID, Detective Superintendent Peter Diamond, a man well used to dramas, but not of the theatrical sort. He wasn't by any stretch of the imagination a theatre-goer. He was already putting up barriers.

'We're in danger of getting ahead of ourselves, aren't we, ma'am?' he said to Georgina Dallymore, the assistant chief constable. 'How do we know it wasn't an accident?'

'There are grounds for suspicion,' she said, bringing her lips together in a way that didn't invite debate. 'I'm not proposing a full-scale investigation yet, but we must be primed and ready to spring into action. If this *is* a crime, it's a particularly nasty one. The poor woman may be scarred for life.'

'As bad as that?'

'So the papers say. In case you're about to remind me that you specialise in murder, I must tell you that this is a kind of death.'

'In what way?'

24

'The end of her show-business career. She's very well known.'

He nodded, thinking she was making a meal out of this. 'Even I've heard of Clarion Calhoun. Daft name, but you don't forget it.'

'She's brilliant at what she does. It's not my kind of singing, but I can't deny her talent. The tabloid press are out in force. If there was foul play, we must get on to it before they do. We can't tag along behind.'

Pressure as always, he thought. One of these days she'll tell me to take my time over a case. And pigs might fly.

He hadn't yet fathomed Georgina's interest in the matter. She was talking as if she had a personal stake.

'What's Clarion saying?' he asked. 'Does she blame anyone?'

'She's refusing to be interviewed. The official line is that she's in no state to receive visitors. Her lawyers have brought in a private security firm to guard the hospital room.'

'Lawyers are involved already?'

'Anything like this and they home in like sharks. They'll sue the theatre for millions if it can be held responsible.'

'The theatre can't afford millions. Are they insured?'

'I hope so, or Bath may end up with no theatre at all.'

Even Diamond regarded that as not to be contemplated. He'd survive, but the city would be a poorer place.

Georgina said, as if reading his thoughts. 'To me, it would be a personal loss.'

25

He lifted an eyebrow.

'I joined the BLOGs this year,' she said.

'Really?' he said, not impressed. 'Rather you than me, putting your private life on the internet.'

'Not blogging,' she said. 'Singing. The Bath Light Operatic Group. You know I've been in various choirs. Well, I thought I might go solo this year, in a small way. I'm hoping to get a part in *Sweeney Todd*, their annual musical. They take over the Theatre Royal for a week in September.'

That was the hidden agenda, then. The BLOGs could not be deprived of their week on the professional stage. Diamond had a vision of Georgina as Mrs Lovett, the pie lady. He did well to keep his face straight.

She continued, 'If, God forbid, the dear old theatre were to shut down, we'd all be devastated.'

'It won't come to that,' he said in an automatic response.

She said through her teeth, 'It had better not. I hope you can steer a way through this mess.'

'Me, ma'am?'

'It won't be easy.'

He could see that. A victim unwilling to speak. An injury of uncertain origin. And a potential lawsuit. 'Whoever takes it on,' he said, meaning anyone except himself, 'getting started won't be easy. Everyone's going to be on their guard.'

'Uniform managed to get some interviews at the theatre this morning.'

'That's something, then. Who did we send?'

'Sergeant Dawkins.'

Diamond's face creased as if caught by a sudden Arctic gust. 'Him, of all people? That's not good.'

'What's the matter with Dawkins?'

26

'How long have you got? Five minutes in his company would tell you. He keeps asking to join CID. He thinks it's personal each time I turn him down.'

'And is it?'

Diamond blew a soft raspberry. 'He'd be a nightmare.'

Georgina said, 'My contacts with him have always been agreeable. In my estimation he's a man of culture.'

In Georgina's estimation most policemen were not cultured, and some were uncouth, Peter Diamond more than most.

'Opinionated.'

'I don't hold that against him. But enough of Dawkins. It's your case from now on. Handle it with kid gloves, Peter.'

His case? This wasn't how she'd started. Hadn't she talked about being primed and ready to spring?

'I'd rather not. Theatre people aren't my cup of tea.' How feeble was that? he berated himself as the words came out. Working in a theatre is your worst nightmare. Tell her there's no way you're getting lumbered. But he was too late.

'They're very friendly,' she said.

'That's half the problem. I'll delegate.'

'What?'

'A good opportunity for one of my more experienced people.'

'No.' A flat, unqualified negative. 'I want you for this, Peter.'

He changed tack. 'I'll call in forensics, then.'

She gave a gasp of disapproval. 'We're not being as obvious as that. The make-up is being analysed

27

in the hospital lab. There was a towel Clarion pressed to her face after she left the stage. Quite a lot of the greasepaint, or whatever she was wearing, rubbed off. They need to know if it was contaminated in some way, so that they can give the right treatment. We'll find out soon enough.'

'It's strange,' he said, getting drawn in, in spite of all his misgivings.

'What is?'

'If the make-up was responsible, why didn't it hurt her when it was first put on? She got on the stage before the pain kicked in. She must have been made up—what?—ten minutes earlier. Twenty? If it was acid, or something, you'd expect her to have been screaming long before she made her entrance.'

'It is rather hard to understand,' Georgina said.

'To me it sounds more like an allergic reaction that took time to develop.'

'If that's all it was, we can breathe again. I hope you're right, Peter. But can a skin allergy be as violent as that? Does it actually burn the flesh?'

CHAPTER THREE

There were lunchtimes when Diamond escaped from Manvers Street police station and found sanctuary in places where no one would bother his head about targets and budget reports and activity-based costing. The city of Bath had enough pubs to suit all his moods, from the Old Green Tree, sedate as a private club with its home cooking and wood panelling, to the garish Hobgoblin, where the boneshaking beat of heavy metal was enough to drive out anybody's demons. Today he'd decided on the Garrick's Head, adjoining the Theatre Royal. A couple of beers with the backstage lads would be an agreeable way to check Georgina's story.

Originally—in about 1720—the building had been a private house, the home of Beau Nash, the Master of Ceremonies who made the city fashionable. It became a drinking house in 1805 when the theatre was built next door. Outside, a bust of the actor David Garrick dignifies the façade, but Diamond wasn't looking upwards. He stepped in, ordered his pint of British Red and took it to the black sofa under the window. The dark wood panelling, board floor and traditional fireplace fitted his expectation of what a public bar should be. He didn't care for patterned wallpaper and fitted carpets. Even better, someone had left the *Daily Telegraph* on the sofa, so he opened it and read about the 'indisposition' of the star of *I Am a Camera*. Restrained, even by *Telegraph* standards. The tabloids no doubt trumpeted Clarion's agony scream by scream.

He hadn't yet briefed his team. Truth to tell, he wasn't confident he had the facts straight. Illusion and special effects were the stock-in-trade of theatres, so he was wary of anything that happened on a stage in front of an audience, even when it was unscripted. Several hundred theatre-goers believed they'd witnessed an acutely painful and distressing incident and probably they had, but it couldn't be taken as fact without investigation. Clarion's burns were real according to the hospital reports, yet the way they had been inflicted gave

29

cause for uncertainty. If, as everyone supposed, the make-up had caused the damage, why hadn't she screamed in pain at the time it was applied, or immediately after?

His other concern was the possibility of fraud. By all accounts, Clarion the pop singer was on the skids and looking for alternative employment. She'd been hired by the theatre to play a nightclub singer. Typecasting, you might say, and a one-off. Did anyone expect she would go on to a second career in acting? As things had turned out, she'd done the minimum of acting and was expected to sue the theatre for a huge sum, enough for a long and comfortable retirement. Of course the scarring would need to be permanent to convince a court. A grim possibility: had she injured herself for the prospect of a multi-million-pound settlement?

Two conversations were in progress and one was getting interesting. Diamond put a hand over his ear to block out the woman at the next table talking about last night's *EastEnders* and tried instead to listen to the man on a bar stool in dialogue with the barmaid.

'It's obvious she's deeply troubled.'

He heard the barmaid say, 'I wouldn't know.'

'You work here, love, so you can't ignore it.'

'Try me. She hasn't been in for a drink.'

'Don't be like that,' the man said. 'Personally, I find the whole thing heartbreaking. She's there on stage and this gorgeous man in one of the upper boxes seems to be giving her the come-on, so she tries to signal that she's interested. In fact she's a lot more than interested. She's practically shinning up the curtain to get at him. And this meanie doesn't even ask her out. He cuts her dead, so in

30

desperation . . . we both know what she did.'

'If you want to believe it.'

'Now, come on. It's common knowledge round here. Do you know which door she used?'

'Door? Oh, I get you. No, and I haven't asked.'

'It may be the one behind you. I couldn't stay in the job if I were you.'

'It doesn't bother me.'

'If you saw her, it would.'

'But I haven't.'

'Never smelt jasmine around the bar?'

The girl laughed. 'You get all sorts of smells in this place. Why, is jasmine what she uses?'

'Exclusively. I've smelt it myself.'

'Where?'

'In the corridor behind the royal circle.'

Curiosity got the better of Diamond. He turned in his chair. 'I couldn't help overhearing what you're saying. This woman you're talking about. Who is she?'

'I wouldn't call her a woman if I were you,' the man said.

'I misheard, then.'

'The grey lady,' the man said, smoothing his tie and treating Diamond to a dazzling smile. He didn't fit Diamond's image of a scene-shifter, but he seemed to know what he was talking about. 'She's our theatre ghost.'

'Ah.' Spooks didn't interest Diamond, and the letdown he felt must have been obvious.

'Don't look so disbelieving,' the man said. 'She's real enough. We know precisely when she topped herself and where.'

'Tell him, then,' the barmaid said, and winked at Diamond. 'Pretend you're shaking in your shoes.'

31

The man said, 'She strung a rope over a door right here in the Garrick's Head and hanged herself, in the year 1812.'

'And came back as a ghost?'

'Any number of people have seen her. Are you old enough to remember Anna Neagle? Probably not, if I'm any judge. Dame Anna had her feet on the ground if ever an actor did. She was playing in something in the nineteen-seventies and she and the entire cast saw the grey lady in the upper box, stage right, just as the curtain rose. Imagine that.'

'They probably did.'

The barmaid cackled with laughter.

'Be like that,' the man said in an injured tone. 'If you don't want to know, why ask me?' This had turned personal and he was ruffled.

Diamond gave an honest answer. 'Just now I thought you were talking about Clarion Calhoun.'

'That poor creature? There's nothing spooky about her. I shouldn't say this, but the accident is a blessing in disguise. She was dreadful in rehearsal.'

The barmaid said, 'Titus, that's unfair.'

Titus ignored her. His focus was sharply on Diamond. 'Are you a fan, then? Without wishing to offend, you don't look like one.'

Diamond was well practised at giving nothing away about himself. 'I was just reading about it in the paper. They say she's in hospital and receiving treatment for burns, so it must be serious.'

'Yes, I shouldn't have been flippant. No one wishes that on her. A visitor, are you?'

'To the Garrick's Head, yes.'

'I thought I hadn't seen you before. I'm Titus O'Driscoll, dramaturge.'

'Peter Diamond.' He played the last word over

in his head. 'What's that—dramaturge?'

'Consultant on the theory and practice of writing drama.' Titus O'Driscoll paused for that to be savoured and for Diamond to volunteer more about himself, which he didn't. 'Do you have any theatrical connections, Peter?'

Everything up to now suggested that the man was gay and interested in finding out if Diamond was. He had himself to blame for getting on first-name terms. 'No. I came in for a drink, that's all. Were you in the audience last night?'

There was a disdainful sniff from the dramaturge. 'I took a squint at the dress rehearsal and decided to pass my time more productively in here.'

'But it's clear you know what goes on in the theatre.'

The barmaid said, 'And how! It keeps him going.'

Titus gave Diamond a sharp look. 'You're not press, by any chance?'

'Lord, no.'

'It was panic stations this morning,' Titus said. 'Absolute mayhem. The police were here, would you believe? Hedley Shearman, our theatre director, was having kittens.'

'Why? Is he responsible?'

'Quite the opposite. He didn't want the Clarion woman playing on his stage, but they twisted his arm, saying that bringing in a pop star was a sure way to sell tickets. And now he's having to make a show of sympathy for her whilst bracing himself for the lawsuit to come.'

'Who did the arm-twisting?'

'The trust. Certain of them, anyway. You know

33

how theatres work? Most of them are run as charitable trusts and usually they keep at arm's length, leaving the artistic decisions to the people who know, but if two or three individuals get together and want to wield power, they can. After a rather indifferent season, the pressure was on for a commercial success, so they leaned on Hedley to revive this clunky old play and give Clarion the star part. And to be fair it looked as if it was going to pay off. The pre-production publicity was sensational.'

'They'll be regretting it now.'

'Too right they will. The box office is under siege with people returning tickets.'

'The show's continuing, is it?'

'With the understudy, Gisella, yes. She's a far better actor than Clarion, but nobody cares. It's the end of the Theatre Royal.'

The barmaid said, 'Don't be so melodramatic, Titus. It hasn't burned down, or anything.'

'It may as well have.'

'He's like that,' she said to Diamond. 'Never looks on the bright side. When the *Blues Brothers* was on he was telling everybody they'd bring the house down, literally.'

'It was only thanks to me that it remained standing,' Titus said. 'I was responsible for those notices in the foyer: "Due to the historic nature of this building kindly refrain from stamping." My forethought saved us, without a doubt.'

'Getting back to last night's accident,' Diamond said, 'does anyone know the cause?'

'If you ask me,' Titus said, 'it's open to suspicion.'

'Go on.'

'Well, she was hopeless in the part and she knew it, and now she's out of it and planning to sue.'

'But there's no argument about what happened, is there? She's in hospital, so the injury must be real.'

'That's for the doctors to decide,' Titus said.

'Don't you believe it?'

'I believe this much: she's displaying symptoms of some sort and the screaming was very convincing and the hospital are taking it seriously.'

'By "symptoms" you mean the skin damage?'

'Whatever that amounts to.'

'It must be serious, for her to be kept in hospital,' Diamond said, doing his best to keep this discussion going. 'How do you get skin damage on the stage? I suppose it's down to the make-up.'

Titus said in an interested tone, 'Do you know about make-up, Peter?'

'Not at all.' Diamond had walked into that. He wasn't homophobic and he didn't want to raise false expectations. 'Hardly anything. I'm saying it's a possible cause, no more.'

'You could be right if something like chilli powder was mixed in with the foundation.'

'Chilli powder?' the barmaid shrieked in disbelief.

'I don't know for certain,' Titus said. 'Some irritant that would itch and bring her face up in blotches and make it impossible for her to continue.'

'I'm speechless,' the barmaid said. 'How could she possibly get chilli powder in her make-up?'

'Deliberately. She was looking for some reason to drop out of the play so she mixed it in herself. Unfortunately for her, the ingredients reacted

35

badly and caused the burning.'

'If it was self-inflicted, she'll have no claim against the theatre,' Diamond pointed out.

The barmaid laughed again. 'There you go, Titus. You've proved yourself wrong.'

Diamond didn't gloat. He'd already decided Titus might be a useful ally. Whatever his duties as the dramaturge amounted to, he appeared to have some status in the theatre. There was one small concern, the risk of raising unreal expectations. 'We were just exploring theories. What Titus was saying sounds possible.'

'You see?' Titus seized on it at once. 'When people listen carefully, they discover truth in my remarks. Peter, how would you like to join me on a ghost hunt?'

'The grey lady?' He gave a token smile, about to turn the offer down. 'Inside the theatre, you mean?' Instinctively he baulked at the prospect and it wasn't the ghost that troubled him. Old reactions were stirring, a profound resistance to stepping inside the place. Yet as a professional he knew he ought to take up this chance. 'Would they allow us in?'

'My dear, I'm on the strength. I can take you in.'

He turned a deaf ear to the 'my dear' and swallowed the rest of his beer and with it some of his anxiety. 'All right, Titus. You're on.'

The barmaid had seen all this with amusement and drawn her own conclusion.

'Mind how you go,' she warned Diamond. 'Watch out for things that go bump.'

Titus led the way outside, left into Saw Close and through one of the arched entrances to the theatre foyer. Inside, people were queuing at the box office on the left, although whether to buy tickets or return them was not clear. Various others, probably press, filled most of the remaining space, looking bored. With a curt, 'Do you mind?' Titus made a beeline for the steps to the royal circle entrance. He had such an air of authority that no one challenged him or took photos, and no one gave Diamond a second look.

If they had, they would have seen a face taut with stress.

Titus tapped out a code on the digital lock and pushed the door open. 'I'll begin by showing you the corridor where she's often been sighted.'

Diamond followed, deeply uncomfortable. The magic of theatre had always eluded him. His mother had never tired of telling friends and family how she'd taken the children to a theatre in Llandudno for a birthday treat only to have young Peter make a scene of his own even before the curtain went up. It wasn't as if it had been *Dracula*; it was a seaside variety show. He'd run out of the theatre and couldn't be persuaded to go back in. Years later, he'd been caned at grammar school for escaping from a trip to see *Julius Caesar*, a set work for his English Lit exam. He'd failed the exam as well. He'd told himself he wasn't minded to believe in people dressed oddly and speaking lines against painted backdrops. There was drama enough in the real world. He didn't have to go to the theatre to experience it. But in his heart he knew there was something else behind his unease, something visceral.

In the low-ceilinged corridor, Titus spoke in a hushed tone. 'The door to your right is the bar. Let's see if it's open.'

'Good suggestion,' Diamond said.

'The door, I mean. We won't get a drink at this time of day.'

They went in and switched on some lights. Diamond's spirits lifted a little. This could be a saloon bar in any classy pub. He could forget where he was.

Titus stepped inside, took up a stance with hands clasped and launched into his tour guide routine. 'I'm taking us back to June, 1981, the week before the theatre was closed for the major renovation. A production of the Albee play, *Who's Afraid of Virginia Woolf?* with Joan Plowright and Paul Eddington. The audience are streaming in here at the interval. Suddenly a woman screams, points at that wall behind you and demands to know what is wrong with the wallpaper. Everyone looks and sees an uncanny spectacle. The wall is shimmering as if in a heat haze.'

A summer evening, Diamond was thinking. All those people packed into this small bar.

'Ah, but that is followed by a sudden icy draught. All the heads turn, sensing that something not of this world has rushed past them to the door. In its wake is a distinct smell of jasmine perfume.'

'The grey lady?' All of this build-up demanded a polite response and he supplied it.

'The doors are flung open and then banged shut. In the corridor, one of the cast is walking by and she steps in here, ashen-faced, and asks what on earth it is that has just swept past her.'

'Impressive,' Diamond said, still playing along. 'Were you present?'

Titus smoothed his hair. 'Too young. But there were numerous witnesses still around to attest to what they experienced.'

'Can't be dismissed, then.' That was more than enough of indulging Titus. 'Where next? The dressing rooms? Was she ever seen there?'

'Before that, allow me to show you the box where she was seen by Dame Anna.'

Leaving the bar, they crossed the corridor to the circle itself. The horseshoe-shaped auditorium was in darkness. Its crimson, cream and gold decorations were just discernible, the silk panels, gilded woodwork, garlands and crystal chandelier giving a sense of the antique theatre that this was, essentially no different from the interior known to the actors who first played here in the reign of George III. Without an audience, and with the curtain down, the space looked smaller than Diamond remembered from his one previous visit. Anyone but he would have been thinking this was the prettiest theatre in the kingdom. His main thought was how quickly he could get out. To his embarrassment he was starting to get the shakes.

'The house curtains were a gift from Charlie Chaplin's widow, Oona,' Titus said. 'Chaplin loved this theatre. If you look in the corners you'll see his initials in gold thread.'

Diamond muttered something in courtesy, but couldn't bring himself to look at the curtains.

Titus flitted down the steps of the centre aisle and beckoned to Diamond to join him at the front of the circle. Nobody else seemed to be about. In this light, and without an audience, it was more claustrophobic than Diamond remembered from his only other visit, when he'd summoned the inner strength to take his friend Paloma Kean to see *An Inspector Calls.*

Making a huge effort, he joined Titus and forced himself to look at the upper box where the grey lady was alleged to appear. 'You told me the story in the pub,' he reminded him. 'You don't have to repeat it.'

'Don't worry, there's another version,' Titus insisted on saying. 'Some believe she wasn't an actress, but one of the audience who occupied the same box night after night to watch the actor she adored. Which do you prefer?'

His thoughts were in ferment. The ghost wasn't high in his priorities. 'I don't have a view. Whatever you say.'

'Some say the man was killed in a duel, but I think that's over-egging it.'

'I agree. Shall we move on now?'

'I hope I'm not boring you. Each of the boxes is endowed, you know. The grey lady box is named in memory of Arnold Haskell, the balletomane. Do you enjoy the ballet, Peter?'

'Not in the least. It isn't my thing at all.'

Titus chuckled at that. 'You'd be happier in the Jolly box, I dare say.'

'The what?'

'The one on the prompt side, named after Jolly's department store.'

'That I can relate to,' Diamond said. 'I wouldn't expect to see a ghost in the Jolly box.'

'And this will intrigue you. The one opposite is the Agatha Christie. You may not expect to see a ghost there, but you might find a bunch of suspects, or even a murderer.'

'Did Agatha Christie sponsor it?'

'Her grandson, in her memory. Dame Agatha died some years before the renovation. There are

40

no reported sightings of her ghost.' He turned to face Diamond. 'Do you believe in the supernatural, Peter?'

'I keep an open mind.' A touch of mischief made him add, 'Don't you?'

'Me? I'm a firm believer,' Titus said.

'Have you actually seen the grey lady?'

'I've sensed her presence and smelt the jasmine more times than I care to remember.'

'I don't think I'd know one perfume from another.'

'Believe me. I can tell.'

Diamond did believe him.

It was a huge relief to quit the auditorium. Ghosts weren't the problem.

At the end of the dress circle corridor, Titus used the code system to open a door marked private and started confidently down some uncarpeted stairs. 'She's been known to terrify actors in their dressing rooms,' his voice carried up the staircase to Diamond. 'And that's before anyone has told them about her.'

'Incredible,' Diamond said, taking the steps with care. He wished no disrespect to Dame Anna Neagle or any other actors, but he knew they thrived on publicity. The sighting of a ghost was a sure way to get a mention in the local press and possibly the nationals, too.

'Incredible, indeed. You'll say that again when you view the dressing rooms.'

'I can't wait.' Actually he felt more at ease now he was out of the auditorium. He needed to be alert for this part of the tour, a chance to see where Clarion had got ready for her performance.

They were backstage now and it became obvious

41

that Titus wasn't just an armchair dramaturge. He knew his way around this place. 'We're fortunate in having eleven dressing rooms on three floors, and most of them are big enough for several actors,' he said. 'It means when you put on a small play like *I Am a Camera*, with a cast of seven, there's no need to double up unless the actors prefer to share. If it were me, I would be happy to fraternise. I'm sociable by nature, as you may have gleaned.'

'Which room was Clarion's?'

'The number one, naturally, with shower and WC ensuite, although I think the number two is more luxurious. However, this is known as the Alec Guinness because Sir Alec himself endowed it.' Titus opened a door. 'Voilà. Pause for a moment and reflect on all the great bottoms that have warmed the seat of that chair.'

It was not a thought Diamond cared to dwell on. 'Clarion must have felt honoured to be in here.'

'Or intimidated.'

'True.' Spacious, and with a huge dressing table and ornate gilt mirror, the room would surely have satisfied the most exacting of actors. A chandelier, chaise longue, wash basin with gold fittings, draped curtains, vases of flowers, electric kettle and a view from the window of the lawn fronting Beauford Square. For Diamond, it came as a relief to see daylight.

'It cost Sir Alec rather more than he'd bargained for,' Titus said. 'When he first stepped in here to inspect the decor, the paint hadn't dried. He didn't know and got a patch of red on his cashmere overcoat. He was gracious enough to dismiss it with a theatrical aside that he would have made an appalling Macbeth.'

'Oh yes?' The point of the story escaped Diamond. No doubt a man of culture would have appreciated it.

'"I am in blood stepp'd in so far," et cetera,' Titus murmured, more to himself than his companion.

Diamond crossed the room for a closer look at the dressing table. He was starting to function again as a detective, the thing he was paid to do. 'I don't see any make-up here.'

'Clarion didn't need it,' Titus said. 'The dresser was under instructions to make her up and she would have brought her own.'

'And taken it away after.' He bent to look more closely at the surface.

'What are you doing?' Titus asked.

'Checking to see if there's any residue.'

'Oh, I shouldn't think so.' Titus stepped over and put out a hand to check for dust.

Diamond grabbed him by the wrist. 'Don't.'

'Why?'

'Could be a crime scene. We don't want your prints all over it.' He wished he'd sounded less like a policemen.

'I would never have thought of that,' Titus said, giving him a long look before adding, 'That's a firm grip you've got, Peter. Strong hands.'

Diamond backed away and looked at some clothes hanging on the wall. 'I suppose these belong to her. She'll have been wearing her stage costume when she was taken to hospital.'

'Yes, they can't be the understudy's. Gisella has her own room on the OP side, number eight, the Vivien Leigh. Would you like to see which of the others are open?'

43

'Not yet.' He hadn't given any thought to security. Dressing rooms were like hotel rooms for the duration of a run. Actors would be entitled to lock up when they were out of the building. 'Is there a key?'

'Clarion will have one and so will the cleaning staff.'

'I don't see her bag here. I suppose someone was thoughtful enough to see that it travelled in the ambulance with her. The place ought to be locked.'

'Because it could be a crime scene?' Titus said, echoing Diamond's words, and with heavy irony. There wasn't much doubt he'd guessed the real incentive behind this tour.

At this point it didn't matter. Diamond got on his knees and looked under the dressing table and the chaise longue. A tissue with some make-up left on it might have dropped out of sight in the confusion. But it hadn't. Or the cleaner had been by.

'What are we looking for now—a hidden clue?' Titus asked.

Diamond hauled himself upright. 'You're thinking I'm here on false pretences, aren't you? I didn't say what my job is and I didn't say it was anything else. You were kind enough to suggest a short tour and I took you up on it. I'm sorry if I gave you the wrong idea.'

'No offence taken,' Titus said. 'Is the ghost hunt at an end?'

'Thank you. It is.' He moved across to the sash window. 'Here's a small tragedy.'

'What's that?'

He pointed to a dead butterfly on the sill.

44

'Looks to me like a tortoiseshell.'

Titus gave a gasp, rolled his eyes upwards and fainted.

CHAPTER FOUR

Hedley Shearman tried phoning Frenchay Hospital for the fourth time that afternoon and was told all calls about Clarion Calhoun's condition were being referred to her agent, Tilda Box.

'I'm not press,' Hedley said. 'I'm the director of the Theatre Royal. I have a right to know what's going on.'

'We're not at liberty to say anything over the phone,' the hospital spokesman said. 'Ms Box is personally handling all enquiries. Would you like a note of the number?'

'Personally' turned out to be misleading. The agency had installed one of those infuriating filter systems. 'If you are enquiring about Miss Clarion Calhoun, press four.' When Hedley obeyed, he got an insipid rendering of Greensleeves for six minutes interspersed with assurances that he was moving up the queue, followed finally by another recorded message: 'Miss Clarion Calhoun remains in Frenchay Hospital. There is no change in her condition. She is unable to speak on the phone or receive visitors. We thank her many friends and fans for their good wishes for her recovery and will update this message as and when we have more news.' So much for the age of instant communication.

'They've put up the shutters and I'm not sure

why,' he told Francis Melmot, the human steeple, who was back, making him feel even more like a dwarf.

'Doing their job,' Melmot said as if he had inside knowledge. 'They don't want hordes of fans trying to see her.'

'Yes, but we're not fans. We have every right to know what's going on.'

'Look at it from Clarion's point of view. She'll be distressed. The first instinct of any woman whose looks are blemished, however slightly, is to hide herself away. It's understandable, Hedley. You drove her to the hospital. Just how badly is her face affected?'

'I couldn't see. For one thing I was driving and for another she kept the towel pressed to her face.'

'Surely you got a better look when you got to A & E?'

'No, they took her straight inside, still covering up. But it must have been serious for them to transfer her to Frenchay.'

'They'd be ultra-careful with a patient as famous as Clarion.'

'I don't know if that's true. They make their decisions entirely on medical grounds, don't they?'

'Hedley, if I was a young doctor presented with a superstar hysterical about the state of her face I'd be only too pleased to refer her to someone else.'

'What are you suggesting—that she might not be as badly hurt as we fear?'

'That's a possibility.'

'A hope, more like. They've retained her in Frenchay and all I get on the phone is that there's no change.'

'No change from what? Red cheeks?'

'It must be more serious than that. One of the cast tried visiting her this morning and was turned away by a security guard.'

'I wouldn't read too much into that. These celebs surround themselves with security.'

'But why?'

'She's buying time while she considers her next move.'

This possibility plunged Shearman into greater panic. 'I think we've got to get our own house in order. I had to speak to Martina, the press officer. She was giving statements off the cuff. A few words out of turn and we could find we're admitting to negligence.'

Even Melmot's self-possession took a knock. 'There's no question of that, is there?'

'I'm afraid there is—if, as we suspect, the make-up caused the damage. The police spent some time questioning Denise Pearsall. She's gone home, very anxious.'

'I'm not surprised. Is she coming in tonight?'

'She has to. Gisella the understudy will need all the support we can give her.'

Abruptly Melmot changed tack. He was all vigilance now. 'Be sure to see Denise the moment she arrives and impound her make-up. We don't want anyone else ending up in Frenchay.'

'Gisella's a professional,' Shearman said. 'She'll do her own make-up.'

Melmot gave him a sharp look. 'I hope you're not implying that Clarion was out of her depth.'

'That's not what I said.'

'You're right about publicity. Make it clear that no one speaks to the press except the press officer and she must get everything vetted by you.

47

Incidentally, what did you say to the police this morning?'

'That was very bizarre. They don't have a clue what's going on. The sergeant was all mouth and trousers, quoting Keats and strutting around my office like Olivier doing *Henry V*. The theatre has that effect on some people. It's a good thing some of us have our feet on the ground.'

'What did they want? It's no business of the police.'

'Apparently they follow up anything unusual that shows up in Accident and Emergency. It was a routine visit, as far as I could make out.'

'They won't be back?'

'I hope not.'

Melmot made an effort to sound calm again. 'We can get through this if we act responsibly. Tomorrow's headlines will be about something else. Performances continue, don't they?'

'Absolutely.'

'Business as usual. That's the way forward.'

*   *   *

When Peter Diamond walked into the Garrick's Head with Titus O'Driscoll hanging on to his arm for support, there was a collective intake of breath not unlike the scene in *Lawrence of Arabia* when Lawrence enters the officers' mess in Cairo accompanied by a native tribesman. The barmaid called out, 'Ooh, look at these two. Are we an item already?'

'A glass of water and a cup of weak tea,' Diamond said through clenched teeth.

'On a bender, are we?' she said, and then, after

a closer look, 'What's up, Titus?' She added with a giggle, 'You look as if you've seen a ghost.'

'He'll be fine,' Diamond said, after helping Titus into a chair. 'He passed out. Plenty of sugar in the tea.'

'Sorry, love. I had no idea,' she said as she dropped a teabag into a pot and filled it with water from the urn. 'What could have caused that?'

'It was all those stairs backstage,' Diamond said. 'The blood runs from your head, makes you giddy. How are you doing, Titus?'

The voice was little more than a whisper. 'Coming round, I think.'

'Hurry up with the tea,' Diamond said.

She brought it to the table and set it in front of Titus. 'Did you see something?'

'I don't remember.' He turned to face Diamond. 'Where were we when this happened?'

'In the number one dressing room.'

'It's all a blur.'

'We'd just about finished the tour,' Diamond said.

'I thought it was supposed to be a ghost hunt,' the barmaid said.

'Yes, we toured the places where the grey lady is said to appear. Titus was in good form, telling me everything. Then out of nowhere he rolled his eyes and his knees went. Luckily I managed to catch him before he fell.'

Titus said with a flicker of animation, 'Did you? How gallant.'

'I didn't have much choice. You fell into my arms.'

'Oh my word. And I don't remember any of this. Is that how I recovered—in your arms?'

49

'No, I let you sink to the floor. When anyone faints, they recover quickly in the horizontal position. You soon came round.'

Titus remained grateful. 'Peter, I can't thank you enough. I was in good hands, literally. Let me buy you a drink.'

'Not just now.' He looked at the clock. 'Is it as late as that? I must get back to work.'

'Do you have a card, or something? We must meet again.'

'No, I don't.'

Titus fished in his pocket. 'Have one of mine, and do give me a call. There's a lot more I could show you—of the theatre, I mean.'

Diamond glanced at the card. There was an icon of two theatrical masks. As well as a dramaturge, Titus was an MA (Oxon) and a freelance lecturer. Below his name were the words 'The Paragon'— which only a Bathonian would recognise as a street name. 'Thanks for showing me round.'

'Next time, we'll arrange for the grey lady to materialise.'

'I doubt if she'll do it for the likes of me.'

After Diamond had left, the barmaid said, 'Seems a nice fellow. I wonder what he does for a living.'

'That much I do remember,' Titus said. 'He's some sort of policeman, unfortunately.'

'What, without a uniform?'

'A detective, I expect.'

'What's unfortunate about it?'

'They can never leave the job behind. They're not encouraged to make friends outside the police.'

'Do you fancy him, Titus?'

50

'He has a certain butch quality that may mean anything, or nothing. And I had a sense that he lives alone. Do you think I did the right thing, giving him my card?'

'Who can say? One thing is certain.'

'And what is that?'

'You're known to the police now.'

*　　*　　*

Back in Manvers Street, Diamond decided to update two of his colleagues, DCI Keith Halliwell and DC Ingeborg Smith. 'All of this could come to nothing,' he summed up, 'but as Georgina put it to me, sitting behind her desk, we must be primed, ready to spring into action.'

Halliwell, his deputy and mainstay, said, 'Just because Georgina doesn't want to miss her chance to sing in *Sweeney Todd*.'

'Be fair,' Ingeborg said. 'The story is all over the papers. If there *is* a crime involved, we'll be in the thick of it.'

'Sorry I spoke.'

Diamond said, 'Let's cut to the chase. Suppose it really is a crime. Who's in the frame?'

'The dresser,' Halliwell said at once.

'Too obvious,' Ingeborg said.

'Who do you suggest, then?'

'The understudy.'

'Isn't that obvious, too?'

'Makes sense,' Diamond said. 'She gets the leading role for the rest of the week. But how would she get to damage Clarion's face?'

'By adding something to the make-up,' Ingeborg said. 'We'd need to know who got made up before

51

Clarion.'

'All of them did their own except Clarion,' Diamond told them. 'She isn't used to stage make-up, so she got help.'

'Do we know the understudy's name?' Halliwell asked.

'Gisella Watling.'

'She'll be one of the cast, as like as not,' Ingeborg said. 'Understudies usually have a small part in the play, ready to step in when necessary.'

'Done some acting, have you?' Halliwell said.

She gave him a sharp look. 'No, I was a critic.'

'A *critic*?'

'If you're a journo, as I was, it's a good way to get complimentary tickets.'

Diamond steered them back on track. 'There are four women in *I Am a Camera*. I can tell you that much.'

'So there it is,' Ingeborg said. 'Our understudy has a dressing room of her own. How about this? Before the show, while Clarion is being made up, this Gisella calls at the number one dressing room to wish her luck and switches the foundation so that Clarion gets a faceful of vitriol.'

'What's that?' Halliwell asked.

'Sulphuric acid, but I wasn't speaking literally.'

Halliwell exchanged a look with Diamond. Sometimes Ingeborg was too clever by half. 'The motive being . . . ?'

'Ambition,' Diamond said. 'Acting brings it out in people. They all want the star role.'

'It's a vicious way to get it.'

'I'm sure the damage was worse than Gisella intended,' Ingeborg said. 'She didn't think it would disfigure Clarion for life.'

52

'Before we pin it on the understudy, let's think who else could be a suspect,' Diamond said. 'Do we know anything about Clarion's personal life?'

'Don't look at me, guv,' Ingeborg said. 'I'm not a fan and never was.'

'But you know where to look?'

'On any newsstand. She's one of those celebs with a paparazzi following.' She gave a shrug and a smile. 'Okay, I should have seen that coming. I'll do a profile.'

'Some rival singer could have got to her,' Halliwell said.

'Would they bother?' Diamond said. 'I get the impression her career was on the skids.'

'A crazy fan, then?'

'The problem with these suggestions is that the rival or the fan would have to get backstage before the show. Not impossible, but it's much more likely it was an inside job—someone who could get past the stage-door keeper without being challenged.'

'Plenty of people work backstage,' Ingeborg said. 'It isn't just the actors. The director, for one.'

'Hedley Shearman.'

'He's the theatre director. I meant the director of the play. Sandy someone.'

'Block-Swell. Sandy Block-Swell. He wasn't even there on the first night. After the dress rehearsal he said he was certain everything would be all right, and he pissed off to Hollywood to direct a film.'

'Sod you lot, I'm all right.'

'Apparently he's like that. But you're right, Inge. We need to find out who was around on the night it happened.'

'I sense a job coming my way,' Halliwell said.

They knew Diamond's methods, these two. He shook his head. 'Not a job exactly. We don't have a case yet.'

'Call it what you like, guv, it amounts to the same thing.'

'More like a perk than a job. If you happen to be free this evening I'll treat you to a theatre visit, the pair of you.'

'Me and him?' Ingeborg said, turning pale. Keith Halliwell was at least twenty years her senior, and married. She had an image to keep up.

'What's wrong with that?' Halliwell asked.

She didn't say. She'd already thought of a get-out. 'Can we get tickets as late as this?'

'They won't be hard to come by, with all the returns,' Diamond said. 'Aisle seats at the back if possible, leaving you free to move about.'

'It isn't just a chance for her to date me, then?' Halliwell said, with a superior look at Ingeborg.

'What do you think?' Diamond said. 'Before the show, test the security backstage. See if you can enter by the stage door. Failing that, there's a way down from the royal circle. I want to know which dressing rooms are in use and where everyone is.'

'What if we're challenged?' Halliwell asked. 'Do we own up to being cops?'

'Why do you think we wear plain clothes?'

'What's our cover, then?'

'They'll take us for press,' Ingeborg told Halliwell. 'We can say we've been promised an interview.'

'Good suggestion,' Diamond said. 'Inge can be the reporter and, Keith, you'd better carry a camera.'

'Some treat, this.'

54

'A night at the theatre?' Diamond said. 'CID doesn't get better than that. And in case you think I'm getting off lightly, someone has to cosy up to that fruitcake Sergeant Dawkins and find out what he got from the theatre director and the dresser who applied the make-up.'

Neither would have volunteered for that.

*   *   *

The theatre seemed to be returning to normal as the day went on. Most of the press had given up and gone. The first rush of people wanting to return tickets was over. The box office manager reported that tonight's house would be down in numbers, but not embarrassingly so. Hedley Shearman, still agitated, went down to the stage door on a mission he regarded as difficult, but necessary.

Basil, the doorman, had seen it all in his time from *Oh, Calcutta!* to *The Rocky Horror Show,* and was trying to be a tower of strength. 'I wouldn't worry, Mr Shearman. Theatre people are far too excitable for their own good. Some of them live off their nerves. You get a crisis like we had last night and everyone seems ready to panic, but they don't. When the shit hits the fan, if you pardon my French, they're professionals. Look at what happened. That Gisella was word perfect. I was told she was better than Miss Calhoun.'

Shearman hadn't come for a pep talk. 'I'm going to ask you a question about last night, Basil. Think carefully before you answer. Were you here all evening?'

'Always am, Mr Shearman.'

'And do you remember admitting anyone you wouldn't have expected?'

Basil shook his head.

'No strangers? No one asking to go backstage on some pretext?'

'Nobody gets past me unless they're staff, or in the show.'

'It's frightfully important. Do you know each of the cast?'

Basil nodded. 'There's only seven of them.'

'What about the technical people, scene-shifters and the like?'

'There aren't many of them this week. This one is a bread and butter show. Small cast, no set changes or special effects.'

'Is Denise in?'

Basil shook his head. 'She was here all morning. She's entitled to a little time off.'

'I know that.'

'She isn't back yet, but I expect she won't be long.'

'The minute she arrives, tell her to report to me. On no account is she to do anything with make-up. And one other thing, Basil.'

'Yes, sir?'

'Because of what happened, I'm making more use of the security people this week. This is no criticism of you, but I've asked them to man all the entrances tonight and for the rest of the week. That includes the stage door.'

Basil's face creased into a frown. 'You're putting a security man on my stage door?'

'That's what I said.'

'As well as me, you mean?'

'Instead of you.'

Basil blinked. 'Eh?'

'I'm giving you the rest of the week off.'

Outraged, he said on a rising note, 'Laying me off?'

'On full pay.'

'I've done nothing wrong.'

'I just made that clear, Basil. It isn't personal. We value your experience.'

'Just my point—experience. Security men won't know any of the actors.'

'They'll be given a list, and a copy of the programme with the actors' pictures. I want a uniformed presence on the door.'

'Are you expecting more trouble, then?'

'It's not a case of that. I want everyone to know that we're serious about security. You can take a few days off.'

'As you wish, Mr Shearman,' Basil said with dignity, as if he were Gielgud overlooked at an audition.

*   *   *

The eccentric Sergeant Dawkins entered Diamond's office with a faint smile playing on his lips. 'You sent for me.'

'I did. Have a seat.' Diamond already felt blighted. Whichever way he started with Dawkins, awkwardness took over. 'You were at the theatre this morning checking on what happened last night. Would you give me a quick rundown?'

'That depends,' Dawkins said, looking at the back of his hand as if checking for liver spots.

'Depends on what?'

'How quick is quick.'

'A summary, then. You don't have to tell me every word.'

'Nor shall I,' Dawkins said, settling into the chair. 'First of all . . .'

'Yes?'

'First of all, may I be so bold as to ask the subtext.'

'The what?'

'The subtext.'

'You're losing me.'

'The hidden agenda.'

'I don't know what you're on about.'

Dawkins gave a broader smile and said nothing.

'You're talking in riddles, man,' Diamond told him. 'Subtexts and hidden agendas. Explain.'

The sergeant turned to look out of the window, as if the answer might be in the car park below. 'Powers of observation, analysis, deduction.'

'You don't have to make a meal of this. All I want is a short report on what was said. You spoke to the theatre director. Did anything emerge?'

'Hey ho.'

'I'm losing my patience, Sergeant.'

'Hey ho, I said.'

'I heard you.'

'Hey ho to your question: "Did anything emerge?"'

'You're talking like one of the Seven Dwarfs and you're wasting my time.'

'Not at all,' Dawkins said. 'It was a comment, sir, a compliment, in fact.'

'I'm not looking for compliments.'

'Quite so. The "hey ho" should have been silent, a tap of the cue on the snooker table.'

The man was round to snooker now. Diamond

58

despaired of getting any plain statement. Without thinking, he put his hand to his head and tugged at the precious patches of hair he had left. What was the point in trying for straight answers?

'The hidden agenda,' Dawkins said, 'so well disguised.'

Diamond reached into his in-tray, picked up the minutes of a Police Federation meeting and tried blocking out this pointless conversation.

But Dawkins had more to say, and he spoke the words slowly, as if they carried a momentous truth. 'Put it this way: I can see where you're coming from.'

'I wish I could say the same.'

'The place I'm coming from is the theatre.'

'We can agree on that,' Diamond said. 'So why don't you tell me in plain words what you found out there?'

'Because of where you're coming from.'

Diamond gripped his desk and made one more try. 'Listen, Sergeant. There's no subtext, as you put it, no hidden agenda. I'm not coming from anywhere. I'm here, face to face with you.'

'Not coming, but come?'

'If that makes any difference, yes.'

'And if my report is satisfactory, may I look forward to going there?'

'Going where?'

'Where you're coming from.'

'And where is that?'

'CID.'

That was it. This pain in the arse thought he was being assessed for a plain-clothes job. Hell would freeze over first. 'No chance.'

Dawkins blinked in surprise.

'You've got more front than the Abbey,' Diamond told him. 'Get on with your report.'

Finally Sergeant Dawkins appeared to accept the inevitable. 'In plain words?'

'Plain and to the point.'

He cleared his throat. 'First I questioned the director, Mr Hedley Shearman. He was at pains to convey that the incident is being treated as an internal matter. They are dealing with it themselves, with a definite intention of carrying out an enquiry. It's a family matter, to quote him. He didn't see Miss Calhoun before the show, but he was in the audience and watched her on stage. When the curtain came down he went backstage and drove her to hospital himself.'

'So he takes it to have been an accident?'

'Indeed, preferring accident to incident.'

To stop Dawkins from starting on another tedious bout of wordplay, Diamond said, 'You also spoke to the dresser.'

'Ms Denise Pearsall, yes. Six years' experience at the Theatre Royal. She made up Ms Calhoun. When I say "made up" I don't mean—'

'What's she like?'

'As a dresser? I wouldn't know.'

'In interview, I mean. What impression did she make?'

'Anxious, nervous, on her guard.'

Who wouldn't be, faced with you? Diamond thought. 'Suspiciously so?'

'Difficult to tell. In her position, anyone would be entitled to feel vulnerable. If there is blame, she is the prime candidate.'

'True.'

'However . . .' A finger went up.

60

Diamond had to wait. The man was like an actor playing to an audience of one.

'However, one other thing of interest emerged.'

'What's that?'

'On Sunday they had a dress rehearsal in full make-up. Nothing untoward was reported.'

'Worth knowing,' Diamond said, nodding.

Dawkins almost purred at the praise. 'May I therefore . . .'

'Therefore what?'

'Look forward to a transfer?'

'I didn't say that.'

'Pardon me, but you appeared to approve of my report.'

'When you finally got round to it, yes,' Diamond said. 'You were simply doing your job, a uniformed officer's job. It wasn't a secret test for CID, whatever you may have thought.'

Dawkins looked as if he'd walked into a punchbag. 'I don't understand.'

'I made myself clear. This isn't a job interview. It's routine.'

'But you sent for me.'

'To get your report, yes.'

'The mere facts?'

'Right. Have I got through to you?'

Dawkins shook his head. 'If you had wanted the facts, you needn't have asked me. You could have got them from PC Reed. She writes everything down.'

Diamond smouldered inside. How he wished he'd thought of that.

*   *   *

Backstage in the theatre, the male lead was the first to arrive for the next performance. Short for a leading actor and with a nose a pigeon could have perched on, he'd had to settle for character parts for most of his career. The role of Christopher Isherwood, a man of slight build and less than slight nose, presented a fine opportunity to get the name of Preston Barnes in lights, second only to Clarion Calhoun's. The resemblance to Isherwood was striking, and he'd cultivated his hair to get the authentic parting and cowlick. 'Has Basil been sacked?'

Hedley Shearman, on patrol in the dressing room area in case Denise Pearsall arrived, was thinking of other things. 'Basil?'

'The stage-door keeper. Some jobsworth is on the door. Very officious.'

'I've installed a security man, for all our sakes. Basil will be back when the present emergency is over.'

'Is that what it is—an emergency?'

'It is for the management. Something went badly wrong last night, and we can't risk a repeat.'

'A repeat? God help us all if it happens a second time. Do you blame Basil, then?'

'I don't blame anyone. It was unfortunate, that's all.'

'It was bloody unfortunate in performance, I can tell you. I'm pretty experienced at covering up when other actors miss their lines, but that was impossible. If you ask me, there was something dodgy with the make-up. The rest of us used our own and we were all right.'

'Did Clarion say anything about it before you went on?'

62

'I didn't see her. I'm on stage when the play opens, as you know. The first I knew there was anything wrong was when she came on and missed her cue and started grimacing. I gave her the line again and she screamed in my face. How is she now?'

'Progressing, I understand, but we ought to assume she won't be back this week. Are you okay playing opposite Gisella?'

Barnes gave a shrug. 'She was adequate last night. Better than Clarion has ever been in rehearsal. Between you and me, we were saved from being savaged by the critics. But the play won't transfer now. We'll all be looking for work after Saturday night.'

'You'll be snapped up,' Shearman said.

'Do you think so?' Barnes enjoyed that. The vanity of actors is legendary, and he was a prime example. 'I'll be glad to get a normal haircut. This silly Isherwood look is too much. I can't think why he persisted with it for so long.'

'You look the part, that's for sure,' Shearman said, eyeing him.

'It doesn't come without years of experience. Character is the actor's overarching responsibility. I inhabit the role I'm playing and the resemblance is created in the process.'

'Like one of those TV impressionists?'

Barnes winced at the suggestion. 'I was thinking of the late Sir Alec Guinness. It's from inside, you know. It isn't the hairstyle or the make-up. It's the self-belief. Speaking of which, I must get to my dressing room and begin my preparation.'

He'd spoken before of his preparation. He arrived early and spent at least an hour in contemplation 'connecting emotively with the role', as he put it. His door was closed to everyone.

'When you arrived last night, was anyone about?' Shearman asked.

'Who do you mean?'

'Denise, for example.'

'The dresser? I've no idea. She doesn't look after me. I'm perfectly capable of dressing myself. I wear that grubby sports coat and revolting blue shirt and all I have to think about is changing my tie.'

'I know that. I was wondering if you remembered seeing anybody.'

'I expect there were technical people. It was a first night, for God's sake. I wasn't registering who was here. I went straight to my room to prepare.'

'That would have been early?'

'Five thirty or thereabouts.'

'Your dressing room is close to Clarion's.'

Barnes frowned. 'Does that make me a suspect?'

'Not at all. You've no reason to harm her. Quite the reverse. I was wondering if you heard anyone visiting her.'

'Certainly not. The walls in this old building are two feet thick. Anyway, I was concentrating on my role and, if you don't mind me saying so, you should do the same. I don't think you should play detective. It's a job for an expert. Let's hope we don't have need of one.'

CHAPTER FIVE

Lately, instead of meeting for pub meals, Diamond and Paloma Kean had taken to going for walks. The suggestion had come from Paloma after Diamond boasted that he hadn't needed to buy a new belt for some years. She'd pointed out that it wasn't the size of belt that mattered, but the bulge above it. They still had the pub meals, but now they walked first, on the understanding that they finished at a recommended watering hole. He hadn't yet given up pies and chips and she was tactful enough not to suggest it.

That evening found them on the Widcombe Flight, which has nothing to do with aircraft. They were walking the towpath of the Kennet and Avon Canal, tracking the seven locks built in the early eighteen hundreds to drive the waterway uphill, out of central Bath and eventually all the way to Reading. Their objective was not so far off: the George Inn at Bathampton.

His friendship with Paloma was still just that. Neither of them wanted to co-habit. They slept together sometimes, finding joy, support and consolation in each other's company. You could have taken them for man and wife, but you would have been wrong. Diamond's marriage to Steph had been written in the stars and her sudden, violent death had made a void in his life that no one could fill. He would go to his grave loving her still.

Paloma's situation couldn't have been more different: she'd gone through a disastrous marriage

65

to a man in the grip of a gambling compulsion. She had tried all ways to reform him and not succeeded. Through her own efforts at building up a business they had stayed afloat financially and raised a son, but ultimately Gordon had dumped her for an older, richer woman willing to fund his bets. Her son, too, was irreparably lost to her. After the divorce she had immersed herself in her career, amassing a unique archive of fashion illustrations used by film and television companies around the world. The business had become the source of her self-esteem. She trusted it, identified with it. She couldn't imagine marrying another man.

Their conversations didn't often touch on business. The history of costume had little in common with crime. But this evening it dawned on Diamond that his tour backstage might amuse Paloma, so he told her about the ghost hunt, quite forgetting that she must have helped the Theatre Royal with research for costume dramas.

He told it well, the story of the grey lady, making it last from Abbey View Lock to the tunnel under Cleveland House.

'She didn't materialise, then?' Paloma said as they entered the stretch through Sydney Gardens.

He laughed. 'Ghosts don't appear for me. I'm not psychic.'

'Good thing. I wouldn't want to be around you if you were. What were you doing at the theatre?'

'Didn't you hear about Clarion Calhoun?'

She'd been working long hours on a major project and missed the whole story, so he updated her. 'It may come to nothing,' he said finally, 'but my boss Georgina has an interest in keeping the theatre going, so . . .'

'She's an enlightened lady.'

He smiled to himself.

'And you chummed up with Titus?' Paloma said.

'I don't know if "chummed up" is the right way to put it. He offered the ghost hunt.'

'He must have taken to you.'

That nettled him. 'If he did, I didn't encourage him.'

'I'm teasing. I've met Titus. I've researched costumes for several of their productions and he always wants to be involved.'

'As the resident dramaturge?'

She laughed. 'Right. He takes himself seriously, but then most of them do.'

'Is his health okay?'

'My word, you're sounding serious now.'

'Now come on. I'm not looking for a date with the guy. The reason I asked is that he fainted in the number one dressing room.'

Her smile vanished. 'Poor Titus. What is it—his heart?'

They were passing under the first of the cast-iron Chinese bridges. Along this stretch the canal curved through the gardens.

'I hope not, for his sake. I helped him out of there and back to the Garrick's Head and he seemed to be getting over it.'

'Did this happen suddenly?'

'We were talking normally, as I recall. It was the room Clarion had used, so I was looking to see if any traces of the make-up were left. There was nothing obvious on the dressing table or under it. I went to the window and found a dead butterfly on the sill. I mentioned it to Titus and that was when

67

he passed out.'

'You're kidding.'

'I'm not saying the butterfly had anything to do with it.'

Paloma was wide-eyed. 'I bet you any money it did. What sort of butterfly?'

'Not rare. Orange and yellow with black smudges. Tortoiseshell, isn't it?'

'You're sure? And it was dead?'

'Well dead.' He turned to look at her. 'Does it matter to anyone except the butterfly?'

'It explains why Titus fainted. Didn't he tell you the story of the butterfly and the Theatre Royal?'

'It didn't come up, no.'

'It's more impressive than the grey lady, take my word for it. And it's always a tortoiseshell.'

'Go on. Scare me.'

'Years ago, before the war, a family called Maddox held the lease and ran the theatre and each year they put on a marvellous pantomime that ran for three months, almost through to Easter. Nellie Maddox made the costumes and Reg and his son Frank wrote the shows and produced them. They had a terrific reputation and the big variety stars queued up to get a part. In 1948 they put on *Little Red Riding Hood* and there was a dance scene, a butterfly ballet, dancers in butterfly costumes moving around a big gauze butterfly that lit up and glittered.'

'It caught fire?'

'No. But during rehearsals a real butterfly, a dead tortoiseshell, was found on the stage and shortly afterwards Reg Maddox, who was working the lights, suffered a heart attack and died.'

'I think I can see where this is going.'

68

'As a mark of respect they decided to cut the ballet from the pantomime. But just before they opened, a tortoiseshell was spotted backstage.'

'Another?'

'But this one was alive.'

He was frowning. 'This was the pantomime season. Funny time of year to see a butterfly, wasn't it?'

'Totally, but there it was, fluttering about. Everyone got very excited and said it must be a sign from Reg. They reinstated the butterfly ballet and the show was a big hit.'

'Nice story.'

'There's more. The Maddox family decided to keep the gauze butterfly for good luck and it's been hanging in the fly tower almost ever since. You can see it to this day. The reason I say "almost" is that when the theatre was refurbished in 1981 they removed it so it wouldn't get damaged.'

'And it fell on someone and killed him?'

'Peter, I don't think you're taking this seriously.'

'Sorry.'

'In all the clearing up, the workmen found an old store cupboard with a wooden box inside. When they opened the lid, six tortoiseshells flew out. Inside they found a photo of Reg Maddox.'

'Spooky.' He tried to sound convinced.

'Isn't it? A butterfly has appeared for almost every panto they've put on.'

'In the depth of winter?'

'It's taken to be an omen of success. Sometimes they appear on stage. When Leslie Crowther was in *Aladdin* one Boxing Day, the butterfly actually perched on his left shoulder. At the end of the show he told the audience why it was so special.'

'Always a tortoiseshell?'

'Always. Most of the stars will tell you their butterfly story if you ask. Honor Blackman, June Whitfield, Peter O'Toole.'

'O'Toole? What was he doing in pantomime?'

'Sorry. I'm not telling it right. In his case it was *Jeffrey Bernard is Unwell*. But this was in October, when the butterfly season is supposed to be over. On the opening night he was on stage and the butterfly settled on the newspaper he was reading. Being such a pro, he ad-libbed a chat with it, saying it was welcome to stay there if it didn't get pissed and make a noise. When it finally fluttered off, it got a round of applause.'

'That was a first, I reckon.' He was starting to be impressed. 'The butterflies are a tad more persuasive than the grey lady.'

'Only a tad?'

'I can believe in butterflies out of season. I've seen them myself. Never thought of them as good omens, but why not? Actors are superstitious, aren't they?'

'You're not wholly convinced, then?'

'I'm an old sceptic, as you know. Something is going on, for sure. What matters is that people in the theatre believe it. And I suppose if a live butterfly is good news, a dead one isn't. I can see why Titus fainted.'

'Does he remember why?' Paloma asked.

'He didn't say a word about it, and he's not the sort to keep quiet. I expect the fainting acted like concussion and blotted out the immediate memory.'

'It'll prey on his mind if it does come back to

him.'

'What do you think? One dead butterfly. Is it like Death knocking on your door?'

'I don't know,' Paloma said. 'We're only too pleased to spot the good omens, but if we believe them we ought to be concerned about the bad ones. Have you told anyone?'

'No, and I don't think I will.'

'What about the butterfly? Is it still there?'

'It will be unless the cleaner has been by. I wonder how long it's been there. Apparently the room was full of people trying to be helpful after Clarion got hurt. Someone will have noticed, surely. From all you've just told me, plenty of people have heard the story.'

'Everyone who works there gets to hear it.'

Diamond found himself thinking about the mischief that could be done among superstitious theatre people. One dead butterfly could create quite a panic. 'I wonder if the understudy has moved into the number one dressing room. It's a status thing, I believe.'

'They may not want the room disturbed,' Paloma said. 'Like a crime scene.'

'But it isn't a crime scene. There's no official investigation. The management were playing it down this morning.'

'They would, wouldn't they?'

'Carry on as usual. The show must go on. That's why I'm thinking the understudy may have moved in.'

'On the other hand, if they're playing it down they may decide to keep the room undisturbed in case Clarion gets over her problem and is ready to return before the end of the run.'

71

'How long is the run?' His brain was racing.

'Only a week. They move on to some other theatre after Saturday night.'

'I doubt if she'll be back.' He took the mobile from his pocket. 'Do you mind? I need to call Ingeborg urgently.'

Paloma sighed and shook her head. Their walks were supposed to be the chance to get away from it all. And how ironic that she'd bought him the phone as a present. 'Go on. It must be important.'

He got through and issued instructions to Inge.

After the call was over, Paloma said, 'You could have gone yourself instead of sending Ingeborg.'

'But I'm with you.'

She smiled. 'Has that ever got in the way of police business?'

They walked in silence for a short way, each reflecting on that last remark. They'd reached the other end of the gardens and the towpath stretched ahead through an eighty-metre tunnel under Beckford Road. There was light at the end, but it was not an inviting place to walk through. 'I'm not proud of this,' he said, 'but to tell you the truth I don't like going into that theatre. It has an effect on me.'

'I noticed, the only time we've been there together,' she said. 'You made a huge effort that evening, didn't you? I appreciated it.'

'It's not as if I'm a wimp. I've attended some gruesome scenes in my time and not turned a hair. Step in there and I can't wait to get out. I'm sure my body temperature drops several degrees.'

'Is it just the Theatre Royal?'

'Any theatre.' He sniffed. 'But we don't have to talk about my hang-ups.'

72

'There must be a reason for it.'

'Whatever it is, it's deep-seated. My parents gave up trying to take me to pantomimes.'

'You must have had a bad experience as a child.'

'If I did, I don't remember. No, it's more about my personality. Theatre is make-believe and I've never wanted to have anything to do with it. I'm a logical guy. I prefer the real world.'

She shook her head. 'Forgive me for saying this, Peter, but that's bunk. You're rationalising, giving in to this hang-up, as you call it.'

He was silent. Not many people could talk to him like that and get away with it.

'And you're missing so much. For me, that moment when the house lights start to dim is magical. I'd hate to be deprived of it.'

'Bully for you and I understand why, but it doesn't alter the feeling I get each time I go there.'

'How are you going to head this investigation, then?'

He laughed. 'With difficulty.'

'Would you like to overcome your problem?'

Now he exhaled sharply. He was wary. 'I'm not sure. What do you have in mind?'

'I know someone who helps people with phobias—'

'I wouldn't call it a phobia,' he said at once, 'and I certainly don't want to see a shrink.'

'Raelene isn't a shrink. She's an earthy Australian, probably the wisest person I know. She can help you, I feel sure, but you have to be willing to unblock whatever it is that your brain is hiding from you.'

'I don't want to do this.'

'Fair enough. Think it over.' She looked away,

across the canal, and changed the subject. 'I may be stating the obvious, but could the Clarion incident be a case of stage fright?'

He shook his head. 'The burns must be genuine, or she wouldn't have been moved to Frenchay.'

'I mean if she was terrified of appearing, really terrified, she could have induced the burns herself. How's this for a theory? She makes her entrance, does the screaming fit, gets off the stage and covers her face with the towel, giving her the chance to apply some chemical that burns.'

'There must be less painful ways.'

'It would explain the delay in her reaction. You said the make-up was thought to be the cause, but if that was the case, she'd have been hurting before she got on stage.'

'You're quite a sleuth yourself,' he said. 'Yes, the delay has to be explained, but until we get the make-up analysed we won't know for sure.'

'You must be champing at the bit.'

'We're ready to go, yes.' They had almost reached Candy's footbridge, spanning the canal and the railway. 'Shall we change the subject?' he said. 'What's the project that's taking up so much of your time?'

'Oh, it's a costume piece. *Sweeney Todd.*'

*   *   *

Outside the Theatre Royal was a Morris column, one of those cylindrical billboards common in Paris and beloved of Proust. It was plastered with posters of *I Am a Camera* showing Clarion smoking a cigarette in a holder. Leaning nonchalantly against it, waiting for Ingeborg, was

74

Keith Halliwell. He had borrowed a camera from one of the police photographers and was carrying a professional-looking shoulder bag that was supposed to be filled with camera equipment. In reality it contained his raincoat and the camera. He wouldn't know how to change a lens or what to do with a light meter.

'Yoo-hoo.' Ingeborg stood only a pace away from him, making a circling movement with her hand.

He hadn't spotted her in the crowd in front of the theatre. She had her hair pinned up and was wearing a black velvet skirt, the first time he'd seen her in anything but jeans.

'Did you get the tickets?' She sometimes forgot she was the DC and he the DCI, but it was obvious that on the present mission she would have to take the lead.

'Royal circle, back row.'

'Shall we do the biz first? I've brought my old press-card.'

'Will I need one?'

'Not if you tag behind me with the camera in your hand. Where is it?'

'In the bag.'

'No use there. The whole point is to have it on view. Let's check the notices in the foyer.'

Halliwell wasn't sure why. He thought they were supposed to try and get backstage before the show. But Ingeborg found what she was looking for, a board with an announcement that for this performance the part of Sally Bowles would be played by Gisella Watling.

They left the foyer. Outside again, they turned right, past the drinkers outside the Garrick's Head.

The stage door stood open, but didn't look like an invitation to go in. They went up some stairs to the point where you had to declare yourself or turn back. Ingeborg tapped on the window and a heavy-jowled, unfriendly face appeared. 'Press,' she said in a matter-of-fact tone, allowing a glimpse of her card. 'May we go in?'

'Who are you?' the doorkeeper asked.

'Ingeborg, independent.' She made it sound as if Borg was her surname and the *Independent* was her employer. A national paper had to be treated with respect by any provincial theatre.

'The press night was yesterday.' Not a lot of respect there.

'I know, but yesterday the story was all about Clarion,' Ingeborg said. 'Tonight it's Gisella.'

'Who?'

'The understudy playing Sally Bowles.'

'The curtain goes up shortly. She won't want to do an interview now.'

'Not an interview. We're taking some pictures backstage for an exclusive. It's all been cleared. We won't get in the way.'

'No one cleared it with me.' The voice was deeply discouraging, and it added, 'I'm not the regular man, you know. I work for the security team. Everything has to be authorised with us.'

'Didn't she let you know? So much on her mind, poor lamb. It's been that sort of day for us, too. We were only given the job this afternoon.'

Halliwell had to admire Inge's sales pitch, and some of it was the truth. She must have learned how to blag in her days as a hack.

She then excelled herself by asking this plonker if they could get a picture of him in uniform to go

76

with the feature she was writing.

'You don't want me in your paper,' he said in a tone disclosing he wouldn't mind at all.

'Keith, why don't you get the picture of—what's your name, sir?'

'Charlie Binns.'

'Of Charlie Binns, while I go ahead and let Gisella know we're here. We don't want her panicking tonight, of all nights.'

The man had bought it. He was fastening his silver buttons. 'I'd better put my cap on.'

And now it was up to Halliwell to work the camera. He wasn't even sure which button to press. He was struggling to get the thing out of its case.

'I'll leave you guys to it,' Ingeborg said, 'if you wouldn't mind letting me through, Charlie.'

The man adjusted his peaked cap, the door was unfastened and Ingeborg went backstage.

Halliwell touched each button he could see and one of them produced a flash. 'All in order,' he managed to say and pointed the lens at Charlie Binns and pressed the same button again. 'Nice one.'

'So when will it appear?' Binns asked.

'Could be in the magazine this weekend. The editor decides.' Halliwell was improvising quite well himself. 'May I go through now?'

He was admitted to a passageway with several noticeboards. At the far end Ingeborg was talking to a large-bosomed woman who didn't look as if she was about to go on stage. She had a modern hairstyle with blonde highlights and was in a low-cut top and jeans. She was holding a dress on a hanger.

'This is my photographer,' Inge said as he

77

approached. 'Keith, this is Kate, who runs the wardrobe department. I was asking which dressing room Gisella uses now, and she's still in number eight upstairs. I thought we might get a picture of the number one room first.'

'That's stage left, on the prompt side,' Kate from wardrobe told them, pointing. 'Are you sure you have permission to be here?'

'Yes, we have clearance from Mr Binns on the stage door.'

'Keep your voices down, then, and don't go anywhere near the stage.' She headed off in the other direction.

'Do we really want a picture?' Halliwell asked Ingeborg as they made their way up the corridor. 'I'm not even sure if there's film in the camera.'

People mostly dressed in black were moving about with a sense of urgency as curtain up approached.

'We only need to get in there. Instructions from the guv'nor. He called me on the way here. You wear specs sometimes, don't you?'

He didn't follow her thread. 'For distance, yes.'

'Did you bring them?'

He patted his pocket. 'I manage pretty well without them, but I thought I might need them for the play.'

'Are they in a case?'

He nodded, still mystified.

'Not one of those soft ones?'

'Metal.'

'Ideal. Well done.'

He didn't ask why.

Quicker than expected, they were approaching the back of the stage itself. There was no other way forward, so they crossed behind the scenery, trying to look as if they had a function in the production. Above them was the cavernous fly tower with its complicated system of grids and catwalks. They turned right towards the wings where someone was perched on a higher level looking at a screen and working a console. Stagehands hurried past.

Praise be: a sign pointed to dressing rooms 1–7. Ingeborg gave a thumb up.

She was off again like the White Rabbit. When he caught up with her she had opened the door of number one and gone in. No one was inside. Some clothes were on a hanger beside the dressing table. 'We're looking for a dead butterfly.'

'You're kidding.'

'Them's the orders.'

Halliwell said no more. If the boss had asked them to find a dead butterfly, so be it. He had faith in Diamond's decisions.

'It should be on the sill, or the floor, if it's blown off, so look where you're treading,' Ingeborg said. 'Voilà.' She pointed to the window. A small, speckled butterfly was lying on the sill. 'Definitely dead, I'd say. This is where your specs case comes in useful.'

'Yes?' He took it from his pocket and removed the glasses.

'A perfect little coffin,' Ingeborg said as she gently slid the tortoiseshell off the sill and into the case and snapped it shut. 'Keep it level at the bottom of your bag and it shouldn't get too shaken up.'

Then a voice shocked them both by saying, 'Beginners, please.' It came from a loudspeaker attached to the wall.

'Should we get to our seats?'

'Still got a couple of things to check,' Inge said.

'What things?'

She crossed to the door and looked out. Other dressing-room doors were opening and actors emerging dressed in thirties costumes. 'Let's hang back a moment,' she said. 'I'd like to meet Clarion's dresser if possible.'

'Is that another request from the guv'nor?' Halliwell asked. He had a suspicion Ingeborg was acting on her own initiative here.

'The one who did the make-up.'

'I know who you mean, but is that a good idea? She's the main suspect and we're not acting officially.'

'He asked us to check if she turns up.'

'That isn't the same as meeting her. We could blow the investigation doing that.'

She saw sense. 'Let's find out from someone else, then.'

'After the show has started.'

They waited in the dressing room with the door ajar. The passageway went quiet and the only sound was the voice over the tannoy giving the countdown to curtain up. The play itself began to be broadcast, a man talking about Berlin.

'Time to move,' Ingeborg said.

She seemed to have an inbuilt compass as well as a strong impulse to get results and Halliwell found himself trailing behind her, avoiding eye contact with everyone else who came by. Everyone backstage had a job to do, a sense of purpose. Any intruder would stand out.

Dialogue was being spoken and it wasn't over the sound system. Halliwell was alarmed to find himself on the prompt side of the wings only a few yards from the actors speaking on stage. Several people were standing in the shadows, watchful and waiting. He recognised one of the actors he'd seen leaving a dressing room. A young woman of elfin size was facing the man, using a soft brush on his face. She looked too young to be the dresser, Denise—but then this was territory peopled by the young. Anyone over forty, as Halliwell was, stood out.

He touched Inge's arm and gestured to her to move back a few yards. Any closer and they'd get in the way of the performance.

The actor getting the last-minute dusting must have heard his cue, because he eased aside the handmaiden with the make-up brush and stepped behind a set of double doors. A doorbell was rung. The actors could be heard reacting and the doors opened and a buxom female actor carrying a tray with a beer bottle and glass came through. She spoke loudly in German to the waiting man and he responded. Their off-stage voices would have carried to the audience. It was strange to see and hear it from this side of the scenery. The doors opened again and the actor on stage said, 'Fritz.' The cue for the waiting actor to make his entrance. The woman with the tray followed him back on.

This was all too close to the action for Halliwell's liking. He'd taken another step back into the shadows. But as the dialogue on stage developed, Inge was stepping over cables, homing in on the young girl with the make-up brush. At heart, she was still a journalist eager for a story. She tapped the girl on the shoulder.

There was a whispered exchange that Halliwell

couldn't hear. Then Inge turned away and returned to where Halliwell was waiting.

'Let's go.'

She led him right around the back of the stage to the opposite side, up a staircase and through a door. Nothing was said until they were through the stage door and in the street, where she took the mobile from her bag.

'I'm calling the guv'nor,' she said. 'They're all on extra duties. Denise didn't show up tonight. This has got serious.'

CHAPTER SIX

Diamond left Paloma asleep in her bedroom in Lyncombe early next morning. Very early. There was much to do, not least returning to his house in Weston to let the cat out. The wild patch at the end of the garden belonged to Raffles. The litter tray was near the door as a back-up, but as any cat would tell you if it could, indoor facilities are second best.

That duty done, the big man cooked himself breakfast, thinking over what he'd learned from Ingeborg's excited call from the theatre the previous evening. She'd said it was obvious who was responsible for the damage to Clarion's face and it was just a question whether it had been negligent or malicious.

Obvious?

He'd been in his job long enough to know that the obvious can be deceiving.

From the kitchen window he could see Raffles

making a statement about concealment, working the earth with his white paws.

Last night's meat pie at the George had been a good one, but it didn't stop Diamond enjoying a 'full English' less than twelve hours later. Tomatoes and mushrooms joined the back rashers cooked to crisp perfection and the eggs turned over and coated pale pink. He made no claims to haute cuisine, but few could match his morning fry-up. A large mug of tea and toast and marmalade topped it off.

Raffles returned in a beeline to his dish to confirm that at some point in the cooking the guv'nor had stopped to open a pouch of tuna in jelly. The man's erratic comings and goings were forgivable if he provided the necessary at the proper times, night and morning.

It was now certain that the Theatre Royal and its community would loom large in CID's schedule today and probably for longer. Diamond didn't relish the prospect of entering the place again. He'd actually given thought to Paloma's offer of a meeting with her friend Raelene to discuss his aversion. Well meant, he was sure, but no, he wouldn't be taking it up. Even if Paloma was right and his problem was psychological, he'd deal with it himself using his professional skills as one more mystery to be investigated and solved. Meanwhile, he'd grit his teeth and get on with the job. Having found the will power to enter the building yesterday he'd do the same again.

'Count yourself lucky you're not a theatre cat, Raffles,' he said to his unlistening pet. 'They're all nutters, all superstitious. They'd trade you in for a black one.'

These one-sided conversations were a by-product of living alone. Unless the radio or TV was on, something had to be done to break the silence. Usually what he said was banal, but it helped him through.

'But if you were a tortoiseshell instead of a tabby, you'd get a better reception—provided that you weren't dead, of course.'

Raffles raised his head from the dish, stretched, licked his teeth and left the room.

'Sorry I spoke.' Diamond drank the last of his tea, checked the time, found his jacket and left the house.

The drive in was quick and enjoyable, before the traffic became the morning crawl he generally endured. He liked the way the early sun picked out the detail of the Victorian terraces along the Upper Bristol Road. The western approach to the city is not Bath as most people think of it. He had to get close before his first sight of Georgian elegance, John Wood's spacious Queen Square with palatial columns and pediments around a central garden. At this stage of the journey he sometimes reminded himself how privileged he was to be in one of the finest cities in Europe, a boost before moving on to the soulless utilitarian block that was his workplace. He was philosophical about that, refusing to let it get him down. You don't want your police station looking like the Parthenon.

Having parked, he went inside, looking forward to a quiet start, not expecting to find anyone in the open-plan area that was CID's hub. The caseload had dwindled in recent days and there was no need for his team to put in extra time. If they clocked in

84

before eight thirty when the civilian staff started, he was content. So it surprised him to see a figure by the window looking out—no one he immediately recognised. None of the team wore a suit, except himself.

And what a suit. This three-piece wouldn't have looked out of place in a circus ring. Patterned in squares too large to be called check, it was loud, tasteless and, frankly, silly. Its wearer was two sizes too small for it, which made the effect even more odd.

'How can I help you?' Diamond asked.

'The boot is on the other foot. How can I help you?' the visitor said, turning.

He recognised the voice first and the face confirmed it and his greet-the-day optimism evaporated. 'Sergeant Dawkins? What are you doing in here, dressed like that?'

'Nothing yet, your eminence,' Dawkins said, 'but I expect to remedy that.'

He ignored the 'your eminence' in pursuit of an explanation. 'I mean why aren't you in uniform?'

'In a sense, I am.'

'Come off it, Sergeant. I'm not getting into one of these obscure debates with you. That is not your uniform.'

'Not the uniform you expected, I grant you.'

'Are you off duty?'

'Far from it.' Dawkins gave a smile that lit up the room. 'On which happy note, I can declare that in this, of all places, my present apparel passes for a uniform.'

'It does not.'

'No one wears regulation blues here.'

'Yes, but we're CID and you're not.'

Dawkins chuckled at that. 'Have you not heard from the assistant chief constable? I was assigned to your command late yesterday.'

'That can't be right.' Suddenly he knew what it meant to be staring down the barrel of a gun.

'A reinforcement, ACC Dallymore calls me.'

'We'll see about that,' Diamond said. He marched straight through to his office, slammed the door, snatched up the phone and asked to be put through to the ACC and was told she was at a policy meeting at Headquarters and wouldn't be in all day. Even before he replaced the receiver he saw the memo on his desk from Georgina:

Peter, I have assigned Sergeant Dawkins to CID for a probationary period with immediate effect. As you know, he has made several applications for a transfer and I believe the time is now right to give him this opportunity. His individual qualities will, I am confident, strengthen the team. I may add that he comes with the recommendation of his senior officer.

'I bet he does,' Diamond muttered with all the bitterness of a man who has been shafted. With Georgina out all day he couldn't overrule her. He sat for two minutes in stunned confusion. Finally he looked for a get-out in the word 'probationary', telling himself he would make sure it was the shortest probation ever. The man would trip up before he'd taken two steps.

He opened the door and looked out. 'What's your name?'

'Dawkins.'

'I know that. Your first name.'

'Horatio.'

It was all of a piece. 'And is that suit your idea of plain clothes?'

'Civilian wear.'

'But it isn't plain. You're going to stand out in a crowd wearing that. Haven't you noticed what the others wear, casual gear, like T-shirts and jeans and leather jackets?'

'With all due et cetera, sir, T-shirts and jeans and leather jackets are not to be found in my wardrobe.'

'You wear that suit around the house?'

'In point of fact, no. This is my walking-out wear.'

'What do you wear indoors, then?'

'When not in uniform, I favour my dance things.'

'Say that again.'

'Singlets and leggings. I'm often barefoot around the house.'

'You're a *dancer*?'

'I do a certain amount, yes.'

There was a pause. 'As in *Swan Lake*?'

'I prefer flamenco.'

Diamond pictured him strutting around the office in Spanish costume and couldn't see it going down well with the team. 'That's remarkable, but it doesn't solve the problem of the suit.'

'If I may be so bold . . .' Dawkins started to say, and then amended it to, 'If I may presume to comment . . .'

'What do you want to say?'

'I am not alone in wearing a suit.'

'You mean I'm in one? I'm in charge here. Besides, mine is plain grey. I don't know what colour you call yours but it hurts my eyes to look at it. Haven't you anything more subdued at home?'

'Dark blue overalls, for garden duties.'

He pictured that for a second. 'I don't think so. We'll put up with this today and find some office work for you. The public isn't ready for that suit. Take off the jacket and sit behind a desk. Other people will be in soon. Oh, and for your own salvation we'll call you Fred.'

'Fred?'

'As in Astaire, but we needn't say so.'

'May I venture to ask why?'

'The dancing. And because other people can be cruel, that's why.'

A little later, after more quiet reflection and gnashing of teeth, Diamond emerged from his office again and addressed the troops, by now all present and ready for any other shocks the day might bring. They'd taken stock of the new arrival and were keeping their distance.

'Some of you know Fred Dawkins already. He's on secondment from uniform. No doubt he'll make his own unique contribution to the team. And he comes at a critical moment, because we have a new line of enquiry. Keith and Inge went to the theatre last night.'

Some joker at the back made sounds suggesting unbridled sex. Ingeborg turned and gave a withering glare. Normal service had been restored.

'Was the play any good?' Diamond asked.

'Not much,' Keith Halliwell said. 'It creaks a bit.'

'We didn't see the first half,' Ingeborg said. 'We went backstage.'

'How did you manage that?'

'By passing ourselves off as press. There was a security man on the stage door. The regular guy wasn't on duty.'

'And you collected the little item I requested?' Diamond said.

Ingeborg turned to Halliwell, who produced his specs case and opened it like a jeweller displaying a precious stone.

The dead tortoiseshell hadn't travelled well. Damaged at the edges and missing one of its antennae, it wouldn't have been of much interest to a butterfly collector, but at least it was out of the theatre.

'You may be wondering why I wanted this,' Diamond said. 'It isn't my latest hobby. This turned up in the dressing room used by Clarion Calhoun the other night. A dead butterfly is a bad omen in the Theatre Royal. A live one would be good news. Don't ask me why. It would take too long. All you need to know is that theatre people are deeply superstitious. There's enough nervousness in that place already without this making it worse.'

'Did Clarion see it?' Paul Gilbert, the youngest DC, asked.

'We don't know. We're not even sure if she knows about the butterfly jinx.'

'Are you thinking someone placed it there to scare her?'

'Let's keep an open mind on that. This sad little critter may have been trapped in the room.'

'How did you know it was there, guv?' DI John Leaman asked.

'I was given a tour yesterday lunchtime.'

'So you're not the only one who saw it?'

89

'My guide saw it. He fainted and appears to have no memory of the incident.'

'Fainted when he saw the butterfly?'

'Right.'

'Bit extreme.'

'Titus is a bit extreme.' He added in a tone that didn't encourage a comeback from anyone, 'And we were on a so-called ghost hunt at the time. But let's get back to reality and Clarion's injury. I called Frenchay Hospital just now and she's still in the burns unit receiving treatment. There can be no question that the skin damage is real.'

'Wounding with malicious intent?' Leaman said.

'That's a possibility. Inge, tell the team.'

She nodded. 'After we found the butterfly, we went backstage and met Kate, the wardrobe manager. She was on extra duties because Denise Pearsall called in earlier to say she was too upset to carry out her duties properly.'

There was a sound like a liner being launched: Dawkins clearing his throat.

'You want to say something, Fred?' Diamond had a sense of dread.

'If you please, Superintendent.'

' "Guv" will do if you want to call me anything at all.'

'Pardon me. Such an appellation smacks of over-familiarity on one's first day.'

Looks were exchanged around the room.

'Get on with it, man.'

'This may or may not be significant . . . guv.'

'Spit it out, or we'll never know.'

'I interviewed Ms Pearsall yesterday morning.'

'I know.'

'DC Smith just said she was too upset to work

last night.'

'Correct.'

'Then it is possible that the interview with me was instrumental.'

Smiles all round the room, unappreciated by Dawkins.

'Conceivably being questioned as a suspect caused her some alarm and she decided to stay away.'

'It can't be discounted,' Diamond said, adding with a straight face, 'and I can understand how it might have happened. Not all of you know this. Fred was the officer who made the first contact with the theatre after getting a report of the injury from A & E. This Denise isn't answering the phone or her doorbell this morning.'

'Has she done a runner?' Leaman said.

'We'll find out. The theatre is playing it down, not wanting us to get involved. They can't stop us if she's gone missing.'

'Bit strong, guv,' Ingeborg said. 'She phoned in only yesterday afternoon.'

'Acting suspiciously.'

'Can we get a warrant?' Leaman asked.

'What for?'

'To search the house.'

'We wouldn't get one. We don't have anything on her for sure,' Ingeborg said.

'We treat her as any other missing person,' Diamond said, 'ask around, find out her movements. See if she runs a car and if she does we put out an all-units order to trace it. That's your job, Keith, with help from Paul. We also step up the pressure on the hospital, insist on getting a statement from Clarion. Inge, you and I will go

91

there together. And it's high time the hospital lab reported on the traces of make-up on the towel. I'll give them a rocket at Frenchay. We'll get our own analysis done by forensics. Not that they're any quicker, but they know what they're up to.'

Another bout of throat-clearing came from Dawkins.

'Ah, Fred,' Diamond said, thinking rapidly to keep this short. 'You're going to ask me what I want from you. You're confined to barracks, for reasons we discussed. Can you use a computer?'

'Use?' Dawkins said as if he'd never heard the word.

'Like work the keyboard.'

'That much I gleaned.'

'So the answer is yes?'

'One's keyboard performance is accurate, but not the quickest,' Dawkins began. 'At the most basic level—'

'Spare us that. The civilian staff will help you. Get Denise's statement on file, and Shearman's. When anything else comes in, every item relevant to the investigation, see that it gets into the system. You're acting as receiver. That's a key post, so don't let me down.'

Fred Dawkins looked apprehensive and said no more.

*   *   *

Frenchay Hospital, north-east of Bristol, was developed in the grounds of an eighteenth-century estate. Grand Georgian buildings have been adapted to medical needs and sit among functional wards and corridors. Diamond hadn't phoned

92

ahead to announce his visit. He had the impression that informality was going to work best. The burns unit was easy to locate and Clarion's private ward was just as obvious thanks to a grey-uniformed security man seated outside.

Diamond showed his ID and the guard picked up his mobile phone.

'Is that necessary? We'll just go in.'

'She's with someone,' the man said. 'I'll have to clear it.'

He was about to push past when Ingeborg touched his arm. 'She may be having treatment, guv.'

'Is she?' he asked the guard.

'I'm checking now.'

The upshot was that the 'someone' came out and she didn't appear to be a doctor or a nurse. She was in a black suit with red tights and patent leather shoes. Her hair was dark, with red streaks, and she wore black shades with a retaining chain. To Diamond's eye, she was in her forties, confident and businesslike. 'You'd better not be press,' she said.

Considering that the guard had already said they were police, this was not a good beginning.

Diamond held up his ID again and introduced Ingeborg. 'And who are you?'

'Tilda Box, Clarion's agent. She's not seeing anyone.'

'Why? Has she gone blind?'

Tilda Box pursed her lips. 'There's no need to be facetious. She's suffering from third-degree burns and severe shock. She's been through a traumatic experience and she's far too distressed to have visitors.'

93

'We're not visitors,' he said. 'We're on an investigation.'

'That's being taken care of.'

'Who by?'

'Private inquiry agents employed by her insurance people. You're not needed here.'

Staying civil with this lady wasn't easy. 'It's not a private matter, Ms Box. It appears a criminal offence was committed Monday evening and we have a duty to investigate.'

She folded her arms. 'Speak to me, then. I'm aware of all the facts.'

'We'll speak to Miss Calhoun.'

'I told you. She's not speaking to anyone.'

'She's spoken to you, apparently, or you wouldn't be aware of all the facts. Are you going to step aside, or do we charge you with obstructing the police?'

'That's blatant intimidation,' she said, and then, as the last words sank in, capitulated. 'For God's sake. Wait here. I'll see what state she's in.'

'No need,' Diamond said. 'We're going straight in. Inge, you go first.'

Tilda Box was incandescent, but stopped short of wrestling with them. Inge went through two sets of swing doors, turned and gestured to Diamond and he followed her into a large room and got his first sight of Clarion Calhoun. He was prepared to find a figure swathed in bandages with apertures for the eyes and mouth. Not so. The patient wasn't bandaged and wasn't in bed. Dressed in a white bathrobe, she was in an armchair looking at a television. Her face, neck and what was visible of her chest appeared to be coated in a yellowish ointment or healing agent. To be fair, the damage

94

to her skin was evident, flakes of tissue hanging from raw burns. She tugged at her long, blonde hair to screen her face from the intruders. 'Who are you?'

Diamond showed the ID and introduced Ingeborg.

'I'm not speaking to the police,' Clarion said. 'Tell them, Tilda.'

The agent had come into the room behind them. Diamond swung around and said, 'Out.'

'I absolutely refuse to leave you alone with her,' Tilda Box said.

'You can absolutely get lost, or I'll absolutely do you for wilfully obstructing a police officer.'

He had Tilda's measure. She quit the room without another word.

'Now, Clarion,' he said. 'I take it you didn't do this to yourself, so it's our job to find who is responsible.'

She appeared to think about playing dumb. There was a lengthy pause. Then she couldn't resist saying from behind the hair, 'The theatre is responsible and we intend to sue.' The voice was easy on the ear. She would have got by as Sally Bowles.

'It may not be so simple,' he said.

'Explain.'

'If someone wanted to harm you, they're mainly to blame.'

Startled, she let go of the hair and turned, giving them a front view of her damaged face and neck. Skin has a marvellous capacity for healing, but it was hard to imagine that the scarring would ever disappear. 'Nobody wants to harm me. That's ridiculous. This is a clear case of negligence. They

95

used some defective product that ruined my skin. These are chemical burns.'

'I doubt if any cosmetics firm would sell a product as harmful as that.'

'In case you're not aware of it, the doctors here are world experts and they're treating me for burns.'

'I'm not arguing with that. I'm saying we don't know how the make-up got to be so dangerous. Was something added to it? That's what we need to find out.'

'Added by mistake, you mean?' She frowned and it was obvious that the flexing of her skin caused pain.

'Or intention. Do you have any enemies, Clarion?'

'No.' The denial was total. Immediately she'd made it, uncertainty showed in her eyes.

Ingeborg said, 'Someone as mega-famous as you is going to have enemies. You don't get to the top without making people jealous.'

She enjoyed the flattery. It showed in her voice. 'Envious, perhaps, but I can't accept what you're saying. No one could hate me that much. This is the end of my career.'

'Has anyone threatened you recently or in the past?'

'I'd remember, wouldn't I? Of course they haven't.'

'Crazy fans? Someone else's fans?'

'I'm coming up to thirty. My last album was two years ago.'

'Three, I think,' Ingeborg said, and got a glare for her accuracy.

'I was about to say my fans have grown up with

96

me,' Clarion said. 'People of my age don't do crazy. They've grown out of all that hormonal silliness.'

'How did the theatre people treat you in rehearsal?' Diamond asked, moving it on, but not confident of shaking the self-esteem of someone who'd basked in admiration for years. She couldn't believe anyone would want to harm her. 'You're an outsider, in a way.'

'I was at drama college, a good one. I'm not a total novice.'

'Yes, but you're not known for your acting and you walked into a starring role. How did they take it?'

'With good grace. They're professionals. My name sells tickets. Few of them would pull in an audience. That's how it is in the commercial theatre and they accept it.'

'Jobbing actors,' Ingeborg said.

'I wouldn't say so in their presence, but yes.'

'So do you recall any hostility while you were rehearsing?' Diamond asked. 'I'm thinking of others besides the actors. Anyone from the management down to the stage hands?'

'If there was any bad feeling, I didn't pick it up.'

'Let's talk about Monday evening,' he said. 'You arrived at the theatre at what time?'

'Before five. I went to my dressing room and sat going over my lines until about a quarter to six. Then I changed into my first costume.'

'Was the dresser there?'

'Denise? She came later with the clothes. She had to collect them from wardrobe. There are six changes between scenes.'

'What time did she turn up?'

'When she said she would. About forty-five

97

minutes before curtain up.'

'Did anyone else come in?'

'There were two or three interruptions from call boys delivering bouquets from well-wishers.'

'Certain flowers can cause allergic reactions, can't they?' Diamond said, more to Ingeborg than Clarion.

'Oh, come on, I didn't bury my face in them,' Clarion said. 'I think I'd know if they were responsible.'

Ingeborg showed by her expression that she, too, thought the flower theory was garbage, so Diamond abandoned it. 'You'd met Denise before?'

'Never.'

'In rehearsal.'

'I see what you mean.'

'She made you up for the dress rehearsal the previous day?'

'Yes.'

'And did your face react then? Any discomfort?'

'None whatsoever. And I didn't notice her doing any different on the opening night. She brought her box of colours and brushes with her. She cleansed my face of day make-up and then put on a thin layer of moisturiser followed by the foundation and the highlights and the liners for the eyes and mouth and so on. I felt no discomfort.'

'What cleanser did she use?' Ingeborg asked.

'Cold cream and astringent, she told me. It all felt normal.'

'What make was it?'

'How would I know that, for Christ's sake? I was thinking about my lines.'

'Then what? The moisturiser?'

98

'Didn't I just tell you? The stage make-up feels dry without it.'

'And the foundation? Cream or pancake?'

'Cream in cake form. She applied it with a sponge. She told me she was experienced and I'm sure she was.'

'So there was this delay before you felt your face burning,' Diamond said. 'How long?'

'Between twenty minutes and half an hour.'

'You were all right until you got on stage?'

'Perfectly.'

'This is the mystery,' he said. 'If we're right in assuming the make-up damaged your skin, why didn't it happen in the dressing room when it was being applied?'

'Slow-acting,' Clarion said.

'We'll get advice on that, but I've got my doubts.'

Her glare could have drilled a hole through his head. 'You can doubt all you want. I'm left with a face like a fire victim and there's no doubting that. I'm suing for loss of earnings and disfigurement and you won't stop me.'

CHAPTER SEVEN

Clarion hadn't endeared herself to Diamond. He sympathised with her injury and understood her anger at the probable loss of her looks and career. He also knew no member of the public welcomes being questioned by the police. Even allowing for that, she'd come across as hostile and unappreciative of the need to get to the truth. She obviously thought her lawyers and her private

99

security people were better placed to take care of her interests. Almost every statement she'd made had been barbed with reproach. But it's impossible to put yourself in the place of someone who's had such a shock, he told himself, trying to be charitable. Easier to feel sorry for the dead victims he usually dealt with. They weren't capable of striking attitudes.

'Back to Bath now?' Inge said, to jog him out of his silence.

'Not yet. Call Bristol police and ask them to supply a round-the-clock guard for her.'

'She has her own guard, guv.'

He gave her a look that said all she needed to know about the competence of private security guards.

She took out her phone.

'And now we'll find the pathology lab,' he said.

'We'd better ask.' She stopped a porter wheeling an oxygen cylinder along the main pathway and they were soon heading in the right direction.

The technician who greeted them inside the door was clearly a junior, but he showed them in to the scientist in charge, a large, bearded man called Pinch, who was sitting on a bench eating a banana. He eyed them as if they'd come to ask for money. When they showed their IDs he jumped to attention, tossed the peel into a bin, wiped his hands and offered them coffee.

All Diamond wanted was the test result, but Ingeborg accepted for them both. The kettle was hot and the coffee was instant, so it shouldn't delay them long.

Pinch explained that his staff supplied their own mugs and there weren't any spares. 'Hope you don't mind drinking from a glass beaker. I promise you, they're clean. Haven't contained anything of human origin. Not today, anyway.'

Diamond wouldn't touch his, he decided.

'So how can I help?'

They asked about Clarion's towel.

'That's been tested, yes.'

'With what result?'

'Traces of glycerine-based make-up, for sure, and face powder, but also a corrosive I wouldn't recommend putting anywhere near your face.'

'Acid?'

'Alkali, in fact, but no less dangerous. Sodium hydroxide.'

'Caustic soda,' Ingeborg said with a sharp intake of breath.

A shocked silence followed.

Finally Diamond, appalled, said, 'Isn't that what they use to unblock drains?'

'Right. We didn't believe it at first, so we repeated the tests. That's why we took so long.' Pinch poured the coffee. 'Help yourselves to sugar.'

Neither reached for the spoon. Ingeborg's face had drained of colour.

'There's no question, then?' Diamond said.

'It's caustic soda for sure, available from your friendly, neighbourhood hardware store. As you doubtless know, it comes in powder form as tiny flakes or granules. Add a solvent such as water and you'll remove most blockages.'

'And most of your skin.'

'If you come in contact with it. In these safety-conscious times it's a wonder the public is still allowed to buy the stuff.'

101

'How does it work?'

'It's inert until added to water.'

'So it could be mixed with something dry, such as face powder, and it wouldn't react?'

'Correct.'

'And being white in colour it would blend in with powder,' Ingeborg added. Horrible as it was, the presence of caustic soda on the towel had to be fitted into a scenario.

'What would have activated it?' Diamond asked.

'Assuming it was applied to her skin?' Pinch said. 'The surface moisture may have been enough. If she was wearing a moisturiser, that would certainly have done it.'

'She had another layer over that, the glycerine-based cream you mentioned,' Ingeborg said. 'If it was mixed with that—'

'I'm not sure it was,' the scientist said. 'We recovered a number of dry particles from the towel. Actors powder their faces, don't they?'

'If they do, it's over some layers of make-up.'

'Okay,' he said. 'I understand it gets warm under the theatre lights. If she started sweating, the process would begin for sure and she might not be aware at first. It forms a slime on the surface and the action can take out the nerve endings as well as the skin tissue. By the time she became aware, it would already have been well advanced.'

'This may explain the delay we've all been puzzling over,' Diamond said. 'Nasty.'

'Worse than nasty,' Ingeborg said. 'It's fiendish.'

'Does she know yet?' Diamond asked.

Pinch shook his head. 'We needed to confirm the results. This is tricky territory. We report to the medics, not the patient or her representatives. We informed the doctor treating her after we ran the first tests, but when there's likely to be legal action, you have to be certain.'

'The medics will tell her?'

'Have to.'

'And it can't have been an accident,' Diamond said. 'The lawyers will be aware of that. You don't add caustic soda to face powder through carelessness. This was deliberate.'

'And vicious,' Ingeborg added, her voice thick with emotion.

When they left, they took the towel with them in a sterile box that served as an evidence bag. It would go to the forensics lab at Chepstow for them to run their own tests.

In the car, Diamond said, 'Are you okay?'

'I thought I was going to throw up when he told us,' Ingeborg said. 'I can handle a murder scene, but this is worse, considering we just spoke to the victim. What a thing to come to terms with, learning you were hated this much by somebody.'

'I know. It's repulsive and impossible to justify. But our job is to find out why it was done and who is responsible.'

'Okay, guv. I won't let it do my head in. What do we do about this?'

'We've got enough now for a search warrant to get into Denise's house and seize her make-up kit. And we need to know a whole lot more about her.'

'Do you want to call Keith?'

He called CID on Ingeborg's phone and got Dawkins, that windbag, announcing that the department was at his service, as if it was menswear in Jolly's.

'Diamond here. Is Keith in the office?'

103

'Keith?' From the bemused way Dawkins repeated the name, it could have been Julius Caesar.

'DI Halliwell.'

'Would he be the gentleman with sideburns?'

Diamond gripped the phone harder. What could have possessed Georgina to dump such a nutcase in CID? 'That's Leaman. If he's there, hand the phone to him.'

'He is not.'

'This is urgent, Fred. Is anyone with you?'

'There is another officer with a more restrained haircut and by what you said I can only deduce he is DI Halliwell.'

'Put me on to him, for God's sake.'

Halliwell was on message at once. He said he'd organise the warrant directly. There was no shortage of local magistrates to contact.

'Any success tracing her car?'

'She owns a silver Vauxhall Corsa. It's not on the street right now. The neighbours say that's where she parks it when she's at home. They're pretty sure it wasn't there overnight. I've got the registration and put out an all units as agreed.'

'What's the address?'

'Excelsior Street in Dolemeads. By the time you get back here, the warrant should be ready.'

'We'll join you as soon as we can.'

He updated Ingeborg.

She said, 'I can't think why Denise would do something as dumb as this. She'd know we'll soon catch up with her.'

'We've yet to find out the background,' he said. 'I sense a history of ill-will behind this. You get people with a grudge and they lose all sense of proportion. This could have been a personal spat with Clarion, or something quite different, like a grievance against the theatre.'

'So she scars Clarion for life?' she said on an angry, rising note.

'Stay cool, Inge. Up to now, nobody has said a word against Denise.'

'Because she's only known to us as a functionary. The dresser. We'll find out a whole lot more shortly.'

* * *

They got to the end of the Keynsham bypass and started the Bath Road stretch of the A4. Ingeborg was driving too fast by Diamond's reckoning. 'You can take it more steadily now,' he said. 'We've made good time. I haven't heard what you dug up on Clarion.'

'I can talk as I drive, guv, and I'm inside the speed limit.'

'Not my limit.'

'It's open country for some way ahead.'

'I'll look at the country. You keep your eyes on the road. Does she have any obvious enemies?'

'I can only go by what's on the internet and in print. She's not controversial, like some pop stars.'

'Relationships?'

'There was a live-in boyfriend for a couple of years. He was Australian, supposedly touring Europe after getting his degree. They split up when he wanted to go back to Sydney and do a Ph.D. He's still out in Oz, as far as I'm aware. If there's anyone else she's serious about, she's kept them well hidden.'

'Does she do drugs?'

She laughed faintly. 'Don't they all at some point? Put it this way: she's not well known for it.'

'How does she spend her money then?'

'Property. She has apartments in London and New York and a manor house near Tunbridge Wells.'

'A home-loving girl, then.'

'It doesn't stop her from eating out and clubbing.'

'Who with?'

'Lately with the agent we met, Tilda Box.'

That intrigued him. 'They go to nightclubs together?'

'There are plenty of magazine pictures to prove it. Tilda entered her life last year when the singing career seemed to be on the slide. She steered her into acting.'

'Is Tilda successful as an agent?'

'I wouldn't know, except she doesn't seem to have any well-known clients apart from Clarion.'

'And she's very protective of her. Is Clarion bi, do you think?'

'I haven't seen it suggested anywhere. The media are quick on anything like that.'

'If she's straight, she'd surely not want Tilda with her on a regular basis.'

'You could be wrong there, guv. A lot of women feel more comfortable with their own sex as company. If the break-up with the Australian guy hurt her, she may be pleased to coast along for a bit with this Tilda, who smooths the way and makes her feel better about herself. Do you want to hear her sing? I picked up one of her singles last night. Top of the stack.'

'What do I do?'

She told him how to insert the disc, and Clarion's chirpy notes took over, balanced by an energising drumbeat. The words were hard to follow and the voice didn't sound anything special to Diamond's ear, but pop music wasn't one of his strengths.

'Is this from the latest album?'

'To be fair, it's not her best. She's trying for a hip-hop sound and it doesn't come off.'

'This was made before Tilda came on the scene?'

'Right.'

'Who was advising her then?'

'There would have been a creative team looking after the music. She had a manager called Declan Dean and he should have been on top of the business side. Somewhere it wasn't working and she left him.'

'At some point every singer's career tails off,' he said. 'It's a competitive market.'

'Highly. Yes, it may just have been the laws of commerce working, but someone has to carry the can.'

'She blamed this Declan?'

'It wasn't so obvious at the time, but it's been seeping out since, in her blog.'

'She has a blog?'

'They all do and most of them are dire. It's about digital exposure in the pop landscape. If you don't blog, you won't survive.'

'What kind of stuff does she write in the blog?'

'You wouldn't find it instructive. Films she's seen and would tip for an Oscar. Good meals she's eaten.'

Clarion's singing was getting too much. 'How do I turn this down?'

She pointed to the volume switch. 'She was a tad more interesting last week, doing her best to plug the play. She was on about learning lines and rehearsing. Of course the blog stopped on Monday. She could easily start up again now, but I guess the lawyers will have closed her down.'

'How would she blog from a hospital bed?'

'Using her iPhone. It would ease the boredom.'

They drove back into Bath and Manvers Street. Before anything else, Diamond arranged for the box containing the towel to be driven to the Home Office forensic lab at Chepstow. He'd been impressed by Pinch, but he still needed official confirmation of the findings.

As promised, Keith Halliwell had the authorised search warrant ready.

'Inge will drive us to Dolemeads,' Diamond said.

'Actually, guv, I was hoping for a few words in private,' Halliwell said.

'No problem. You can drive me there and we'll talk on the way. I'll tell Inge to meet us. I want her in on this.'

In the car, it emerged that Sergeant Dawkins was the problem.

'He's an oddball,' Halliwell started to say.

'Tell me something new,' Diamond said.

'I can't think how he managed to convince the ACC he was CID material. He means well—I think—but he says the strangest things. Our civilian women got the idea he was put in to spy on them. He was going on about time and motion. You remember when every business brought in time and motion experts to improve efficiency?'

This angered Diamond. 'Bloody nerve. He's got no right to talk to my staff like that. Time and motion. It's old hat, anyway.'

'I know, but it made everyone nervous. I told him to shut up about it and he didn't seem to understand what the fuss was about.'

'I'll tear some strips off him. I thought leaving him in the office was the best option. Now I'm not so sure.'

'He's in a world of his own.'

'It's when his world collides with ours that things go belly up.'

They crossed the river to the cheap housing of the Dolemeads estate, on the flood plain of the Avon. Excelsior Street was one of the first to be built after the clearance of a notorious Victorian slum known locally as Mud Island, where the houses were chronically damp and regularly flooded. In the first years of the twentieth century the site was raised by as much as twelve feet and a prestigious new council estate erected, not in the local stone, but red brick.

Ingeborg was waiting outside Denise Pearsall's narrow terraced house. She said she'd tried the doorbell and got no response. She'd spoken to the neighbours who described Denise as a very private lady. They hadn't seen her since the weekend.

Halliwell had brought an enforcer, the miniature battering ram used to open locked doors. 'Before we use that,' Diamond said, 'let's see if there's an easier way.' By sliding a loyalty card between door and jamb, he freed the latch and opened up.

In the narrow hallway, the morning's post of junk mail showed Denise had not been there for a day or two. Ingeborg was sent to search upstairs while the men inspected the living room and kitchen. The interior was clean and decorated in pastel shades of pink and blue. The only messages on the answerphone were several from the theatre asking Denise to make contact as soon as possible.

The tidiness made for an easy search. If her home was any guide, Denise was organised to the point of compulsion. Even the fridge magnets were in rows you could have checked with a ruler.

It didn't take long to discover that her professional make-up kit wasn't in the house. Ingeborg found some lipsticks and creams in the bedroom that were obviously for personal use and there were a few sticks of greasepaint in a drawer downstairs that they put into evidence bags.

'She'll have her main stuff in the car,' Diamond said. 'We've got to find that soon.'

Halliwell picked a magazine from the rack in the living room. 'How about this, guv?'

Clarion was on the cover of a celebrity mag.

'Good spotting, but it's hardly incriminating. Show me a page with her picture defaced and I might get excited.'

Ingeborg came downstairs carrying a three-ring binder with photos of actors Denise had dressed, most of them autographed with gushing compliments about how wonderful she'd been. She'd listed each production she'd worked with and the leading actors. The handwriting was as neat as the house, and as uninformative.

'We'll take this,' Diamond said. 'Is there a computer up there?'

'In the small bedroom she uses as an office,' Inge said. 'I checked. She seems to delete the e-mails after she's read them and there's very little to see. I get the impression she doesn't use it much.'

Diamond went upstairs to see the rooms for himself. The place looked as if it awaited a house guest—and a finicky one. The bed apparently hadn't been used overnight. Crisp, clean bed linen, surfaces free of dust, carpets hoovered, all in marked contrast to his own chaotic living arrangements.

He picked up a doll from the chintz-covered armchair in the corner. 'A bit like Clarion, would you say?'

Ingeborg smiled. 'I can't see it, guv.'

'No, and no pins sticking into it either.' He left the room and started down the stairs. 'Did you search the bathroom?' he called back.

'The shower surfaces are dry. Nothing much in there except toothpaste and showergel,' Ingeborg said from the bedroom. 'She makes herself up in here.'

'The cupboards, I mean. Cleaning materials. I'm thinking of caustic soda to clear the drain in the shower.'

'She doesn't use it. There's a bottle of Sink Fresh. Not the same thing at all.'

He checked the kitchen and all the cupboards downstairs, reflecting as he studied the labels that the absence of any caustic soda didn't mean Denise was in the clear. She would have taken the stuff to the theatre.

He decided they'd seen enough and failed to turn up anything of significance. They hadn't even come across an address book or a phone with stored numbers.

111

                    *   *   *

Back in Manvers Street, finding Denise and her car
remained the priority even though there was little
anyone in the building could do about that.

After the fruitless search in Excelsior Street,
Diamond felt ready to get some frustration out of
his system. He asked Fred Dawkins to step into his
office. 'What's this I hear about you upsetting the
civilian staff?'

'With the best of intentions—'

'Don't burble, man. Answer my question.'

'I can't,' Dawkins said.

'Why not?'

'You asked me what you hear about me
upsetting the civilian staff. What you hear is in
your head.'

The logic was correct, but inflammatory. 'You
know bloody well what I'm talking about.'

'That, too, is questionable.'

'You were out of order talking about time and
motion. Don't deny it, Fred. People don't lie about
stuff like that.'

'Time and motion?' Dawkins scratched his head
and seemed genuinely at a loss. 'Ah, I have it. I was
quoting Ford.'

'Henry Ford?' Diamond said, thinking of car
production.

'John.'

'*Stagecoach*?' He knew his old films and he was
damn sure John Ford the director wasn't into time
and motion.

' *'Tis Pity She's a Whore.*'

'Sergeant, there's something you'd better get

                         112

very clear. We don't go in for personal abuse in this department.'

'It's Jacobean.'

'It's offensive.'

'It's the title of a play.'

'I'm not on about plays. This is about you stirring up trouble in the department.'

'By speaking of time and motion?'

'You've got it.'

Unexpectedly, Dawkins made a fist and raised it. Briefly, Diamond thought he was about to strike him, but it was a theatrical pose and the man started speaking lines. ' "Why, I hold fate clasped in my fist, and could command the course of time's eternal motion, hadst thou been one thought more steady than an ebbing sea." '

One thing, and one thing only, was clear. Manvers Street nick wasn't ready for Jacobean drama.

' "Time's eternal motion," ' Dawkins repeated.

'Ah.'

'I can explain.'

'Save your breath. I'm beginning to cotton on. Do you make a habit of quoting lines from plays?'

'I would characterise it as an occasional indulgence.'

'Knock it off, for all our sakes. It caused confusion and near panic. The only quoting we do in CID is the official caution.'

'I shall curb the habit,' Dawkins said, and added with an earnest look, 'I trust I haven't blighted my prospects . . . guv.'

They were blighted the moment you stepped in here in that clown suit, Diamond thought. 'So are you a theatre-goer?'

113

'One of my indulgences,' Dawkins said.

'I suppose it comes with the dancing. Do you know the play Clarion was in?'

'Know it, no. Know of it, yes. I haven't seen it, which is a pity. I was at some disadvantage questioning Mr Shearman, the manager, but I formed the impression that he wasn't all that familiar with the script himself.'

'It's the same story as *Cabaret,* I'm told.'

'Then you were not told the whole truth. There's no music in *I Am a Camera*, no dancing and no changes of scene. The only changes are of time and costume. Putting it on at all was a risky venture.'

'A vehicle for Clarion Calhoun.'

'That, I think, goes without saying.'

'You also spoke to Denise Pearsall. What did you make of her? Was there any aggro towards Clarion?'

'Aggravation? None that I noticed. I saw anxiety in plenty.'

'Denise was troubled?'

'Exceedingly.'

'From guilt, would you say?'

'Difficult to divine. Conscience, possibly. She appeared to accept that her make-up was the likely cause of the occurrence.'

'Did you question her about it?'

'Minutely. She told me she used new materials.'

Diamond's eyebrows shot up. 'Some new brand?'

'She meant "new" in the sense of unopened. The brand was the same she had used before without ill effect. That was made clear.'

'She wasn't blaming anyone else, then?'

114

'The question of blame didn't arise. If you care to look at a transcript of the interview it is now stored in the computer, as you instructed.'

'Good. I will.' Somehow, Dawkins was coming out of this so-called roasting better than he came in. 'Watch what you say in future.' Even as he spoke the last words, Diamond knew he'd used the faulty logic the man revelled in dismantling.

But Dawkins had the sense not to comment. He nodded and left the room. If there was a faint smile lingering it may have been only in Diamond's imagination.

*   *   *

The notices were in and Hedley Shearman was relieved. The critics praised Gisella Watling's performance and didn't make too much of Clarion's collapse. The sensational stuff had all been covered in news stories the previous day. UNDERSTUDY'S SUCCESS IN DEMANDING ROLE, went one headline. Another: GISELLA'S STARRY NIGHT. Reviews like that would keep the show afloat until the end of the week. Nobody now expected it to transfer to London unless Clarion made a miraculous recovery.

He clipped the reviews. Anything good for morale was to be encouraged. They would be pinned on the stage-door keeper's noticeboard where everyone would see them as they arrived. Before that, however, he would use them to boost his chances with Gisella. He was waiting inside when she arrived for the matinee.

'Have you seen these?' he said. 'They loved your performance.'

115

She hadn't. She was over the moon, even if she tried to appear casual. In all the mayhem after Clarion broke down, he'd missed an opportunity to get to know this young woman who had been thrust into the limelight and performed so ably. She was taller than Clarion, with less of the showbiz glamour about her. For the play, her dark hair was styled with waves and cut short at the back, a style he could quickly get to like. She wasn't a starry-eyed beginner. She must have been on the stage some years. The concept of ensemble casting in the modern theatre ensured that she knew the role and didn't need to appear on stage with the book in her hands. Even so, it had taken courage to go on.

'It's a big step up the ladder,' he told her with a fatherly show of encouragement that often did the trick with young actresses. 'All sorts of people will read this, especially casting directors. You never know where it will lead. Clarion's misfortune is your opportunity.'

'I don't think of it like that,' she said in a voice that could have come from a twelve-year-old. 'I certainly wouldn't have wanted to get the part this way.'

'My dear, the theatre is one long story of actors seizing the moment. Did you know Shirley MacLaine was just a dancer in the chorus of *The Pajama Game* and doubling as understudy when the star, Carol Haney, broke her ankle? She was thrust into the limelight, took the audience by storm and got the movie role as well, because Hal Wallis happened to be in the audience. You never know your luck.'

'I still feel bad about Clarion.' Her eyes

confirmed it. To Shearman, she appeared utterly sincere.

'Why should you? You're not responsible.' After a pause he added, 'I hope.' He laughed. 'Ignore my twisted sense of humour. You could move into the number one dressing room if you wish. You've earned the right.'

'I'm happy where I am, thanks.'

'Which room is that?'

'Number eight. The one with the gloves and handbag in a frame on the wall.'

'They belonged to Vivien Leigh, you know. It's endowed in her name.' He stopped himself telling her that eight had the reputation of being haunted. Various unexplained phenomena had been reported over the years by actors who had used it. 'If it ever feels cold in there, be sure to ask for a fan heater.'

'Thanks, but it's comfortable. I'd better get up there now.'

'Do you do your own make-up?'

She nodded. 'I'm used to it.'

'Well done. Hope there's a good house in this afternoon with at least one butterfly. You know about the Theatre Royal butterflies?' He was being over-friendly now, doing his best to charm her. He'd got lucky like this a few times over the years.

'Yes, I heard the stories.'

'I'll come with you and show you something. It's on the way. It won't hold you up.'

She had to pass the fly tower to get to her dressing room. He walked close behind her, enjoying the swing of her hips. 'Back in the nineteen-forties, when the whole butterfly thing started,' he said, moving closer, 'the man who had

117

my job was called Reg Maddox and he designed a butterfly ballet for the pantomime and because of what happened one of the big gauze butterflies made as the backdrop was kept hanging in the flies as a kind of talisman. You wouldn't know it was there unless someone told you where to look.'

They had reached the fly floor, the area immediately behind the stage, where the peeling walls, old props, unwanted arc lamps and looped cables were in sharp contrast to the plush public areas of the theatre. Above them, the steel-framed fly tower, with its intricate single-purchase counterweight system of grids, lines and pulleys, rose eight metres clear of the rest of the building.

'The lighting isn't so great here, but if you look straight up, you'll get a sight of the lucky butterfly right at the top.' He pointed upwards with his left hand and at the same time curled his right over her shoulder. 'Do you see it?'

Gisella tilted her head back and didn't flinch when Shearman touched her. She was taller than he, but he didn't mind that. As he sometimes said when he'd got a woman into bed, the length that mattered wasn't from head to foot. He'd moved so close that he could feel her hair against his cheek. The sensation pleased him. He wasn't looking up at the damn butterfly. He knew where it was.

Suddenly she tensed and her whole frame shuddered.

He jerked his hand away from her shoulder. 'It's okay,' he said.

'It isn't,' she said in a shocked voice. 'Can't you see what I can? It's anything but okay.'

118

CHAPTER EIGHT

A police car and an ambulance were parked in front of the triple-arched theatre entrance in Saw Close. The whole area was congested with people arriving for the matinee.

'The stage door,' Diamond said to Keith Halliwell, and headed along the paved passage, past the tables outside the Garrick's Head. His negative feelings about entering the theatre had to be ignored. When you get the shout in CID you can't stop to think. Up the steps into the dim interior, they found their way through the backstage honeycomb and emerged under the fly tower, where an assortment of actors and technicians were gazing upwards at two paramedics and a uniformed police officer who had made their way along a narrow catwalk close to where a body was jackknifed over a pair of battens suspended from the grid under the roof. One arm hung down. The other must have been trapped.

'Do we know who it is?' he asked a stagehand.

'It must be the dresser. She went missing earlier.'

Missing no longer. He hadn't met Denise Pearsall and wouldn't have recognised her. All he could make out was that whoever was up there was dressed in jeans and black trainers. There was no indication of life.

He stood for a moment in silence. Violent death of any sort is a desecration, deserving of pity. A fall on to steel battens, almost certainly fracturing the spine, was chilling to contemplate. Here was a woman who had been in the prime of a useful, creative life. Who could say what hopes, memories, disappointments had been prematurely ended by this act?

A short, stout, self-important man in a striped suit came over and put an end to compassionate thoughts. 'Plain-clothes police, are you? I'm the theatre director, Hedley Shearman. I made the emergency call.'

'Was it you who found her?'

'I was with Gisella, one of the cast, and we happened to look up and had the shock of our lives. That arm, hanging down. Dreadful.'

'Are you certain who she is?'

'It has to be Denise, Clarion's dresser. You can't see her face from here, but some of her long red hair is visible. I knew she was upset by what happened on Monday. She phoned yesterday and told me she couldn't face coming in for last night's performance. God forgive me, it didn't cross my mind that she was suicidal.'

Diamond turned to Halliwell and asked him to pass the news to Manvers Street, making clear that although the missing person enquiry would shortly be called off, the dead woman's car still needed to be found. 'Where does she park?' he asked Shearman.

'The nearest is right across the street, but it's so small you hardly ever get in there on a weekday. Most of us use Charlotte Street or the multi-storey in Corn Street.'

Halliwell used his personal radio.

'When did you spot her?' Diamond asked Shearman.

'Twenty minutes ago. Gisella—who is playing Sally Bowles now—had just arrived for the matinee and I wanted to point something out to her in the fly tower. She looked up and saw the arm. She's profoundly shocked, as I was. She wants to go on, though. I'm not planning to cancel the performance.'

'We'll see about that,' Diamond said.

'It's all right. Nothing is visible to the audience,' Shearman added in earnest support of his decision. 'There are no scene changes. The set is all in place. You and your officers can remain at the back here throughout and you won't disrupt the show.'

A cancelled performance was anathema to theatre people. And from a police point of view it might suit to have the minimum of fuss. Yet how bizarre to have an audience enjoying the play while a corpse was behind the backcloth.

'No. Send them home.'

Shearman was appalled. 'What—cancel, at this late stage? Impossible. Denise wouldn't have wanted that.'

'Denise is out of the equation. It's my decision.'

'I don't know about that. I'm in charge here. What can I possibly say to people?'

'Unforeseen circumstances. The truth will have leaked out anyway. They've seen the ambulance and the police cars as they came in.'

'We've got coach parties coming in from miles around.'

'Bath isn't short of other attractions. They'll think of something else to do. Teashops, pubs, shopping. I suggest you make the announcement now if you want us out before the evening performance.'

121

Red-faced and angry, Shearman caved in and used his phone to issue instructions.

'Make sure the staff don't leave as well,' Diamond told him. 'I may need to question them.'

For all his bluster, Shearman wasn't going on stage to announce the cancellation. He delegated that thankless task to his front-of-house manager.

'Did anyone see Denise arrive this morning?' Diamond asked.

He shook his head. 'Someone would have told me. I was trying to contact her.'

'So when do you think this happened?'

'I've no idea how long she's been up there. People are walking through here a lot, but you don't look up unless you have a reason.'

'What was your reason?'

'I told you, I was with Gisella. She's the understudy who took over from Clarion. I wanted to show her the lucky butterfly—as encouragement.'

Diamond's interest quickened. 'Butterfly, you said?'

'Not a real one. A piece of scenery from way back. You can see it yourself right up near the roof if you stand in the right place. A dusty old thing more than sixty years old, but we value it as an emblem of good fortune.'

'Show me.'

Shearman moved a few strides to the left and pointed upwards, across the tower and at a higher level from where the corpse was lodged. A flashlight would have helped. Fortunately the thing suspended among other strips of scenery was colourful enough to make out. Red, purple, green and yellow and with scalloped edging, it didn't look like any species of butterfly known to biology.

'The scene painter enjoyed himself by the look of it.'

'It was for a pantomime.'

'Ah, I heard about this from someone else. So you looked for the butterfly and saw the body?'

'Gisella spotted it first. To her credit, she didn't scream. I almost did myself when she pointed.'

'Gisella stayed calm?'

'I wouldn't say calm. She was in control, but obviously shaken.'

'So you're saying the body could have been there some hours without anyone noticing?'

'Quite possibly. It's dark up there, as you see.'

'Nobody goes up between performances?'

'There's no reason to. The scenery for this production is all in place and we won't be changing it this week.'

'I'm trying to work out when it happened. She wasn't at home overnight. We searched her house this morning.'

'Then it's not impossible she did this some time yesterday. She phoned in about two in the afternoon.'

'And spoke to you? How did she sound?'

'Exhausted, really. She said she was sorry but she'd have to let us down because she couldn't face the evening performance. Denise is not a skiver. I knew it was genuine. I told her to get some rest and we'd cope without her, which we did.'

'Who was the last person who spoke to her here?'

'One of yours.'

'A police officer?'

'A sergeant in uniform with a policewoman

123

taking notes. He was doing all the talking.'

'Sounds like Sergeant Dawkins.'

'With a rather abrasive style of speech.'

'Definitely Dawkins.'

Shearman was quick to add, 'I'm not suggesting your sergeant said anything that caused Denise to take her own life.'

Privately, Diamond reserved judgement on that. He'd been driven near the limit by Dawkins. 'Why did she come in yesterday morning?'

'It was the obvious thing to do after what happened to Clarion. She felt responsible, being the one who made her up. I don't think she'd slept much. Neither had I, come to that.'

'Did she appear depressed?'

'Anxious, certainly. Depressed, probably. Whether suicidal is another question. I had no inkling of that, I assure you. But I can imagine how it preyed on her mind as the day went on and we had no better news of Clarion. Listen, can't we bring her down from there?'

'Not until the pathologist has seen her and photographs are taken.'

'It's obvious how she died. She jumped.'

Diamond didn't comment. He was psyching himself up for a duty he didn't relish. 'How would I get up there?'

'Do you want to get closer?'

'Well, I wouldn't be doing it for nothing.'

'The quickest way is up the iron ladder in the corner.'

He eyed the ladder, close to where the counterweight-carrying arbor moved up and down a track parallel to the wall. A vertical climb with the rungs spaced a foot apart looked a stern test of

124

an overweight detective's agility. He was in two minds. He could ask Halliwell to do it. In truth he needed to see the set-up for himself.

Shearman said, 'There's a little platform at each level, about every ten feet. Do you see?'

He was already having second thoughts. 'I'll wait for the paramedics to come down.'

'It looks as if they're on their way.'

With mixed feelings, he saw that they were, and so was the police officer. 'She's well dead,' one of the paramedics said on reaching the ground. 'Her neck is broken. Are you police as well?'

Diamond introduced himself. 'No indication how long she's been there, I suppose?'

'I wouldn't know. Are you going up to see?'

Duty demanded that he did. 'I'd better.'

'How are your knees? We can't do much for the lady, but we'll run you into casualty if need be.'

Bloody cheek, he thought. 'I played rugby for ten years. My knees are as good as yours.'

'Just asking.'

He was canny enough not to show off by shinning up the ladder like a sailor. By pausing between levels, he got to the catwalk breathing heavily, but without mishap.

Now it was a matter of edging out to view the body, making certain he clung on to the single handrail. What he saw was Denise Pearsall's body lying face up along the battens, her head skewed into an unnatural angle, the hair red, the face deathly white. Her eyes and mouth were still open, the tip of her tongue protruding, and a line of dried blood running from the edge of her mouth to her jawbone. Traces of eye make-up and lipstick on features that had once been attractive made the

125

death scene more grotesque. Had she prettied herself for her final act?

She'd stood no chance. She'd dropped from the loading bridge where the counterweights were added or removed, a distance at least ten metres higher, and hit the metal hard, snapping her spine at the neck. It would have been instant death, he told himself. But to see where she'd fallen from, he'd need to climb a stage higher.

It had to be done. He hauled his overweight frame up the last set of rungs until, gasping for breath, he reached the bridge, a catwalk with access to the steel cables and pulleys. Spare weights were ranged along the length of it. With only the briefest of glances downwards, he edged out to the position directly above the corpse. She'd have needed to step over the handrail. It couldn't have been accidental. Presumably she had intended to hit the floor, not the battens below. His blood ran cold.

Over to the other side was the piece of butterfly scenery, a psychedelic monster as tall as he, probably the last thing Denise saw before she died. It hadn't brought her much luck.

He'd seen as much as he needed. With painstaking care he picked his way down the sets of ladders.

An aroma of coffee wafted upwards. He was thinking he could do with some after that morbid duty. On completing the descent he saw Dr Bertram Sealy, the local pathologist, with his flask open. 'Should have guessed.'

'You should invest in one of these,' Sealy said, holding up the flask. 'Indispensable in my work. You're sweating, Superintendent. Did you go up to

126

the very top? You want to watch your blood pressure, doing stuff like that in your condition.'

'Coming from you, that's rich.'

'So what did you discover? I've heard of corpsing in the theatre, but this is excessive.' Sealy fancied himself a master of the black humour exchanged between pathologists and policemen to make the job bearable.

'This wasn't a cry for help, that's for sure. If you take a jump like that, you mean to do the business.'

'Was she a headcase?'

'Not known to be. But it seems she may have blamed herself for an incident here two evenings ago.'

'The Clarion what's-her-name thing? I saw it in the paper. Nasty.'

'If you can give me an estimate of when death occurred, doctor, that would be useful.'

'Said he, always the optimist. Do I need oxygen climbing that high?'

'You ought to make it.'

'I hope so. My wife knows I'm visiting the theatre and she told me to ask for complimentary tickets. Is it a good play?'

Sealy showing off his self-composure.

'I haven't seen it.'

'You should ask for a ticket. Perks of the trade.' Pathologists have to be positive, and Sealy lived up to the challenge. He screwed the empty cup back on to the flask and walked over to the ladder. 'I'll need someone to carry my bag. Do you want to go up again?'

Diamond snapped his fingers at a young uniformed constable. Then he turned his back on Sealy. 'Does she have a room of her own somewhere?' he asked Hedley Shearman, thinking a suicide note might exist.

'No. Dressers do their work around the dressing rooms. The nearest thing to an office would be wardrobe.'

'She worked out of a wardrobe?'

Shearman didn't turn up his nose, but his eyes said a lot. 'It's one of the biggest places backstage, where all the costumes and wigs are stored.'

'Beverages, too?'

'What?'

'I'm parched.'

'You won't get a drink in wardrobe, but the bars were doing some trade until we sent the audience away.'

'Show me to the nearest, then.' He told Halliwell to keep an eye on things and got a moody look back.

*   *   *

'It's a jewel of a theatre,' he forced himself to say to soften up Shearman over a beer in the dress circle bar. 'Are the finances in good nick?'

'Reasonably good. Mostly we play to full houses.'

'What's the seating capacity?'

'Eight seventy-five. We used to seat more, but we removed some capacity when we last refurbished the main house in 1999. Necessary, though. It was a tight fit before, I have to admit. The present seating is the best you'll find anywhere, by Quinnet of Paris, who fitted out the Royal Opera House. You're a big man, but you'd be comfortable, I assure you.'

128

The personal reference wasn't welcomed by Diamond. 'I've never had trouble fitting into seats.'

'More leg room, I meant.'

'I once sat through an entire evening here.'

'Congratulations.'

Ignoring the sarcasm, Diamond aired more of his limited theatrical know-how. 'You need well-known actors to bring in the audiences.'

'Yes, but we're not tied to the star system. We have the Ustinov Studio as part of the complex and we can put on more experimental, contemporary productions there.'

'Clarion Calhoun was chosen for her box-office appeal. Is that right?'

Shearman glanced away momentarily. 'She wasn't my personal pick.'

Diamond didn't miss an opening like that. 'You'd have gone for someone else?'

'I had reservations about Clarion. She went to drama school, but hasn't done much since. It was a top-level decision, the choice of play and the casting. Anyway, that's water under the bridge. The poor woman won't be doing any more acting in this run.'

'How did Denise feel about the choice of Clarion in the main role?'

'No idea. I never discussed it with her. Why should I? She was only a dresser. They're pretty low in the pecking order. No way would they have a say in casting.'

'But she was on the permanent staff. If there was a general feeling that Clarion wasn't up to the job, it would have fed through to Denise.'

'You're losing me.'

'There's a sense of unity in this theatre,'

129

Diamond said, playing to Shearman's vanity. 'You sense it as soon as you step into the place. An outsider like Clarion—not known as an actor—is given the star part. There must have been some muttering in the ranks.'

'How does this affect the tragedy of Denise's suicide?' Shearman asked.

'I'm thinking aloud. She was well placed to get Clarion sidelined.'

'Deliberately? Oh no.'

Diamond nodded.

Shearman dismissed the suggestion with a flap of his hand. 'By making her up with something that damaged her face? No chance.'

'You may as well know. It was caustic soda.'

The man jerked back so suddenly that he spilt beer on his trousers. 'That isn't possible.'

'It is. It was analysed.'

After a moment of silence he said in a strangled voice, 'I can't accept that Denise would have done such a thing.'

'Why else did she kill herself, then?'

Shearman thought about that and released a long, audible breath. 'God almighty.'

'How well did you know Denise? Was there any malice in her?'

'Malice?' He repeated the word as if it was foreign. 'None that I ever noticed. We never had any complaints from actors.'

'We'll need to inform her next of kin. Presumably you keep her personal file somewhere?'

'All it would have is her letter of application and some contact details. We're a theatre, not the civil service.'

130

'I'll see it, just the same. Does she have any family?'

'I couldn't tell you. We weren't on close terms.'

'She's been here six years, Mr Shearman.'

'I keep telling you. She was only a dresser.'

'It's about rank, is it? There must be someone in this theatre she was on speaking terms with. Who did she know best?'

He hesitated. 'She worked for Kate, the wardrobe mistress. I wouldn't say they were the best of friends. You'd better speak to Kate. She objects to the official label, by the way. She likes to be known as Kate in wardrobe.'

'Is she in the building now?'

'I'm sure she is. They wash and iron the clothes after each performance. This is all such a shock. I'm still coming to terms with it. Caustic soda? I can't believe Denise would do such an abominable thing, yet why else would she have killed herself?'

'Will you manage without her?'

'Of course. Actors are good at coping. Clarion was the exception and that was only down to inexperience.'

'I ought to be getting back.' Diamond drained his glass. 'Just now when we spoke about the choice of play you said it was a top-level decision. You're the boss, aren't you?'

Shearman gave a hollow laugh. 'Don't be deceived. A theatre is full of egos known as managers. House, front-of-house, marketing, production, development. Even kids straight out of drama school are classed as assistant stage managers, or deputies. Basically, if you're not a scene-shifter or a call boy, you're a manager of some description.'

131

'But someone has to make decisions.'

'Not me. Not this time.'

'Who's the big cheese, if you aren't?'

'The chairman of the board. Francis Melmot.'

'He signed up Clarion?'

'There was consultation, so-called. I was asked what I thought, but the decision wasn't mine. He outranks me, and so do all the trustees, come to that.' The bitterness wasn't disguised.

'So it's run as a trust?'

'Most theatres are, these days.'

'And is it usual for the board of trustees to decide on the play?'

'Not in this theatre. Artistic decisions are generally left to the salaried staff. We're employed for our expertise . . . supposedly.'

'You're saying she was foisted on you by the board?'

'I wouldn't put it like that. You mustn't misquote me.' Suddenly, Shearman regretted what he'd revealed. 'We're very fortunate in having the trustees we do.'

'Their decision could have a bearing,' Diamond said.

'No, I don't think so. Not at all.'

'If an exception was made and an edict was issued from on high that Clarion had to be given the role—'

'You're not listening. I told you there was consultation.'

'But the decision wasn't yours. I'd better speak to Francis Melmot.'

Shearman's face flushed crimson. He'd given too much away. 'Oh dear. I don't think this is wise. The casting has no bearing on what happened.

132

Denise wasn't involved in theatre politics. She got on with her job like the rest of us. There must have been some dreadful error.'

'Caustic soda in the make-up?'

Shearman fingered his tie as if it was choking him.

They returned to the scene of the fatal incident.

*   *   *

High in the fly tower, photographs were still being taken of the body, but Dr Sealy was back on ground level. 'We'll have her down presently and I'll do the autopsy tomorrow morning.'

'Anything I should be told?' Diamond asked.

'Not really. The cervical spine appears to have snapped at the point where she hit the metalwork. Death would have been immediate.'

'Time?'

Sealy looked at his watch. 'Two twenty.'

'Ten minutes ago?' Diamond said in disbelief.

'The legal time of death, when I confirmed that life was extinct. If you're asking for the estimated time, the moment she died, you're asking for the moon, old boy. I took a temperature reading, but it means very little really. There's obvious hypostasis in the arm that hung down, so I can tell you it was some hours ago, but how many is another question.'

'Will you know any better tomorrow?'

'Frankly, I doubt it.'

'Where would I be without your expert help?'

Sealy gave a shrug. 'Now who do I see about those complimentary tickets?'

Kate, in wardrobe, sighed heavily. 'Denise was my senior dresser. I can't think what drove her to this.'

'She used this room as her base, I was told.' Diamond couldn't see where. He was wedged between an ironing board and a washing machine. Every surface was covered in layers of dress materials. Racks of costumes, hatboxes piled high, wigs on dummy heads and sewing machines filled all the other space.

'She did, but you wouldn't know. She always brought her own things with her and took them away at the end of the show.'

'What things?'

'Her bags, I mean, with all she needed. Dressers are expected to deal with any emergency from a missing button to a false moustache that won't stick.'

'Make-up?'

'In rare cases, yes.'

'Like Clarion?'

'Yes.'

'Did Denise supply the make-up for Clarion?'

'That's right. Her own. She had a special bag for it.'

'Describe this bag, would you?'

'Black leather, rather like an old-fashioned doctor's bag, with all the pots and brushes inside. I expect you'll find it in her house.'

'We already searched. It isn't there.'

'In her car, then.'

'Do you know where she parked?'

'Anywhere she could. Finding a place is a lottery at this time of year, with all the summer visitors.'

He looked across the heaps of costumes and materials. 'I was wondering if she left a note somewhere.'

'A suicide note? I haven't found one. I don't think she'd leave it here. Things get covered over. I'm always losing scissors.'

'It's worth a check.'

'If it's anywhere, it would be somewhere near the door where you're standing. She'd hang her coat there and chat, just like you are.'

He didn't class his questions as chat. After lifting everything within reach and finding no note he asked, 'Did she seem anxious about anything?'

'Anxious? Not Denise. She wouldn't mind me saying she was as tough as old boots. She'd done all sorts. At one time when she couldn't get theatre work she helped out at an undertaker's, prettifying the departed for their relatives to see them. She also toured with a theatre company in Bosnia when the war was going on. And when she was just a slip of a girl she was involved with a prison drama group in Manchester, murderers and rapists. She was no wimp, bless her.' She produced a tissue and blew her nose, but Diamond had the impression it was more about self-pity than sympathy. The loss of the senior dresser would add to the workload.

'Did she talk to you about the current production?'

'I talked to her. As one of the dressers she works for me, you see.'

The pecking order again. 'Are there others?'

'Usually, yes, but not for this production apart from one little student who helps out. There are only seven actors and not many costume changes.'

'Did Denise have anything to say about the

casting?'

'We consulted over the costumes and make-up.' A guarded answer.

'Yes, but did she say anything about *I Am a Camera*? Personalities, the actors in particular? You can be frank with me.'

The last words were a mistake. Kate shook her head before he'd finished saying them. He had an instinct that this big-eyed, blousy woman who didn't like being known as the wardrobe mistress would be a rich source of gossip if only he could tap into it.

'Come on, Kate,' he said. 'You just told me she liked a chat. You both had to work with the same set of people. Actors are fascinating to be around, aren't they?'

'Tell me about it,' she told him, rolling her eyes, and then appeared willing to say more now that the focus had shifted from Denise. 'They're like kids, most of them. It's all "me, me". And if they're not full of themselves they're sucking their thumbs in a corner, wanting to be mothered. It depends.'

'How was Clarion getting on with everyone?'

'Clarion?' She spoke the name as if it had no connection to the cast. 'All right.' Said without conviction.

'Nervous?'

'She was confident in one way, used to dealing with people, but it stood out a mile that she was terrified of acting. She's used to going in front of an audience, huge audiences sometimes, but not speaking lines. She kept telling us she'd had drama training, and I think she was trying to convince herself more than us. She wasn't much good in rehearsal.'

'Forgetting her lines?'

'More the way she spoke them. Trying too hard. It's not an easy part, Sally Bowles.'

'Was there a sense that the play was going to flop?'

Kate hesitated. He'd pressed too hard again. No one admits they're involved in a turkey until it's too late.

'More nervousness than usual, then?'

'I suppose.'

'And how was Denise taking it? Was it personal for her?'

She was even more twitchy now that Denise's name had come up again. 'What do you mean—personal?'

'She worked here a long time. She was proud of the theatre, wasn't she?'

'It was a job like any other. There's this idea that theatre people are like a family. Sentimental tripe.'

'You get dysfunctional families.'

'Too true.' She busied herself brushing the front of a jacket with such sudden force that it was a wonder the lapels stayed put. 'But we're professionals and we do the job we're paid to do, or try to.' There was strong resentment here, but what about he couldn't tell.

'If a play flops, you all work hard for small audiences and a blasting from the critics,' he said. 'I get the impression there was a lot of nervousness about this one. I'm wondering if Denise took it to heart.'

'She felt we'd been short-changed with Clarion getting the role, and quite a number of us shared her opinion.'

'But then it's all over at the end of a week,' he

said. 'Didn't justify killing herself. Was she well balanced?'

'I always thought so.'

'Maybe there were other strains in her life.'

Again, she was shaking her head before he'd got the words out. 'I doubt it.'

'Was she romantically involved with anyone?'

'In the theatre?

'Or outside.'

'If she was, she never said a word about it. I'm sure I'd know. I've talked to her often enough about my own love life. It's a standing joke that I wear my heart on my sleeves. Sleeves—geddit? I find being upfront, as I am, encourages other people to share their secrets.'

People's self-image is often at variance with reality. Diamond wouldn't have called this lady upfront. 'She lived alone.'

'Her choice. Some of us think a man is for pleasure, not for life.' Surprisingly in the circumstances, she was giving Diamond the eye. Maybe that was what she meant by upfront.

'Did she have any other secrets I should know about?'

'What are you hinting at? She wasn't gay. Plenty of people in this profession are, but Denise wasn't.'

'On Monday when the play opened, did she call in here?'

'Always does, about six, in time to deliver the costumes to the actors. She was no different from usual, just anxious about the first night, as we all were.'

'Can you recall what was said?'

'Not much. She was doing the rounds of the dressing rooms. It's not a time for chat. I think we

138

both said we hoped it would go better than the dress rehearsal. When the time came to sort Clarion out, she picked up her case and tootled off, as calm as a lake in heaven.'

'Her case. You're speaking of the make-up case?'

'Yes.'

'I want to be clear about this. Denise arrived with the make-up. Had she come straight here from her car?'

'I assume so. She was still wearing her coat. Like I said, she always hung it on the door behind you.'

'So no one could have tampered with the make-up before she got to Clarion's dressing room?'

'That's for certain.'

Useful information. Suspicious as always, he'd been toying with the possibility that some other person could have added caustic soda to the make-up before the show. This seemed to scotch the theory. 'Did you see her after the incident on stage?'

'No, she went to the hospital with Clarion. I was way too busy helping Gisella. There was a swift decision to get her on as understudy, and my job was to get her into one of the Sally Bowles costumes.'

'And make her up?'

Kate shook her head. 'She was playing Natalia, so she was done already.'

'She performed well, I gather?'

'She was marvellous, considering. We had an ASM understudying her part—two small scenes—and she had to step up as well. Fortunately for me they're similar in build. All it needed was some pinning here and there.'

139

'What troubles me about all this,' Diamond said, 'is the phrase you used just now. You said when Denise left this room to go and see Clarion, she was "calm as a lake in heaven".'

'It's Gilbert and Sullivan,' she said. 'I forget which one. Just a phrase that came to mind. Put it this way. She was her normal, placid self, well in control. What's wrong with that?'

'I'll tell you. She was on her way to smear caustic soda on Clarion's face and cause acute pain and third-degree burns, so how could she be so calm?'

'You'll have to work that out for yourself.'

One thing he had worked out. The wardrobe mistress and the dresser had not been on the best of terms.

CHAPTER NINE

Diamond had a strong dislike of being fobbed off. After seeing Kate in wardrobe, he asked to meet Francis Melmot and was told that the chairman was unavailable for the rest of the day.

'What does that mean?' he asked Shearman.

'I assume he has a prior engagement.'

'Priority over the police? I don't think so. What do you know about his plans, anyway?'

'I'm just passing on the information. He's out of reach.'

'Climbing the Matterhorn, is he?'

'What?'

'Channel swimming? Bungee jumping? How is he out of reach?'

'All I can tell you is what he said to my secretary

140

before he left the building.'

'So he was here today?'

'And yesterday. And the day before. The chairman is taking a keen interest in what's happened.'

'So keen that he clears off as soon as the police arrive. Does he work for a living?'

'He has a number of directorships, I know for certain.'

'You'd better give me his phone number.'

On trying the number, he got a recorded message telling him what he'd already heard: that Mr Melmot was unavailable. He had the same result from the mobile.

'Where does he live?' he asked Shearman.

'I don't think that's wise.'

'I didn't ask if it was wise.'

Shortly after, with arms folded and jaw jutting in Churchillian defiance, Diamond was driven by Keith Halliwell through the leafy lanes of Somerset towards Wellow, about five miles south of the city. They were looking for Melmot Hall, where Melmots had lived since the Restoration.

For Diamond, getting out of that theatre was like being released from some hypnotist's instruction. Only now did he fully understand the paralysing effect the place had on him. This couldn't go on. If he didn't deal with it, he'd be forced to drop the case.

'Funnily enough,' Halliwell said, trying to lighten the mood, 'I've never been to Wellow.'

'You wouldn't have much cause,' Diamond said. 'It's not the crime capital of the south-west.'

The sat-nav directed them through the quiet village and across the Wellow Brook towards the unexpected: a line of parked cars stretching to infinity, making two-way traffic an impossibility.

'What's going on?' Halliwell said, slowing up.

'We are,' Diamond said, still in warlike mode. 'We're going on. If anything comes the other way, they'll have to reverse.'

Knowing you didn't argue with the boss when he was like this, Halliwell moved the car on fifty yards to an imposing gateway with stone eagles: the entrance to Melmot Hall.

A line of cones barred anyone from driving in.

'He *is* playing hard to get.'

Forced to move on, they despaired at the sight of more cars parked solidly along the left side of the narrow road.

'You could have set me down by the entrance,' Diamond said.

'Sorry, guv.'

Much to Halliwell's relief another driver moved out and left a space. He reversed in promptly and opened his door.

Diamond didn't move. 'How am I supposed to get out?' His side of the car was against the hedge. A slimmer passenger might have managed it. His deputy had the tact not to say so.

'Can you slide across and use my door?'

'And damage my wedding tackle on your gear lever? No thanks.'

Halliwell drove out again to allow the big man to alight without mishap. The car was parked for the second time and they walked back to the entrance. Inside, people were strolling around the edges of an immaculate lawn in front of a large gabled house with tall Tudor chimneys. Halfway along the drive an elderly woman in a straw hat and pale yellow muslin dress was seated behind a trestle table. 'You've brought some sunshine with you, gentlemen,' she said when they reached her. 'Two? That'll be six pounds, please.'

'Sorry to disappoint you, but it won't,' Diamond said. 'What's going on?'

'Aren't you here to visit the garden?'

'We're visiting the owner, Mr Melmot. Is he home?' He thought the name would get them in, but it didn't.

She eyed them with suspicion. 'I'm Mrs Melmot and I don't recall meeting you. Everyone has to pay today. It's all for charity. Teas are being served on the terrace.'

Halliwell had picked a pamphlet off the table. He passed it to Diamond. It was about openings in Somerset under the National Gardens Scheme.

'We didn't come to see your garden, ma'am,' Diamond said.

'I guessed as much by the look of you,' Mrs Melmot said in a tone that wasn't complimentary, 'and you're not the only ones. They come from miles around for a slice of my famous lemon drizzle cake, but the entrance fee is the same whatever you're here for.'

'Is your husband on the premises?'

'I hope not. He's dead.' She announced it as if talking about a felled tree, in the matter-of-fact tone of the well-raised Englishwoman.

There wasn't anything adequate Diamond could say, so he waited for her to speak again.

'He shot himself in 1999. Six pounds, please.'

After another pause, Diamond said, 'It must be your son we've come to interview. Sorry about the misunderstanding. I haven't made myself clear.

143

We're police officers.'

'Do you have a warrant?' she asked, unfazed. She'd evidently watched police dramas on TV.

'We don't require one. We want to speak to Francis Melmot, that's all.'

They could have ignored her and stepped past, but in this quintessentially peaceful setting it seemed churlish to cause a scene. Actually one was brewing behind them. Some American visitors had been kept waiting in line. One of them asked what the hold-up was.

'These gentlemen seem to think they can come in without tickets,' Mrs Melmot said.

'It's for charity, for Christ's sake, and cheap at the price,' the man said, handing across a twenty-pound note. 'Here, this should take care of it, and let's all get started while the weather holds.'

'That isn't necessary,' Diamond said, but the money was already in the cashbox. Mrs Melmot was no slouch with the cash. She'd also pressed yellow stickers on their lapels and their sponsor was pocketing his change. This farce had gone too far to reverse.

'Settle up with the gentleman, Keith, and I'll see you right.' He marched up the drive towards the entrance porch and was stopped by a man in a green blazer with both hands raised.

'The house isn't open, sir.'

'Are you the owner?'

'I'm staff. Mr Melmot is in the orangery, around the building to your left.'

'What's he wearing? We haven't met.'

'You can't miss him.'

This begged a question Diamond didn't ask.

Now that the awkwardness of arriving was over,

144

he found himself mellowing a little. He couldn't fail to respond to the glories of an English garden on a summer afternoon, a precious break from the dark confines of the theatre. The owners of all those cars were scattered across several acres of lawn and it didn't seem crowded. His mood was improving by the minute.

He found the orangery, a large octagonal Victorian structure. No oranges were visible, but there was a sizeable lemon tree and a sizeable man—around six foot eight—in a white linen jacket and pink shirt was standing beside it speaking to visitors with an air of authority. Showing patience that was unusual for him, Diamond awaited his turn.

'This isn't a question about the garden,' he said when his chance came. He introduced himself.

'Detective superintendent? What on earth . . . ?'

'Following up on the fatality in the theatre.'

'The dresser? Tragic, yes, but hardly a matter for the police. She took her own life.'

'We still have to check in case it's a suspicious death.'

'I can't see how. She jumped, obviously. And you've driven all the way here to talk to me?'

'I was hoping to catch you at the theatre, but you'd left.'

'There was no more I could do, I'm sorry to say.' Francis Melmot made an effort to be more agreeable. 'Extremely distressing, the whole thing. Shall we speak somewhere else? One's voice carries in here.' This was true, particularly as he was so tall that nothing obstructed his outflow of words.

Somewhere else: Diamond's thoughts turned to

the terrace and the famous lemon drizzle cake. Instead, Melmot steered him through a walled vegetable garden to an open area with a sunken lawn.

'We use this as an open-air theatre for local groups. You've heard of Storm on the Lawn, I expect?'

'No.'

'Good Lord! Where have you been living? It's been running more than ten years. The Youth Theatre summer school, a series of marvellous open-air productions at Prior Park. The first was loosely based on *The Tempest*. Hence the name Storm on the Lawn. It stuck and has been used as an umbrella title ever since. Well, the Melmot Hall open-air shows aren't up to that standard. We get the local am-dram groups. Farce on the Grass, we call it in the family, whatever the show, and it's usually the *Dream*. Muddy fairies and mosquitoes.' He grinned. The extreme distress he'd mentioned seemed to have evaporated.

'You're heavily involved in the theatre,' Diamond said.

'Yes, everyone says I should have played some kind of sport, for obvious reasons, but I've always been drawn to the footlights. The trouble is that there aren't many actors male or female comfortable going on stage with a beanpole like me, so I have to make my contribution in other ways. Even then, it's difficult. Pity the unfortunate person seated behind me in the audience.'

'So you became a trustee?'

'When one is in a position to help out, one should, I feel.'

'A responsibility, being chairman?'

146

'Indeed, and much more so in times of crisis.'

'I was told that the trustees had a hand in the casting of Clarion Calhoun.'

The first hint of ill-humour surfaced on Melmot's face. 'Who told you that? Shearman, no doubt. Theatre politics. He's touchy on this subject.'

So are you, Diamond thought. 'But is it true?'

'Broadly, yes.'

'And is it usual for the board to make decisions like that?'

'Commercial decisions. This was a commercial decision. She's hugely popular, as I'm sure you're aware. It was democratically decided. The trustees are realists. They know we need at least one sell-out production as well as the pantomime to stay solvent.'

'You get Arts Council support?'

'Not a penny. We're truly independent, very good at fund-raising and constantly raising our sights.'

'*I Am a Camera* is a sell-out, I was told.'

'Absolutely.'

'I was also told that Clarion can't act.'

Melmot's blue eyes bulged suddenly. 'That's hardly fair. She didn't get the chance.'

'I heard she was poor in rehearsal.'

'That's not unusual. You know the superstition. Bad dress rehearsal, good first night. She went through drama school.'

'A long time ago. The critics would have savaged her. You were putting the theatre's reputation at risk.'

'You shouldn't take everything Hedley Shearman says as gospel. His pride took a

147

hammering. He thought he was in overall charge of the casting and he usually is. I don't accept that Clarion was heading for poor reviews.'

'I didn't get it only from Mr Shearman,' Diamond said. 'Everyone I've spoken to says she was rubbish.'

'The wardrobe mistress, I suppose,' Melmot said. 'Kate is not a happy woman. This is the problem. People are quick to take sides in a community like ours that lives off its nerves. You get cliques and conspiracies all the time. You've heard only one side of the argument.'

'Are you telling me you had a hit on your hands?'

He gave an impatient sigh. 'This isn't getting us anywhere. Why don't you concentrate on the matter in hand, the suicide?'

'All right, let's do that. It isn't entirely clear why Denise Pearsall, an apparently well-adjusted, happy woman, decided to end it all.'

'That's plain enough, isn't it? She was responsible for the damage to Clarion's face. Apart from the personal tragedy, it has deeply worrying implications for the theatre.'

'The possibility of a lawsuit?'

'For obvious reasons, I'd rather not discuss that.'

'Clarion seemed ready to discuss it when I spoke to her this morning.'

He took a step back and almost fell down the slope in his surprise. 'You've seen Clarion?'

'At Frenchay.'

'I was told she was surrounded by security.'

'She is. She wouldn't want a visit from anyone else. She's instructing her lawyers, she told me. Suing for disfigurement and loss of earnings.'

148

A sigh that was almost a groan marked Melmot's reaction. 'I feared as much. Years of good housekeeping and fund-raising could be undone by this.'

'You heard about the caustic soda?'

'Yes, I did, and I was speechless. Madness. I can't think what drove the woman to it. She was with us for six years.'

'Happy in her work?'

He gave a shrug that was meant to be reassuring. 'There were some personal issues in the wardrobe department, but we'd dealt with them. By all accounts she was good at her job and in command, as you say. Was it a dreadful error? How could it possibly have happened?'

Crucial questions, as yet unanswerable, as Diamond showed by spreading his hands. 'Let's talk about Clarion. You said the decision to use her was democratic. Who was it who first suggested her for the part?'

'I did.'

'You?'

'I'd better qualify that. I suggested her as a name for the summer season. The choice of play came later.'

'What gave you the idea?'

He smiled. 'I'm a fan.' Difficult to credit, but the way his face had lit up seemed to make it believable that a middle-aged owner of a stately home should be into the pop scene. 'Followed her career almost since she started. She's an amazing performer. I remembered reading somewhere that she'd been through drama college and also that she thought Bath was the loveliest city in England. Putting two and two together, I mentioned her name at a board meeting and they were as excited about it as I was. The next thing was choosing a part that would tempt her and someone came up with Sally Bowles.'

'Why didn't you go for the musical?'

'*Cabaret*? Far too expensive, and not her style of singing.'

'So who made the approach?'

'Yours truly.' He smiled. 'I can be persuasive.'

'Had you met Clarion before?'

'No, this was my chance. I asked her out to lunch in London and sold the idea to her. She leapt at it. Neither of us mentioned that it's been a while since she had a big hit, but it was a factor. And she still had the acting bug. Tough negotiations followed with the agent, of course.'

'Tilda Box. I met her at the hospital.'

'You did?' Melmot was beginning to treat Diamond with caution, if not respect. 'Miss Box is a hard bargainer. Eventually we got the terms reduced to a realistic figure. God knows what we'll have to pay now.'

'Only if they can prove you were negligent,' Diamond said. 'I'm no lawyer, but these were special circumstances.'

'Denise Pearsall was in our employment, unfortunately. If the fault was hers I can't see us avoiding a substantial payout. Is there anything else you need to know? I really ought to be meeting my visitors.'

Diamond suggested walking back to the orangery, talking as they went. 'When Clarion came to Bath to start rehearsing, was anyone with her?'

'Tilda, making sure she was satisfied with the

arrangements.'

'No one else? Where did they stay?'

'I don't know about Tilda, but Clarion put up here for a couple of days.'

'Here?' Diamond pointed a thumb at the stately home. 'You had her as a house guest?'

'I suggested it early in the bargaining process, as an incentive. One of the things I know about millionaire pop stars is that it pleases them to mingle with old money. It makes them feel more secure.'

'A couple of days, you said?'

'Yes, when they started rehearsing until late in the evening she moved to the Royal Crescent Hotel.'

'For you as a fan, it must have been a dream come true.'

The colour rose in the fan's cheeks. 'It was all very proper. My mother lives here too, you know.'

'I met her when we arrived,' Diamond said. 'Famous for her cake.'

Melmot clicked his tongue. 'Is that what she tells people as they arrive? She's incorrigible.'

'I was also told about your late father.'

'The whole family saga? Oh my word. It makes one cringe. She'll talk to anyone. Father had an accident while cleaning his shotgun. Mother was typically calm about the whole thing, I have to say. They weren't close.'

Diamond could understand why. 'Are any other members of your family living here?'

He shook his head. 'Just mother and me. I'd offer to show you round, but I'm supposed to be available to answer questions about the plants and if you don't mind I really ought to be more visible

151

now.'

They'd reached the orangery. Diamond thanked him and went looking for Halliwell.

He found him at a table on the terrace overlooking the south lawn. He had a cup of tea in front of him and an empty plate that he slipped deftly under the saucer. 'I thought if I waited here, guv, you'd come by sooner or later.'

Diamond pointed. 'Was that the lemon drizzle?'

'It was.'

'Good?'

'The best ever. I was lucky. I had the last piece. You can still get a cup of tea and a digestive biscuit.'

'Are you serious?'

'There could be flapjacks.'

'I break my teeth on them.' Muttering, he went over to where the tea was being served by the Wellow Women's Institute.

'I don't want you thinking this has anything to do with the cake I missed out on,' he said to Halliwell when he returned to the table, 'but tomorrow morning you're standing in for me at the post-mortem.'

CHAPTER TEN

Late the same afternoon in Manvers Street, Diamond shut himself in his office and sank into the armchair he rarely used. On the face of it, the case could now be closed. Denise's suicide could only mean she held herself responsible for the damage to Clarion's face. What other

152

interpretation could be put on it? By some freakish oversight she had used caustic soda with the regular make-up. It was unlikely to have been deliberate. Nobody knew of any feud between them. Everyone spoke of her as a balanced, conscientious member of the full-time staff, good at her job. Her horror at what had happened must have driven her to take her own life.

It was tempting to leave the lawyers to discover the truth about the scarring episode and argue over who was responsible. They were going to make a long-running, expensive court action out of it for sure. He'd only been drawn into this at Georgina's insistence, and she would be content if *Sweeney Todd* went ahead as scheduled. There was no reason why it shouldn't. The legal process would be slow to start.

But his self-respect as a detective wouldn't let him walk away. There ought to be a better explanation. He reached for one of the forensic textbooks on the shelf behind him. What would be the use of caustic soda in a theatre? Presently he learned that sodium hydroxide, as it was known to the scientists, was much more than a remedy for blocked drains. Destructive as it was to human tissue, it had useful applications, mainly because of its action on unwanted fats and acidic materials. Soap manufacturers depended on it for converting fat, tallow and vegetable oils. It was used in the processing of cotton and the dyeing of synthetic fibres, in the manufacture of pulp and paper, biodiesel and PVC. The recycling industry needed it to de-ink waste paper. Incredibly even food producers and water-treatment firms made use of the stuff.

For all that, he thought, the simple power to unblock drains seemed the best bet. A theatre with eleven dressing rooms—most with shared washing facilities—was certain to experience problems with waste water. Actors would be showering and washing away hair and make-up after every performance. It would be an ill-prepared theatre that didn't have drain-cleaning products at the ready. A cheap, effective product such as caustic soda might be preferred to something with a fancy name that cost three times as much.

But where had Denise picked up the chemical, and why? He'd found none in her house. The theatre cleaning staff would have a store somewhere. He was wondering if supplies of the stuff also lurked in her workplace among the clutter of the wardrobe department, where costumes were laundered daily and drains might well need unblocking. Equally, some might be tucked away under a sink in one of the dressing rooms she visited.

The biggest mystery was how she could have made the mistake. Pure caustic soda came in sturdy containers with child-proof lids and a printed warning. Could a professional like Denise have muddled one with a tin of talc? The fine, white powder might appear similar, but the packaging was distinctive.

Early on, he'd speculated whether someone else had tampered with Denise's make-up and this still seemed possible. Various people were unhappy that Clarion had the starring role. If one of them had decided to injure her and put her out of the play, they knew she was the only cast member being made up by Denise. Doctor the make-up and it was obvious who would take the rap.

This line of thought presented two problems he hadn't resolved: opportunity and timing. First, Kate in wardrobe had said Denise arrived with her black leather make-up case and didn't open it or leave it lying around. She went straight from the wardrobe room to Clarion's dressing room. And second, there had been a delay of at least twenty minutes before Clarion reacted.

There had to be a way through this. Deep in thought, he clasped his hands behind his neck and stared at the ceiling. Finally he tapped the chair arm and stood up. He was no Sherlock Holmes. He needed to ask for a second opinion.

He got up and put his head around the door. 'Is Ingeborg still about?' She could well have gone home. It was late in the afternoon and she always got in early.

The only response came from Sergeant Dawkins, still at his desk in the hideous check suit. 'Did you wish to see her?'

'That's the general idea.'

'Will anyone do?'

'If I'd wanted anyone, I'd have said.'

'I'm ready for any assignment.'

'You're not, dressed like that,' Diamond told him. 'And there ain't no assignment, as you put it.'

'Am I grounded?'

'If that's how you want to think of it, yes. On essential office duties, as I told you. Do you know where Inge is?'

'Does that make me a groundling, I wonder?'

'Fred, I'm too busy for word games.'

'I've also been busy. I transferred all the witness statements to the computer as instructed. My "to

155

do" list is now a blank.'

'Did she say where she was going?'

'She did not and I didn't ask.'

'But she hasn't gone home?'

'With all due respect, that's not a question you should ask a groundling about a colleague.'

'For crying out loud, man, I'm not checking up on her.'

'An informed guess, then. She may have gone to powder her nose.'

Powder her nose? Which century was this stuffed shirt living in? 'I give up.'

This was the moment Ingeborg came through the door.

'In here,' Diamond said like a headmaster, pushed to the limit.

Ingeborg shrugged, looked towards Dawkins for a clue as to what was wrong, and followed Diamond into his office.

'If I have to put up with that pillock much longer, I'm taking early retirement,' he told her.

'I thought it was me in the firing line,' she said. 'He's not too bad if you make allowance.'

'Believe me, I've made all I can manage. I want to tap your brain. I had a thought about the dead butterfly we found in Clarion's dressing room. The reason I asked you to collect it the other night was simply to avoid an outbreak of hysteria. You know what theatre people are. The butterfly curse, and all that garbage. The obvious explanation is that the thing flew in from outside, got trapped and died, right?'

'That was my reading of it,' Ingeborg said.

'There is another possibility, of course: somebody put it there.'

156

'Why?'

'Out of mischief, or worse.'

'In what way?'

'To add to the panic over what happened to Clarion.'

'Who'd want to do that?'

'Someone with a grudge against the theatre, or the management, giving the impression the play was cursed.'

She was frowning. 'Denise, you mean? What would be the point of that?'

'I don't know. This is why I'm asking for your thoughts.'

She twisted a coil of blonde hair around her finger and then let it go. 'If she did, I can't think why. Damaging Clarion's face was enough to jinx the production without this extra touch.'

'Let's take another option then,' he said. 'Someone else planted it.'

She let that sink in before replying, 'But what for, guv?'

'To distract us. When a dead butterfly is found, so the legend goes, something bad is about to happen.'

'Well, it had already. Clarion was in hospital.'

'This is exactly what I'm getting at, Inge. This wasn't about Clarion. I don't think the butterfly was in the dressing room on Monday night. Someone would have noticed. People crowded in there to see if they could help. One of them would have spotted it on the window sill and created more hysteria.'

'You're saying it was put there later?'

'It was Tuesday lunchtime when I was shown around by Titus O'Driscoll. The room wasn't

157

locked. Anyone could have gone in there late Monday night or Tuesday morning.'

'Why?'

'To stoke up superstition. At the time I saw the butterfly and you collected it, we were assuming Denise was still alive.'

For a moment he thought she'd missed the point. Then she took a sharp breath. 'The butterfly was supposed to be an omen predicting her death?'

He nodded.

She was staring at him. 'Everyone is meant to think the butterfly curse has struck again—that she was doomed to kill herself.'

She'd got it. But would she go the extra mile?

'When in fact she didn't,' he said. 'The person who left the butterfly in the number one dressing room murdered her.'

She flicked her hair back from her face as if in denial. 'That's a whopping assumption, guv. It opens up all kinds of questions.'

'Okay. Let's hear them.'

'Why would anyone want to kill Denise? She wasn't unpopular, was she? From all I hear, she was difficult to dislike. And how would they do it? I've been backstage as you have, and seen the height of the fly tower. They'd have to persuade her to climb I don't know how many sections of a vertical iron ladder and jump off. It's all but impossible.'

'Back to the drawing board, then,' he said, not meaning it.

The note of irony caused Ingeborg to reconsider. 'There may be *something* in it, even so.'

He watched her face.

She nodded to give him a shred of credit. 'If

158

Denise was murdered—and I don't believe for a moment that she was—it would suit her killer nicely to have everyone assuming she did it because of guilt over Clarion. Case closed. We don't look at anyone else as a suspect. How convenient for this killer of yours.'

'This hypothetical killer.'

She smiled. 'This impossible hypothetical killer.'

'You're sounding more and more like Fred Dawkins.'

'It's catching.'

'It's a peculiar thing,' he said, 'Dawkins talks a lot of rubbish but just now he made a remark that for one split-second gave me an idea, and then it was gone. I can't remember what.'

'He's added some experience to the team,' Ingeborg said. 'He knows a lot about the theatre.'

'And dance.'

'Poetry.'

'Self promotion.'

She smiled. 'But not what the well-dressed man is wearing. Maybe I should take him clothes shopping tomorrow.'

'Good thought. I might view him differently as a smart dude.'

She was enjoying this. 'And we'll give the clown suit to a charity shop.'

'Safer to burn it. Are you serious?'

'About what?'

'Getting him some sensible gear.'

'Well, he's desperate to get out of the office. The only outings he gets are to the little boys' room.'

He snapped his fingers. 'Got it.'

'What?'

159

'What Dawkins said. I asked him where you were and after rabbiting on about himself he said you may have gone to powder your nose. I had a mental picture of you in front of a mirror with an old-fashioned powder puff.'

'And did that inspire you?'

'It put a useful thought in my head. Well, it may be useful. Earlier I was trying to think of a way round one of the main puzzles in this case. How come Clarion wasn't in pain until she got on stage, at least twenty minutes after she was made up?'

'The pancake?' she said.

He frowned. 'Come again.'

'Theatrical make-up. They apply it thickly for the stage. In this case it acted as insulation. The caustic soda went on last and only began to work when she got under the lights and started to sweat.'

'Twenty minutes is still too long,' he said.

'How do you know that?'

'Caustic soda is highly active. I've got a book on toxicology here and it talks of absorbing the moisture from the air, even. I doubt if she'd have left the dressing room before it started destroying the tissue. But I think I know what happened, thanks to Fred Dawkins.'

'And me supposedly powdering my nose?'

'Right. The caustic soda wasn't in the make-up Denise used in the dressing room. Before the actors go on, when they're waiting in the wings, isn't someone there to touch up the make-up to stop them shining under the lights?'

She blinked in surprise.

'Am I right?' he said.

Now she stared as if he'd performed the three-card trick. 'You are, guv. I saw it going on last night

160

when Keith and I were backstage. A young girl was there with a make-up brush.'

'That's when Clarion got it.'

One mystery solved. To give credit where it was due, he'd had help, unwittingly, from Fred Dawkins. But he doubted if he'd tell the man.

'Got anything planned for tonight?' he asked Ingeborg.

She gave a slow smile. 'Depends. I was going to wash my hair.'

'Because I'd like to see this young woman at work and I need—'

'A sidekick?'

'A guardian angel.' And he meant it. A visit to the theatre was a test of nerve. Talk about stage fright. He had his own form of it.

After fortifying himself with a coffee he returned to the privacy of his office and phoned his sister in Liverpool, his only blood relative. Jean was three years older than he and they'd never been close. They each scribbled a short update on Christmas cards and that was their only communication these days. But after Steph's death she had surprised him by travelling down for the funeral and he'd appreciated her presence there.

He didn't spend long over the small talk. A polite enquiry as to her husband's health ('Physically, he's fine. No problems at all.' Leaving open the matter of Reggie's fragile mental state) and then he plunged in.

'I'm going to test your memory if you don't mind. You remember how I hated being taken to the theatre as a child?'

'Do I just?' Jean said. 'It ruined a birthday treat for me, as Mum never stopped reminding us. You

161

got over it eventually, I hope?'

'Actually no. I'm better than I was, but I still get uneasy. I wouldn't visit a show unless I'm really pushed into it. Just now I'm on a case involving theatre people and the same old problem is getting to me.'

'But you're a tough old cop. You see all sorts of horrible things in your job.'

'This is different. It's involuntary. I get the shakes each time I enter the theatre. It's stupid. I've got to get over it. Something way back must have started me off, but I seem to have blanked it out. If I knew the cause, I could deal with it.'

'You're asking me?' Jean said. 'You didn't discuss your peculiarities with me. You wanted me and everyone else to see you as a tough little tyke—and you were, believe me, except for this one chink in the armour. I don't think Mum and Dad ever worked out why you were like that. In those days nobody bothered with counselling or child psychology.'

'I was hoping you might throw some light.'

'One thing I can tell you is that you weren't born like it. When you were a little kid you really enjoyed all that stuff, strutting around on a stage. You were Joseph in the nativity play and you volunteered to help the conjurer in a magic show. It made me squirm with embarrassment. Proper little show-off, you were.'

'Now you mention it, I remember. I would have been five or six, then.'

'And you did some acting.'

'Me? Get away!'

'In that one-act play at Surbiton.'

Another memory came back. His art teacher at

162

junior school had recruited him for a costume piece about Richard III. He'd played one of the boy princes murdered by the king in the Tower of London. 'You're right, except I wouldn't call it acting. All I had to do was pretend to die. Fancy you remembering that.'

'It got up my nose, that's why. Mum and Dad had booked that holiday in North Wales, a week on a farm to coincide with my eleventh birthday, and we were supposed to be leaving home on the Friday and driving through the night, but thanks to you and your play we lost two days and finally did the journey on the Sunday.'

'And it rained. I remember that.'

'Did it rain! Every day. The whole holiday was a washout. We didn't even get much sleep through that cow making pathetic sounds all night because the farmer had separated it from its calf.'

'That's coming back to me now.'

'And to cap it all, on the day of my birthday for a treat they took us to the Arcadia theatre at Llandudno to see a variety show and that was when you came over all peculiar and absolutely refused to stay in there. The show hadn't even started. You were fighting with Dad to get out. We had to leave. Oh yes, that was a birthday to remember.'

'I wasn't allowed to forget it,' he said. 'I can only think something upsetting must have happened in the play the weekend before, but I can't work out what. I remember it as a bit of a laugh. There were two of us. I wish I could recall the other boy's name. What age would I have been at the time?'

'Easy. It was my eleventh birthday, so you were eight.'

'I wonder if the actor playing the king scared

163

me. They were only amateurs.'

'You wouldn't know this, Pete, not having had kids of your own,' she said, 'but young boys of that age don't show their fears. They have this shell of bravado or just plain cheek, but under it are all sorts of insecurities.'

She'd touched a raw nerve, speaking of parenthood. 'It doesn't take a parent to know that,' he said. 'I was a boy myself.'

'Why have you called me then, if you know it all?'

'Calm down, big sister.'

'I must admit it still irks me,' Jean said. 'Llandudno wasn't the only place it happened.'

'I know,' he said. '*Julius Caesar* at the Old Vic when I was fifteen. I was in real trouble for ducking out of that.'

'And some other shows we might have gone to as a family. It's a shame, but there's no point now in making an issue of it.'

Even so, he'd heard the resentment coming down the phone. 'We did get to one Christmas show.'

'*Treasure Island* at the Mermaid Theatre with Bernard Miles as Long John Silver,' Jean said at once.

'Your memory is phenomenal.'

'It was a rare treat. How did you get up the courage for that?'

'The theatre hadn't long been opened and we were taken on a tour as part of a school trip, so I knew what to expect, I suppose.'

'We all wondered if you'd make a dash for the exit, but you were fine.'

'I enjoyed it.'

164

'You see? It's all in the mind.'

He didn't need telling. 'You've been helpful.'

'Ring me again if you ever get to the bottom of this,' she said. 'I'm rather curious.'

Rather curious? It's not a crossword clue, he thought.

*   *   *

The call to Jean had stirred some memories, but it made no difference to the mounting tension as he walked from his car to the theatre that evening. The only consolation was that he and Ingeborg were going backstage and not into the auditorium. A notice on the stage door said *Autographs Wait Here Please* and he would have been happy to do so . . . indefinitely. He swallowed hard and followed his assistant up the steps. The security man, Charlie Binns, gave Ingeborg's warrant card a longer look than Diamond's, and passed no comment. The eyes registered much, however, not least that he wouldn't, after all, be gracing the *Independent* colour section this week or in the foreseeable future.

Inge went first, moving confidently past the theatre notices, down more steps and across the fly floor, the area behind the scenery. Diamond, tense, but trying to appear as comfortable as she was, glanced upwards to make sure the body had been removed from the catwalk, and it had. On the prompt side, they stood in the shadows. The pre-show activity, crew members in black criss-crossing on various duties, brought home to him how many anonymous helpers were involved in the play, apart from the actors. He'd thought there would be a closed circle of suspects backstage. Quite some circle.

Above them, in a precarious cubbyhole reached only by ladder, the deputy stage manager was directing operations from a console. They heard him call the five minutes and then overture and beginners. Preston Barnes, the actor playing Isherwood, appeared from behind them and walked straight on stage, his eyes expressionless as if all his thoughts were turned inwards.

'He's there when the curtain goes up,' Ingeborg said in a low voice to Diamond. 'Now watch.'

They edged forward for a view of the stage. Barnes had seated himself at the table downstage. And of crucial importance to the investigation, a young woman moved in to dust his face with a make-up brush.

'Who is she?' Diamond whispered.

'Belinda. Straight out of drama school, I expect. This is how they get experience. This way now.' Ingeborg tugged at his sleeve.

'No. We must question her.'

'Shortly. Trust me, guv.' She steered him away and right around the back of the set to the OP side. Everything was dimly lit, even the stage.

'If you don't mind,' someone said in a stage whisper that was more of an angry hiss. A large woman in a pinafore, black dress and carpet slippers wanted to pass them. She was carrying a lace tablecloth.

'Fräulein Schneider,' Ingeborg muttered to Diamond after they'd stepped aside.

'Big star?'

'Just big.'

The make-up girl came off the stage and

166

checked Schneider with a mere two flicks of the brush—as if to confirm that she was a minor player. Diamond noticed that the powder came in a black cylindrical box.

Some accordion music was playing. 'And curtain up,' a low voice said through the tannoy.

The mechanism whirred and the curtains parted and the stage came alight. For a moment no words were spoken. Preston Barnes as Christopher Isherwood was in the spotlight at the desk, writing.

Rather than looking at the stage, Diamond had been watching the young make-up artist. He didn't want her to vanish as suddenly as she'd arrived. Helpfully, two more actors, a man and a woman, both young, were ready to go on. She was attending to one of them with more than the token flicks of the brush.

'Gisella,' Ingeborg murmured. 'Overnight star.'

His first sight of the understudy, the fledging actress with a clear motive for ousting Clarion. Similar in figure, she was prettier, he thought, and didn't look at all nervous. She'd been given generous reviews, the first big break of her career. How much would an ambitious young actor dare to do for stardom?

Barnes spoke his first lines, reading back the words his character was supposed to have written, about Nazis rioting in the streets of Berlin. This opening speech gave some background on Isherwood's attempt to scrape a living as a writer. He moved seamlessly into the 'I am a camera' line and was only interrupted by Fräulein Schneider's knocking on the double doors.

'Come in, Fräulein,' Barnes said, and the big woman entered and started tidying in preparation

167

for Sally Bowles and getting a few guarded laughs from the audience as she spoke of her own love life and how sad it was that her bosom only grew large after the death of her partner, 'a man for bosoms'.

Diamond continued to watch Gisella in the wings. She was in a black silk dress with a small cape over it and patent leather high heels and was carrying a handbag. A pageboy cap at a jaunty angle completed the look. She turned her head and their eyes met and Diamond was the first to look away. Under her gaze he felt reviled, like a Jew in Berlin in the thirties. Either she was in the role already or she wasn't nice to know.

He had to remind himself that he'd come to see the girl with the make-up brush now attending to the young male actor playing Fritz. But a problem was emerging. If each of the actors was given the last-minute touch-up from the same powder box, there was an obvious flaw in his theory.

He was still brooding over this when sound effects rang a doorbell. The make-up girl stepped back and the actor playing Fritz approached the doors.

From the wings, the flurry of action on the brilliantly lit stage was compelling. The business of the door being opened by Preston Barnes, Fritz entering with hat and cane and Fräulein Schneider coming out with an empty beer bottle, glass and plate, all within touching distance, absorbed Diamond. When he looked away, the make-up girl had gone.

'Where'd she go?' he asked Ingeborg.

She, too, had been dazzled by all the action. 'I'm not sure. Up the stairs, I think.'

'That's a guess, isn't it?'

168

She nodded, biting her lip. 'Trust me,' she'd said earlier. A mistake.

'You go up. I'll try round the back.' The urgency of getting this right pushed his own disquiet out of court. He swung right, straight into an avalanche of hot flesh: Fräulein Schneider's enfolding bosom.

'Do you mind?' she said.

'I didn't see you.'

'A likely story.'

An angry 'Ssshhh' came from behind them. Diamond backed off, jigged left and moved as fast as he could across the fly floor towards the prompt side. In the near darkness at the back of the scenery he thought he spotted the pale gleam of the young woman's face on the far side, turning right. A shout might have halted her. It might also have halted the play. In his haste to follow, he tripped on a cable and just avoided falling face down. As it was, he staggered two or three steps to save his balance and somehow remained on his feet.

On the other side, eyes down for a whole obstacle course of cables, he saw nobody like the make-up girl and he now had a choice of routes. The dressing rooms seemed the better way. He dodged past some waiting stagehands and away from the wings. No one was in the narrow passageway ahead. She must really have shifted to be out of sight already, unless she was still over the other side where Ingeborg was searching.

A man wired up with headset and mike appeared from the number two dressing room. Diamond asked if Belinda had come this way.

'Who's that?'

'The make-up girl. Small, dark hair. She was in

169

the wings just now with a face brush checking the actors.'

'Why don't you ask in wardrobe?'

Good suggestion—if he could find it. Wardrobe was part of the undercroft suite, along with the band rooms and the company office. Earlier, when he'd interviewed Kate, he'd got there by another route.

The headset man pointed the way.

Simple.

Downstairs, around a couple of turnings, he recognised the door and opened it. Kate was at the far end grappling with what he took to be one of her tailor's dummies until he spotted that her dress was pulled up to her waist and the dummy had a head of curly black hair with a bald spot and was the back view of Hedley Shearman without trousers humping her against a wall as if there was no tomorrow.

With his police training, Diamond first thought rape was being committed and it was his duty to intervene. Just in time, he registered that Kate was shouting, 'Yes!' with every thrust.

Belinda wasn't in the room. In the circumstances it would have been odd if she were.

He left them to it, too involved to have noticed him, and closed the door.

Where now? After that distracting spectacle, he needed to refocus on the search for Belinda. His ignorance of the layout backstage was a huge handicap. He took the steps up to stage level intending to look into the main dressing rooms. Before he got there the phone in his pocket vibrated. He put it to his ear. 'Found her?'

Ingeborg's voice told him, 'Yes, guv. First floor,

170

dressing room ten. Can you get here?'

'Try and stop me.'

He knew his way to the OP side and there he asked one of the crew. The nearest stairs were pointed out.

'Dressing room ten. Is it somewhere nearby?'

'You can't miss it.' The promise that guarantees the opposite.

In fact there was only one dressing room and Ingeborg must have heard his heavy tread.

'Guv?'

He found her standing beside the make-up girl, who looked about sixteen and terrified. Short, and slightly built, with dark, cropped hair, in a black T-shirt and form-fitting trousers, she was still holding the brush and box.

'Exactly who are you?' he asked.

'Belinda Craigie. I work here.'

'What's in the box?'

'Talc.'

'Are you certain?'

'Positive.'

'Hand it across.'

'But I need it for later.'

He opened the box and sniffed. Tentatively he touched the powder with his little finger. There was no reaction. He wetted another finger and made a light contact. Nothing happened. 'Where did you get this, Belinda?'

'The wardrobe department. It's a fresh box, opened this afternoon. I took the wrapper off myself.'

'So you know why I'm asking?'

'Clarion Calhoun?' Alarm showed in her eyes. 'I had nothing to do with that.'

171

'Is it your job to touch up the actors' make-up before they go on?'

'One of my jobs. I help out in the box office and take phone calls.'

'And were you here Monday evening?'

She nodded.

'Checking the actors' faces?'

'Not all of them. Only those who needed it.'

'Clarion?'

A vigorous shake of the head. 'Her dresser looked after her. Denise.'

'Are you certain of that?'

'Hundred per cent. I watched her.'

'Denise putting powder on Clarion's face while she was waiting in the wings?' This was dynamite if it was true.

'Yes.'

'Was she using the same stuff as you?'

'I don't know. She had her own powder box.'

'From the wardrobe department, like yours?'

She spread her hands. She didn't know.

'Did it look the same?'

'I can't say for sure. There wasn't much light.'

He checked the tip of his little finger again. The skin was unharmed. 'You just said you opened a new box today.'

Belinda nodded. 'Strict orders from Mr Shearman: start with fresh powder every performance.'

'But was that the rule on Monday, before the incident happened?'

She blushed. 'No, I used the box I'd opened for the dress rehearsal. I didn't want to waste it.'

'And where had it been kept overnight? In the wardrobe department?'

'Yes.'

'Was there a second box beside it—the one Denise used?'

She shook her head. 'I don't think so. She brought her own.'

'In a bag, or what?'

'I don't think she had a bag. I just saw her working on Clarion before she went on.'

'Did you speak at all?'

'We're supposed to keep quiet.'

This young girl came across as a convincing witness. More and more, suspicion was returning to Denise as the cause of Clarion's scarring. Diamond could see how impressed Ingeborg was. His hypothesis that Denise was innocent and a murder victim was unravelling by the second.

He asked about Belinda's background, something he should have started with. 'Did you know Clarion before you started working here?'

'I knew about her. Everyone does. Well, everyone with an interest in music.'

'Personally?'

She sighed. 'I should be so lucky. I don't mix with pop stars.'

'Would you call yourself a fan?'

'To be honest, she's more for people over thirty.'

'Not cool, then?'

'Not any more.'

'And you. Where are you from?'

'Twickenham.'

He perked up. 'I know Twickenham. I played rugby there for the Metropolitan Police.'

Ingeborg smiled at Belinda in a sisterly way and said, 'That's all some people know about Twickenham.'

173

Diamond gave Ingeborg a sharp look. 'How much do you know about it?'

'Eel Pie Island, Alexander Pope—'

'Okay, I shouldn't have asked.'

Belinda said, 'I was named after a character in a poem by Pope.'

'It crossed my mind. It's an unusual name,' Ingeborg said.

It hadn't crossed Diamond's. He wasn't going to ask which poem. There were times when he found himself in agreement with the CID gripe that Inge was too clever by half. 'So what brought you to Bath?'

'The job. After drama school, I applied everywhere. I want to act, but when you're starting out you take anything you're offered, front-of-house, part-time, anything. Mr Shearman saw me helping in the box office and said he'd do his best to find me something backstage. I got lucky.'

Shearman no doubt thought he'd got lucky, too. Before long he'd be offering something more backstage. 'It's tough for young actors, I've heard. How did you feel when you heard about Clarion walking into a starring role?'

A catch question she dealt with. 'I was told she went to drama school.'

'But not one of the better ones,' Ingeborg said.

'All I'm hoping is to be picked as a spear-carrier or something. I can't be jealous of someone getting the lead.'

'Not many spear-carriers in this play,' Diamond said.

Belinda smiled.

'You'd better get back to your duties,' he said.

'May I have my talc back?'

174

He handed it across and she took off fast.

'Not a serious suspect, but a useful witness,' he told Ingeborg.

'Agreed.'

'It's pretty obvious Denise was brushing caustic soda on Clarion's face while she was waiting to go on. One mystery solved.'

'The delay?'

'Yes, and if we can find the box she was using we'll get the contents analysed.'

'Is it worth searching wardrobe?' she asked.

'We'll have to—but my guess is that if Denise knew what she was doing she wouldn't be so careless as to leave it lying about.'

'We could look now.'

He passed a hand thoughtfully over his head. 'Should be okay by now.' He told her about the scene of passion he'd stumbled into.

'What an old goat,' Ingeborg said. 'I thought he fancied Gisella.'

'He fancies anyone willing to have him.'

CHAPTER ELEVEN

An alert policeman spotted Denise's Vauxhall Corsa late the same evening when the huge Charlotte Street car park was just about empty. It was in the top section near the path linking with Royal Avenue, below the Crescent.

Bath Central phoned Diamond at home. He hadn't been in for long and was microwaving a TV dinner. He turned it off and said he'd come at once. 'You can never relax,' he told Raffles, who

175

had just been fed and was actually quite relaxed. 'You know the real reason I'm going hungry tonight? Because Georgina wants to tread the boards in *Sweeney Todd*. That's the hidden agenda here.'

It was dark when he arrived. Keith Halliwell was there with a torch and so was the young constable credited with the find.

'Nice work,' Diamond said, trying to raise his own spirits. 'Have you looked inside?'

Halliwell shone his torch over the interior. 'Nothing to see.'

'Let's have the boot open. Got the tools?'

Halliwell unfurled a cloth containing a set that had belonged to a housebreaker. He selected a jemmy.

With the job under way, Diamond told the constable they could manage without him now. 'Top result,' he added as an afterthought.

'Thanks, sir.' But the young officer lingered, shuffling. 'Would you like my torch?'

'Don't you need it? You're still on patrol, aren't you?'

'I can easily get a spare.'

'All right, then.'

'I was thinking . . .'

'No harm in that.'

'Well, wondering, actually, if there are any openings in CID.'

'You what?'

'That's my ambition, sir, to do plain-clothes work.'

'Bloody hell. Another one. What's your name?'

'Pidgeon, sir. PC George Pidgeon.'

'Well, Pidgeon, I'll bear you in mind, but right

now we're trying out Sergeant Dawkins. Do you know him?'

'I've worked for him, yes.' From the tone, the experience hadn't been a rip-roaring success.

'And it may be a while before we take on anyone else.'

'Understood.' George Pidgeon's face said it all. He nodded and walked off into the darkness.

Halliwell meanwhile was bending metal, mutilating the car. One extra heave on the jemmy and the boot-lid sprang open to reveal a large, soft bag and the leather case Kate had described.

'Huh,' Diamond said with satisfaction. 'You know what this means?'

Halliwell shook his head. It was near the end of a long day. 'You'd better tell me, boss.'

'She had no intention of reporting for work when she returned to the theatre or she'd have taken this lot with her.'

'She'd made up her mind to kill herself already?'

'Looks that way.'

'Why not do it at home?'

'What with?'

'Sleeping tablets.'

'There weren't any. She didn't take them. The theatre was a better place.'

'Like her second home, you mean?'

'For the jump.' Sentiment didn't wash with Diamond. But he wasn't always clear-headed in his personal actions. He was in the act of reaching for the make-up case when Halliwell said, 'You ought to be wearing gloves.'

'Raw caustic soda? You're right. These fingers are old friends.'

'I was thinking about handling the evidence.'

'Think what you like. I'm never too proud to take advice.'

Halliwell didn't say a word.

Better protected, Diamond reached for the leather case and shone the torch inside, over a neat arrangement of brushes, combs, lipsticks and eye-liners strapped to the side. Lower down, jars and tins, a roll of cotton-wool pads and a black cylindrical box that he lifted out. 'Remarkably like the one Belinda was using.'

'Careful, boss.'

He handed Halliwell the torch. 'Hold this.' Then he opened the box. A small amount of white powder lay inside.

'I wouldn't sniff it if I were you.'

'Could be harmless.' He moistened his gloved forefinger with spit and dipped it in the powder. 'It's supposed to form a viscous slime that burns through skin.' He rubbed thumb and finger together. 'Doesn't feel slimy.'

'We'd better get it tested properly,' Halliwell said.

'Only if they're quick about it. I'm not waiting a week for results. Can you get some of this to an analyst first thing tomorrow and stay with him till it's done?'

A shake of the head. 'Sorry, guv. I'm down for the post-mortem, remember?'

A fixture not to be altered. The only other detective of senior rank was Diamond himself. 'So you are. We'll get one of the others to visit forensics. Anyone will do as long as they insist on an instant result.'

'Fred Dawkins?'

There was a pause for thought. 'I don't think so.

178

He makes a song and dance out of anything. Give it to Paul Gilbert.' He replaced the lid and put the powder box aside.

The cloth bag was the other part of Denise's dresser's kit, a collection of sewing materials, sticky tape, clothes brushes, scissors, paper tissues and medical items for almost any emergency. He didn't spend long with it once he had checked for caustic soda and found none. 'Can you force one of the doors? I want to see if there's a parking ticket.'

'She'll have taken it with her,' Halliwell said. 'At one time this car park was pay and display. These days you take your card to the machine when you return.'

'Which is why the car wasn't noticed before this by a parking attendant,' Diamond said. 'I still want to check the glove compartment.'

The jemmy was put to use again. The interior, when they got to it, contained nothing of genuine interest. Denise had been too organised and too tidy.

'Where would she have left her handbag, I wonder?' Diamond said. 'I reckon it contains the parking ticket, her credit cards and her mobile phone, any of which could settle this.'

Halliwell gave him a faintly amused glance. 'In spite of all, you're not a hundred per cent confident about the suicide, are you?'

He ignored that. 'Women hate being parted from their handbags.'

'She wouldn't have climbed up the ladder with it.'

'It wasn't lying around there. Maybe someone picked it up.'

'Nicked it?'

'Or handed it in as lost property. It could be as simple as that. We'll make enquiries in the morning.'

The meal was uneatable when he got home. He settled for his staple fare of baked beans on toast and went to bed. Raffles was already curled up asleep in the centre of the quilt. Getting in without disturbing him was a tricky manoeuvre and then he was left closer to the edge than he liked. He wasn't sure why he gave that cat more respect than any of his team. Maybe it was because it had belonged to Steph.

*   *   *

On Thursday morning he woke late and with a headache. For much of the night he'd been unable to sleep and had finally got off about five. His brain had been in overdrive, trying to remember things from his childhood. The phone call to his sister Jean had raised more questions than it had answered. What could have triggered the incident at Llandudno when he'd first exhibited signs of this panic about theatres? It had been a variety show, for pity's sake. What was sinister about that? More than a year later he'd been able to face *Treasure Island* at the Mermaid. No qualms about Long John Silver and the black spot and poor Ben Gunn, which you'd think might have unsettled a nervous kid. Then there was that one-act play about Richard III that Jean had recalled. It hadn't been a school play. The art teacher—whose name he couldn't remember—had belonged to some amateur dramatic society in Surbiton. They'd needed two boys and he'd been recruited along

180

with another kid from his class. They'd rehearsed in some old army hut and the performances were one weekend in a church hall and that was as much as his memory would dredge up. He couldn't even bring back the name of the other boy. He felt it was somewhere in his brain. It began with G, he thought. He wouldn't remember the first name; boys all called each other by surnames then.

In the small hours when he should have been asleep he was going through the alphabet, trying different letters after G. When he'd been through the vowels he tried consonants. At G with L he felt he was getting closer. Not Glass, but something roughly like it. Gladstone, Glaister, Glastonbury.

And then it came to him: Glazebrook.

Having got the surname, the rest followed. Mike Glazebrook.

At three in the morning, he was downstairs going through phone directories looking for Glazebrooks. Ridiculous. He didn't have directories for the whole country and anyway a lot of people were ex-directory these days. He made tea and went back to bed and still didn't sleep. In the night hours a simple query can easily be magnified into a compulsion. It became a matter of urgency to find Glazebrook. How would you trace a schoolboy more than forty years later? Secondary schools mostly had old boys' associations, but primary schools seemed not to bother. He'd heard of the Friends Reunited website and never looked at it until this night at 4.15 a.m. No joy. No Glazebrook. His contempt for websites was confirmed. It was beginning to seem a lost cause. If only Mike Glazebrook had progressed at the age of eleven to the same

181

grammar school as Diamond, he'd have been sharper in the memory. He must have gone to some other school. Go through the local schools, then, and see if they had any record of the boy and what had become of him.

Before setting off for work he was phoning schools in the Kingston area. The second he tried came up trumps. 'We have a Mr M.G. Glazebrook on our board of governors,' the secretary said. 'I believe he attended the school as a child.'

'The M—does that stand for Michael?'

'I believe it does.'

'And does he live near the school?'

'I'm not at liberty to tell you where he lives.'

'If you're worried about Data Protection, I'm a police officer and a one-time friend of Mike's. He's not in any trouble, by the way. What age would this gentleman be?'

'Fiftyish, I would say.'

'He was ten when I saw him last. Listen, I'm not going to press you for his contact details, but would you do me a great favour and phone him now and tell him his school friend Peter Diamond would like to hear from him today if possible? I'm at Bath Central police station.'

*   *   *

He was late getting in and slow to get a grip. Worse, the CID office was empty except for a civilian computer operator.

'Am I missing something? Was there a bomb alert?'

'They were all in first thing, sir.'

That comment shamed him into checking the

182

clock. Already Halliwell would be an hour into observing the post-mortem, getting to the gory stage, and Paul Gilbert would be standing over a forensic scientist analysing the contents of the powder box. Someone else, presumably, was at the theatre searching for Denise's handbag.

'Sergeant Dawkins ought to be in.'

'He was, but earlier, sir. He's out on an assignment with Ingeborg Smith.'

'Doing what, for Christ's sake?'

'They didn't say.'

He had his answer five minutes later when Ingeborg walked in with a fashion plate: Fred Dawkins, transformed, in a black leather jacket, white T-shirt and jeans.

'Strike a light!'

'Cool?' Ingeborg said.

He couldn't bring himself to say so. 'He needs a haircut and the brown shoes look wrong. Aren't they the same ones he was wearing yesterday?'

'Give me a break, guv,' she said. 'I can't fix everything.'

'Where did you go?'

'Charity shops mostly. The jacket is Oxfam.'

'How do you feel?' Diamond asked Dawkins.

'Like the proverbial pox doctor's clerk,' the fashion victim answered. 'However, if it gets me out on active duties, I shall be more than compensated.'

'It's taken ten years off you,' Ingeborg said.

'It's added ten to me,' Diamond said. 'I'm promising nothing, Fred. We'll see how the day develops. Is John Leaman in?'

'At the theatre with two from uniform searching for the handbag,' Ingeborg said. 'Keith said you

183

suggested it last night.'

The nitpicking Inspector Leaman was ideal for that job. If the bag was lying anywhere, John would find it. 'Okay. By the end of the morning we may be able to put this case to bed. The evidence is stacking up that Denise used the caustic soda on Clarion and killed herself when she realised the full extent of her action. Any ideas why?'

'Why she wanted to maim Clarion?' Ingeborg said. 'Can we agree it couldn't have been a mistake?'

'The intent is clear,' Dawkins said. 'Malice aforethought.'

The phrase conjured a momentary image of Fred as a judge. With his ponderous delivery he'd be well suited. Ermine would have looked better on him than black leather. 'It's not a particularly intelligent crime, is it?' Diamond said. 'Anyone could work out who did it.'

'Angry people lose all sense of proportion,' Ingeborg said. 'We don't know her motive. She may have been at her wits' end, wanting to stop Clarion.'

'But why?'

'God knows what went on between them. Denise had worked there as a dresser for six years. She was under instructions to nursemaid Clarion. She may have felt her effort wasn't appreciated. Clarion is used to people idolising her.'

'A lot of actors are prima donnas,' Dawkins said. 'A dresser would be able to cope with that.'

'Yes, but most actors are good at what they do. They're entitled to some respect. Clarion was no good in the role and still wanted the star treatment.'

184

'Allow me to propose another motive, then.'

A sigh. Tolerant as she was, even Ingeborg showed signs of losing her patience. 'Go on.'

'It requires an open mind.'

'We can manage that, I hope,' Diamond said, exchanging a look with Ingeborg.

Dawkins said in slow time, as if addressing a jury, 'By sabotaging Clarion just before she went on she was doing her a good turn, saving her from a mauling from the critics.'

'Saving the theatre, too,' Diamond said and admitted, 'That's not bad, Fred.'

Ingeborg shook her head. 'No woman behaves like that, deliberately damaging someone's face as a so-called good turn.'

'We're assuming she didn't expect the stuff to leave permanent scars,' Diamond said. 'When it happened, and she realised the theatre could be sued, she was devastated.'

'Driven beyond all,' Dawkins added in a sepulchral tone.

Ingeborg shook her head. 'You guys need to get out more.'

*   *   *

The call from Mike Glazebrook came soon after eleven. Diamond wouldn't have known the voice, but it didn't take long for the two to convince each other that they were the former princes in the Tower. 'And you're a detective,' Glazebrook said. 'I think I know what this is about.'

'I'll be surprised if you do,' Diamond said. 'Anyway, what's your line of work?'

'Surveying and structural engineering. I look at

old buildings and assess their safety. I'm often in Bath, as it happens. We have the contract for the Abbey.'

'And where are you now?'

'Finishing off a job in Lacock. If you'd care to meet, I could see you this afternoon, say in front of the Abbey about three? It's on my way home.'

'How will I recognise you after all this time?'

'Look for the short, fat guy in a pork-pie hat.'

*　　　*　　　*

At the theatre, DI John Leaman failed to find the missing handbag. Kate in wardrobe gave him a description—a shoulder bag in pale calf hide about the size and shape of an A4 filing wallet. She also allowed him to search the wardrobe room. The disruption of her overstocked headquarters must have horrified her, but she took it without complaint. Leaman didn't do things by halves. He upset a few others backstage as well by insisting on being admitted to every room in the entire complex. The actors wouldn't like it when they found out. Dressing rooms are supposed to be sacrosanct. The cast are given their own keys and they bring in their own comforters, ranging from teddy bears to joss sticks to racks of wine to personal friends.

Hedley Shearman demanded to know what the search was all about. 'Why would she have her handbag with her if she was intent on killing herself?'

'It wasn't in the house or her car, so where is it?' Leaman asked, as if Shearman ought to know.

'Don't look at me like that. I didn't take it,' the

186

little manager said.

'Maybe one of your staff did.'

'I take offence at that. We're not dishonest here.'

'I wouldn't count on it.' Tact wasn't John Leaman's middle name.

Shearman offered to mention the missing bag at a meeting he'd called at noon. Asked about the purpose of the meeting, he said he wanted to give everyone a chance to talk through what had happened and generally to reassure them it was business as usual. 'Your poking around this morning had the opposite effect,' he told Leaman. 'People are behaving as if a crime has taken place, alarmed that they're coming under suspicion.'

Leaman phoned the police station and told Diamond about the meeting.

'I'll come,' Diamond said at once without even a thought about his aversion. This opportunity couldn't be missed.

'I don't know if they'll welcome you, guv.'

'I'm not asking for a red carpet.'

*　　　*　　　*

But even before Diamond arrived, psyched up and with pulse racing, the meeting had been cancelled. He wasn't the only one in a state of tension. The entire place buzzed with it. 'What happened?' he asked.

'I've been trying to find out,' Leaman said. 'No one is saying. All I know is that the theatre director has been given a bloody nose.'

'Shearman? Literally?'

'Yes, it's a right mess, I was told. He had it

187

coming to him, if you ask me. Bumptious little sod. I didn't get much co-operation out of him.'

'Where is he now?'

'In the wardrobe department being patched up. The woman in charge won't let anyone near him.'

'We'll see about that.'

Diamond tried the door of wardrobe and found it locked.

'Piss off, will you?' Kate's voice yelled from within.

'It's the police. Superintendent Diamond. Open up, please.'

There was a pause, followed by her voice again. 'He says it's not a police matter. He doesn't want to lodge a complaint.'

'Unlock the door.'

'It's not him you should be coming after. He's the victim here.'

'If you don't open it, I'll force my way in.'

More hesitation and voices inside followed by the sound of unlocking.

'He can't speak,' Kate said, blocking the way. 'He's in no state to see anyone.'

'I'll be the judge of that,' Diamond told her, pushing the door wider.

He was presented with the bizarre spectacle of Hedley Shearman lying face upwards on an ironing board holding a bloody tissue to his nose.

'Vicious and unprovoked,' Kate said. 'It won't stop bleeding. Is it broken, do you think?'

'I'm not a doctor. Has he tried pinching it?'

'What for? That will cause more pain.'

'It has to form a clot. Try gentle pressure against the side the blood is coming from.'

Shearman did so, and groaned.

188

'Who did it?' Diamond asked Kate.

'Preston.'

'Preston Barnes?'

'You'd think he'd learn to control himself. He was with the Royal Shakespeare.' She leaned over Shearman and said, 'How are you doing, duckling? Has it stopped yet?'

'I don't know,' Shearman said without opening his eyes. The fact that he could speak was enough for Diamond to start the questioning.

'What was this about?'

'About Preston's dressing room being searched,' Kate said.

'I'll hear it from Mr Shearman,' Diamond said and got closer. 'Preston objected, did he?'

Shearman responded on a low, nasal note, pitiful to hear. He was a different creature from the rampant stud seen in wardrobe the previous evening. 'He said some of his personal things had been moved. He blamed me. I told him everyone's room had been searched and he said I should have stood up to the police.' A pause. 'He didn't say "police", in point of fact.'

'Where did this fight take place?'

'It wasn't a fight,' Kate said. 'It was a brutal, unprovoked assault.'

'In the auditorium,' Shearman said.

'In front of several witnesses,' Kate added. 'Hedley was getting ready for the meeting, having the house lights put on.'

It was impossible to shut her up.

'I didn't stand a chance,' Shearman said. 'He was in a blazing temper before he started.'

'You'll make yourself worse with this talking,' Kate said.

189

Diamond said, 'It's your talking that bothers me, ma'am. If you don't button it, I'll ask you to wait outside. Now, Mr Shearman, what is it with Preston? What's behind this?'

'I don't know,' he said. 'He was secretive from the first day of rehearsals, insisting he was given time to psych himself up for the role. I'm not sure what he does, but he's there in the dressing room at least an hour and a half before curtain up and he turns off his phone and refuses to answer the door.'

'Weirdo,' Kate added.

'I won't warn you again,' Diamond told her. He turned back to Shearman, now with his eyes open and looking as if he might survive. 'When you secured him for the part was he okay about acting with Clarion?'

'That was never an issue.'

'There's no history between them?'

'They hadn't met before coming to Bath. This is about Preston and his obsessions, not Clarion. He came with a reputation for awkwardness. I should have paid more attention, but we have a tradition here of welcoming all sorts. We're friendly.'

More than friendly in your case, Diamond thought, recalling last night's romp. He continued to ask about Preston. If the man had been acting secretively, he might be a serious suspect. 'How was he in rehearsal?'

'I've no complaints about him as an artist. He does his job and does it well. In fact, until this morning we were on civil terms.'

'I'd better speak to him.'

'Don't,' Shearman said in a horrified gasp, trying to raise his head. 'It will only make matters

190

worse, and we have four more performances to go. The theatre comes first. As far as I'm concerned, the episode is closed. It didn't happen.' He removed the tissue. 'Look, it's stopped bleeding.'

'Sorry, but my show has to go on as well as yours.'

'I don't want the board to know.'

'Who said anything about the board?'

*　　*　　*

Another locked door—to Preston Barnes's dressing room—frustrated Diamond, but not for long.

'Shall I ask for the pass key?' Leaman said.

'No need.' He knew the layout. Along the corridor he went and through the side door that had once been the theatre entrance in Beauford Square. The principal dressing rooms are at ground level and look out on a quiet lawn enclosed by railings. He picked the right window. As he'd anticipated, the casement was open at the top for ventilation. Nothing was fastened. He slid the lower window up and climbed in. Leaman followed.

Barnes was on the chaise longue wearing only a pair of jockey shorts. A tarantula might have crawled on to his chest from the way he sprang up. 'What the fuck—?' He was across the room and grabbing a bathrobe before they spoke a word. He wrapped it around himself as if playing the storm scene from Lear.

Rather than trading obscenities Diamond made a point of introducing Leaman and himself, adding, 'It was obvious you weren't going to open

191

the door. We need to speak.'

'If that little turd has reported me, I'll kill him.'

'I wouldn't issue death threats, not in my hearing. As it happens, Mr Shearman wants to forget the incident.'

He switched the attack. 'You've no right breaking in here.'

'Nothing is broken. What's your problem, Preston?'

Actually Diamond had noticed one problem in the short interval before Barnes had wrapped himself up. Another was that this young man would never be right for the classical roles. He was too small and too long in the nose. If he stood up, he wouldn't be much taller than Hedley Shearman. Very likely there was bitterness here as well as a hot temper.

'I like to prepare before I go on. Is that asking too much?'

'What form does the preparing take?' There were no obvious props, no incense burners, violins, tom-toms, chest-expanders. Plenty of space, though. It looked a bigger dressing room than the number one.

'That's personal.'

'Someone said you psych yourself up.'

'It's much more than that.'

'You'd better tell us, then.'

'I need to school myself for the test to come. Focus my energy, my emotions. Visualise the role. Become the character. Have you heard of Stanislavsky? Brecht? Lee Strasberg? I think not. What's the point in trying to make a policeman understand the guiding principles of my art? Oh God.' He gave an exaggerated yawn. 'I'm a method

192

actor, if that means anything. In simple terms, I take a mental journey to Berlin in the thirties. By a supreme exercise of will power Preston Barnes becomes Christopher Isherwood, or as close as any actor is capable of getting. Does that make sense to you?'

'All this is going on before the show?'

'It's fundamental.'

'To you—or all actors?'

'Not all. We're individuals, each with his own style. Some choose to go on without the sort of preparation I undergo.'

'Richardson,' Leaman said, surprising each of the others.

Barnes shot him an ill-tempered look. 'Which Richardson is that?'

'The late Sir Ralph.'

'What do you know about Ralph Richardson?'

'He was a biker, like me. Rode a Norton for some years, then a BMW. He'd turn up at the theatre, go on, do his stuff, get on his bike and ride home.'

Barnes and Diamond were too stunned to comment.

Leaman added, 'I don't think he was a method actor.'

Diamond picked up where he'd meant to be. 'With all this preparation, you guard your privacy, obviously.'

'That's no crime,' Barnes said.

'It is, if it leads to an assault.'

'But you said—'

'Yes, Mr Shearman is willing to overlook it, he told me.' He glanced about him. 'What's so special about this room?'

'It's mine. That's what.'

'Inspector Leaman didn't find the handbag he was looking for.'

'Are you being offensive?' Barnes said. 'I'm as straight as you are.'

'Denise the dresser's handbag. It's missing.'

He almost spat out the words, 'So I was informed.'

'You think we used it as an excuse to get in here? We're not as subtle as that. Did you know Denise?'

'We met. She was Clarion's dresser, not mine. I don't need one.' He pointed with his thumb to the shabby sports coat and grey flannels on a hanger beside the dressing table. 'That's the only costume I wear in this production. I change my tie a few times and that's it.'

'Did you know Clarion before joining the cast?'

'No, and her singing sucks, but it doesn't mean I wished her any harm.'

'Were you worried about the play? I'm told she wasn't much good in rehearsal.'

'Wasn't much good? She was crap. But I've been in the business long enough to know it *can* be all right on the night.'

'But it wasn't. What an experience you must have had.' Deliberately Diamond was playing to Barnes's ego. This was all about him.

'It wasn't something I want to repeat,' he said. 'One minute she seemed to have forgotten her lines and the next she was screaming in pain. I defy any actor to cope with that.'

'After the curtain came down, were you one of the people who went to her dressing room?'

'No. I waited in the wings to see what would

194

happen next. They gave Gisella the part, as you know. I steered and coaxed her through it in ways you wouldn't even begin to appreciate.'

'She was ready to go on?'

'Scared, obviously. In fact, she saved the night from total disaster. And she gets better with each performance. Have you seen it?'

'Not yet.'

'You should.'

'Your own performance is worth seeing, I was told.'

'Thanks.' The actor glanced in the mirror. Flattered, he was off guard.

'What do you inject before the show?' Diamond asked in a matter-of-fact tone.

'What?' He swung back to stare at Diamond.

'I noticed the needle marks.'

'I'm diabetic.'

'I don't think so, Preston. And I don't believe the horseshit you told us a moment ago about locking yourself in to visualise the role. You come here early to jack up.'

'You can't prove a damn thing.'

'I'm not investigating your habit. I know why you flew into such a rage over the search. You thought we'd find the syringe. And why you were so quick to cover your arms when we came in just now.'

He'd turned ashen as Diamond was speaking. 'You people have no idea of the stress actors are under night after night.'

'Heroin?'

'Methadone, on prescription.' His manner switched from aggression to supplication. 'I'm fighting the addiction. I can give you my doctor's name if you keep this to yourself. I don't want the

195

management finding out. Please.'

'Does anyone else in this theatre know?'

'Absolutely not. It would destroy my career.'

'We can count on your co-operation, then?'

In a voice otherwise purged of defiance he managed to say, 'Bastards.'

CHAPTER TWELVE

'She definitely broke her neck,' Keith Halliwell reported on his phone from the mortuary.

'We know that,' Diamond said. 'I saw for myself, but was that the cause of death?'

Halliwell took a moment for thought, a moment that didn't yield much. 'Must have been.'

'Not necessarily.'

'Are you kidding me, boss?'

'She could have been dead already.'

This didn't persuade Halliwell. 'What—and somebody pushed her off the loading bridge? Difficult. How would he have got her up there?'

'There are pulleys and lines for hoisting things.'

'He'd need help.'

'Possibly.' Unknown to Halliwell, the word that had first sprung to Diamond's mind was 'definitely'. His confidence was shrinking. Now that he'd spoken, his theory did sound far-fetched, if not totally off the wall.

'If she died by some other method it would have shown up in the post-mortem,' Halliwell pointed out.

'You mean a bullet through the head or a dagger in the heart? There are more subtle ways of

196

misleading a pathologist, Keith.'

'I was impressed by Dr Sealy. He said because of the position she was found in, she must have been falling backwards. Therefore she climbed over the rail and held on to it with both hands before letting go. Suicides often do it that way, not wanting to look down. He said that's why she didn't end up on the floor. She didn't see the battens that broke her fall.'

'Pretty conclusive, then?' Diamond said without pressing his doubts. 'No other marks or injuries?'

'None that he noticed, and he's thorough. He did add that he'd wait for the lab test on the samples he'd sent. There was some suspicion she'd taken alcohol shortly before she died. Even I could smell it.'

'Dutch courage.'

'I reckon.'

'Whisky? Gin?'

'He calls it ethanol. Same thing.'

Diamond was unimpressed. 'Typical bloody Sealy. Alcohol to you and me. Ethanol to him.'

'He couldn't tell what drink it was. You get the same sharp, sweet smell whether it was cheap beer or vintage bubbly. When you're alive, alcohol metabolises, but after death it gets trapped in the blood.'

The science didn't interest Diamond so much as the how, when and where. 'And what did he say about the time of death?'

'Not much more than he said before. Probably between eight and twenty-four hours before she was found.'

'No use to us. But thanks, Keith. How's the stomach?'

'Mine?'

Diamond smiled at that. 'I'm asking if you could manage a sandwich after the post-mortem.'

'I don't see why not.'

Which is why you always get the job, he thought. 'If you fancy a bite to eat, John Leaman and I are about to call at the Garrick's Head. There was a punch-up at the theatre this morning. Tell you about it then.'

He was trying to be realistic. The theory he'd flirted with had withered away. Dr Sealy would surely have picked up some indications of murder. Post-mortems rarely add much to what is already obvious. True, Sealy cared more about covering his back than giving pointers to the police, but he was good at his job, and Keith Halliwell was a sharp-eyed observer. An unexpected discovery had never been likely. The case was moving to a conclusion. All it wanted was confirmation that Denise took responsibility for the Clarion incident. If her powder box contained traces of caustic soda, the suicide would be hard to deny. Paul Gilbert should soon report on the lab result.

'Do I need a drink!' he said to Leaman.

*   *   *

They were greeted in the pub by the barmaid announcing, 'Here's your friend, Titus. I told you he'd be back.'

The dramaturge, Titus O'Driscoll, at a table by the fireplace, looked up from the book he was reading. 'My cup overfloweth. Well, it would have, if he hadn't arrived with someone else.'

Diamond, trying to be tolerant, raised a grin.

198

'John Leaman works with me.' He turned to the barmaid. 'We'd each like a pint of your best.'

'Are you off duty, then?' Titus asked.

'At this minute, yes. And how are you, Titus? Fully recovered, I hope.'

'The head, yes,' he said, 'but the heart remains in intensive care. I'm not used to being in the arms of strange policemen.'

Leaman's eyes gleamed like the brass fittings on the bar.

'Titus fainted and I caught him before he fell,' Diamond explained, as if catching gay men was as commonplace as tying shoelaces.

'And the reason I fainted is one of the great unsolved mysteries,' Titus said. 'I have a theory of my own too embarrassing to mention in present company. Well, I will.'

This had gone far enough. 'No, you won't,' Diamond said at once, 'because it wouldn't be right.' With the case just about to be put to bed there was no need to hold back. 'You passed out because you saw a dead butterfly in Clarion's dressing room.'

For a moment Titus was speechless. Then: 'Oh my word!' He had lost so much colour that there was danger of another fainting episode.

'You still don't remember?'

'Now tell me it was a tortoiseshell. It was? No wonder I collapsed.' His blue eyes widened and he said in a doom-laden voice, 'The curse strikes again.'

'Nobody ever mentioned a curse that I'm aware of.'

Titus was in Hammer Horror mode. 'The death of Reg Maddox all those years ago after the dead

199

butterfly was found on the stage. If that doesn't have the force of a curse, I don't know what does.'

'But Clarion didn't die.'

'Denise did, the day we discovered it. Why didn't you tell me?'

'I know what theatre people are like about superstitions. It could have caused a panic.'

'Really.' Titus rolled his eyes and made an expansive gesture with his arms. 'As if we're the sort of people who panic. Where is the butterfly now?'

'In a drawer in my office,' Diamond said. 'It's been there since Tuesday, and I'm still breathing.'

'Mock the dark forces at your peril. I'm in urgent need of a drink.'

Diamond nodded to the barmaid, who said, 'Water, Titus?'

He pursed his lips and turned away, so she poured him a glass of wine. She was enjoying every second of this.

'It's summer,' Diamond said. 'Butterflies get trapped all the time in places like this.'

'That's not the issue,' Titus said after taking a sip. 'They become an omen when they die.'

'They're short-lived anyway. I dare say there are others lying around the theatre.' He turned to Leaman for support. 'When you were doing your search, did you notice any?'

Leaman shook his head. 'I wasn't looking for butterflies.' A simple statement and a reminder how single-minded he was.

'What did you hope to find?' Titus asked Leaman.

'A handbag.'

'Any particular handbag?'

200

'The one belonging to Denise Pearsall.'

Diamond said, 'I suppose you wouldn't know where it is?'

Titus cocked an eyebrow. 'Are you implying that I picked it up? No, I did not.'

'What would Titus want with a handbag?' the barmaid said and shrieked with laughter. She could get away with stuff like that.

Diamond wasn't amused and didn't smile. His thoughts hadn't moved on since the remark about butterflies. Painstaking as John Leaman was in tracking anything down, he could have missed other items of importance. Tunnel vision, they called it in CID. 'Titus,' he said.

'Yes?'

'Our tour backstage was cut short. Would you mind showing me the rest?' An inner voice shrieked that he must be crazy, volunteering to go back into the theatre, but he'd been steeling himself for this. Backstage was less of a problem for him than the auditorium itself.

'As I recall it,' Titus said without enthusiasm, 'we weren't on a tour. We were ghost-hunting.'

'So we were.'

Titus softened a little. 'True, we didn't look at all the dressing rooms. Number eight is renowned for psychic phenomena.' He sighed. 'But I don't believe you're interested in the occult.'

The barmaid said, 'He could be interested in you, Titus.' She was making mischief and Diamond let it pass. She was an unlikely ally.

Titus drank most of the wine at a gulp. 'What about your colleague?' he asked Diamond.

'He'll wait here.'

'Just the two of us?'

'That's it.'

'If you insist, then.' He drained his glass and left it on the bar.

On their way through the foyer, Titus said, 'I'm under no illusions, Peter. You're a detective on a case. What I don't understand is why you need me to show you around the building.'

'There's a double incentive,' Diamond said. 'It's a warren backstage. I'd soon be lost on my own. And I get a man-to-man talk with you.'

'Really?' Titus pressed the combination on the digital lock and they passed into the red-carpeted corridor behind the royal circle.

Diamond's nerve came under immediate test. The auditorium was visible through several entrances. He looked away, avoiding even a glimpse of the curtains. 'Shall we start with that haunted dressing room you mentioned?'

'We can't go in. It's in use,' Titus said.

'Who by?'

'Gisella, the young woman who understudied Clarion.'

'She gets the spooky room?'

'It's comfortable and close to the stage and I don't suppose she knows about the manifestations,' Titus said. 'After the accident she was offered the number one and turned it down.'

'Everyone was called for a meeting this morning, so she may be in,' Diamond said, refusing to be put off. 'She'll invite us inside, won't she? How well do you know her?'

'We've spoken.'

'Cordially, I hope?'

'Of course. Unlike some I could mention, I'm not a prickly personality.'

'Which way, then?'

They had reached the pass door to backstage. Titus worked the digital lock again.

'Is there one combination for all the doors?' Diamond asked.

'No, they're different. Newcomers are given a plastic card with the numbers. I long ago committed them to memory.' He pushed the door open and they went through. 'Dressing room eight is on the OP side. We have to cross behind the stage.'

A passing stagehand smiled at Titus and winked.

'People are obviously used to seeing you here,' Diamond said. 'I expect they'd notice a stranger.'

'You're being a detective again,' Titus said. 'This is supposed to be a ghost hunt.'

'A stranger could turn out to be a ghost.'

'Or an evil person who maims famous pop singers. If you really want to know, it would be almost impossible for a stranger to pass through here unnoticed.'

'They'd get lost as well.'

'Very likely.' In the passageway close to the stage, Titus stopped and pointed ahead. 'Dressing rooms eight and nine, usually occupied by some of the principal actors, but not the leads.'

'Let's see if she's in.' Diamond knocked on number eight.

'It's open,' a childish voice came from inside.

He raised a thumb at Titus and turned the handle.

'Oh,' Gisella said from her chair in front of the dressing table. 'I thought you were the boy bringing more flowers.' She was looking at them through everyone's idea of a theatrical mirror, fringed with light bulbs. All they could see of her was the permed nineteen-thirties haircut above a slender, white neck. 'If you're press,' she said, 'it isn't convenient now. I've done so many interviews already that I need a break.'

'Now come on, Gisella,' Titus said. 'You know me, the dramaturge. And this is my friend Peter.'

'I'm sorry, guys, but I don't have time to socialise.'

'That goes without saying,' Titus said. 'We're only here to look at the room.'

This unflattering comment seemed to intrigue her. She swivelled in her chair to look at Diamond. 'Peter who?'

He told her his name.

'Are you an actor?' Before he could answer she added, 'Do you have a stage name?'

He realised what this was about. She thought he was being shown the room because he'd be using it when the next production got under way.

He was about to deny it, but Titus got in first. 'One could easily mistake him for Timmy Spall. Is that who you're thinking of?'

'No.'

'Kenny Branagh? Martin Shaw?'

'I'm a policeman,' Diamond said to get realistic. 'Do you mind if I look round?'

Gisella was definitely surprised, but she had the wit to make a melodramatic gesture out of it, pressing a hand to her brow. 'The police! I am undone.'

'Don't be like that,' Titus said. 'He's a nice policeman.'

She said in a more serious voice, 'If you think I had anything to do with Clarion's accident, you're

204

mistaken. Just because I was understudying doesn't mean I wished her any harm.'

'Have you noticed how cool it is in here?' Titus said with a look at Diamond heavy with significance. 'Unnaturally cool, I mean.'

'I haven't complained,' Gisella said. 'I like it.'

'It's always cool, even in a heatwave,' Titus said. 'No one has ever explained why.'

More supernatural hokum, Diamond decided. Ghost-hunters were always going on about drops in temperature.

'Do you see the handbag?' Titus said.

'Where?' Diamond said, all attention.

'Behind you on the wall.'

He swung around, and was disappointed. Framed in a glass case were a bag and a pair of gloves.

'They belonged to one of the most exquisite beauties ever to grace the stage,' Titus said. 'Vivien Leigh. The room is named in her honour. I don't think there's any suggestion that she is the visitor here.'

'I don't know what you're talking about,' Gisella said. 'She died at least forty years ago.'

'Precisely.' Titus gave Diamond another piercing glance.

The room's spectral possibilities didn't impress Diamond at all. He was more interested in Gisella's unease at having a policeman in her room. 'You said you wished Clarion no harm. Was she a friend?'

'In the sense that we're all in the same company,' she said. 'We got along well. Most people here are friendly, some over-friendly.'

'A certain theatre director?' Titus said.

205

She gave a shrug that seemed to answer the question.

'He was with you when you spotted Denise's body,' Diamond said, wanting to hear her account.

'Yes, I knew what was going on. He was cosying up to me on the strength of some nice reviews I'd got. Men of his sort aren't subtle. He offered to show me the theatre mascot, that butterfly in the wings, and I could feel him pressing against me as I looked up. He was taking advantage for sure. The old, old story of a man thinking he has power over a woman.'

'Has he tried it on since?'

'Not yet, but I'm sure he will. I watched him trying to hit on Clarion last week when we were in rehearsal. She brushed him off like some ugly little insect. It creased me up.'

'Did you know Clarion before you were picked for this play?'

'I knew of her. Doesn't everyone? But we'd never met.'

'You must have met her in rehearsals.'

'Sure. She shared all the director's notes with me and showed me the moves, as you do with an understudy. And we practised lines together.'

'Was she nervous?'

'A bit. Well, a lot, actually, even though she wouldn't admit it. You see, it was years since she'd done any acting. Our director, Sandy, kept telling her she was marvellous and heading for a huge success, but then he left us all to it after a far-from-smooth dress rehearsal and flew out to Hollywood.'

'He couldn't be bothered?'

'I wasn't going to say so, but yes.'

206

'That was my impression, too,' Titus said. 'Sandy came with a reputation for looking after number one.'

'You're the beneficiary,' Diamond said to Gisella. 'You stepped up, grabbed the opportunity and got rave reviews. Just about everyone else came off worse: Clarion, Denise, the rest of the cast, looking forward to a long run, the management, facing a possible lawsuit.'

'So I got lucky,' she said with a defiant stare. 'In this job, sweetie, you take whatever chance comes your way.'

There was a simmering resolve to this young woman. Four days had turned her from a bit-part actor into a leading lady—with attitude.

'Have you heard from Clarion since you took over?' Diamond asked.

'Clarion has bigger things to worry about than me.'

'Why don't you move to the number one dressing room? It's better than this.'

'It was offered, but I still think of that as hers. This is perfectly serviceable.'

'Cold,' Titus said.

'It's not midwinter. I told you it doesn't bother me.'

The reason didn't ring true to Diamond. Here was a deeply ambitious actress turning down the star dressing room. Was there something about this less salubrious room she was reluctant to leave behind? It was furnished for two, with a second mirror and dressing table almost hidden behind enough bouquets and sprays to fill a florist's.

He pointed. 'Is there anything of yours in the drawers?'

'Not those, no.'

'Mind if I take a look?'

'What for?'

He opened the top drawer and found it empty. So was the other. He crossed the room to inspect the hand basin. 'Does this ever get blocked?'

'What do you mean?'

'The plughole. Make-up. Hair and stuff.'

'Not while I've been here.'

He opened the cupboard underneath. No caustic soda. Not so much as a dead butterfly. 'We'll leave you in peace, then. Are you performing tonight?'

'Every night.'

'Break a leg.'

In the corridor outside, Titus said, 'Peter, that was a fearful old cliché, if I may say so.'

'Break a leg? I thought it was what you say to actors instead of wishing them good luck.'

'It went out with kitchen-sink drama, about nineteen sixty.'

'We'd better get through before I embarrass you some more. Something is puzzling me. This was dressing room eight. One, two and three are on the prompt side. What happened to four, five, six and seven?'

'Upstairs on the prompt side. And ten and eleven are above us.'

'Who uses them?'

'In a small-cast play like *I Am a Camera,* scarcely anyone. There's no need.'

'Above us, you say. I haven't been upstairs. Some of my team have.'

'There isn't much to see.'

'But I'll see it.'

They climbed the narrow staircase to dressing room ten, distinctly less glitzy than the ground-floor rooms. The mustiness testified that it hadn't been used for some time. Titus informed him it was supposed to take up to four actors and was probably home to more when big-scale productions like musicals and pantomimes were put on. Diamond opened some cupboards and drawers and then asked if there were more rooms on this floor.

Titus shook his head. 'It's the only one this side. You don't want to bother with eleven. It's up another flight of stairs and hasn't been used in weeks.'

'Take me to it.'

'No one has ever seen a ghost there.'

'There's a first time for everything.'

Dressing room eleven, when they got up there, short of breath, turned out to be a barn of a place, with nine mirrors and dressing tables, bare of anything else except chairs and a clothes rail. 'Fit for the *corps de ballet* or the chorus,' Titus said with disdain. 'I don't come up here.'

After a cursory check that included a glance into the WC and shower, Diamond had to admit that Titus had been right—any self-respecting theatre ghost would shun this one.

'Down all those stairs again?' Titus said in a superior tone when they stood in the passageway.

'You said this was the only room?'

'On this floor? Yes.'

He pointed across the passage. 'What's that, then? The cleaners' store?'

'I haven't the faintest idea.'

Whatever the door was for, it needed

209

redecoration. Numerous scrapes and dents could well have been made by buckets and vacuum cleaners.

Diamond pushed the door open and got a shock. He was looking straight across the dark chasm that was the fly tower. This was the loading bridge, the same catwalk cluttered with counterweights that he'd reached previously by climbing vertically hand over fist from floor level. Why hadn't he noticed the door then? Because after the white-knuckle experience scaling the ladder he'd given all his attention to Denise's broken corpse.

'Should have thought of this,' he complained more to himself than Titus. 'The scene shifters need to get access.' He leaned over the metal railing and reminded himself what a long way down the floor was, but vertigo wasn't his problem in this theatre. Already his mind was working on new scenarios. A major objection to his murder theory had been the difficulty of getting the body up to this level without assistance. Now he knew how it might have been done.

Equally—to be less fanciful—Denise could have used the back stairs herself in her suicide plan. As an experienced dresser, she would have known all about room eleven and the door across the passage.

'Peter, I'm lost in admiration,' Titus said from behind him. 'I thought I knew this theatre like the back of my hand. I wouldn't have looked behind that door unless you had.'

Diamond didn't answer. He was still weighing the possibilities this had opened up.

Finally he turned away. 'I'll take another look at

that dressing room.'

'There was nothing in there,' Titus said.

'Nothing obvious.'

They returned to number eleven and its nine dressing tables and it still gave the impression of long disuse. Diamond stood in the centre with the air of a prospective buyer trying to visualise the place fully up and running. 'Do the cleaners come in here most days?'

'How should I know?' Titus said, his voice piping in protest. 'I'm not the caretaker.'

Diamond answered his own question. 'Likely they wouldn't when the room isn't in use.' He moved closer to the line of tables and crouched like a bowls referee judging a closely contested end.

'Have you found something?' Titus asked.

'No.'

'What are you doing, then?'

'Looking at the table tops.' He took two steps to his left and assumed the same position, eyes level with the surface.

Consumed with curiosity, Titus came closer and tried to ape Diamond's stance. 'There's nothing I can see. Are you a sensitive?

'A what?'

'Certain people have extra sensory perception.'

The man never let up. Diamond straightened up. 'Be honest with me, Titus. Have you ever seen a ghost?'

'Up to the present time, no. But I'm sensitive to emanations like the grey lady's jasmine.'

So tempting to shoot him down in flames, but in a mysterious way Diamond didn't care to dwell on, he had formed a liking for Titus. Back to reality. 'I

211

was right. The place hasn't seen a duster for some time.'

'It's a dressing room, not an army hut.'

Unfazed, he moved on again to the next table, the last along that side. 'When we came in just now we didn't touch the tops of these, did we?'

'I certainly didn't,' Titus said. 'I watched you from the doorway. You looked into the shower room. You didn't open any cupboards.'

'Because there aren't any,' Diamond said. 'It's built for economy.' He completed his examination of each of the surfaces on the facing side. Then he stood back. 'What we have here are nine dusty tables and one over there'—he pointed to the one farthest from the door—'has a distinct curved shape in the dust at the front edge. You've heard of fingerprints? That looks to me like a bum print.'

CHAPTER THIRTEEN

'Talc, pure talc, and nothing else.'

'That's a pain. I thought we were getting somewhere.'

Diamond, Halliwell and Leaman had returned from their liquid lunch to find DC Paul Gilbert waiting in the CID room to report on the contents of Denise's box of powder. It wasn't the result anyone wanted to hear.

'I could have had my feet up watching a film last night instead of standing in a car park kidding myself we'd found solid evidence.'

Young Gilbert hung his head as if he was personally responsible.

'But we can use this,' Diamond said, more in charity to the young cop than real confidence.

Gilbert looked up. 'Can we?'

'If Denise's talc was harmless, how did Clarion come into contact with the caustic soda?'

'It can't have been accidental,' Halliwell said, picking up the point. 'We're talking about a dangerous substance with all kinds of warnings on the container. Someone was hell-bent on damaging Clarion's face. If Denise didn't do it, who did?'

'I can name some people with an interest in stopping Clarion.'

From across the room, Ingeborg said, 'We've been over this, guv, and we got nowhere.'

'Yes, but since we spoke I've met some of these characters.'

'The understudy?' Ingeborg said without enthusiasm.

'Only four days into the run and already behaving like the prima donna. Clarion's misfortune is Gisella's big break. Very little sympathy there and huge ambition. For some reason, though, she hasn't moved into the star dressing room.'

'Feels safer where she is?' Halliwell said.

'Could be as simple as that.'

'Now she's got the part, she doesn't want to get unpopular with the rest of the cast, lording it over them?'

'I can believe that, too. I pointed out that she's the only person to benefit from Clarion's exit from the play.'

'What did she say to that?'

'Basically, that actors ride their luck and take any chance they get.'

'Doesn't she understand she's a prime suspect?'

'She rules out foul play. They all do.'

'That's actors for you,' Halliwell said. 'Turn their backs on real life and put on a show.'

Diamond didn't comment. He'd started on this update and he meant to complete it. If Ingeborg showed signs of disenchantment, the entire team needed firing up. 'I also met the male lead, Preston Barnes, after he punched the theatre director on the nose.'

'Punched him? What for?' Ingeborg said, all interest again.

'For allowing John Leaman to search his room this morning. Barnes had things to hide. Turns out he's a junkie.'

'Really? What's he on?'

'Methadone, he says. He needs a fix before each performance.'

'But is he also a suspect? Why would he want to hurt Clarion?'

'Maybe like me she saw the state of his arms and worked out what he's doing to himself. He's fearful of anyone in the theatre finding out.'

'But where's the logic in damaging her face?'

'To be shot of her. She's not going to give any more thought to his drug habit. She's out of it now.'

'I suppose.' She didn't seem wholly convinced.

Undaunted, Diamond moved on. 'Another one in the mix is Hedley Shearman, him of the bloody nose, who incidentally is quite a goer. I opened a door and saw him having it away with Kate, the wardrobe mistress.'

'Before or after the punch-up?' Leaman asked.

'The night before, during the play.'

'A lot of it goes on behind the scenes,' Ingeborg said, speaking as the ex-journo.

Even so, her inside knowledge prompted a few smiles.

'Did they know you saw them at it, guv?' Halliwell asked.

'No.'

'What did you do, shut the door?'

'Not immediately. I had to make sure it was consensual, didn't I? And it was. They're still good friends. Kate patched him up this morning after he was hit. But I was speaking of motives. Shearman claims he was railroaded into having Clarion in the play. He was sure she'd flop and he'd take the blame.'

'Who railroaded him?'

'Francis Melmot, chairman of the board of trustees. Melmot is a Clarion fan. He came up with the idea of using her in a play and got the board on side. Met Clarion for lunch and invited her to stay at Melmot Hall.'

'Get away,' Halliwell said with relish. 'Did she go?'

'She did, for a couple of days, he said.'

'Couple of nights.' Halliwell got a laugh for that.

'I wouldn't count on that,' Diamond said. 'There's a domineering mother living there.'

'He's a mummy's boy at his age?'

'Mummy is quite the duchess. I wouldn't care to cross her.'

'Then she wouldn't be troubled by bourgeois values,' Ingeborg said. 'Upper-crust mothers positively encourage their sons to get laid.'

'Is Melmot seriously in the frame?' Halliwell asked.

215

'He must be,' Diamond said.

'He's a fan, you said. What's his motive?'

'It became obvious in rehearsal that Clarion was going to screw up. She was no Sally Bowles. His own reputation was on the line. He had to find a way of stopping her.'

'By scarring her?' Ingeborg said with disbelief. 'What sort of fan is that?'

'Might I venture an opinion?' a voice said from close to Diamond, reminding him of things he'd been trying to forget. Sergeant Dawkins in his leather jacket and jeans had blended with the team.

'Go ahead.'

'Regarding the fun and games.'

'I don't think I mentioned fun or games.'

'Rightly so,' Dawkins said, and nodded as if that ended the exchange.

'Fred, if there's something you want to say, out with it.'

'There are ladies present.'

There was a sharp intake of breath from Ingeborg.

'"Fun and games",' Dawkins said, 'is a euphemism.'

'For fuck's sake, Fred,' Ingeborg said. All the good will he'd earned with her had just drained away. 'Do you mean sex?'

'In a word, yes.'

'Say it, then.'

Dawkins tugged the leather jacket more tightly across his front. 'What if those nights in Melmot Hall didn't turn out as Mr Melmot hoped? If the'—he paused—'sex was unsatisfactory, or a disaster, he may have panicked that Clarion would

216

tell everyone and he'd be a laughing-stock.'

No question: this new man brought fresh thinking to the team.

'Good point, Fred,' Diamond said. 'It's true she didn't stay long.'

'Perhaps he didn't.'

'Didn't what?'

'Stay long.'

'What?'

Halliwell said, 'It's a joke, guv.'

'Is it? Oh, I get you.' Not many in CID had caught on.

Leaman said, 'Those are our suspects, then?'

'For my money, yes,' Diamond said.

'What about the gay guy?'

'Titus?'

'He knows his way around the theatre.'

'He would. He's the dramaturge. Advises on the scripts, or something like that. Yes, he goes backstage. He's toured me round a couple of times. What are you driving at, John? You think Titus had a motive?'

'I don't know about a motive. He had the opportunity for sure if he can come and go without anyone asking what he's up to.'

'Agreed, but I can't see why he'd want to damage Clarion's face.'

Leaman backed down. 'Just me thinking aloud, guv.'

'No harm in that. I doubt if Titus has it in him to do anything like this. He's full of stories about spooks, but when he saw a dead butterfly he passed out.'

Now Ingeborg thought it was worth pursuing. 'As someone who cares about the theatre, he could

217

have decided to stop her.'

'But not like that.'

'You don't think he's capable of it?'

'Don't get me wrong, any of you,' Diamond said, 'but I have some respect for Titus.'

No one in the room had any doubts about the big man's sexuality and no one sniggered. Yet there was a moment of awkwardness that lasted until Dawkins cleared his throat.

Diamond turned to him. 'You want to say something else?'

'It popped into my head . . . guv.'

'What did?'

'A thought.'

Everyone waited. They were getting used to the slower delivery of this new man. He sometimes made sense, given a hearing.

'The box of talcum powder in Denise's bag was harmless.'

Diamond nodded.

'But the fact remains that Clarion's face was damaged by caustic soda.'

'Correct.'

Ingeborg drummed her fingers on the desk in impatience.

Dawkins was not to be put off. He was into his stride now. 'What if there was a second box?'

Diamond frowned. 'There wasn't, not in her bag.'

'A box she used for last-minute powdering, when Clarion was waiting to go on, one she kept in the wings on some ledge where she could reach for it when needed? It could still be there.'

'Possible, I suppose,' Diamond said, weighing the suggestion. He and Ingeborg had watched the young girl Belinda brushing the actors' faces and she'd said Denise had been there the first night. 'Yes, definitely worth checking. Inge, you can take this on.'

'Now?' Ingeborg asked.

'Sooner the better. And take Fred with you.'

Her eyes doubled in size. Insubordination threatened. She'd already done more than her share of mothering Dawkins.

But the man himself was ecstatic. 'You're sending *me*?'

'Yes, but keep a low profile. Leave the talking to Ingeborg. Any problem with that, Inge?'

She said with an effort at control, 'No, guv.'

Galvanised, Dawkins was already making for the door.

After they'd left, Halliwell said, 'He's keen.'

'Keen to get out of here, anyway,' Diamond said. 'Well, people. How has it been? Busy this morning?'

One of the civilian staff spoke up. 'A number of phone calls. Sergeant Dawkins handled them.'

'In his inimitable style, no doubt.'

'There was one message from the assistant chief constable.'

'Georgina? He didn't say.'

'It's logged.'

'What do you mean—logged?' He had a mental picture of felled trees.

'Stored in the system. I believe the ACC wants to speak to you.'

'Why didn't someone tell me before this?'

'If you look at your in-box, sir, you'll find Sergeant Dawkins marked it as priority.'

'My in-box? He's got a tongue in his head. He

was here until a few minutes ago.'

'I think he may be shy.'

'Have you seen the suits he wears? Shy he is not.'

The blood pressure soared to a dangerous level. It was a good thing Dawkins had left the building.

*   *   *

In her eyrie on the top floor, Georgina was in a benign mood when Diamond entered and muttered an apology about not responding sooner.

'It isn't urgent, as I thought I made clear to Horatio.'

He was thrown by the name. He had to dig deep to recall who Horatio was and when it came back to him, he wasn't thrilled. How was it that the so-called shy man, Dawkins, was on first-name terms with the assistant chief constable?

Georgina was thinking of other things. 'All the trouble at the theatre—did you get to the bottom of it?'

'Not yet, ma'am,' he said. 'It's more complex than I first thought.'

'The suicide?'

'I'm not a hundred per cent sure it was a suicide.'

Her eyebrows lifted like level-crossing gates.

'She left no note,' Diamond said.

'I expect she was too distressed. People with suicide in mind aren't always so organised.'

'And we haven't been able to prove a definite connection with the caustic soda incident. We're still working on it. Denise Pearsall doesn't seem to have had any grudge against Clarion.'

'I'm not sure I'm following you,' Georgina said. 'Are you suggesting she died by accident?'

'I'm wondering if she jumped at all.'

'Now you've lost me altogether.'

'She may have been pushed.'

Georgina blinked. 'I can't think how.'

'Neither could I until this morning when I had another look backstage. Foolishly I'd assumed she climbed a ladder to get up to the loading bridge. Today I learned there's a way on to it from the second floor.'

'Is that significant?'

'It is if someone wanted to murder her. Much simpler than climbing a vertical iron ladder.'

'*Murder?* Peter, are you serious?'

'There's a dressing room up there, just the one, not in use in the present play. I found clear evidence somebody was in there recently. It would make a useful base for anyone intending to ambush her.'

Georgina let him know she would need a lot more convincing. 'It's far more likely she went in there herself prior to taking her own life.'

'Even so, I'm having the room checked by a scene of crime team.'

'You're reading a lot into this.'

'I want to know who was in there and why.'

'What would be the point of killing Denise? She was a nice woman, from all I heard, respected by people in the theatre.'

'I know.'

'And she'd struggle with an attacker, surely. There would be marks on her body that would be obvious in the post-mortem. Was anything mentioned by the pathologist?'

'No, but there was alcohol in her system.'

'She may have taken a drink to get her courage up.'

'Or someone gave her a cocktail of drink and drugs.'

'Drugs were present as well?'

He cleared his throat. 'That's speculation on my part. We won't know until the blood is tested.'

'And if, as I suspect, the results are negative?'

'I'll look at the possibility of more than one killer being involved.'

Georgina clicked her tongue. 'This is in danger of becoming an obsession, Peter.'

'If you remember, ma'am, you got me started on this.'

'Only because I could see the theatre being closed down. That seems less likely now, even if Clarion sues.'

'Do I sense that you'd like to call off the hounds?'

She looked away, out of the window. 'No, you can finish the job. I'm more confident than I was.' She turned to face him, eyes shining more brightly than her silver buttons. 'I was chosen last night for *Sweeney Todd*.'

'Nice work, ma'am.' He couldn't resist asking, 'What part are you playing?'

'Not one of the principals. I have the voice, but as a newcomer to the BLOGs, I can't expect a major role this year. I'll be strengthening the company.'

In the chorus, in other words. 'And it's to run at the theatre?'

'The third week in September. Rehearsals have been under way for some time. I'm joining late.'

'Where do you rehearse? Not in the theatre?'

'No, we don't have the use of it yet. Our rehearsal room is a church hall.' But she took his enquiry as a pledge of interest. 'Do you sing, Peter?'

He laughed. 'Like a corncrake.'

'Well, if you wanted—if you were looking for a way to get involved—you could be an ancillary.'

'What's that?'

'One of our back-up people, using whatever talents you possess, designing the programme, making props, painting scenery. There are jobs galore.'

'Theatre isn't my thing.'

'Fair enough. I only mentioned it in passing. Living alone, as you do, you might want to join something outside the police.'

If I do, he thought, it won't be anything you belong to.

'Horatio doesn't do any singing,' Georgina added, 'but we couldn't stage a production like *Sweeney* without him.'

There was a pause for thought.

'Dawkins?' he said, feeling the blood flushing his face. 'Sergeant Dawkins is in the BLOGs?'

'Hasn't he told you? He's our movement director. All the action sequences are co-ordinated by him. Dances, fights, stunts, swordplay.'

'Movement director?' His head reeling, Diamond was reduced to echoing her words.

'He's a trained dancer, you know.'

'He told me that much. How long has he been doing this?'

'Before I joined.'

Now it was revealed why Fred Dawkins had

been plucked from the uniformed ranks and foisted on CID. He'd got to know Georgina through the BLOGs and worked his ticket. What a shaft.

'I know exactly what's going through your head,' Georgina said, 'and I have to tell you I moved him into CID on merit. He impressed me long before I joined the BLOGs. In fact, I'm surprised you hadn't spotted him.'

'I knew him,' Diamond said. 'He stood out.'

'He's a rising star.'

'Risen.'

'Don't mistake his slow speech for woolly thinking. He's got a quick brain. You need to be sharp to choreograph an entire show like *Sweeney*.'

'He's sharp, all right.'

She was missing all the irony. 'You can safely send him off the building on an operation. I gather he's frustrated being confined to barracks.'

'Has he been complaining to you, ma'am?'

She backtracked a little. 'It may have been mentioned in passing. He's too gifted to be on the end of a phone all day long. Let him off the leash and I predict he'll not let you down.'

'He's off the leash right now, making another search of the theatre with Ingeborg Smith.'

'Splendid. If anyone can get results for you, Horatio will.'

He'd heard as much of this as he could take. 'Is there anything else?'

On his way downstairs he forced some perspective into his thinking. Nothing fundamental had changed. He was still stuck with Dawkins and he'd have to give the man a chance. Everyone works the system and there were infinite ways of

224

doing it. Fred hadn't joined the BLOGs to cosy up to Georgina. He was already installed there. He'd got lucky and cashed in. Who wouldn't have?

CHAPTER FOURTEEN

Hedley Shearman was on duty again in the Theatre Royal, bruised, but no longer bleeding, demanding to know what the devil the police were up to, poking around in the wings.

'Searching,' Ingeborg told him. A short answer can be a good riposte to bluster.

'That's obvious.'

'Yes.'

'But what do you hope to find?'

'Make-up.'

'The stuff Denise was using Monday night? I don't think you'll find it here. She was very organised. She wouldn't have left anything lying around.'

'She may have been so organised that she kept some handy in the wings for use before the show. That's why we're checking.'

'Well, it had better not take long. We have a performance tonight and I don't want you getting in the way of the actors.' He took a second look at Dawkins and frowned. 'Aren't you the man in uniform who was here Tuesday morning putting me through the third degree?'

Dawkins had been obeying orders, keeping that low profile Diamond had decreed. Faced with open hostility, he broke his vow of silence. 'I wouldn't characterise it as such.'

225

'You look and sound awfully like him.'

'It was not the third degree. It wasn't even the second.'

'Oh, you don't like the term,' Shearman said, getting some of his bounce back. 'I was on the receiving end and I know what it felt like. Why aren't you in uniform today?'

Ingeborg was quick to head off an elaborate explanation. 'He's joined CID.' She looked at her watch. 'If you want us out before the show, better let us get on with it.'

Another glare and then Shearman moved off towards the dressing rooms.

Basic stage scenery is constructed as flats, canvas over a wooden framework, and when it is in position some of the horizontal battens form ledges. Small objects are sometimes lodged there, lucky mascots, bits of chalk, pens and torches. But it was doubtful if anything as big as a powder box would fit. More likely they'd find what they were looking for tucked away in a corner at floor level. Plenty of areas backstage needed checking. They went about the search systematically, each working at a different side of the stage, dividing the space into sections, lifting props, discarded cloths and coils of cable.

'I'm getting less confident,' Ingeborg called across the stage after twenty minutes. 'If it's here, it ought to be obvious.'

Dawkins didn't answer and it wasn't clear whether he disagreed or was still observing the embargo.

'Putting myself in Denise's place,' Ingeborg went on, 'if I had some powder laced with caustic soda I wouldn't leave it lying around. I'd get rid of it.'

Still there was no answer from the opposite side.

'But then,' she added after more thought, 'if someone else doctored the stuff, Denise wouldn't have known.'

This time Dawkins couldn't resist. 'Don't you think the someone else would also have got rid of it?'

'In that case we're wasting our time.' Deadpan, as if she didn't remember, she asked, 'Whose idea was this?'

Dawkins became silent again.

*   *   *

Diamond had an in-built resistance to computers and he didn't make a habit of checking for on-screen messages. If his own staff had anything to report, he expected to be told. Most of them knew this. To be fair to Fred Dawkins, anyone new on the team might have acted as he had, thinking it wasn't unreasonable to expect the top man to make regular checks.

Dawkins was out of the office now, so Diamond stopped complaining about the call from Georgina he'd almost missed. Still the thought nagged at him that there could be other information waiting for him. Unseen by the team, he stepped into his office to check the in-box.

There wasn't much. Headquarters had issued a new online procedure for budget reports. Stuff that, he said to himself. Keith Halliwell had called in from the mortuary. Old news. He'd seen Keith since then. Clarion Calhoun was moving out of the burns unit to a private hotel in Clifton called the

Cedar of Lebanon and would become an out-patient. Nothing remarkable in that. There was always pressure on bed-space in hospitals. Finally, there was a note that the crime scene investigation team had started work in dressing room eleven.

He regarded one oval-shaped button on the keyboard as his friend. A tiny image of the moon put the computer into sleep mode. He pressed it and watched the screen go dark. Magic.

With two separate searches now under way, he could keep the appointment with his old school friend. On this fine afternoon, he chose to walk to the Abbey Churchyard and treated himself to the carnival atmosphere as he zigzagged between crocodiles of French schoolkids waiting to tour the Roman Baths and cheering the buskers balancing on unicycles juggling flaming torches. He didn't have time to watch, unfortunately. No matter, he thought. Later, he'd do some flame-throwing of his own when he caught up with Sergeant Dawkins.

The short fat guy in a pork-pie hat was standing below the bottom rung of the famous ladder to heaven carved into the Abbey front, and not realising the symbolic stance he was making. The years had been kind to Mike Glazebrook; he could have passed for forty-five. Diamond shook his hand and suggested they had tea at one of the outdoor tables on the sunny side.

'You've put on some weight since I saw you last,' Glazebrook said. 'Is it fattening, this police work?'

'I was going to ask the same about structural engineering.'

'Oh, I wouldn't get a safety certificate, but I hold up, just about.'

The banter was a useful way to roll back forty

years and revive the matiness that passed for friendship at school. They chose a table and each ordered a cream tea as if to affirm that healthy eating wasn't for them.

'I wasn't sure you'd remember me,' Diamond said. 'It wasn't as if we were at secondary school together.'

'Spotted you straight away. It's the onset of senility,' Glazebrook said, straight-faced. 'The short-term memory goes, but we can recall trivial details from our childhood.'

'Are you calling me trivial?'

'Sorry. Make that significant.'

Straight to business, Diamond decided. 'My recollection is that we got to know each other through that play we were in as the boy princes.'

'*Richard III.*'

'Except they didn't call it that. Wasn't it *Wicked Richard,* so as not to confuse it with the Shakespeare version?'

'Shakespeare?' Glazebrook rocked back and laughed. 'Who did they think they were kidding? Even at that age I could tell it was crap. But you're right about the title. Didn't one of the actors write it?'

'Very likely. Maybe the art teacher who recruited you and me. Now what was he called?'

'Mr White—Flakey, to us kids.'

Diamond raised his thumb. 'Of course.' This was promising. The man had a reliable memory.

'I don't remember him doing any writing,' Glazebrook added.

'He painted the scenery, I expect.'

'He must have, and probably did the posters and the programme.'

229

'He would have been useful to them with his art skills and his link to the school,' Diamond said. 'That's how we got roped in. There was no audition. I can't think why he picked you and me out of all the kids.'

'Can't you?' Glazebrook said with a suggestive smile.

'We must have looked the part. Princely.'

Glazebrook laughed again. 'No chance. We were two miserable little perishers. I used to have a photo of us in costume and we didn't look overjoyed in our breeches and tights. My mother tore it up when she read about Flakey in the *News of the World*.'

Diamond tensed, played the words over and felt a vein pulsing in his temple. 'Read what?'

'Didn't you hear? He wasn't called Flakey for nothing. He was sent down for five years for interfering with schoolchildren, as they called it then. Dirty old perv.'

The pulsing spread through his arms and chest. 'I heard nothing of this.'

'Really? And you a cop? We'd long since left the school when he was found out. It must have been five or six years later. I was put through the inquisition by my parents, wanting to know if he'd got up to anything with me. He hadn't, but I wouldn't have told them if he had. You try and forget stuff like that.'

'Right,' Diamond said automatically, his thoughts in ferment.

'He didn't try it on with you, did he? You'd have told me at the time, wouldn't you?' He gave Diamond a speculative look. 'I guess not, if I wouldn't discuss it with my parents. But at this distance in time we can be open with each other.'

'Sure.'

But he wasn't. He was trying to remember.

'In my opinion weirdos like that should be locked away indefinitely or offered the chance of chemical castration,' Glazebrook was saying. 'You can bet he didn't serve five years. He'd have been out on probation, back in society, looking for more little kids to abuse.'

'They wouldn't have allowed him to teach again,' Diamond said.

'With his art, he could get other work, no problem. When he surfaced again at one stage he was illustrating books—for kids, no doubt. I mean, you don't get pictures in books for grown-ups, do you?'

'Covers?'

'Covers is right,' Glazebrook said. 'Covers for pervy behaviour.'

'Did you keep up with any of the others?' Diamond asked, to move on. He couldn't take any more of this.

They talked for another ten minutes, exchanging memories, but Diamond's heart wasn't in it. He was reeling from the shock. After he'd settled the bill, they shook hands and went their separate ways.

This time, he paused and stood with the crowd watching the unicyclists performing in front of the Pump Room. In fact he saw nothing. All of his perceptions were directed inwards. His brain was surfing incomplete memories of that time as a boy. He wanted the truth, however sickening it was, but it was elusive. Everything connected with school and that play took on a new and sinister

231

significance. Yet he was finding it difficult to pinpoint any one incident. The brain has ways of blocking traumatic experiences, particularly from childhood. He understood that. The one certainty was that he couldn't enter the theatre without fear. The whole truth wasn't revealed yet. He could still only guess at what happened, but the guessing was more informed and more unpleasant.

A shout from the crowd brought him out of this purgatory. Time was going on and he needed to get his head straight, somehow put the conversation with Glazebrook to the back of his mind. He was required back inside the theatre, expected to function as a detective. He watched the buskers juggling with fire, keeping their balance. Then he moved on.

*   *   *

Francis Melmot was outside the stage door, chatting to some front-of-house people who must have thought they'd escaped for a smoke. He hailed Diamond with his usual bonhomie. 'What a pleasure this is, Inspector.'

Not for Diamond.

And 'inspector' was a demotion, but the matter wasn't worth pointing out. Diamond touched his grey trilby and said he hadn't expected an official welcome from the chairman of the board.

'I just looked in to share some wonderful news with our loyal and much valued staff,' Melmot said, at the same time despatching the much valued staff with a flap of the hand.

'What is it?' Diamond said with an effort to be civil. 'A five-star review?'

232

'Actually, no, even though we've had some excellent ones.' Melmot drew his shoulders back and seemed to grow even taller. 'I was advised an hour ago that Clarion has withdrawn her threat to sue.'

'Who by?'

'Her lawyers.'

'That is good,' Diamond said, and meant it, his mind speeding through possibilities. He could see this whole investigation coming to a swift end. 'What happened? An out-of-court settlement?'

'No, we're not paying a penny. It's unconditional.'

'What a turnaround. When I saw the lady yesterday her mind was made up.'

'Yesterday she was still in shock,' Melmot said. 'She's had time to reflect since then. There's even better news. She will be making a substantial private donation to the theatre.'

'Did you talk her round, then?'

'I haven't spoken to her.'

Mystified, Diamond refused to believe him. 'You're on close terms. I thought a word in her ear may have worked this magic.'

Melmot blinked. 'I'm not sure what you mean by close terms.'

'She stayed with you in Melmot Hall.'

'As a house guest. She didn't sleep with me, Inspector, if that's what you're suggesting.'

'Dream on, eh?'

'What?' Melmot reddened.

'You said you were a fan. Didn't sex cross your mind when you invited her to stay?'

'That's downright offensive.'

'I can't think why. Personally, I'd take it as a

compliment. Anyway, what happened in the bedroom isn't my concern, except I just wondered if there was a falling out, something that made her leave Melmot Hall in a hurry.'

'Absolutely not.' His cheek muscles twitched. 'Just to put the record straight, Inspector, there are twenty-two bedrooms and mine is in another wing. When the rehearsals started in earnest, Clarion wanted to be nearer to the theatre, so she moved into the Royal Crescent. Pure convenience.'

'Thanks for putting me right,' Diamond said and trailed a warning. 'I was going to ask the lady herself and now there's no need, but I'll visit her just the same. I'd still like to know why she's changed her mind about suing.'

The triumphant manner had gone. Melmot tried to sound more conciliatory. 'I daresay her lawyers talked some sense into her. I understand she's left the hospital.'

'I did hear. It doesn't mean her face will ever be the same again. She'll have to go back for treatment.'

'Believe me, Inspector, she has the heartfelt sympathy of everyone in the Theatre Royal. Now that the threat of legal action is removed, we sent her some more flowers and our wishes for a full recovery and she'll be listed in the programmes as a patron.' He seesawed from largesse to a lament. 'Of course the saddest thing of all is that the dresser took personal responsibility and did what she did. I've no doubt she killed herself because she feared for our future, as we all did. She was deeply committed to this wonderful old theatre.'

'Yes, I've heard that,' Diamond said.

'Will you draw a line under the investigation?'

Melmot asked, sounding as casual as he could. 'I believe some of your people are backstage at this minute.'

'Enquiring into Denise Pearsall's death,' Diamond said, conceding nothing. 'That continues until we find out exactly what happened.'

'It's academic, isn't it? Nothing can bring her back.'

'But I'll be giving evidence to a coroner. I need all the facts.' He took a step towards the stage door. 'I'd better see what progress they've made.'

'I don't know how you get inside the mind of a suicide victim.'

'We can't and we won't.' Diamond nodded and moved on and into the building.

Clarion's decision baffled him. Her career was in ruins but she could still afford a lawsuit and she had a strong chance of winning. If Melmot hadn't persuaded her to drop the case, who had?

The back stairs to dressing room eleven were testing for a man of his bulk, yet easier than the iron ladder in the fly tower. He paused at the top to draw breath. He could hear voices ahead. Pleasing to know that the crime scene people were at work in number eleven; less pleasing when he saw who was in charge, an old antagonist called Duckett.

'What's the story so far?' Diamond asked as he raised the tape across the door to bend under it.

'Stop right there, squire,' Duckett called across the room through his mask. He looked risible in the white zip-suit and bonnet that was de rigueur for crime scene investigators. Two others, a man and a woman, were similarly dressed and on hands and knees under the dressing tables. 'Don't take another step. You'll contaminate the evidence.'

Diamond chose not to disclose that he'd been in here with Titus at lunchtime. He waited for Duckett to come to the doorway by the least obvious route, hugging the walls. 'You may not know this, but it was me who called you in.'

'I guessed as much,' Duckett said with a superior tone. 'A dressing room as large as this and filled with trace evidence from I don't know how many people is about the most complicated scene any investigator can have to examine. Thanks for that.'

'I won't need to know its entire history,' Diamond said. 'If you can tell me who was here most recently, that would help.'

'Apart from two lumbering detectives in size ten shoes, you mean?'

One detective and one dramaturge, Diamond was tempted to point out, but it wasn't worth saying.

'It's true there's about three weeks of dust over every surface,' Duckett said. 'You asked who was here and I can't tell you, of course. All I'm able to say at this stage is that within the last few days two people were in here and one at least had long reddish hair.'

Two people, one of them Denise. This had huge potential importance. 'The dead woman had long red hair.'

'We're in a theatre. I wouldn't jump to any conclusions as to gender. They weren't here long, going by what we found, but they seem to have done some drinking. The marks in the dust look like the bases of wine glasses and a bottle.'

'You haven't found the bottle?'

236

'Taken away, apparently. As were the glasses, the cork and the wrapping. Someone extra tidy, or secretive. The owner of the red hair sat in that chair at the end while the other individual perched on top of the dressing table opposite.'

'Didn't they leave any other traces?'

'People always leave traces. It's the principle of exchange. When two objects come into contact, particles are transferred. How informative those particles may be is another question. We'll examine everything and let you know in due course.'

He heard the 'in due course' with a sinking heart. 'Fingerprints?'

'A few so far, not of much use. Paradoxically, the best prints come from a clean surface, not one coated with several weeks of dust.'

'Signs of violence?'

'None that we've discovered. All the indications are that the people came in, made themselves comfortable, enjoyed a drink and left. It's not what I call a crime scene.'

'A woman fell to her death from the loading bridge across the passage,' Diamond reminded him.

'I know, and we'll examine that, too.'

'If they left with the bottle and glasses it must be because they didn't want them discovered later.'

Duckett shrugged. 'Or simply that they didn't finish the wine and took it with them.'

'Is there anything you can tell me about the second person, the one who sat on the dressing table?'

'Average-sized buttocks.'

'Average? What's that?'

'Slimmer than yours.'

'Oh, thanks.'

'You asked.'

'Nothing else?'

'We have a mass of trace evidence to examine in the lab. I can see this taking two to three weeks.'

'*What?* It's only dust.'

Duckett was equally outraged. 'This dust, as you call it, is made up of millions of particles and they may include skin and hair capable of giving DNA evidence, fibres from clothing, soil brought in on people's shoes, each with potential to establish who was here and what happened. I don't know if you appreciate how much work is involved. Each specimen has to be put through a battery of tests from simple magnification to infrared spectrophotometry.'

Science never intimidated Diamond. 'Three weeks, though. It's not as if you have a corpse in here. It's an empty room. All right, there's dust. Don't start on me again. Just get on with it. I've got other fish to fry.'

Crime scene types were like that, he reflected as he started down the stairs. They feed you one titbit and then keep you waiting for weeks. The news that two people had definitely been in there fitted his theory, but the absence of violence did not. He couldn't reconcile the wine-drinking with the death leap. Had Denise become suicidal after a couple of glasses of wine with a friend? Who was the friend? No one had come forward to say they were the last to see her alive.

For now, he turned his thoughts to the search downstairs.

His people weren't in the wings. He found them

238

on the stage behind the closed curtain, Ingeborg in Isherwood's writing chair and Dawkins horizontal on the sofa. Ingeborg got up guiltily, but Dawkins remained where he was.

'Didn't know you were in the building, guv,' Ingeborg said. 'We were just deciding what to do next.'

'I can see. Are you comfortable, Fred?'

'We completed the search, your worship,' Dawkins said without turning his head, 'and I proposed a pause for rest and recuperation. Union rules.'

'Which union is that—the layabouts? What did the search produce?'

'Diddley squat, I'm sorry to tell you,' Ingeborg said. 'We looked everywhere, guv. Only stopped a few minutes ago.'

'Do we now admit that the theory of the extra powder box was mistaken?'

'It looks that way,' she said.

Dawkins, whose theory it had been, said nothing.

Diamond crossed the stage and sank in the high-backed chair beside the tiled stove. He, too, had earned a break. 'There's news,' he told them. 'I saw the chairman of the trust, Francis Melmot, and he told me Clarion has withdrawn her threat to sue. What is more, she's making a donation to the theatre.'

'Praise the Lord,' Dawkins said. 'Our ship is saved, and all who sail in her.'

'You took a message on the phone this morning,' Diamond said to him. 'Did she say anything about this?'

'The message was from Bristol police, who were
239

guarding her. They informed me she was leaving the hospital for a private hotel in Clifton.'

'The Cedar of Lebanon. Good thing I happened to check my in-box. In future, Fred, speak to me.' He mimed jaw action with thumb and fingers. 'Is that clear?'

'Clear and duly noted.'

In an obvious attempt to improve the atmosphere, Ingeborg said, 'What changed Clarion's mind, I wonder? Do you think the damage to her face is not as bad as it first appeared?'

'It wasn't mentioned.'

'She'd look silly trying to sue if she made a full recovery before the case came to court.'

'Which would make a sad mockery of Denise's suicide, if suicide it was,' Dawkins said.

'Speaking of which,' Diamond said, 'I've just been up to dressing room eleven.' He told them about the evidence of two people drinking wine there, one a redhead, like Denise.

'Then suicide it wasn't,' Ingeborg said.

'Why not?'

'Two people, and one ended up dead.'

'Hold on,' he said. 'Suppose the other person agreed to meet her for a drink and said something that so upset her that she went straight over to the gallery and took her own life.'

'Her lover,' Dawkins said from the sofa.

'Did she have one?' Diamond asked, thrown by the suggestion.

Before Dawkins could respond, Ingeborg said, 'Now you're talking, Fred. I reckon she was dumped. Hedley Shearman seems to have been everyone's lover and, if he wasn't, it wasn't for want of trying,'

'Don't get carried away, Inge,' Diamond said. 'Shearman likes the ladies, agreed, but is he that much of a catch? Gisella is unimpressed and she told me Clarion gave him the elbow as well. There's no evidence Denise or any other woman liked him enough to kill herself for him.'

Dawkins had another theory. 'Here's a more down-to-earth scenario. She was told her services were no longer required.'

'Her job, you mean? By Shearman?' Ingeborg said.

'Or the chairman of the board.'

'Melmot?' She seized on the possibility. 'Yes, perfect. He's the smarmy sort who'd pour you a glass of wine and sack you at the same time. I can see it.'

Diamond was less enthusiastic. 'Why would Melmot invite her up to an empty dressing room? There's a management office.'

Nobody had an answer.

The flow of suggestions dried up. Diamond looked at his watch. It wouldn't be long before preparations started for the evening performance. It was a strange experience sitting here on the stage among the scenery and bits of furniture. He could imagine the curtain going up and the lights on and the actors speaking their lines, creating a drama out of words someone else had written. He found it hard to credit that people did this from choice.

'Let's get out of here. You finished the search, you said?'

'We looked everywhere,' Ingeborg said. 'Shake a leg, Fred.'

Dawkins heaved himself off the sofa and performed a theatrical bow.

Ingeborg said, 'Why don't you show us a few steps? You're in the right place.'

'Wrong shoes.'

'A soft shoe shuffle. Go on, Fred. The boss doesn't believe you can do it.'

'Difficult on a carpet.' But the showman in Sergeant Dawkins couldn't resist. He performed a few stylish steps, a double turn and a slick finish. No question: he'd done this before. He was a good mover.

Ingeborg clapped and Diamond gave a grudging nod. 'Where did you learn?'

'The obvious place.'

There was never a straight answer from this man.

'It was a simple question, Fred.'

'Let me hazard a guess about you, guv. In your youth you spent Saturday mornings kicking a football in the park.'

'Sometimes.'

'My parents sent me to dance school. At the time I didn't appreciate the opportunity, but later I saw some Fred Astaire films and took it up again.'

'*Top Hat*?'

'That was one of them.'

Diamond was more at ease now. 'And less well known, *Flying Down to Rio*, *The Gay Divorcee*, *Follow the Fleet*?'

Surprised that he could reel off all these titles, Ingeborg said, 'Are you a dancer as well, guv?'

'Get real, Inge.'

'You seem to know a lot about it.'

'Old films, I know about. If you haven't seen

Astaire dancing with Ginger Rogers, I'm sorry for you.' Now that he'd started, Diamond couldn't suppress the nostalgia. 'He would have danced all over this set, and I mean all over—the sofa, the chairs, the bed.' He looked around the set and his eyes lighted on the tiled stove. 'The only thing that might have defeated him is that ugly great object. Does it have a part in the play?'

'It's a period piece, I expect.'

'Typical of Berlin in the thirties, is it?'

'Probably,' Ingeborg said and took a couple of steps towards it. 'I don't think it's ugly. The tiles are quite pretty.'

'But you wouldn't want it in your living room. Is it real, or made specially?'

Dawkins spoke up. 'It can't be genuine.'

'How do you know, cleverclogs?' Ingeborg said.

'The genuine *kachelofen* is built of masonry, to conserve the heat passing through. It would be too heavy for the stage. The tiles may be real.' His expertise was impressive, but didn't cut much ice here.

'It looks real to me,' Ingeborg said, with a wicked urge to prove him wrong. She reached for the handle of the small square oven set into the tiles and was shocked by the door coming away in her hand and falling on the floor. Dawkins had been right. It was wood, painted to look like metal. 'Jesus, I've broken it.'

'No, you haven't,' Diamond said. 'Pick it up and push it back in the slot.'

He could have saved his breath. Ingeborg had suddenly become more interested in the space she'd uncovered. She reached inside. 'Hey, what's this?'

243

'The powder box?'

'No. Various bits of paper.' She took out several sheets and glanced at the top one. 'It's only the stage plan for this set,' she said in disappointment. 'And a couple of pages from a script. I expect someone was cleaning up and put them in here rather than binning them.'

'I don't suppose they're needed now,' Diamond said.

'I'll put them back, in case.' She was still holding one item, an envelope. 'This looks like a letter. *To All at the Theatre Royal.*'

'Is it sealed?'

'No. Shall I see what's in it?'

'Let me,' Diamond said.

She handed it across.

He took out a sheet of paper and gave it a rapid look. 'This is a suicide note.'

CHAPTER FIFTEEN

My Dear Friends,

This theatre has been my life and you have been my family, all of you, for six happy years. I can't thank you enough for all the warmth and support you have given me and the wonderful moments we shared. I had no idea everything would change overnight, but it has, through my own stupidity. I'm deeply sorry now about what happened to Clarion and I pray that it won't be permanent. I hope by some miracle the theatre and all of you can survive this. But for me there can be no future in my beloved Theatre Royal,

my home, and this is where I have chosen to
put an end to it, backstage where I belong.
Please don't mourn. No black clothes. No
prayers at my funeral. If my ashes could be
scattered in the theatre garden that would be
more than I deserve.
  Goodbye and blessings.
  Denise

Diamond handed the note to Ingeborg. Fred
Dawkins stood beside her and read the words at
the same time.

'Poor soul,' Ingeborg said.

'Brave soul,' Dawkins said.

'True.'

'Blaming no one else.'

'Yes, I've heard suicide called a coward's way
out, but I don't agree with that.'

'Even to think about one's own funeral.'

'It's been written on a computer and printed
out,' Diamond said, unwilling to join in the
fatalistic talk and already querying this as reliable
evidence. 'Suicide notes are usually written by
hand.'

'Guv, we're in the computer age now,' Ingeborg
said. 'No one writes anything by hand apart from
shopping lists. If I were doing one of these I'd use
my laptop. She's signed it by hand.'

'We'll get the signature checked,' he said and
then, as he thought about forensics, 'If I'd been
sharper, we wouldn't have handled it. They can get
prints from paper. Someone is going to rap my
knuckles over this.' With a shrug and a wry smile,
he started to fold the note.

'Don't, guv,' Ingeborg said. 'The more you

245

touch it, the less chance there is of finding anything. We need an evidence bag.'

'Did anyone think of bringing one?' he said with a look that said it was more their fault than his.

Dawkins was never stumped for a suggestion. 'Place it between two of the other sheets of paper.'

'Good thinking, Fred,' Ingeborg said.

Outnumbered, Diamond didn't argue.

*   *   *

The same evening when he called for Paloma, she was in her office scanning pictures of frock-coated Victorians for the costume designer of *Sweeney Todd*. 'Could you lower the lid while I hold this engraving in place? Gently.'

The scanner hummed and another image was stored. The BLOGs would have more than enough authentic illustrations to work with.

'Did I tell you my boss has made it into the chorus?' Diamond said.

'Georgina? Good for her. She'll be one of the Fleet Street women in a bright bodice and skirt.'

'More out of the bodice than in. She's a well-built lady.'

'Front row for her, then. The BLOGs maximise their assets.' She picked up a book and opened it at the page she wanted. 'One more, and we're done. I hope this damn show goes ahead. I've invested a lot of time in it.'

'It's on. The theatre has a future.' He told her about Clarion deciding not to proceed with the lawsuit.

'Sensible woman,' Paloma said. 'The only people who make money out of the courts are the

246

lawyers. Who told you this?'

'Francis Melmot, the chairman of the trust. They can't believe their luck.'

Then he told her about finding the suicide note.

'Not a bad day all round,' she said. 'The theatre is in the clear and the note proves what happened to Denise. Case closed.'

'If the note is genuine.'

'Why shouldn't it be?'

'For one thing it was hidden away inside a piece of scenery.'

'But you explained about that. Someone found it lying about and tidied up. That German oven was a useful place to tuck some papers out of sight.'

'Why would Denise leave her suicide note lying about?' he said.

'Come on, Peter. To be noticed. It's a theatre. Where do you put something you want people to find? Centre stage isn't a bad idea, is it? She was about to hurl herself off the gallery and hit the stage floor. I know she didn't fall all the way, but that was clearly the intention. They'd find the body and see the note nearby.'

Put like that, it made sense.

'Denise killed herself. It's over, Peter. You can relax.'

How he wished he could. He'd been debating with himself whether to tell Paloma what he'd learned from Mike Glazebrook. There was a powerful instinct to stay tight-lipped and battle with his own demons. Innocent as he must have been at eight years old, he still felt tainted. On the other hand, he'd told Paloma about the panic attacks he'd been getting at the theatre. She was sure to ask at some point soon if he'd worked out

247

why they happened.

Would he have confided in Steph, his wife?

Certainly.

Then why not Paloma?

'I met someone I was at school with today.' When he'd finished telling her, he felt some relief. It hadn't been good to bottle it up.

Paloma had listened in silence, only her eyes expressing concern. 'You don't know for certain that the art teacher abused you,' she pointed out.

'I won't unless I can let the memories in. My brain is acting as a censor. It doesn't take a Sigmund Freud to work out that something deeply upsetting is locked in there. White was a convicted paedophile and he recruited us for that play I was in. My theatre phobia—or whatever we choose to call it—kicked in immediately after that weekend.'

'But do you really want to remember?'

'It's more than a want. It's a need. I have to overcome this, not have it forever as a no-go area.'

'The school friend . . . ?'

'Mike Glazebrook.'

'He told you Flakey White didn't abuse him. Do you believe him?'

'Yes, he convinced me.'

'Yet you feel sure you were taken advantage of? Why you?'

'I've thought about this. Paedophiles are devious. If I was the kid he set out to entrap, he may have used Mike as a cover, so that it wasn't obvious, to let me feel safe knowing there was another boy. Our parents would also be more confident if there were two kids, not one.'

'Where do you think the abuse happened?'

'Don't know. His car? The changing room at the

248

hall? I can't—or won't let myself—remember.'

'But you're sure it took place?'

'It's the only explanation. I don't scare easily, Paloma. This has undermined me.'

'Is White still alive?'

The question unsettled him. Up to now he'd been focusing on the past. 'No idea. He'd be over seventy.'

'Plenty of people are. You're in the police. They keep track of sex offenders, don't they? You could find out. You could meet him.'

She was pushing him to the limit and he wished he hadn't started this. 'I don't know if I could trust myself. He'd deny it, anyway.'

'Some way, you need to know the truth. It's a festering wound, Peter. If you can find him, it's the best chance you've got. Do you know his real name?'

'It was something fancy. Morgan O. White, I think.'

'That should make him easier to find.'

'I expect he changed his identity. Most of them do.' He was putting obstacles in the way and it did him no credit.

'But the Sex Offenders Register would list all the names he's used.'

'You have a touching faith in the system,' he said. 'He was convicted in the sixties, thirty years before the register was started and it isn't retroactive.'

'There must be criminal records.'

'You're right. They're kept at Scotland Yard by the National Identification Service.' Keen to bring this conversation to an end, he added, 'I'll call them from work tomorrow and get them to run a

249

check. Let's go for a meal and talk about other things.'

'You've got your mobile. Why not do it now?'

She could have been Steph talking. After a moment's hesitation he reached into his pocket.

Once he'd passed the checks on his own identity, the information was quick in coming. The helpful civil servant at the Yard told him that Morgan Ogilby White, a teacher, aged thirty-one, had been convicted on three counts of indecency with minors at Winchester in 1965 and sentenced to five years, of which he had served three in Shepton Mallet prison. The offences had been committed at a private school in Hampshire called Manningham Academy. White must have moved there from the junior school in Kingston where Diamond had known him. He'd been released on probation in 1968.

Hearing the details like this made it more real than getting it at third hand from Glazebrook's Mum.

'Is that it?' he asked.

The voice said, 'That's all we have.'

'I was expecting more.'

'He hasn't re-offended—under that name, anyway. Paedophiles are crafty at changing their identities and re-offending, as you know.'

'I was hoping to trace him.'

'Difficult. You could try the probation service. But your best bet would be the police authority where he offended. Before the new legislation came in, they kept their own intelligence on sex offenders.'

*   *   *

The house was more than three-quarters full that evening. Not bad, considering how bleak the prospects had been after Clarion had left the cast. Although numerous fans had returned their tickets on the Tuesday, the generous reviews and news coverage of Gisella's success as understudy had boosted sales and many of those empty seats were filled.

Chairman Melmot had made sure everyone knew of Clarion's decision not to sue. The mood backstage was upbeat as the countdown to curtain up was relayed at intervals over the tannoy. Gisella herself couldn't wait to go on stage. She'd heard that a casting director from the National had come to see her as Sally Bowles. They were looking for someone to play the main role in a revival of *Irma la Douce*. If she was asked, it would be a huge opportunity, she'd informed the other leading actors. Preston, as usual, was incommunicado an hour before the show, so she'd pushed a note under his door. She didn't have any worries about him. He could be relied on to give a strong performance. An actor was allowed to be self-absorbed off stage as long as he played his part like a professional. Whatever his secret pre-show build-up might consist of, it worked. The way Gisella saw it, Preston's Isherwood was a perfect foil for her Sally Bowles.

Little Hedley Shearman looked in at one stage with a bunch of roses when Gisella was doing her make-up. 'You look radiant,' he said. 'These are for you, my dear.'

She thanked him for bringing them up, assuming they'd been left by some admirer at the stage door.

'They're from me,' he said with a smirk, 'to spur you on.'

'Oh . . . well, thanks.' A guarded response. She hadn't enjoyed him pawing her the day before.

He continued, oblivious. 'We're expecting a VIP out there tonight.'

'I heard. Don't make me nervous.'

'You'll be marvellous, no question.' And now he revealed the reason for the flowers. 'How about a spot of supper afterwards? I know what you actors are like. You'll be on a high. You can't face sleep for hours.'

'Thanks for the offer,' she said, 'but I don't like eating late. I'll just have a sandwich at the hotel. And I have no problem sleeping, as it happens.'

'Can I join you?' He grinned. 'For the sandwich, I mean. I'm supposed to be dieting.'

'Mr Shearman—'

'Hedley to you.'

'Hedley, please don't take this personally, but I don't want company tonight or any night.'

This awkward exchange was quickly forgotten as the beginners left the dressing rooms to take their positions. The buzz of expectant conversation out front had been audible over the tannoy and was exciting to hear from the wings. The old theatre with its gilded panels, crimson drapes and crystal chandelier created an ambience. Every performance started with favourable conditions for a good hearing. The anticipation on both sides of the curtain was positive.

Preston Barnes was already in his usual place at the table on stage, having his appearance checked by Belinda, the make-up girl. Gisella tried to catch his eye to check that he'd seen her note, but he

252

didn't look her way. His concentration was total, almost intimidating.

In the wings the large woman playing Fräulein Schneider waited with the lace tablecloth she would set in preparation for Sally Bowles. Everyone in the cast spoke of her as Schneider, rather than using her own name. She had an air of overweening importance on and off stage. All the other actors stood nearby, lesser lights so far as she was concerned.

'And curtain up,' came the voice of the DSM from the prompt corner. Thursday's performance got under way. No evening in the theatre is ever exactly like another, even though the cast speak the same lines and make the same moves. This night would stand out.

I Am a Camera was written as a three-act play, but in the modern theatre a single interval is preferred, so the decision had been made to stop once, at the close of Act One, and run Two and Three together, dimming the lights between to show the passage of time. Act One ends with Sally Bowles, who is pregnant, about to go to an abortionist recommended by Fräulein Schneider. Isherwood is not the father, but he offers first to marry her and then to pay for the operation.

Shortly before the interval curtain was lowered, Schneider had an exit, followed soon after by Sally. On each other evening they had gone straight to their dressing rooms to prepare for the second half. Tonight, in the wings, Schneider blocked Gisella's way. Something was clearly wrong. She was out of character and apparently eager to speak. Gisella's first thought was that she must have committed some gaffe, missed a cue or blocked a sight line. It was soon clear something else was wrong.

'Did you see it?' Wide, startled eyes locked with Gisella's.

'See what?'

'Out there. The top box, stage right.'

Gisella's role was so demanding that she never had a chance to look anywhere beyond the footlights. She was aware of the audience, as any actor is, yet her concentration had been all on what was happening on stage. 'I wasn't looking.'

Schneider's part involved a lot of business moving about the set, tidying up, picking garments off the floor, answering doorbells, so that was how she had opportunities to sneak a look at the auditorium. 'I didn't believe my own eyes,' she said, 'but there's no question. Look at me. I'm not suggestible.'

This had seemed self-evident up to now.

'I don't know what this is about,' Gisella said, 'but I must get to my room. If you don't mind—'

'The lady in grey. She was there.'

There was a pause while Gisella tried to overcome her disbelief. 'The theatre ghost?'

'Staring at me, watching.'

'That's what an audience does. They stare at us all.'

'She was not flesh and blood. She was quite alone.'

'In the box? I expect it's just some member of the public.'

'The boxes haven't been used all week,' Schneider said. 'The sight-lines are too restricted. That box is where the ghost is always seen. I promise you, she was there, pale as death, and all in grey. What does it mean if you see her? Is it bad luck?'

'I've no idea, but . . .' Gisella looked around for support, anything to shake off this crazy woman. The curtain had just come down and Preston Barnes was walking off.

Schneider caught him by the arm. 'Did you see her?'

'Who?'

'The grey lady.'

He wasn't as polite as Gisella. 'Let go of me.'

'The theatre ghost.'

'For Christ's sake, I don't have time to piss around.' With that, he marched on, past them both.

Gisella wished she'd been as firm as that. She needed the interval break herself, and more than ever on this important night. She had to be on again from the opening of Act Two. All Schneider had to do was announce a couple of visitors. 'I'd forget about it if I were you,' she said, taking a step away. 'You don't want it affecting your performance.'

'I'm scared,' Schneider said in a little-girl voice. 'Doesn't anyone believe me?'

'There's nothing to be scared of.'

'Someone else must have seen her. I'll ask stage management.'

'Do that. I must get to my room.'

Soon, the news of the sighting circulated backstage. Scene-shifters tried peeping through the slots in the curtain. The grey lady was no longer on view. 'She must have gone for her interval drink,' was the quip. The word got through to the Garrick's Head, where Titus O'Driscoll was

255

holding court with a few friends. Titus was never going to treat the theatre ghost lightly.

'This has to be investigated at once. A sighting of the grey lady is an event.' He left his half-finished wine and hurried round to the foyer. The interval was still on and the usual smokers were standing in Saw Close. None looked as if they'd seen a ghost. The royal circle bar was the obvious place to check first and Titus headed there. The talk in the bar was all about the play, not the grey lady. Deeply disappointing to a ghost-hunter. Recalling that earlier sightings had been from the stage itself, Titus hurried to the pass door at the end of the corridor and let himself through to the backstage area.

He had an immediate success. One of the crew who recognised him told him exactly what Schneider claimed to have seen.

'Marvellous,' Titus said. 'This has all the hallmarks of a classic encounter. Where is she now—in her dressing room?'

'Probably on her way back. The second half starts in five.'

'Is she on at the beginning?'

'Quite early in the scene.'

Torn between getting Schneider's account at first hand and trying for a sight of the ghost, he chose the latter, returning through the pass door to the royal circle. The five-minute bell had gone and the audience were coming back to their seats. The house lights were still on. A clear view of the box could be had from here. Disappointing. No grey lady. The box was unlit and to Titus's keen eye had a look of disuse. He asked some people who had just returned if they'd noticed anyone occupying the upper box before the interval. They had not, but then they were foreign tourists and all their attention must have been on the play, trying to follow the dialogue.

He was deeply frustrated by knowing someone had reported a sighting just a short time ago. Perhaps he was fated never to see the grey lady, to be an expert reliant on other people's experiences. He went backstage again, still hopeful of a first-hand account from Schneider.

No question: the place was charged with nervous energy. Preston was on stage ready for the second half and Gisella stood in the wings ready to make her entrance. The deputy stage manager's urgent voice was coming over the tannoy system. 'I'm not raising the curtain without her. We've been through this a dozen times. She has to be out here and ready. Will someone please put a bomb under her?'

'Who does he mean—Schneider?' Titus asked a stagehand.

'Wouldn't you know it? Old bossy-boots. She's not in position and we're running late already.'

'I'll check. Which dressing room is she in?'

'Nine, on the OP side. It's being taken care of.'

'I'll still check. That's where she's got to be.'

He crossed behind the scenery. Out of consideration for her below-average mobility, Schneider had been given a ground-floor dressing room that by rights should have been occupied by a leading actor. The door was open. Two stagehands were trying to coax her back to the stage, but she was in her chair with arms folded showing no intention of budging.

One of them was saying, 'You can't stop the

show. It isn't fair to the rest of the cast.'

Schneider was implacable. 'I won't be treated as a half-wit. I know what I saw. Mr Shearman was downright rude to me. He seems to think I imagined it. Well, if that's what he thinks, he can rot in hell and so can the rest of them.'

'Wouldn't it be better to make your point after the play is over?' the other stagehand said. These two young women were almost certainly drama students getting experience, and they would learn from Schneider's behaviour, but they weren't competent to reverse it.

Titus took over. 'I understand you had a sighting of the lady in grey. I'm Titus O'Driscoll, dramaturge.'

'If you're here to drag me kicking and screaming on to the stage, you'd better think again, because it won't look pretty.'

'Madam, I have no such intention,' Titus said. 'I have the utmost sympathy for you.'

'Bad cop, nice cop, is it?' she said with a glare. 'That won't wash with me.'

'What was her appearance?'

The more vocal of the stagehands said, 'Sir, we don't have time. She's needed for her first entrance.'

'Grey. She was all in grey, with cold, glittering eyes I shall never forget so long as I live,' Schneider said.

Titus asked, 'Was she wearing the costume of a nineteenth-century lady?'

She became more animated. 'Yes! It looked like a cloak, the sort of thing they used to wear over their ball gowns, with a cowl, all grey.'

Titus gasped and his voice faltered in

258

excitement. 'This is truly momentous.' After a moment's thought, he said, 'We need to speak for longer. Why don't you go on stage now and meet me afterwards to talk about this amazing occurrence?'

'I've made my position clear,' Schneider said. 'I've been through a terrifying experience and was given no sympathy whatsoever. Until that horrible little manager man goes on his knees and apologises to me I'm not moving from here.'

'Find Mr Shearman,' Titus said to the stagehands with more drama than anything heard in the play. 'Get him here fast. Tell him he's needed by the dramaturge.'

'There isn't time.'

'Young lady, if you want to stay working in this theatre, do as I say. I don't care if you drag him feet first. Do it!'

Both of them hurried out.

'You're a gentleman,' Schneider told Titus.

The DSM's voice over the tannoy said, 'We'll have to manage without her.'

'Fat chance,' Schneider said with a smirk.

'All she does is step on stage and announce people,' the DSM went on.

Schneider drew in a huge, affronted gasp.

'We'll have to improvise. Isherwood must answer the doorbell himself. Are you okay with that, Preston?'

'The hell he is!' Schneider said, rising from her chair. 'They're going to axe me from the scene. They can't do that.'

'You'll be redundant,' Titus said, sharing her outrage.

'It's underhand. It's blackmail,' Schneider said.

259

'You'd better deal with it fast,' Titus said. 'We can talk about the grey lady later.'

The protest came to an abrupt end. Schneider swept out of the room and beetled towards the wings, elbowing Hedley Shearman aside as he arrived to plead with her, flanked by the stagehands.

'Is she going on?' Shearman asked. The emergency had exacted an extraordinary toll from him. He was sweating and he'd changed physically, drained of colour, jowls quivering, voice thinner, as if he'd seen the ghost himself.

'Under protest,' Titus said. 'I doubt if you've heard the last of it.'

'Whatever you said it appears to have worked.'

'The lady has my sympathy,' Titus said. 'The supernatural is extremely unnerving. I've no doubt in my own mind that the theatre ghost was among us tonight.'

'Auto-suggestion, I expect,' Shearman said.

'Unlikely.'

One of the stagehands said, 'She convinced me she'd seen something.'

'Me, too,' Titus said, 'and I propose to go into the box and check for proof positive: the scent of jasmine.'

'Not now,' Shearman said, close to panic.

'Why not?'

'There's a performance in progress. I won't have the audience distracted. It isn't fair to the performers.'

'All I need is to open the door and sniff.'

'You won't. The box is locked on my instructions. As soon as this daft rumour started I knew some idiot would want to get in there. It isn't

260

going to happen.'

'You can unlock it for me,' Titus said. 'I'm not "some idiot", as you put it. I'm on the staff, and, what is more, on the creative team, not mere management.'

Even in his depleted state, Shearman wouldn't relent. 'For God's sake, I'm not getting into an argument about status.'

'See some sense, then. If I wait for the curtain, the jasmine will have dispersed.'

'There is no ghost and there never has been,' Shearman said, practically stamping his foot. 'It's a myth put about by people who ought to know better. This has been one hell of a night, and my job is to restore sanity to this theatre. I suggest you return to the Garrick's Head, or wherever it is you came from.'

'There's gratitude,' Titus said, knowing he'd lost this skirmish.

*   *   *

The play resumed seven minutes late, barely enough to register with the audience. Schneider may have appeared subdued compared to other performances, but she didn't miss a cue or dry or scramble her lines. Gisella was in fine form as Sally Bowles and this seemed to inspire Preston. The second half sparkled.

From the back of the royal circle, Titus kept a vigil on the box opposite, and was disappointed. The grey lady failed to appear for him.

In the stalls, the casting director from the National Theatre studied Gisella's performance and made a few notes. Francis Melmot loomed in

261

the aisle, studying the casting director.

In the understage area, Kate from wardrobe found Hedley Shearman alone in the company office, hunched over his desk, his hands covering his face. The loudspeaker in the corner of the room was relaying the dialogue from upstairs.

'Someone obviously needs some therapy,' she said, putting an arm around his shoulders and nudging his face with her breast. 'As a matter of fact, I feel the need myself. How would Hedley like to give his Kate another good seeing-to?'

He tensed. 'Leave me alone.'

Stung by the reaction, she snapped back, 'What's your problem? Not in the mood? That's got to be a first.'

'We're in deep shit,' he said.

'Why? What do you mean?'

'There's been another death.'

CHAPTER SIXTEEN

Diamond and Paloma were debating whether to finish a vintage Rioja or have it corked and take it with them. Truth to tell, he wasn't a wine man. He'd started the evening with a beer. The wine was mainly for Paloma and he'd restricted himself to less than a glass, keeping her company. They had eaten well in the Olive Tree at the Queensberry Hotel and his thoughts were turning to a taxi ride to Paloma's big house on Lyncombe Hill and a romantic end to the day. He was trying to persuade her to finish the bottle at home and she was arguing that he hadn't drunk his share.

'I know my limit,' he said. 'You don't want me turning grouchy.'

'Is that what happens?' She was laughing.

'Even more grouchy, then.'

'Funnily enough, I quite enjoy your grouchy moments. You can be amusing and curmudgeonly at the same time.'

'It's a rare talent.'

'So what are you going to do about Flakey White?'

Put on the spot, he said, 'From what the Yard told me, it won't be easy to trace him after more than forty years.'

'But you'll try?'

'I suppose. I can try Hampshire, where he was convicted, and some of the adjacent police forces. Not sure what good it will do. He may have emigrated, or died. He'd be an old man now.'

'You need to know. This can't be shelved. It goes deep. I see it in your eyes each time it's mentioned.'

'I'm on the case.' He released a long breath. 'But it's not an after-dinner topic.'

'If my friend Raelene can be of any help the offer is still open.'

He was about to wriggle out of that one when they were interrupted by an old-fashioned phone bell.

'Sorry,' he said, fishing in his pocket. 'Didn't know I had it with me.'

Paloma watched in amusement, half expecting him to produce a phone set with receiver, cord and stand. In the event, he took out the mobile she herself had given him over a year ago. Some playful member of his team had programmed a

263

ring tone from the nineteen-sixties.

He switched off and raised an apologetic hand to the people at the next table.

'Who was it?' Paloma asked.

'No idea.'

'You can find out.'

'I have better things to do.'

'Like?'

'Like asking for the bill and getting them to call a taxi. Did we settle what to do about your wine?'

'Our wine. All right, let's take it with us. But I think you should check that call.'

He handed the mobile across.

Paloma pressed two keys. 'Bath Central.'

He winced. 'At this hour?'

'Hadn't you better call them back?'

A few minutes later, two taxis left the Olive Tree. One took Paloma home to Lyncombe; the other, Diamond to the Theatre Royal.

*   *   *

Saw Close was crowded when he arrived. The theatre crowd had not been out long and many were waiting for transport. His taxi was hired before he stepped out of it.

This time he didn't pander to his anxieties by using one of the side doors. Taking a grip on his nerves he marched straight into the foyer, braced for the personal challenge of entering the auditorium. But there was no need for heroics. After making himself known, he was directed down some stairs and along the red-carpeted passageway leading to the front stalls and boxes. Through open doors to his right he couldn't avoid

264

glimpsing the stage itself, yet he was relieved to see that the house lights were on, the safety curtain down and the cleaning staff at work along the rows. The access to the boxes was up the curved stairs at the end of the passage. This little theatre was an obstacle course of different levels. Grabbing the rail, he climbed upwards, passing the box on the royal circle level and then higher to where a uniformed female constable guarded the door of the upper box. She recognised him and actually gave a cursory salute.

'No need for that. Who are you?' he asked.

'PC Reed, sir.'

'I expect you have a first name.'

She blinked in surprise. 'It's Dawn.'

'Who's inside, Dawn?'

'DI Halliwell and the manager, Mr Shearman. Oh, also the deceased.'

'Bit of a squeeze, then. Don't let anyone else in.'

He pushed open the door. The single wall light didn't give much illumination. Keith Halliwell was bending over the body of a woman, shining a torch on the face. Shearman was in shadow on the far side.

'Have you checked for a pulse?'

Halliwell looked up. 'Ah, it's you, guv.'

'I wasn't asking about me.'

'She's been confirmed as dead by the paramedics.'

'Any idea who she is?'

Halliwell sidestepped the question. 'Mr Shearman identified her.'

But at this minute Shearman was reluctant to repeat the name. He was looking deathly pale himself. 'It's a nightmare,' he said, 'and just when I

265

thought we were getting over our difficulties.'

Diamond moved in for a closer look. He wasn't often thrown by surprises. This ranked high in the register and he took several seconds to absorb it. He knew the features at once and the torchlight showed the skin damage. The dead woman was Clarion Calhoun.

'For the love of God. She's only just out of hospital.'

'Discharged this morning,' Shearman said.

'What's she doing here?'

'She called Mr Melmot with a special request. She wanted to see the play before it closes, but not from the public seats where people would recognise her. She was brought in through the side door wearing one of those hoodie things and given this box for the evening.'

'Did you know about this?'

Some colour returned to his face. 'I was in on it, yes. Mr Melmot told me.'

'Who else knew?

A shrug. 'Now you're asking. Word gets round, even when you try and do something in secret.'

'Who brought her up here?'

'One of the security people, name of Binns.'

'I've met him. Security so-called.'

'Fair comment. Anyway, I was waiting in here for them. I welcomed her.'

'How was she looking?'

'I couldn't see much. She was holding the scarf across her face, to hide the damage, I suppose. She seemed calm and said she'd be all right. I offered to send up a drink, but she didn't want one. It was obvious she wanted to be left alone, so I didn't linger.' He shook his head. 'What the press will

266

make of all this, I dread to think.'

'Do they know?'

'I haven't told anyone except you, but it's certain to leak out.'

'I can't disagree with that,' Diamond said. 'Look, this is ridiculous, using a hand torch. Why don't we get proper lighting? It's a theatre, for God's sake. They can point a spotlight straight in here.'

'I'll see to it at once,' Shearman said, eager to be out of there.

'Careful. Keep close to the wall.'

The little manager's voice turned even more panicky. 'You don't think this was a crime?'

'We can't see unless you fix the bloody spot.'

Sounding as if he was hyperventilating, Shearman edged around the wall and hurried out.

'Give me that torch,' Diamond said to Halliwell.

No question: this nightmare was true. She was definitely the woman he'd visited at Frenchay Hospital. The scarring was still apparent, even if most of the redness had faded. As to a cause of death, he could see no bleeding at the mouth or nostrils. Although a grey chiffon scarf was around her neck, it wasn't tight and there were no obvious ligature marks. She appeared to have fallen sideways from a chair that was still upright.

Sudden deaths can and do happen to people in the prime of life, but they are rare. This one had to be suspicious, to say the least.

'Has anyone else been by?' he asked Halliwell.

'The two paramedics.'

'When?'

'Before I got here. A pathologist is on his way.'

'Right. And who discovered her?'

267

'The theatre director, I think.'

'Shearman. Did he say what time?'

'I got the impression it was when the show ended. I suppose he came up here with the idea of escorting her to a taxi.'

' "Got the impression"?'

Halliwell looked uncomfortable. 'I haven't asked him yet.'

'Why not?'

'I haven't been here long.'

Diamond bit back the impulse to find fault. 'It's all very odd, Keith. If she was murdered—and we'd better assume she was—it throws new light on the previous incidents.'

'The dresser's fall?'

'And Clarion's scarring. Is someone responsible for all three?'

Halliwell didn't answer. He'd worked with Diamond long enough to know guessing wouldn't do.

As if cued by Diamond's remark about new light, the spot came on, dazzling them, and after their eyes adjusted they found the box deprived of its lush look. Cracks in the paintwork, old stains on the carpet. Even a cobweb on the ceiling was exposed in the glare, and tangled in it was a dead butterfly, a tortoiseshell.

Diamond gave it a glance and passed no comment.

The two detectives learned no more about Clarion's death. There was no obvious injury, no sign of a weapon, not even a glass she'd drunk from. In the powerful light her skin was paper white apart from the scar tissue. There wasn't the facial congestion you expect in a violent death like strangulation.

Halliwell spotted a black leather handbag on the floor below the front of the box. It was zipped. If theft had been the motive and money or cards taken, it was unlikely that the thief would have bothered to refasten the zip.

'Leave it,' Diamond said at once. Proper forensic procedure debarred them from handling anything at this stage. 'We're doing everything by the book, right?'

'Right, guv.'

'She's so famous that every action we take is going to be picked over by the media. And what is more, from now on, anyone backstage from the manager down has the chance of making big money by selling exclusives.'

'Christ, they'll be round here with their mobiles taking pictures.'

Diamond nodded. 'It wouldn't surprise me if the lighting guy has already taken a long shot from somewhere up there.'

'And those paramedics may have spoken to the press. You want to seal the building?'

'That would be a start. This theatre has more entrances than Victoria station. I'm sure PC Reed is a good copper, but we need twenty of her. Yes, get reinforcements. Get our team in, everyone you can raise, and a scene of crime unit. Tell them to bring arc lamps and some kind of screen for the open side.'

'There are curtains.'

He cringed at his own stupidity. Crimson velvet and about ten feet long, they were difficult to miss, but he'd managed it. 'Where would I be without you? Pull them across. And where does this other door lead to?'

He opened it and got his answer: the dress circle.

He pushed open the door to the stairs and told PC Reed she now had two doors to guard, so she'd better come inside the box with the body. 'Does that bother you?'

'No, sir.'

'Good answer. You're the speed writer, I believe.'

She nodded.

'Do you get every word?'

'I try to.'

'And is it understandable to anyone else?'

'If they can read my writing.'

'May I see?

She took her notebook from her tunic pocket and opened it at an example.

'What's this, then?' he asked.

'The interview with Denise Pearsall.'

'On Tuesday morning? You and Sergeant Dawkins?'

'Yes.'

He frowned at the first few letters—*hv w mt b4* – and then smiled. 'Neat. I get it. May I tear these pages out? I'd like to read the rest.'

'Take the notebook, sir.'

'No, you're going to need it. We're expecting the pathologist. If he says anything, be sure to get it down. Over to you, then.'

He and Halliwell stepped through to the dress circle and for no obvious reason he felt less troubled than he'd expected by the sight of the auditorium. He looked across to the far side and spotted a movement in the royal circle, one level down. He shouted through his hands, 'Where are you going, Mr Shearman?'

'Backstage, to see if the actors are all right.'

'Make an announcement over the public address. Nobody leaves the building. Everyone still here is to assemble in the stall seats: actors, crew, cleaners, front-of-house people, the lot.'

'It's getting late.'

'That's an order.'

Halliwell, phone in hand, told him CID and uniform were alerted. More officers were already downstairs and security had been told to seal the building. 'But if she was murdered, whoever did it is most likely out and away.'

'Which is one good reason to find out who's still here,' Diamond said. 'Get them listed when they're all together. They're going to be stroppy. Do your best. I'll speak to them as a group.'

Dr Sealy, the pathologist, arrived, grumbling that he'd been watching an old *Inspector Morse* on television and now he wouldn't find out who did it.

'Give me strength! This is the real bloody thing,' Diamond said.

'Without the culture.'

'Do you want me to hum the *Morse* music?'

'Frankly, old boy, if you sang the whole of *Die Meistersinger*, it wouldn't make a blind bit of difference.' Sealy lightened up at the sight of PC Reed, still on duty. 'But here's a Rhine maiden sent to help me into my zip-suit.'

'She won't be doing that,' Diamond said. 'She's working for me.'

'Getting into one of these isn't simple, you know.'

'Tough.'

271

Dawn Reed remained impassive while Sealy struggled into the white suit.

Over the public address, Shearman made his announcement telling everyone where to assemble. There was a definite tremor in the voice.

The crime scene people arrived soon after and set up their lighting. Downstairs, more uniformed police reported for duty. Halliwell went off to supervise them.

From the dress circle, Diamond watched the actors and backstage staff respond to the summons and take seats in the stalls. A hierarchy was observed without any supervision from the police: actors in the front row, stage management behind them, the crew next, then the front-of-house team and finally the cleaners. Among the actors, Diamond spotted Gisella, Preston Barnes and the woman playing Fräulein Schneider. Kate from wardrobe was in the third row. A late arrival from backstage was Titus O'Driscoll and he was uncertain where to position himself until Shearman offered him a second-row seat. There must have been forty to fifty people there already.

Binns, the stand-in doorkeeper, was one of the last to arrive, reluctantly having been replaced by a policeman.

Still upstairs, Diamond opened the door of the box and asked Sealy if he'd found anything of interest.

'Run away and play, will you? I've hardly started.'

Impatient investigating officers don't cut much ice with pathologists. Diamond exchanged a long-suffering look with PC Dawn Reed. 'Tell me when he comes out.' He took the stairs down to the ground floor and was pleased to find most of his CID team already there: Ingeborg was helping Halliwell list the names of all present. Leaman and young Paul Gilbert were in the aisle and the man he thought of as the square peg, Fred Dawkins, was in conversation with one of his recent colleagues in uniform.

Diamond asked Shearman if anyone was missing.

'I think not,' the manager said. 'There's a spare programme here. If you go through the names you'll find all the cast and crew are accounted for. How long will this take?'

This was brushed aside. 'So where's the big man?'

'Who do you mean?'

'Melmot.'

'Francis? He's not in the play.'

'I'm not asking who's in it. Was he in the theatre tonight?'

Shearman pressed a hand to his mouth as if the thought had just dawned. 'He was, yes, doing the hospitality bit with our special guests. It was Francis who told me Clarion wanted to come. We decided between us that a seat in the box was the best way to keep her hidden.'

'But has anyone seen him since the play ended?'

Nobody spoke.

Then Gisella said, 'Did I hear right? Clarion was here?'

Titus O'Driscoll, seated next to Shearman, gave a gasp. 'I knew it, we've been duped.'

Diamond glared. 'What do you mean?'

'The sighting.'

'You're not making sense.'

273

'There was a sighting of the theatre ghost this evening, the same grey lady you and I discussed the other day. A manifestation would be a sensational event by any stretch of the imagination. That's why I'm here. A reliable witness saw her in the Arnold Haskell box, the one with the drawn curtains.'

All the conversations around them had stopped.

'This evening?' Diamond said.

'During the play. She was all in grey. Where's Fräulein Schneider?'

'Here,' a voice answered from the front row. The big woman turned a stricken look on Titus.

'Don't be nervous,' he urged her. 'Tell them what you saw.'

'They won't believe me.'

'Out with it, ma'am,' Diamond said.

Her words soared melodramatically. 'She was here tonight, I swear, staring at me from the upper box where she is known to materialise.'

'Dressed in grey?'

'Totally. In a hooded gown of exactly the sort a lady of fashion wore to the theatre two hundred years ago. Most of her face was veiled in some shroud-like material.'

'She's round the twist,' a voice from the back said.

'You see?' she appealed, hands outspread.

'What time was this?' Diamond asked.

'I don't know. I was on the stage in performance. Before the interval.'

'Was she there after?'

'I can't say. I was too petrified to look.'

'She was not,' Titus said. 'I observed the box for the whole of the second half.'

'Are you doubting me as well?' Fräulein

274

Schneider said in the voice of a martyr.

'Not at all, madam. I hate to say this, but I fear that my friend Mr Diamond can account for what you saw.'

'The dead woman everyone is talking about?'

'Get with it, love,' someone shouted from the third row. By now almost everyone knew why they were there.

Diamond didn't want this potentially vital witness driven into silence or hysteria. 'What you've told us, ma'am, could be important, and I want to hear more from you in a moment.' While he had full attention from everyone he announced what he could about Clarion, stressing that she'd been wearing a grey scarf and dressed in a grey hooded jacket that if seen from the waist up could conceivably have been taken for a cloak.

Fräulein Schneider gave vent to a great theatrical sigh.

Diamond said he expected a number of witnesses had seen Clarion and he would need statements from all of them.

'What the hell was Clarion doing here?' Preston Barnes asked.

He got a dusty answer from Shearman. 'She wanted to see the play. Perfectly understandable considering she was in it until Monday night.'

To avoid this descending into a free-for-all, Diamond said his officers would start taking statements directly.

'Did someone murder her?' Barnes asked.

'It's an unexplained death. We have a duty to investigate.'

'Most of us can't help you at all.'

'We'll be the judges of that. Everyone will be

interviewed.'

'We'll be here all bloody night, then.'

This prompted quite a hubbub of alarm over personal arrangements.

Diamond ignored that and briefed his team. The key points to discover, he told them, were whether anyone had seen or heard anything about Clarion's visit. Those unaware of it would be allowed to leave.

'If one of them killed her, he's not going to put up his hand and tell all,' the hard-headed John Leaman said.

'I'm not expecting a confession tonight,' Diamond said. 'We're collecting facts.' He named his interviewers and sent them to various parts of the auditorium. He was left with one lost sheep, Fred Dawkins.

'Am I not to be trusted, guv?'

'Far from it, Fred. Have you heard of Wyatt Earp?'

He frowned. 'The sheriff?'

'I think you'll find he was a marshal, and so are you, for one night only. Marshal this lot in an orderly way, keep them sweet and send them one by one to whoever is ready to see them. Can you handle that?'

'Only if I get a badge and a gun.'

The man had a glimmer of humour. Given time, he might fit in.

A massive gap in the sequence of events needed clarifying. Diamond took Shearman on one side. 'You've got some explaining to do. You told me you went to the box at the end of the play and found the body.'

The manager had turned pale. 'That is correct

and I called 999 and got the ambulance here.'

'I'm more interested in what you didn't tell me. At which point of the evening did you know she was dead?'

His mouth moved without any words being spoken.

'You heard what O'Driscoll said. No one was visible in the box during the second half. She was already dead, wasn't she?'

Still he didn't answer.

'There she was, your VIP guest. It would be extraordinary if you didn't look in during the interval to see if she was comfortable. The truth,' Diamond said.

Shearman sighed and finally found some words. 'Unless you've been in my position you couldn't possibly understand the pressure I was under. I had a theatre full of people, a performance in progress. To interrupt it would have created mayhem.'

'You haven't answered my question. When did you find out? In the interval?'

'Shortly before the second half started. I knew she'd prefer to remain hidden, so I took her a glass of champagne. I tapped on the door and looked inside and had the shock of my life.'

'Think hard before you answer this. Are you certain she was dead?'

'Definitely. I spoke her name several times, and felt for a pulse. Absolutely nothing. I was petrified. The four-minute bell had gone for the second half to begin again.'

'So you let it run. The show must go on. That's the mantra, isn't it? You had a dead woman lying in the box—'

277

'No one could see her. She'd fallen on the floor. It looked like an empty box to anyone who didn't know.'

'How long is the second half?'

'About an hour and a quarter.'

Diamond was appalled. 'You left her lying dead for all that time and did nothing?'

'What could I do? Empty the theatre? I couldn't get her out without disturbing the audience. I was in a terrible dilemma. I'm responsible for all those people. She wasn't visible to anyone, as Titus told you.'

'You could have got her down the back stairs.'

'Not without being noticed. You heard what Titus said. He was watching the box and no doubt others would have seen us moving her.'

'When this leaks out, as it's bound to, the press are going to hang you out to dry.'

'I had to reach a decision. It seemed the best thing to do. It was all down to me. Francis wasn't about.'

'He'd already left, had he?'

'I've no idea, but he wasn't taking much interest in Clarion at that stage.'

'Did you tell anyone? Kate, the wardrobe mistress?'

'I kept it to myself, I swear. And as soon as the show was over I dialled 999.'

'If Clarion was murdered—and it's quite possible she was—we'll need to know where everyone was during the interval.'

'I can tell you what I was doing for most of it. I was trying to speak sense into Schneider.'

'Schneider?'

'It's the part she plays. Everyone calls her that.

She was ranting on hysterically about the grey lady and not being able to continue. I told her flatly she was a professional actor with a duty to the rest of the cast. She'd obviously noticed Clarion in the box before the interval, but I couldn't tell her who it was.'

'Why not?'

'She's a blabbermouth. She wouldn't keep it to herself. Clarion wanted privacy.'

'Wasn't she visible from the audience?'

'She was sitting well back. Only someone on stage would catch a glimpse.'

'Any one of the actors could have spotted her, then?'

'They may have seen a figure there. Hard to recognise who it was.'

It was clear to Diamond that anyone in the cast or crew might have learned that Clarion had been in the theatre. Melmot and Shearman knew for certain, and so did the security man, Binns. For a would-be murderer, the opportunity had been there: Clarion alone in the box during the twenty-minute interval.

He'd heard as much as he wanted from Shearman. Binns was next up, all silver buttons and defiant, staring eyes, expecting an attack on his professional competence.

'How did you learn about Clarion's secret visit?' Diamond asked.

'Mr Melmot.'

'How exactly—a note, a phone call?'

'Personally. He came to the stage door and told me himself.'

'This was hot news.'

Binns shrugged in contempt at the obvious.

'Tell anyone else, did you?'

He didn't like that. 'What do you take me for? It's more than my job is worth to go blurting it out.'

'So what happened?'

'I carried out his instructions to the letter. Waited out front for her to come in her black limo. Escorted her round to the side door and up the back stairs to the top box. Mr Melmot was already up there and greeted her and my job was done.'

'She arrived by limo, you said?'

'Chauffeur-driven Mercedes, like I was told to look out for.'

'Was anything said when she first got out?'

'Not by her. She had a scarf across her face like one of them Arab women and the hood of her jacket was over her head. I told her to come with me and she did.'

'Did she appear nervous?'

'How would I know when all I could see was her eyes?'

'You're in the security business. You can tell a lot from a person's behaviour, or you ought to.'

'She was in control of herself, if that's what you're asking.'

'Was it busy outside the theatre?'

'It was past the time when they're hanging about outside. The show was almost starting. No one took any notice of her.'

'Was anyone lurking around the stairs to the box?'

'No.'

'After taking her upstairs, where did you go?'

'Back down and round to the stage door. I was there for the rest of the evening.'

Just a functionary. That was his defence,

anyway. If anyone had a case to answer, it wasn't Charlie Binns.

Diamond kept an open mind.

If Binns and Shearman could be believed, the people 'in' on the secret visit amounted only to three. But at the interval Fräulein Schneider was mouthing off to Gisella and Preston and everyone who happened to be in the wings that she'd seen the grey lady in the upper box. Anyone who guessed the truth or simply went to investigate could have attacked Clarion. Her death had taken place in that twenty-minute slot.

Was it murder?

He returned upstairs, fixed on dragging some definite information out of Dr Sealy. The stairs didn't do anything to lower his blood pressure.

'What killed her, then?' he said when he'd got his breath back.

Sealy was still crouched over the body. 'I told you—' he barely managed to say before Diamond cut him off.

'You told me nothing. You've been studying the body for—what?—forty minutes and given me no help at all. I've got all of fifty people down there wanting to get off home. I can't hold them indefinitely.'

'Your call, old boy, not mine,' Sealy said without looking away from the body.

'Is there anything I should be told?'

'About her death? Nothing I can tell you.'

'Are you saying it was natural?'

'No.'

'Unnatural?'

'I reserve judgement. I'll do the PM tomorrow. Do you want to be there?' He knew what to do

281

with a knife, how to twist as well as dissect.

'Not even a suspicion?'

'I'm a scientist, my dear fellow. Suspicion is speculative and I don't have any truck with it.'

'Put it this way, then. Is it possible she was killed and no mark was left?'

'Entirely possible, but don't ask me to list the possible causes or we'll be here all night.' He stood up. 'It gets to your knees, all this stooping. Pity she didn't die sitting up in the chair.'

'Just for your comfort?'

'Well, if she had, she'd have been visible to the audience and I imagine someone would have spotted something was wrong.'

'I don't know. People fall asleep watching dull plays.'

The first glimmer of concern crossed Sealy's features. 'Is it dull? I was given tickets for Saturday.'

'I haven't seen it. Look, if you're not going to tell me anything, I might as well be off.'

'There's something I can tell you,' Sealy said.

'About the cause of death?'

'No. About the victim. Take a look at her arms.' He crouched again and rolled back one of the sleeves of the grey jacket as far as the elbow.

Diamond leaned over his shoulder for a better look. There were scars on the inner side of the forearm. 'She was a druggie?'

'No. These old injuries are not the same as you get from shooting up. She's cut her wrists more than once. Clarion Calhoun was a self-harmer.'

CHAPTER SEVENTEEN

An event as sensational as the sudden death of a major pop star becomes international news in a short time. Well before midnight on Thursday the police switchboard was jammed with media enquiries. Diamond issued a statement confirming that a woman had been found dead in a box at the Theatre Royal and that a post-mortem would be conducted next morning and a press conference would follow.

Early Friday he phoned Ingeborg at home and confided what the press didn't yet know.

He heard her intake of breath.

The shock was still with him too, and gave more bite to his words than he intended. 'When I asked you to bone up on Clarion's life you didn't tell me anything about self-inflicted injuries.'

The criticism hurt. 'Be fair, guv. Don't you think if I'd found even a hint of anything like that, I'd have told you right away?'

As so often, his plain speaking had caused more offence than he intended. 'I'm saying this has come out of the blue, that's all.'

'If you remember, I was looking at websites and fanzines. This isn't the kind of stuff a pop star wants to be known for.'

He backed off a little. 'You'd think the tabloids would have been on to this.'

From Ingeborg's tone, she appreciated the shift of focus. 'She must have kept it well hidden. Thinking about it, all the pictures I've ever seen show her with her arms covered up.'

283

'Well, you can't hide much when you're on the dissecting table. Sealy says he can use ultra-violet light to enhance old scars and give us an idea how long she was doing this.'

'Can we be certain they were self-inflicted?'

'They're classic signs, he says.'

Ingeborg moved on quickly to the key question. 'Are you thinking she may have damaged her own face with the caustic soda?' She paused, shocked by her own statement. 'It changes everything.'

He'd debated this with himself for much of the night. What if no crime had been committed at all and the whole of CID was flat out on a barren investigation? 'Let's find out if Sealy is right. That agent you and I met at the hospital—the dragon. What's her name?'

'Tilda Box.'

'Yes. She must know what her client got up to. Where is she based? London, I suppose.'

'We have her mobile number.'

'You'll get more out of her if you meet.'

'We need someone to identify the body.'

'Neat.' Not for the first time, he valued Ingeborg's quick brain. 'What time is it? Wake her up and tell her we want her here before they start the PM.'

'Now?'

'Call me back as soon as you've fixed it. I'm at home.' He put down the phone.

Raffles was pressing against his leg, reminding him of a duty that couldn't be ducked. There was barely time to open a pouch of tuna before the phone rang.

'She's catching an early train,' Ingeborg told him. 'I'm meeting her at the station and driving her

284

to the mortuary.'

'She'd heard, of course?'

'Oh yes. She's been up some time answering the phone.'

'You can you handle this, can't you, Inge?'

'Getting her to open up? No problem, guv.'

'She's a hard nut.'

'Brittle. I watched you deal with her.'

This sounded like a compliment, but it wasn't. Cracking a difficult witness was a skill Ingeborg had learned in her days as a journalist. There were times when Diamond suspected she could crack him, too. Right now he wanted her opinion on the excesses of her age group. 'You hear quite a lot about self-inflicted injuries among young women. Why do they do it?'

'Guys do it as well.'

He smiled to himself. 'Point taken.'

'It's often a teenage thing,' she said, and then conceded a little. 'I don't know what the stats say, but you could be right that females are in the majority here. As to why, you'd better ask a shrink.'

Perish the thought. 'I was hoping to get an opinion out of you.'

She took a moment to think. 'It's often triggered by stress. Situations they can't cope with. I did see a theory that they're suffering such pain from within that they take to cutting themselves to transfer the pain to the outside.'

'There's something wrong with the logic there.'

'I don't think so. The cutting brings temporary relief.'

'By pain from within, you mean anxieties?'

'Out of all proportion. You know how tough it

can be when you're growing up.'

'Clarion was no teenager.'

'Right, but what kind of adolescence did she have? She was thrown into the world of pop from an early age. Her growing up must have been distorted.'

'Arrested development?'

'If you want to put a label on it. She would have been okay while things were going well but as she sank in the charts she would have been deeply troubled. Her great days as a singer were over. We don't know when she started cutting herself. It may have been when she was younger, but all the recent disappointment must have been hell to endure.'

'Are you saying she was immature?'

A sigh came down the phone. 'Emotionally, maybe. Unable to cope. She had the acting as a back-up, but everyone says she was rubbish in rehearsals. First-night nerves plus the knowledge that she couldn't hack it as an actor must have really got to her.'

'Damaging her own face would be a step on from cutting her arms,' Diamond said.

'I know, but self-harmers use anything that comes to hand, a hot iron sometimes, a lighter, boiling water, acid.'

His flesh prickled.

She went on, 'And she had the extra incentive that scarring her face would save her from being savaged by the critics and all the bad publicity, which she must have been dreading.'

'I thought self-harming was done in secret and covered up.'

'She did cover it up by blaming the theatre.'

'But the pain was very public.'

'No one knew it was her own doing. She would have secretly brushed caustic soda on her face just before going on, so the cause of it wasn't obvious. She had the credit of making an entrance and the agony that followed actually saved her from having to remain on stage.'

'This is getting too deep for me. We didn't find any trace of the stuff in her dressing room.'

'She would have flushed it away, wouldn't she?'

'You really believe this, Inge, don't you?'

'It makes sense to me, guv.'

'Why did she threaten to sue? Wouldn't a self-harmer stay silent?'

'To make her story stand up. She wasn't going to admit that the scarring was self-inflicted or she'd have been crucified by the press. So she had to point the finger at someone else. She waited a few days and then let it be known she was withdrawing the action, but without saying why.'

He was being persuaded, and now he added his own twist. 'I wonder if she ever did instruct her lawyers. That's something else you should ask the agent.'

'Do we agree that the threat to sue was all a bluff?'

'Could well have been, if this theory is correct. Her stay in hospital may have given her pause for thought. The doctors who treated her at Frenchay would have seen the state of her arms and worked out that she had a history of this.'

'Wouldn't they have informed us?'

'Patient confidentiality.'

'I'm all for that,'

'So am I, until it gets in the way of a police enquiry.' He drummed his fingers on the edge of the worktop. 'And so we come to the even bigger question: does self-harming lead to suicide?'

'You mean did she kill herself?' The question hung unanswered for a long interval before Ingeborg said, 'I don't think it follows. Most of them are content to damage their bodies without wanting to destroy them.'

'It's not a slippery slope, then?'

'You'd have to ask an expert, but I don't believe it's inevitable or even likely.'

He'd done enough theorising. 'We have no clue as to what caused her death last night.'

'But we should find out from the post-mortem. Will Keith be sitting in?'

'He's got lucky again, yes. But of course we'll have the usual wait for test results.'

'Is poison a possibility?' Ingeborg said, her voice rising in anticipation.

'She wasn't shot, stabbed or strangled. There were no obvious injury marks, apart from those we've talked about.'

'So it is.'

'The trouble is we won't know if she took poison herself or was given it.'

'Was there an empty cup or glass in the box?'

'I didn't see one.'

'Most poisons are slow-acting, aren't they? I don't think I'm with you on this.'

He let it pass. In fact he hadn't declared for poisoning or any other form of death. He'd simply complained about waiting for results. But he wanted Ingeborg on side. 'Hope it didn't ruin your evening, turning out last night.'

'It wasn't a problem. I was ironing.'

'Ironing?'

288

'And listening to the radio.'

A domestic scene he hadn't remotely imagined. He'd pictured her clubbing at Moles. It seemed even the funky Ingeborg wasn't whooping it up every night of the week.

*   *   *

It was still early. After shaving, he got on the phone again and put in several calls to police authorities in the home counties. He'd given a promise to Paloma that he would follow up on that call he'd made to the Yard seeking information on Flakey White. She was right. For peace of mind, the damage of long ago had to be repaired if at all possible. Everyone he phoned said they would 'look into it'. He suspected that their priority was at a lower level than his.

*   *   *

His first move of the day wasn't to the theatre or Manvers Street nick, but south, into Somerset, with Paul Gilbert as back-up and chauffeur. An early call on Francis Melmot was essential.

The sun came out and Melmot Hall appeared dramatically out of an early morning mist, much of the west wing still obscured. A little over a week ago, Clarion had been driven here to be the guest of her unlikely fan and his sharp-as-nails mother. What had the pop star expected of her stay in a stately home, and what had she experienced? She hadn't remained here long.

'Do you like lemon drizzle cake?' Diamond asked young Gilbert as they approached the pedimented entrance.

'I don't even know what it is, guv.'

'You've led a sheltered life. You could find out today. They're famous for it here.'

Their knock was answered after a long delay by Melmot himself, wearing an ancient brown dressing gown over bare legs and with flecks of shaving foam around his nose and ears. 'Do you know what time this is?'

'Time for some questions about last night,' Diamond said. 'You know what happened in the theatre?'

'Of course. I was there.'

'Not when I needed to question you. May we come in?'

Melmot held on to the large oak door. 'Can't you come back later?'

'That's something you don't say to the police, Mr Melmot.'

'If you must, then. I wasn't expecting visitors.'

'You coped with hundreds the other day.'

'Only in the grounds. That's different.'

When they entered, it was apparent what the problem was. The grounds had been trimmed, clipped and weeded for the open day. The interior of the house, a spacious entrance hall with a curved, cantilevered staircase, was like a tip, cluttered with bulging carrier bags, piles of books and junk mail, all covered in dust.

'As you see, I don't employ staff in the house,' Melmot said, opening a door. 'You'd better come in here.'

They entered a large, high-ceilinged room almost empty of furniture and with patches on the wallpaper showing where pictures had hung.

'Find yourselves a pew.'

The only possibilities were dining chairs heaped with cardboard boxes containing crockery.

'These things are waiting for a valuation,' Melmot said.

'Selling up?' Diamond asked, gesturing to DC Gilbert to clear some space for them all. The prospect of coffee and lemon drizzle cake had all but vanished.

'Not the house. Just some of the contents. You wouldn't believe the upkeep of a place this size. It's death by a thousand cuts. Most of my ancestors' portraits have gone, including, I may say, two Knellers and a Gainsborough. Each time I sell something I have to justify it to my mother, who thinks I'm a wastrel. By the way, she won't interrupt us if you're brief. She remains in her room until eleven. After that, she'll be on the warpath.'

'Let's go for it, then. I was told you were phoned some time yesterday by Clarion wanting to see the evening performance.'

'That's correct.'

'You knew already that she'd dropped the lawsuit. You heard from her lawyers, you told me.'

Melmot nodded, wary of what he might be asked.

'So you were well disposed to the lady?'

'We've been over this before. I told you I was a fan.'

'But your admiration must have been tested by the lawsuit hanging over you.'

'A temporary difficulty. Others took it more seriously than I.'

'Denise, for one.'

'That's a matter of conjecture, isn't it?'

'Not since we found the suicide note.' Diamond watched the reaction before adding, 'Didn't you hear?'

Melmot blinked several times and turned a shade more pink. Plainly, the Theatre Royal's bush telegraph had malfunctioned. But then Diamond remembered that the discovery had been known only to Ingeborg, Fred Dawkins and himself. If three members of CID can't keep quiet, who can?

No point now in keeping back the news.

'How desperately sad,' Melmot said after he'd been told, but it was lip service. Anyone could tell he wasn't either desperate or sad.

'Yes, if Clarion had withdrawn her threat earlier, Denise might not have taken the action she did.' Diamond gave a shrug that would not have disgraced a Frenchman. 'But then a lot of unpleasantness would never happen if we had the gift of hindsight. Getting back to Clarion, can you recall her exact words when she phoned you yesterday?'

'That's asking too much.'

'Near enough to exact, then.'

'I'll try. She had my mobile number from a couple of weeks ago when I made arrangements for her to stay here. She phoned me about three in the afternoon. I was surprised and rather relieved to hear her voice.'

'But you already knew she wasn't going to sue.'

'Yes, but not from Clarion herself. There was no hint of reproach. She used my first name and asked if I'd heard she was out of hospital. She said she was staying at the Cedar of Lebanon in Bristol and was wondering if there was some way she could get to see the play she'd had so much to do with. I took it as an olive branch.'

'Was anything said about the lawsuit?'

'No, we avoided that. I said we'd be delighted to welcome her and she said immediately that she didn't want to make an occasion of it. She wanted to come unannounced and in secret. She wasn't ready yet to meet the cast or any of her fans.'

'Because of the scarring?'

'I suppose. We didn't go into that. I had what I thought was the rather good idea of letting her see the show from a private box. It's not the best sight-line in the house, but it has the great advantage of being discreet. If you sit well back you're invisible to the audience.'

'You suggested this over the phone?'

'Yes, and she liked it immediately.'

'So you made plans?'

'Certainly. I didn't order her car, but she told me to look out for a black Mercedes limo. I laid on everything at my end of things, getting Binns, the security man, to meet her and escort her upstairs.'

'Did you tell anyone else?'

'Only Hedley Shearman. He had to know, as theatre manager. I asked him to look in at the interval and make sure she was comfortable.'

'Didn't you see her yourself?'

'Only when she arrived. She was a little late, just before curtain up, and it was the briefest of conversations. I had other duties in the interval, so I had to rely on Hedley to take care of her.' He rolled his eyes. *Take care of her.* God only knows what happened. It now appears she died during the interval.'

'Where were you?'

'In the interval? In the 1805 Rooms, pressing the flesh.'

'The 1805 Rooms?'

'It's our VIP suite. Named after the year the theatre was built. We had a casting director from the National and several of our sponsors.'

'You were there for the whole twenty minutes?'

'It went on for longer, in fact. Some minor alarm backstage.'

'This would have been Fräulein Schneider reacting to the grey lady—as she supposed at the time.'

'Actors.' He clicked his tongue in disapproval as if speaking of prodigal sons.

'You haven't answered my question: were you in the 1805 Rooms for the whole of the interval? I can easily check, but it would be simpler hearing it from you.'

'The bulk of the time. I slipped out towards the end to find out what the delay was about and while I was making my way backstage the second half started.'

'So there was a period of time when you were between the 1805 Rooms and backstage?'

'A very short period. Is that significant?' He managed a look of innocence that faded when Diamond declined to answer.

'And at what point did you learn that Clarion was dead?'

'After the final curtain as I was leaving the theatre. One of the front-of-house staff told me an ambulance had been called to someone who had apparently collapsed and died in the Arnold Haskell box. Dreadful. I knew who it was, of course. The whole world fell in on me. Couldn't

294

think how it had happened. They told me Hedley was dealing with it. In my state of alarm I couldn't face anyone and I knew there was sure to be an explosion of media interest. Let's admit it: I panicked.'

'You left the theatre?'

'Returned here in turmoil and spent a sleepless night trying to work out what to tell people.'

'People like us?'

'Not you. I've told you the honest truth. It's all those reporters I dread. They'll twist it into a filthy scandal. They always do.'

Diamond was tempted to say not much twisting would be needed and see what reaction that would get, but the last brief comment interested him. 'Why, have you been on the receiving end before?'

'Not in a serious way. This is something else.'

'Yes, it's huge,' Diamond said. 'I'm holding a press conference this afternoon.'

On the drive back to Bath, he asked Gilbert what he'd made of Melmot.

'Didn't like him, guv. He's all front. Chairman of the board and all that.'

'True.'

'There wasn't much real sympathy for either of the women who died in his theatre. All he thinks about is what the press will make of it. He said he was a Clarion fan, but he isn't grieving for her.'

'She let him down,' Diamond said. 'He had great hopes. He saw an opportunity and brought her to the theatre to be in this play, offered to let her stay with him.'

'Hoping to get inside her knickers?'

'I wouldn't express it in those terms. He claims not. He said she stayed in a different wing of the

295

house.'

'He'd say that, wouldn't he?'

'I'm inclined to believe him. He's a mummy's boy, and you'd understand why if you met his mother. Aside from all that he was getting credit from the theatre people for finding a star performer and she was supposed to be grateful for getting the part. But it all turned sour. She didn't stay long in the house.'

'I'm not surprised, seeing the state of it.'

'And she was going to be a flop in the play.'

'His reputation was under threat.'

'You've got it. People of his sort, heirs to a big estate, are often prone to insecurity. They don't like to be thought of as living off their capital and nothing else, so they get involved in business or the arts at boardroom level. The theatre is a perfect vehicle for someone like him to earn extra status.'

'Buffing up the image.'

'And it was in serious danger of collapse. I've been asking myself if that could be a motive for murder. But he let slip another intriguing remark.'

'About being treated unfairly by the press?'

'Yes, there's some skeleton in Melmot's cupboard that we ought to know about. When we get back to Bath, do some digging. See if he's on file.'

*   *   *

Tilda Box had found time to dress in purple and black, an outfit straight out of *Vogue*, but appropriate for the occasion. She spotted Ingeborg in the station forecourt and came over, confident, smiling, swinging her handbag and smelling

296

expensive. She'd obviously refreshed her make-up just prior to arrival at Bath Spa station. She was carrying several celebrity magazines.

'I hope you weren't trying to phone me on the train. I had to switch off. It's been non-stop.'

'It's like that at the nick,' Ingeborg said. 'My boss is giving a press conference some time soon.'

'Really? What will he say?' She was eager for information.

'Not a lot. He'll want to confirm her identity if possible. That's up to you, of course.'

She frowned. 'There's no question that it's her?'

'Not so far as I know.' Ingeborg started the car and headed out into Dorchester Street and west towards the hospital. She had a miniature tape-recorder running under the armrest between them.

Tilda was more uneasy than she'd first appeared. Nobody enjoys the duty of identifying a body, and most find it daunting, if not scary. 'There's no damage to her face, is there? Extra damage, I mean. I should be able to recognise her? I thought this was just a formality.'

'Absolutely,' Ingeborg said, noting how panicky her passenger was starting to sound. This would be as good a time as any to pounce. 'How long has she been cutting herself?'

'Cutting herself?' Tilda made a show of sounding baffled without remotely convincing Ingeborg she was sincere.

'You must have seen the state of her arms,' Ingeborg said as if she had checked the corpse herself. 'You of all people will know about the self-inflicted injuries—as her professional adviser.'

Briefly, there seemed to be a real danger of Tilda opening the passenger door and leaping out.

Then she seemed to think better of the escape option and gave up any pretence of not knowing. 'For some years, in fact. Top performers like Clarion are under enormous pressure that the rest of us will never experience. Have you seen the body, then?'

'My guv'nor has.'

'Oh. Did he say anything else?'

'Anything else?

'About her appearance. I've no idea what to expect when we get there.'

'As you said yourself, it's just a formality,' Ingeborg said. 'Did she talk openly about the self-harming?'

'I wouldn't say openly. To me in confidence, yes.'

'It must have been a huge worry for you, personally and professionally.'

'That goes without saying.'

'But she told you everything. A sympathetic ear.' A touch of flattery from Ingeborg, opening the way for the key question. 'We could see you were very close when we met at the hospital after her face was damaged. Did she tell you she did that to herself?'

Tilda hesitated, as if sensing she'd been forced into a corner, and then the words tumbled out. 'Yes, it was so sad, really. She told me in the hospital. The rehearsals hadn't gone well and she was worried sick about the first night. She needed a get-out but at the same time she was deeply ashamed of herself. She'd used corrosives on her skin before, all part of the self-harming. There was caustic soda under the sink in one of the dressing rooms. I think they used it to clear the drains. She

298

collected some in a tissue and dabbed it on her face before she went on, punishing herself as well as making sure she would have to abandon the performance. I don't think she knew how excruciating it would be. She almost passed out with the pain.'

'And then she blamed the theatre?'

'Poor darling. The doctors told her she was scarred for life. Having to admit to the world that she'd done it to herself was more than she could cope with, so she started this talk of legal action. I don't think she ever intended to see it through, but it relieved the pressure. She even convinced me— and I know her history. That morning when you came to the hospital I was sure she had strong grounds for damages. I called her lawyers and told them what to expect and they promised to see her as soon as she was out of hospital. The meeting never took place, of course.'

'When did she tell you the truth?'

'Later, over the phone. It was preying on her mind. I phoned the lawyers and they advised the theatre she'd decided not to sue. Without disclosing the reason, of course.'

Ingeborg breathed a quiet sigh of relief. One part, at least, of the mystery that had engulfed CID all week was solved.

'Did you see her after she came out of hospital?'

'No, I'd already returned to London. We spoke on the phone and she told me of her plan to see the play. I would have advised against it, but she sounded so depressed that I thought it would provide some distraction, if nothing else. I couldn't see any harm in it, so I didn't try to dissuade her.'

She reached in her bag for a tissue and sniffed into

it. 'If only I had.'

'Would you say she sounded suicidal?'

'Why?' Tilda was all attention again, and her voice piped in horror. 'Oh my God—did she? Do you know something? They haven't already done the post-mortem?'

'No, they won't have started yet. I'm just asking.'

'Oh.' Deflated, she said, 'No, the thought hadn't crossed my mind.'

*   *   *

Outside Bath Central police station, the pressmen, impatient to go in, were taking pictures of everyone who entered, regardless of who they were. 'Can't you let them in?' Georgina, the ACC, said, not pleased at being called love and asked if she was Clarion's mother, in spite of being in uniform.

'I know what they're like, ma'am,' Diamond said. 'Stuck in the conference room they'll get even more bolshy.'

'You'd better think of something. They'll be smashing windows soon.'

It was eleven thirty. The post-mortem should have started at ten. He phoned the mortuary and asked for Halliwell. They said he was still observing.

'Don't they ever take a break?'

'They took one less than twenty minutes ago,' the mortuary keeper said.

'And what were they saying when they came out?'

'That it could take another hour or more.'

'For crying out loud. You'd think it was brain

300

surgery.'

'Well, it is.'

He was forced to admit that this was true.

He left a message for Halliwell to update him at the first opportunity.

At least Ingeborg had delivered. He'd listened to the tape. To have it confirmed by Tilda Box that Clarion had been a long-term self-harmer was a breakthrough. Under all the pressure he hadn't yet worked out the full implications. If Clarion had damaged her own face, why had Denise killed herself and left that suicide note? Get through the press conference, he told himself, and you'll think more clearly.

'Is this a good moment, guv?' Paul Gilbert asked, putting his head around the office door.

'There's no such thing.'

'Sorry.' The head disappeared.

'Come back.'

Even more apprehensive, Gilbert obeyed.

'It had better not be a request for time off.'

'You asked me to check on Francis Melmot.'

'Well? Do we have anything on him?'

'Nothing on record. It never got to court, but there was a complaint of assault that was later withdrawn. It was in connection with his father's death in 1999.'

Diamond gave a nod. 'I know the old man shot himself, supposedly while cleaning his gun.'

'Well, not long after that, a reporter turned up at Melmot Hall and made some remarks Francis didn't appreciate.'

'About the shooting?'

'No, about his father's private life. The old boy was quite a goer. He'd been screwing a barmaid

301

and Mrs Melmot had got to hear of it. The reporter seemed to be suggesting the old lady told her husband to do the decent thing and shoot himself and wanted to see if he could get a quote from Francis. Instead he got his nose broken.'

'He's a big guy to tangle with, is Francis. I suppose the mistress offered her story to the paper.'

'Whatever, it never got into print.'

'This tells us he's capable of violence, but I have some sympathy, especially as it was a poxy pressman. Where did you dig this out?'

'From an old-stager at Frome nick. He remembered taking the statement.'

'Nice work, Paul. Get a note of it on the case file.'

*　　　*　　　*

Around noon, Ingeborg came in. 'Is your phone dead, guv?'

'Could be. I asked the switchboard to give me a break.'

'Keith was trying to reach you from the mortuary.'

He sat forward. 'He was? Is it over?'

'Depends what you mean. You could say it's just beginning. They're saying Clarion was suffocated.'

CHAPTER EIGHTEEN

'Convince me,' Diamond said.

Halliwell gave his humour-the-boss grin. He was

302

back from the mortuary and looking drained, not from attendance at the autopsy, but the prospect of explaining the result to his crotchety superior. 'Dr Sealy wasn't in any doubt.'

'I'm no pathologist,' Diamond said, 'but even I know they turn purple if they suffocate. I saw the body. She was as pale as your shirt. What is more, they get those little blood marks in the eyes and the skin.'

'Petechial haemorrhages,' Halliwell said from his long experience of listening to pathologists.

'Well, there weren't any.'

'He said the so-called classic signs were absent.'

'Great. So how does he know she was suffocated?'

'He found pressure marks at the base of her neck.'

'She was *strangled*? I saw no marks.'

'Will you let me explain, guv? This wasn't a strangling. These marks were here.' He tapped his own shoulders where the collar of his T-shirt met his neck. 'About here, on each side, where the killer pressed into the flesh with thumbs and knuckles. You wouldn't have seen because of that hooded jacket she was wearing. The pressure was through her clothes.'

'To obstruct the arteries?'

Halliwell shook his head. 'You're getting ahead of me again. Dr Sealy said in his opinion she was suffocated with a plastic bag pulled down over her head and held there until she stopped struggling, which happened rapidly.'

There was an interval of silence while the method registered with Diamond. 'An ordinary plastic bag?'

303

'Except most carrier bags have little holes punched into them.'

'Right. This one was airtight?'

'She was already seated,' Halliwell went on, 'so the killer would have entered the box from behind and slipped the bag over her head.'

'Simple as that?'

'Not quite. You and I might think she died from lack of oxygen, but sometimes a neurochemical reaction kicks in and the death is from cardiac arrest. He said in cases like that, the skin turns pale rather than congested and there aren't any of the signs you'd normally expect in asphyxia.'

'As I noted at the scene,' Diamond said with more than a hint of self-congratulation.

'It was a quick death, apparently, and the panic in the victim very likely contributed to the speed of it.'

Diamond exhaled sharply. 'Nasty.'

'And it didn't require much strength.'

'Surely she'd have grabbed at the bag and tried to pull it off.'

'Very likely, but the force downwards is stronger than her trying to get a grip and push it up. By grabbing the bag she was tightening the pressure against her nose and mouth. And she wouldn't have been heard. She was out of sight of the audience, anyway.'

'She may have scratched her attacker.'

'I wouldn't mind betting he—or she—wore gloves.'

Halliwell had sketched the scene vividly enough for Diamond to visualise how the killing may have worked, and it was gruesome in its efficiency. 'And there's no other way to read these marks?'

'He said not. The bruising on the shoulders was definitely man-made, recent and prior to death.'

'We didn't find a bag at the scene.'

'Well, the killer wouldn't have left it there.'

He had to agree. 'You're right, Keith. This wasn't the work of someone careless.'

'Will you tell the press?'

A difficult question. It had crossed Diamond's mind already, without any prompting from Halliwell. The police are trained to be selective with information. Sometimes details known only to the killer are held back for tactical reasons. The news that Clarion Calhoun was dead would get banner headlines. To reveal that she'd been murdered in this manner would put the media machine into overdrive and make his task that much harder to perform. Yet if they weren't told, they'd ferret out the truth in a matter of hours. He could see no advantage in playing the long game. 'I'll lay out all the main facts.'

It was agreed that Halliwell would brief the CID team shortly before Diamond broke the news to the press. 'Tell them to put their private lives on hold. It's overtime for everyone.'

*   *   *

He kept the press conference down to under twenty minutes. His stark opening statement made the strong impact he intended and gave the hacks their juicy quotes. The questions that followed were mostly reactive to the crime rather than targeted to the investigation. He dealt with them in short answers and came out feeling less battered than sometimes.

305

*   *   *

In the CID room he braced himself for a more searching examination. Everyone was there, buoyed up by Halliwell's briefing. Even Georgina had come downstairs to listen.

'It's the most public murder enquiry we've ever had in this city,' Diamond told them. 'We must be razor sharp. Speaking of which, where's John Leaman?'

A hand went up at the back of the room.

'You're in charge of the search of the theatre. The box where she was killed has been gone through by the crime scene people, but the rest of the building hasn't. Comb the place for the murder weapon, the plastic bag. The killer may have dumped it in some bin thinking it wouldn't be noticed. Take as many coppers with you as uniform can spare. If you see anyone acting suspiciously, report it to me. Inge?'

'Guv?'

'Go through all the statements we took in the theatre last night. Look at everyone's movements, especially during the interval. We have three obvious suspects, Shearman, Melmot and Binns. Each of them knew ahead of time that she was coming to the play. See if what they said checks out.'

'Right, guv.'

'Then there's a second tier of suspects, the actors. They had a view of the box.'

'Not a good view,' Leaman said.

'Did I use the word good? They could tell it was occupied if they happened to look and, as I

306

understand it, that box isn't used much.'

'The Schneider woman admitted she saw someone,' Halliwell said.

'A ghost,' Paul Gilbert said.

'Saw something, then. And at the start of the interval she was busy telling everybody about it, enough to alert anyone with half a brain that someone had been sitting there.'

'She told Gisella for sure,' Ingeborg said.

'And Preston Barnes,' Diamond said. 'Find out how they spent the rest of their interval. Did they go to their dressing rooms and stay there? Were they alone?'

'Fräulein Schneider wasn't,' Halliwell said. 'She had people with her trying to calm her down.'

'Which people?'

'Stagehands, she told me.'

'We can't ignore any of the crew,' Ingeborg said. 'They could have heard Fräulein Schneider panicking about the grey lady.'

'The wardrobe woman,' Halliwell said.

'Not to forget the dramaturge,' Fred Dawkins added. 'He was with Schneider towards the end of the interval.'

'Did you take his statement last night?' Leaman asked.

'No. I was Earping.'

'What?'

'Marshalling,' Diamond said, not wanting a bout of wordplay at this stage. 'Fred was making sure everyone got seen. Who was it who took Titus O'Driscoll's statement?'

Halliwell raised his hand. 'He told me the news of the grey lady's appearance reached him in the Garrick's Head and he went backstage for a first-hand account.'

'Do you see what we're up against?' Leaman demanded, his hellfire preacher voice soaring. 'The entire theatre was in on this. Some of the audience always step outside at the interval for a drag on a cigarette, so it was known on the streets as well. Any nutter could have gone up to the box and killed her.'

'Get wise, John,' Ingeborg said. 'They didn't know Clarion was in the building. Only three people knew that.'

'And those three are firmly in the frame,' Diamond said to get on track again. 'We may be close to an arrest. I'm assigning Keith, Inge and Fred to getting the fullest possible profiles of our three main suspects—everything about them, their past, present and, above all, any link, however remote, to Clarion. And you don't have to be too subtle about it. They know they're under scrutiny.'

Fred Dawkins had heard his name and looked as if he'd won the lottery. 'Which one is mine?'

'That's up to Keith.'

'You can take Binns,' Halliwell said at once.

'I shall take him and dismantle him. No portion will go unexamined.'

'Sounds painful.'

'Not for me. I'm a fully fledged member of the team now.'

'I wouldn't say that,' Diamond said. 'Let's see how you cope.'

Then Georgina spoke. 'Please bear in mind, Peter, that Sergeant Dawkins has a rehearsal tonight.'

He jerked back in disbelief. 'Rehearsal? For what?'

'*Sweeney Todd*. We're doing a walk-through of the moves in the rehearsal rooms, the entire cast. As our choreographer, he's indispensable.'

'He's on the strength, ma'am. We're flat out on this murder enquiry.'

'I appreciate that. I'll speak to you presently.'

He felt his blood pressure rocket. He could protest, knowing he had right on his side, but it would get him nowhere. He hadn't asked for Dawkins in the first place. The man was a pain, anyway. Let him do his bloody walk-through— walk through the door and out of CID for good.

With a huge effort, he controlled himself. 'Let's not lose sight of the other unexplained death at the theatre. There's compelling evidence that Denise was not alone in the minutes before she fell to her death from the fly tower. I can't at this moment see a definite link, but two violent deaths in two days make a double murder more likely than not.'

'*Post hoc, ergo propter hoc*,' a voice spoke up. It was Fred Dawkins.

'Did you say something?' Diamond asked, feeling a stronger throb in his veins.

'Merely a warning to the unwary, guv,' Dawkins said. 'It's Latin.'

'What's the use of that? We're English.'

'A rough translation would be: after this, therefore because of this. It articulates the fallacy that because one event follows another, it must be caused by the other. If, for example, a man eats some oysters and then gets indigestion, it may not be the oysters that were responsible. It may have been the rhubarb that he had as the dessert.'

'I don't know what you're on about.'

'Perhaps it wasn't a perfect analogy.'

309

'Better shut up, then.'

'I was trying to inject a note of caution about assuming a link between the deaths of Denise and Clarion.'

'We heard,' Diamond said and went back to addressing the meeting. 'I was starting to say that the investigation into Denise's death won't be pushed into the background just because Clarion was a star performer. It's still high priority. The so-called suicide note has gone for analysis and we should find out if it was genuine. From what we now know about Clarion's self-harming, it appears Denise wasn't responsible for the scarring, so she had no reason to blame herself.'

'A double murder looks likely,' Halliwell said. 'Stuff the Latin.'

'One more thing,' Diamond said. 'With all the media interest, we're all of us liable to be approached by the press, by Clarion's army of fans and every kind of snoop. Keep it buttoned, okay?'

The briefing over, he followed Georgina from the room and tapped her arm. 'About Sergeant Dawkins . . .'

'I hope you're not going to make an issue of this, Peter.'

'Either he's on the squad or he isn't.'

'You're right, of course,' she conceded. 'I spoke out of turn. It's obvious that you're fully stretched. But if you can see your way to releasing him for a couple of hours tonight I'll make it up to you in human resources. We have some bright young bobbies in uniform keen to get CID experience.'

'I'll take Dawn Reed and George Pidgeon,' he said at once.

Georgina looked surprised that he knew any

names outside his own little empire. 'Agreed.' She moved at speed towards the stairs to her eyrie. She hated being outmanoeuvred.

* * *

I Am a Camera was forced to end its run prematurely. The theatre would be dark for the next two nights. Even Hedley Shearman admitted that to have carried on would be insensitive. The actors and crew were asked not to leave Bath, to be available for more questioning if required.

Alone in his office, Diamond studied printouts of the statements made by theatre staff on the morning after Clarion's face was damaged. Thanks to PC Reed's speed writing and Fred Dawkins' faultless typing, they were lucid accounts, but they didn't yield anything new. Both Shearman and Denise had acted responsibly after the incident, losing no time in getting Clarion to hospital. As for their backgrounds, there was nothing on Shearman and not much on Denise. No doubt Fred Dawkins had done most of the talking. All he'd learned from Denise was that she had been with the theatre six years. More information about previous jobs had come later from Kate in wardrobe, a secondary source, not so dependable. A proper check was a high priority, and best left to Halliwell and his team. More would definitely emerge.

In the calm at the eye of the storm, Diamond's thoughts returned to his own early life and what lurked there. He'd heard nothing back from any of the police authorities he'd contacted about Flakey White.

He knew the resources existed online to make

311

an identity check. Still uncomfortable using the computer, he knuckled down and found how to search the death registers for White's unusual set of names. Nothing came of it.

If alive, the man would be in his seventies. Was he known in cyberspace?

When he Googled the full name, it gave several hundred so-called 'hits' that he could tell straight away were nothing to do with Flakey. The entire resources of the internet were no help.

Disappointed, his prejudice against computers justified, he sat back and tried thinking of another way of tracing an ex-teacher with a prison record.

Then he remembered something Mike Glazebrook had said. It had barely sunk in at the time, such had been the shock of hearing about White's court case.

He reached for the phone. Talking to a real person beat staring at a screen.

'Mike? Peter Diamond here.'

'Peter who?'

'Your old schoolmate. The princes in the tower.'

'I'm with you now.'

'When we met and talked about Flakey White, you said something about him surfacing again as a book illustrator.'

There was a pause. 'You don't want to know.'

'Actually, I do.'

'Why? He's a scumbag. Don't have anything to do with him.'

He stretched the truth. 'It's a police enquiry.'

'Is he still at it, then?'

'We don't know until we catch up with him.'

Glazebrook clicked his tongue and gave a snort that could be heard in John O'Groats. 'Couple of

312

years ago I saw something in a magazine in my barber's, a feature about illustrators. There were photos of these guys at work in their studios and one of them was called Mo White. It was definitely Flakey. He was white-haired and wore glasses, but the face hadn't changed much, the beaky nose and the foxy eyes.'

'What was he illustrating?'

'It looked like comics to me.'

'For kids, you mean?'

'Who else reads comics?'

'There are books for adults called graphic novels. They've got popular.'

'Porn, you mean?'

'Not necessarily. I suppose you don't recall where he was working?'

'It didn't say. And there was nothing about his evil past. I bet his employer didn't know.'

'If he was working as an illustrator he must have had a publisher,' Diamond said, thinking aloud. 'They ought to have contact details. They have to pay royalties.'

'Get on the case, then, if you really want to wallow in the mud,' Glazebrook said.

'You said you saw this magazine a couple of years back. Can you recall the title?'

'No chance. And when I say a couple of years I could mean five or six.'

Thanks a bunch, mate, he thought.

'One other thing, Peter.'

'What's that?'

'When you put the boot in, give him one for me.'

Even Diamond was shaken by that. 'He must be seventy-five, at least.'

'So what? He didn't care about the age of the

kids he abused.'

The internet finally came in useful. He found a website devoted to graphic novels and their illustrators. An artist called Mo White was credited with rendering Dickens novels into illustrated books for adults. The latest were *A Tale of Two Cities* and *Bleak House*, both in 2003. The publisher was Stylus of New Oxford Street, London.

The woman at Stylus confirmed that White had produced the two books for them and she believed he'd retired soon after. The 'Mo' stood for his initials: Morgan and some other name beginning with 'O'. She was guarded when Diamond asked for a contact address. It was company policy not to give out personal information.

Silently he cursed the Data Protection Act. 'What a disappointment after all the research I've done,' he said, sounding as if his world had caved in. 'He was my art teacher forty years ago. It's a school reunion. I was so looking forward to seeing the look on his face.'

She melted. White was living in Forest Close, Wilton.

Wilton, near Salisbury. Only about an hour's drive from Bath.

The reunion was a must.

*   *   *

A call came in from an unexpected quarter: Duckett, the crime scene investigator, in a skittish mood. 'How was the fish?'

'What?'

'The last thing you said to me was that you had

314

other fish to fry.'

'Do you want me to laugh?' Diamond said.

'You should be on your knees in gratitude. I have information for you. It's not my full report. You'll get that when I'm ready. But we found something of particular interest in dressing room eleven and I thought I'd pass it on at the first opportunity. You'll recall that we established that two people were in the room, one presumably Denise, and one her possible attacker?'

'Yes.'

'And there were the base marks of a bottle and two wine glasses in the dust?'

One of the many annoying things about forensics experts was that they kept going over the obvious. 'Of course.'

'We analysed the dust nearby and found some particles of a chemical called flunitrazepam.'

'Really?' Another annoying thing was that they talked in a foreign language.

'Better known as the date rape drug, Rohypnol.'

Now Diamond was fully alert. 'Go on.'

'It's a prescription drug ten times more potent than Valium. In its original form it was colourless, odourless and tasteless, but since 1998 the manufacturers have added a blue dye that will appear when it dissolves.'

'That much I know.'

'There are still supplies in circulation of the pure version. This tested neutral, so it must be pre-1998. At least one capsule had obviously been opened to disperse the chemical in the drink. Have you had the blood-test results from the post-mortem on Denise Pearsall?'

'Not yet.'

315

'I would expect them to confirm that she was drugged.'

'For sex?' Diamond said. 'Nothing about recent intercourse was mentioned by the pathologist.'

'No. I wouldn't place too much emphasis on the date rape connection. The purpose would have been to induce passivity. Within ten minutes the subject feels euphoric and relaxed. She would then have allowed herself to be taken across to the gallery from which she fell or was pushed. In other words, Mr Diamond, I have just provided you with potential evidence of malice aforethought.'

'I'm obliged to you.'

'Have you found the glass she drank from?'

'Her killer is too smart to have left it behind,' Diamond said. 'And I don't suppose it's any use trying to trace the source of the drug if it's as old as you say. Who uses this stuff legitimately?'

'People with severe sleep disorders. Personally I prefer Horlicks.'

Shortly after, Diamond stepped into the CID room to tell the team and they seamlessly picked up from where he'd ended the phone conversation with Duckett.

'How do people get hold of this drug?' Paul Gilbert asked.

'It's no big deal,' Halliwell said. 'I expect you can get it on the internet.'

'This was old stock.'

'Plenty of it was changing hands in the nineties and is still in circulation. We've taken it off blokes going into nightclubs. They don't seem to have any problem acquiring it. There are evidence bags downstairs with the stuff.'

'There must have been a lot of it around.'

'How many pharmacies are there in the country? How many doctors over-prescribe?'

'Of more importance to us,' Diamond said, 'who in the Theatre Royal would be likely to have a supply of the stuff?'

Fred Dawkins said, 'The pocket Lothario.'

'Come again.'

'Hedley Shearman. The little man with the large libido.'

'Fred's right,' Halliwell said. 'Shearman is just the kind of shagbag who would use the date rape drug. He has plenty of form as a seducer, as we're finding out. Before coming to Bath, he was front-of-house manager at a theatre in Worthing and got one of the box office ladies pregnant. His second wife divorced him on the strength of it.'

Diamond was less convinced. 'There's no evidence that he or anyone else had sex with Denise.'

'He could have made a play for her some other time,' Halliwell said, clearly liking this scenario. 'Maybe she gave him the brush-off and threatened to report him to the board. He got scared and set this trap for her.'

'Is that enough to justify murder?'

'He's still paying for the divorce. Losing his job would be a disaster. That's the motive and we know the opportunity was there. As manager he could move around backstage without anyone paying attention.'

'But would he risk the theatre closing?'

'It didn't, guv. Everything carried on as usual after Denise's death. He was one of the keenest to let the show go on. He argued with you about the matinee that was cancelled.'

317

'True.'

'He looks the strongest suspect we have,' Paul Gilbert said.

Diamond was reluctant to pin it on Shearman at this point. 'Are you also suggesting he murdered Clarion?'

'He was the man on the spot, wasn't he?' Halliwell said. 'He arranged for her to be seated in the Arnold Haskell box. He could have gone there any time during the play. He was the only one of the theatre staff we know for sure was in there with her. He admits she was dead at the interval and he delayed reporting it until the show was over. If that isn't guilty behaviour, what is?'

'But why? Why murder Clarion?'

Halliwell shrugged. 'He's unstoppable. He fancied his chances with her.'

'Little Hedley Shearman?' Diamond shook his head. 'With an international pop star?'

'You've got to remember how vulnerable Clarion was at that stage. She'd been scarred. She'd come back to the theatre, his territory. He felt he had power over her, placing her in the box. He came on strong with her, she told him to get lost and he snapped and killed her.'

'With a plastic bag he happened to have brought along for the seduction? I don't think so, Keith.'

Halliwell wasn't giving up on his suspect. 'Well, he tried it on earlier, before the interval, and she laughed in his face. He was humiliated, so he went back with the bag and suffocated her.'

'Thanks. I'll bear it in mind,' Diamond said in a tone suggesting the opposite. 'Has anything else of interest been uncovered yet?' He moved around the room looking over people's shoulders. He

318

could be an intimidating presence. Everything went quiet again apart from the tapping of keyboards and the occasional beep of the phones.

One of the civilian staff called him to the phone. 'DI Leaman would like a word, sir. He's at the theatre.'

He picked it up. 'John?'

'Guv, we've started the search here.'

'Any joy?'

'I'm in wardrobe, with Kate.'

'Lucky man.'

'You asked us to look for carrier bags. The thing is, Kate has to do shopping for costumes and materials. She has a stack of bags. So far I've counted forty-seven.'

CHAPTER NINETEEN

Patience was a virtue Diamond didn't have in abundance, but over the years he'd cultivated a little of it. Experience had taught him that you can't rush the people who work in forensic labs. The blood-test results from the post-mortem on Denise Pearsall would be revealed only when the scientists were ready. The men in white coats were well used to dealing with calls from policemen wanting swifter action. However, the same constraints didn't apply to document examiners. They were used less often, so fair game for some badgering, in Diamond's opinion. The suicide note supposedly written by Denise and recovered from the fake stove on stage at the theatre had been sent to an expert in Bristol called Lincroft. He hadn't reported back yet.

'Fearfully sorry, but I can't help you much,' Lincroft said when Diamond phoned him. 'There isn't much to go on.'

'A signature.'

'Half actually. She signed with her first name only.'

'We sent you her real signature to compare it with.'

'Well, I couldn't do much without. If the suicide note is a forgery, it's a good one. Often you can tell under the microscope, for example when there's some shakiness to the writing from the effort to make an exact copy. There is slight evidence of a tremor here, but one has to make allowance for the writer's state of mind.'

'I don't know how you ever reach a conclusion,' Diamond said, hearing himself apeing the laid-back voice.

'Usually there's more to work with. And I don't confine my researches to suicide notes. You'd be surprised what gets referred to me apart from the usual cheques and wills. Degrees, diplomas, even sick notes. Sometimes the deception is obvious, when, say, they trace over a signature in pencil and ink it in after. This certainly didn't happen to the note in question.'

'If this is a forgery—and there's reason to think it is—how do they make it look right?'

'By working from a genuine signature and practising. In that way they avoid the giveaway signs of uneven speed and pressure.'

'But I can't look to you for a firm opinion?'

'I did say it was quite well done if it isn't the real thing. I've spent considerable time, effort and

320

taxpayers' money examining this document. The fact that it's merely a forename makes my task even more demanding. Even if I work on it for another week I'm unlikely to say what you want to hear.'

'Oh brilliant.'

At this point, Lincroft must have been moved by the disappointment in Diamond's voice. 'If I were you, I'd come at this from another direction.'

'Oh?'

'The letter was computer-generated. Did this lady possess her own computer and printer?'

'Yes, but you can't tell anything from printed stuff. It's all done by laser, isn't it? The days are long gone when we all used typewriters with chipped keys.'

'Some modern printers still give information. I noticed some specks down the right edge, very small, deposited by the toner.'

Diamond picked up the photocopy he had of the note. He'd already seen some tiny dots randomly spread and hadn't thought anything of them.

'Cleaning the drum removes them,' Lincroft went on, 'but people tend to wait until the marks get worse and become obvious. There must be enough here to identify the printer that was used. I suggest you run some paper through the lady's printer and then compare it.'

He was impressed. 'Sounds like good advice.'

'Glad to be of service. I'll return the letter with my invoice. Goodbye.'

The phone went dead. There were times when Diamond wished he, too, was self-employed and issuing invoices.

He checked with the store downstairs where

evidence was kept. They had what they called Denise's motherboard, but not her printer. 'Why not, for crying out loud?' he said, and then aired his new expertise. 'Some printers leave marks, you know. Vital information.'

They said it wasn't their fault, but they would send someone to Dolemeads to fetch it.

'Pronto.'

'If that's what you want, sir.'

'What I really want is for someone to run a dozen sheets of blank paper through the thing and have them on my desk within the hour.'

He went down to the canteen. He'd arranged to meet his new recruits there. George Pidgeon and Dawn Reed were waiting by the door, as edgy as first-night actors. Was it his imagination, or were the police getting younger?

'You should have gone in,' he told them. 'Or are you waiting for me to buy you tea and a bun?'

PC Reed started to explain, but Diamond interrupted. 'You'll soon learn that I'm not easy to work for. Whatever you do, it's wrong. Coffee?'

They hesitated as if it was a trick question.

'I'm having tea and a Bath bun,' he said.

'The same for me, sir,' PC Pidgeon said at once.

'But we'll buy our own,' Reed added.

'In that case you can buy mine as well while I bag a table,' Diamond said.

From the far side of the canteen he watched with amusement as they lined up at the counter talking earnestly to each other with an occasional glance to where he was, most likely settling who would pay for his tea and bun.

When they came over with the tray he held out a fiver.

322

'It's on us, sir,' Reed said.

'It isn't. I brought you here. I pay.'

Having worked with Fred Dawkins, this young lady was used to being overruled.

That settled, Diamond said with an effort to be friendly, 'You're asking yourselves why you've been plucked from the ranks. It's because I've seen you in action, both of you, and I liked what I saw. George, when you found that car for me the other evening you asked about the possibility of a transfer to CID.'

'Yes, sir.' Pidgeon's spaniel eyes gleamed in expectation.

'This isn't it. I want two reliable officers for a job I wouldn't care to do myself. And you can stop all this "sir" stuff. "Guv" will do to my face and what you call me behind my back is your affair. Understood?'

In unison they said, 'Yes, guv.'

'This job is secret. Do you know the difference between secret and need to know?'

'If it's secret, no one needs to know,' Reed said.

'Correct. Not your friends, family, brother officers, superiors, the chief constable, not even the theatre ghost. Afraid of ghosts, are you, either of you?'

Unused to this sort of question from a senior officer, they each grinned sheepishly.

'This is something I do need to know,' he said.

They glanced at each other and shook their heads.

'That's good, because you'll be spending the next two nights on duty inside the Theatre Royal, supposedly one of the most haunted buildings in Bath. It will be dark when you go in and I want it to

323

remain in darkness. You'll be alone in that spooky old building, apart perhaps from the grey lady.' He scanned their faces. 'How does that strike you?'

'Not a problem for me, guv,' Pidgeon said.

'Me neither,' Reed said.

And they obviously meant what they said.

'You're too polite to ask what this is all about. Here's the deal. We've had two murders in the theatre in two days. One thing we know for certain about the killer is that he or she is very familiar with the place, backstage as well as the part the audience sees. The digital security system is no bar to this individual. And we believe the first murder may have been done after hours, at night. My idea is to set a trap, persuade the killer to return to the scene of the crime. The time they'll choose will be at night. If this succeeds you'll be lying in wait and you'll arrest them. Does that make sense?'

'What's the bait, guv?' Reed asked.

'Good question. Not yet decided. It has to be something that unsettles them, some giveaway clue they left behind and need to return for. They'll think the theatre is empty. This is why your mission is top secret.'

The start of a frown appeared as Pidgeon asked, 'Will we be armed?'

Diamond shook his head. 'You can carry your batons if you like.'

'I meant firearms.'

'I know what you meant and I said batons. Have you done the firearms course, either of you?'

They shook their heads.

'You'd end up shooting each other. If it's any comfort, the only weapon the killer has used so far is a plastic bag.' He took out one of the cards

324

issued to theatre staff. 'These are the security codes. You enter through the Egg Theatre, which is at the back. Get there by ten. Your shift ends at first light.'

'Do you want us in uniform, guv?' Dawn Reed asked.

'What do you think? Because I treated you to tea and a bun, that doesn't make you CID. I suggest you get some sleep in the next few hours.'

'Are we off duty now?'

He nodded and watched them leave, two kids let out of school early. A touching sight. He hoped his faith in them would be justified.

*   *   *

The sheets of paper that had been run through Denise's printer had some marks along the right side that didn't remotely match the suicide note. Diamond showed them to Paul Gilbert and explained their significance.

'Is this good news, or bad?' young Gilbert asked.

'Good and bad. It's more evidence that we're working on the right assumption, that she was murdered,' he said, 'so that much is good. If she'd printed the note at home, suicide would have been a safe bet.'

'So what's bad?'

'We don't know which machine it was printed on. We can't be sure of anything until we find out.'

'I expect the murderer has a printer,' Gilbert said. 'If we asked each of the suspects . . .' His voice trailed away as he realised why he'd been called in.

'And it's quite possible our crafty killer didn't

325

use his own computer at all,' Diamond said. 'You can start by getting specimen sheets from all the printers at the theatre. I've seen one in the box office. There must be a number of others. When you've eliminated them, start making a nuisance of yourself, going into people's homes. Don't let anyone offer to do the printing for you.'

'Isn't there a flaw in this, guv?' Gilbert said.

'What's that?'

'If I was the killer, I'd already have cleaned my printer so it wouldn't leave marks at all.'

Just when Diamond was starting to feel he'd caught up with computer technology and found its Achilles heel. 'Let's hope he hasn't thought of that. Run these tests as discreetly as possible.'

Gilbert looked as if he'd rather stack shelves in Sainsbury's.

'Look at it this way,' Diamond said. 'You could be the guy who fingers the killer.'

He didn't seem convinced.

*   *   *

Motive would be the key to the murder of Clarion Calhoun.

Alone in his office and sensing that time was running out, Diamond turned to the classic trinity for all crimes: opportunity, means and motive. Opportunity wasn't of much help. In a theatre where so much was going on and with the victim isolated, the opportunity had been there for the taking. The means, a plastic bag, was so commonplace that there was doubt if it was worth searching for. The theatre was full of bags. Leaman had called in again to say he had found another nine in the props room, making a total of fifty-six at the latest count, and it was probable that the bag actually used had been disposed of elsewhere.

Only the motive was worth pursuing. Why would anyone want to kill Clarion when she had withdrawn her threat to sue? The theatre had been saved from a damaging court case. She was everyone's fairy godmother. The good news had been relayed to the entire theatre community by Francis Melmot. But now that Clarion was dead, all bets were off. The future of the place was plunged back into uncertainty. Surely no one wished the theatre to be closed after two hundred years?

There had to be another reason why she was killed. She'd fought her way to the top as a pop star. How many hopefuls had she pushed off the ladder? It was possible someone had harboured a grudge. But when you considered the line-up of suspects, none of them had any connection with the pop world except—very remotely—Melmot, who had been a fan, not a rival.

Who stood to gain financially from Clarion's death? She had property, for sure, and money, though probably not the fortune she'd earned at the peak of her career. She was going to make a substantial donation to the theatre. Was that the trigger that had killed her? Did someone foresee their inheritance being frittered away on wigs and make-up and weird experimental plays?

He made a note to find out the terms of Clarion's will, if she'd made one, and who the main legatees were. There had been a live-in boyfriend at one stage, but he'd returned to Australia after they split up. There was a manager called Declan Dean, and she'd dumped him, too. Anyone else? Tilda Box would probably know. Indeed, Tilda Box might be the beneficiary. She seemed to have been more than just an agent. She and Clarion had been seen clubbing together. But then Tilda had been in London at the time of the murder.

The more he thought about it, the more he was convinced that nothing would be gained by treating the two murders in isolation. The victims were totally unlike each other, yet the theatre had brought them together as leading actress and dresser. Clarion's extravagant act of self-harm had thrown blame on to Denise. The unfortunate dresser had at first assumed like everyone else that she'd made a dreadful mistake. Her death, almost certainly dressed up as suicide, must have been cunningly arranged by the killer, who evidently knew the theatre intimately, the butterfly superstition, the empty second-floor dressing room and the door to the fly tower and the compartment in the stove where the so-called suicide note was discovered.

Equally, Clarion's killing required special knowledge, the news that the injured star was secretly visiting the theatre. Really only three people knew in advance. Others may have worked it out for themselves after the 'ghost' was sighted, but the killing didn't have the feel of a last-minute decision. The murderer had come prepared with the airtight killing bag and chosen the short span during the interval when the curtain was lowered and most of the audience were outside. A muffled cry of distress from the box hadn't been noticed. He or she had left unseen, probably by the rear

328

door. It was hard to imagine one of the actors having committed the murder on the spur of the moment and then going back on stage for the second half.

Realistically, Shearman, Melmot and Binns were the prime suspects. Binns wasn't on the staff, but it was his job to patrol the building and he knew the security codes and could come and go at will.

Reassured that he'd drawn the net as tightly as he could, Diamond looked into the CID room again. 'Anything I should be told?'

'Keith just called from the theatre a minute ago,' Ingeborg said. 'He said to tell you about a fourth suspect.'

Telepathy seemed to have been at work here. Galvanised, he said, 'Who's that?'

'Kate, the wardrobe lady. Like the others, she knew Clarion was on her way to the theatre the evening she was killed.'

'She didn't.'

'Talk to Keith, guv.'

'Has he been talking to her?'

'No. To Hedley Shearman. They're close, those two.'

'I've seen how close. Did he say any more?'

'It sounded as if he was still with Shearman when he was speaking. He couldn't talk freely.'

'I'd better get down there.'

'Would you like someone else to go?' Ingeborg asked in a tone that was almost motherly.

He felt a rush of blood. 'Why do you say that?'

'In case you're needed here.'

They both knew what she was on about. She was the sharpest observer on the squad.

He told himself by now he was over the paranoia or whatever it was that afflicted him each time he visited that theatre. Familiarity breeds confidence. Peter Diamond, detective superintendent, head of CID, scourge of the luvvies, would show them how to make an entrance.

'I'm needed there and I'll go,' he said.

He took his car, left it on the double yellow line outside, took a deep breath, crossed the pavement and . . . felt the first wave of nausea. Nothing had altered. If anything, it was worse. He stopped like a beast smelling blood at the slaughterhouse door.

Ridiculous.

Another gulp of air and he forced himself to go in.

There was a notice saying all performances had been cancelled until next week. The foyer was empty, the box office closed. He could turn round and leave. No one would know.

Instead he gritted his teeth, took the security card from his pocket and pressed the keys that admitted him to the royal circle. Inside it was darker than usual. Only a few side lights were on. He heard voices from the bar and one was Halliwell's. Thank God he wouldn't need to look into the auditorium.

Keith was in there seated across a table from Shearman. 'Are you okay, guv? You look pale.'

'Bit breathless. Out of condition, I expect.'

'Why don't you sit down?'

He pulled up a chair. 'You left a message, something about Kate.'

Shearman twitched and looked away.

'That's right,' Halliwell said. 'Talking to Mr Shearman I discovered that she knew Clarion was

330

in the theatre last evening.'

'How is that?' Diamond said, turning to Shearman. 'You told her?'

The little manager scraped his fingers down the side of his face, leaving white marks. 'I'm sorry. It was stupid of me.'

'You tipped her off about Clarion's visit?'

'I wouldn't put it like that.'

'When? When did you tell her?'

'During the first half.'

Halliwell said, 'Kate and Mr Shearman were at it in the wardrobe room.'

'Shagging?' He shook his head in disbelief. 'Does this happen every night and twice on matinee days?'

'It's not like that,' Shearman said, blushing. 'She's been through a hugely difficult time and so have I. There's no law against it.'

'What exactly was said?'

'I said I couldn't stay long with her because I'd need to go up to the box during the interval. First of all I said it was a VIP I was taking care of, but of course she wanted to know who, and in the end I weakened and told her.' He paused, and then emphasised each word with his forefinger. 'She had nothing to do with Clarion's death.'

'Where is she now? Here in the theatre?'

He shook his head. 'She left earlier, after your man finished his search of wardrobe. She has nothing to keep her here.'

'Tidying up would be good. Wardrobe was a mess when I saw it.'

'Her heart isn't in it any more.'

Diamond leaned closer to him. 'So why did you lie?'

'To protect her. It's no secret now that she and I are close friends. I didn't want her treated as a suspect, put through the mill, as some of us have been. She's no murderer.'

'Do you know where she's gone?'

'Home, I expect. She lives in Warminster, but I hope you're not going to trouble her there. You'd be wasting your time. I'm sure she's innocent.'

Diamond turned to Halliwell. 'Didn't we ask everyone to stay in contact?'

He nodded.

'We have a phone number. Try it.'

Halliwell took out his mobile and dialled. 'Nothing. She's switched off.'

Diamond cast his thoughts back to the interview he'd had with Kate shortly after Denise had been found dead, the obvious coolness, if not open hostility. She'd used the phrase 'tough as old boots' about her colleague and said she was 'calm as a lake in heaven' when going off to attend to Clarion's make-up. He'd questioned how anyone could be calm if they were about to smear caustic soda on another woman's face and Kate had said he'd have to work that out for himself.

He said to Shearman, 'I picked up some tension between Kate and Denise.'

'Did you?' he said, as if it didn't surprise him. 'I wouldn't make too much of that if I were you. Denise came under Kate's supervision in the wardrobe department, but she'd worked here for six years, rather more than Kate had. There was bound to be some professional awkwardness.'

'Kate didn't seem too cut up about Denise's death.'

'I expect she was putting a brave face on it. A

332

terrible thing like that takes people in different ways.'

'Maybe. Just now I commented that wardrobe was a mess and you said her heart wasn't in it. What did you mean by that?'

Shearman hesitated. 'Oh, I was talking about the dreadful things that have happened. It's enough to sap anyone's morale.'

Smart answer, but not convincing, Diamond thought. 'Going by the state of the place, it didn't get like that in a couple of days.'

'I'm sure the disorder is more apparent than real. She knows where everything is—or she did until your search party turned the lot upside down.'

Diamond hadn't been swayed by the manager's defence. Kate was definitely in the frame now. Her strong dislike of Denise had been obvious all along. She'd portrayed her as tough, calm and so indifferent to Clarion's scarring that she could well have inflicted it. Coming from a colleague, that was quite a character assassination. It wasn't beyond her to have lured Denise upstairs, slipped her the drug and pushed her to her death to fake the suicide. Working so closely with Denise, she would be familiar with her signature and well able to forge the note. Up to that point everything seemed to be going to plan. Then she'd found out that Clarion was making this secret visit to the theatre. Did alarm bells go off in her head—that Clarion had worked out the truth and was coming to confront her or even expose her as the killer? How simple to have picked up one of the many plastic bags in wardrobe and gone to the box and suffocated Clarion.

He turned to Halliwell. 'This stinks. I'm going

out to Warminster to see her.'

Shearman was shaking his head. 'You'll send her into a panic. She'll think she's under suspicion.'

'She is. I don't want you tipping her off,' he said and told Halliwell to stay with Shearman for the next hour.

'Don't you people understand that I have a job to do?' Shearman demanded.

'There's no job. The theatre is dark now.'

'That's when things get busy for me. I'll be organising a team to strike the set.'

'To *what*?'

Halliwell said, 'He means moving the scenery, guv. They want to clear the stage so it's ready for the next production.'

Diamond pointed a finger at Shearman. 'Don't even think about shifting it. Leave everything in place, exactly as it is. That's an order.'

CHAPTER TWENTY

South-east of Bath in the thick of the Friday afternoon commute along the A36, Diamond drove at his usual steady forty, heading a procession increasingly desperate to overtake. At his side was a detective sergeant almost his own age who had transferred from Chipping Sodbury a couple of months back, a soft-speaking, dependable type. Lew Rogers had merged into the CID room almost unnoticed. This was a chance to get to know him better. About all Diamond had discovered was that he cycled to work from Batheaston. Either a fitness freak or a green, he had decided.

'I'll be relying on you to guide me to the street where this woman lives,' Diamond said. 'I generally steer clear of Warminster.'

'Why is that? All the sightings of UFOs?'

'No. The bypass.'

They both smiled. Back in the sixties and seventies there had been persistent reports of flying saucers over Warminster and the nearby downs. There were claims that some local residents had been abducted. Books had been written about extra-terrestrial visitors.

'Have you thought about getting a sat-nav?' Rogers asked in his innocence.

'Got one.'

'Where is it?'

'It's you, sat here and navving for me. More reliable, I hope, and with extras, like hands. If you look in the glove compartment you'll find some Softmints. Have one yourself.'

'Thanks, but I won't,' Rogers said. He passed a mint to Diamond. 'Does Kate live alone?'

'As far as I know, yes.'

'Are you going to nick her?'

'If necessary.'

'Is she on the run?'

'Would I be driving at this speed if she was?'

'I was told you don't do more than forty in any situation.'

Diamond looked ahead without even the suggestion of a smile. 'You're well informed. There's a stretch of dual carriageway coming up. They can all overtake if they want. We'll get there soon enough. We're not far off now.'

Two minutes later, all the brake lights started

going on. Both lanes of the carriageway were blocked as far ahead as he could see.

'Shouldn't have spoken. What's this about?' he said. 'One of those idiots who just overtook us, I wouldn't wonder.'

Everything came to a complete halt.

'Could be road works,' Rogers said.

'I don't think so.' He'd heard the two-tone wail of an emergency vehicle from behind. 'Can they get by?'

An ambulance snaked a route through the stationary traffic.

Diamond switched off the engine and took out his phone. After speaking to traffic division he informed Rogers that the problem was half a mile ahead, almost in the town. 'Some idiot managed to turn his car over and the fire service are using their cutting equipment. Fancy a game of I Spy?'

'Perhaps I *will* have one of your mints, guv.'

'Live dangerously.' Fitness was Rogers' thing, Diamond decided.

He dialled CID for an update and was pleased when Ingeborg answered. She was better than any of the team at summing up what was happening, and was just back from interviewing the chairman of the board at Melmot Hall.

'Learn anything new?' he asked.

'Yes, and I would have called you if you'd kept your phone on.'

'You're in danger of nagging the boss, Inge. I was driving.'

'You've got someone with you who could take a call, guv. Anyway, this will make you sit up. Melmot told me Kate is working her notice. He sacked her a week ago.'

336

'Melmot sacked Kate?' he said more to himself than Ingeborg, to gain a couple of seconds while the implications sank in.

'He said there had been problems with her before, not doing the job properly.'

'Now he tells us.'

'She'd clung on because of her relationship with Shearman, who always backs her and says the criticism is unfair. But when Melmot was approached about the state of the wardrobe room he went to see it for himself and was so appalled that he fired her.'

'It was a dog's breakfast when I saw it,' he said, 'but I've no experience of these places.'

'You can't run a theatre wardrobe in such a mess. Everything has to be in place and organised.' That was one of Ingeborg's favourite refrains. She was right, of course, whether it was a theatre wardrobe or a CID office.

'Shearman was silent about this when I questioned him.'

'He would be.'

'He did say at one point that her heart isn't in it any more. That should have alerted me. He doesn't give much away.'

'Do you want to know who the whistle-blower was?'

'Go on.'

'Denise Pearsall.'

He gave a whistle of his own. 'That could be the clincher. Melmot told you this?'

'He said she took some photographs of the wardrobe room with her phone and went to see him with them.'

'She was asking for trouble, shopping her boss.'

The facts were slotting in like the last pieces of a jigsaw. 'Kate must have known who dropped her in it. You can't keep stuff like that to yourself. This is dynamite, Inge. It means she had a red-hot motive for revenge on Denise. And if she thought Denise had mentioned any of this to Clarion, she had a strong reason to kill Clarion as well.'

Ingeborg sounded a note of caution. 'Before we get carried away, guv, let's not forget Shearman. He's Kate's lover. He could have killed Denise. In his case, there was a personal element because Denise ignored him, went over his head and complained to Melmot.'

'Point taken. And he was the best placed of everyone to murder Clarion.' He pressed back against the headrest and released some of the tension with a huge sigh. 'Whoever it is, we're on to them. When I get to see Kate, I'll know. The one small problem is that I'm stuck in a bloody traffic jam. Nothing is moving.'

*   *   *

A further ten minutes went by. The hold-up had reached the stage when people were out of their cars discussing what was going on. Diamond remained seated, thinking of other things, using the time to revisit each stage of the murders, down to such detail as the placing of the butterfly in dressing room one and the secreting of the suicide note in the stove. Nothing conflicted with either Kate or Shearman committing both murders.

'When we finally get moving again and find the house,' he said to Lew Rogers, 'we'll make sure she doesn't see us coming and escape through the back. I've had that happen before. I'll park some distance up the street and you can make the first approach. She knows me. I don't think she's met you.'

'I was in the theatre last night with the others.'

'But you didn't speak to her. Anyway, you're lower profile than I am.'

Ahead there was the sound of doors being slammed and engines starting.

'Thank God for that.'

Progress was still slow, but at least there was movement. It went from a crawl to a sedate ten-mile-an-hour cruise as far as the roundabout and then slowed again on the two-way approach road to Warminster. Rogers looked up from the street atlas. 'There's another way into the town, but it may be just as congested.'

'We'll settle for this.'

Ahead was a police car with its blues flashing and a uniformed cop guiding the line of traffic past the scene of the accident.

'Nasty,' Diamond said as they came alongside a mangled blue saloon being lifted on to a breakdown truck. 'Must have hit that tree. I wonder if it was fatal.' Then he realised he was rubbernecking and gave his attention to the road ahead.

Lew Rogers was good with the map. Away from the town centre, Warminster is a maze of side streets and dead ends. He directed them unerringly off the High Street and over a railway bridge to the estate where Kate lived. The houses there must have been built as army quarters to support the nearby barracks, functional brick buildings without much to distinguish them. Some boys were kicking a football in the road.

Diamond succeeded in reaching the end without running over a child and parked at the kerbside. 'Did you spot the house?'

'I did. It's the one with the yellow door about halfway along.'

The way the houses were sited, an escape route from the back looked unlikely. Tall fences enclosed the back gardens.

'Shall I see if she's in, guv?' Rogers asked.

'Why not? Give me a wave if she is.'

Rogers started the walk back, watched covertly in the rear-view mirror by Diamond and openly by the young footballers.

Rogers went through the gate and rang the bell on the yellow door.

Diamond watched and waited. The footballers had suspended play.

No one came to the door.

Presently Rogers returned to the car. 'Nothing doing. The kids say they know when she's home because she parks her car outside, a blue Vauxhall Astra.'

A disquieting thought popped into Diamond's mind, but he dismissed it.

'What do we do now?' Rogers said.

'We can at least see if she comes along in the next half-hour. She could have been caught in the traffic jam, like us.'

The evening light was still good although the shadows were lengthening. Behind the houses, the downs were turning pink. A fertile imagination wouldn't have had much difficulty in seeing flying saucers.

'Will we wrap this up tonight?' Rogers asked.

'I hope so. Why—do you have plans for the weekend?'

'Not really.'

'Married, are you?'

'Second time around.'

'She'll have plans, then.'

'No doubt.'

Diamond took another look at the house. 'Was that ground-floor window open when you went to the door?'

'I'm sure it was.'

'Careless of her. Anyone could get in.'

'True.'

After a pause, Diamond said, 'We shouldn't leave it unsecured. In fact, we have a civic duty to investigate.'

Rogers clearly understood what the head of CID intended. He may have been shocked, but he had the good sense not to mention it. The two of them approached the house. The security risk in question was a small top window opened for ventilation.

'Your arm is longer than mine,' Diamond said. 'If I give you a hand-up, see if you can reach in and unfasten the catch on the window below.'

The footballers came closer while Diamond was helping Rogers get a foot on the outer ledge. The smallest of them, prompted by the others, said, 'What are you doing, mister? Are you breaking in?'

'It's all right,' Diamond called back. 'We're the police, making sure it's safe.'

'How do we know you're the police?'

'A burglar wouldn't do this in broad daylight with you lot watching, that's why.'

Rogers lifted the catch on the lower window and they both climbed in. The place was appreciably tidier than Kate's workplace. A black sofa covered with a purple throw. Afghan rug. Flat-screen TV.

'Can you work a computer?' Diamond asked.

'Depends what sort.'

'See if you can find hers and run a sheet of blank paper through the printer.'

'It's right here against the wall.' Rogers checked that the paper in the feed was clean and then passed a couple of sheets through and handed them to Diamond. 'I don't know what you're expecting to find, guv.'

'It isn't this,' Diamond said. The sheets were still pristine. 'Mind, she could have used another machine. I'll have a look round.'

A swift tour of the small house revealed no second printer and nothing else in the way of evidence. Up in the bedroom he started in surprise when his own phone emitted its archaic ring-tone. He'd left it switched on after speaking to Ingeborg. The voice was hers again.

'Where are you now, guv—still in Warminster?'

He avoided a specific answer. 'Should I be somewhere else?'

'You don't need to wait there, anyway. Kate was in a car accident on her way home. She turned it right over, only a short way from the town.'

That disquieting thought resurfaced and chided him, gloating: *I told you so*.

'Is she alive?'

'So they're saying. She was taken to A & E at Salisbury Hospital. I don't know what condition she's in.'

'We're halfway there. We'll find out.'

342

*   *   *

Like all main hospitals, Salisbury has insufficient parking. Even detectives on police business have to search for a space. By the time Diamond found one, it was a fair walk to Accident & Emergency. They did, at least, get some priority at the enquiry desk and learned that Kate was not critically injured. She had some minor abrasions and was being assessed for concussion. They were told the way to the out-patients' canteen.

'You know what that means,' Diamond said to Rogers. 'This could take a long time.'

'Shall I fetch some coffee?'

'Good thinking. And a beef sandwich would go down well.'

He called Ingeborg again to update her. The mobile was getting more use in one day than it had in months. 'Will you stay at the hospital?' she asked.

'One of us will, for sure.'

'How did the accident happen?'

'We don't know yet.'

'Is it possible more than one vehicle was involved?'

He sensed at once what she was thinking, that Kate may have been forced off the road in a cynical attempt to kill her. Kate as victim would mean a reversal of the way he was thinking. 'Hard to tell until we get a chance to speak to her. We saw her car being lifted from the scene and there wasn't another at that stage.'

'They'd have driven on.'

'I know what you're getting at. She's being

343

assessed for concussion, so she may have no memory. It'll be up to the accident investigation team to tell us, and they won't be quick. What's going on at your end?'

'Not much, I'm afraid,' Ingeborg said. 'Paul is back from the theatre. He was checking all the printers there. He says he did a printout on every one, but there wasn't a single match with the suicide note. That line of enquiry doesn't look promising.'

'He'd better not give up on it. I expect it was printed at home on a personal computer. He'll just have to visit each of the suspects.'

'He knows, guv. He'll see the job through.'

'Tell him he needn't go out to Warminster for Kate's machine.'

'Why is that?'

'It's been cleared. No specks at all.' He moved swiftly on. 'Who else is around?'

'John Leaman. He finished that search of the theatre and found I don't know how many carrier bags. And Fred Dawkins has just left for that *Sweeney Todd* rehearsal. He's done a solid job on Binns, checking with previous employers. We now have a complete career record. A few blemishes, but nothing of obvious interest. Binns doesn't seem to have had any previous connection with Clarion or Denise or the Theatre Royal.'

'Is Keith still with Shearman?'

'No, he came back an hour ago, wanting to give the little fink enough rope to hang himself, he says.'

'Not literally, I hope. And what's your take on Francis Melmot?'

Her sigh could be heard down the phone. 'I'm in

two minds, guv. He's far from silent, but he gives nothing away. I'm sure he's an excellent chairman of the trustees because he's so discreet. Personally I find him charming and affable and I think he truly cares about the theatre. But his decision to employ Clarion was a disaster. All of this mayhem was triggered by him and I suspect there's more he hasn't told us.'

'Like sacking Kate?'

'Well, yes.'

'How did you wheedle that out of him?'

'I traded.'

'Traded what?'

'I made some suggestive remark about Shearman and Kate and he obviously didn't know what they get up to in wardrobe. He was shocked into telling me she'd already been dismissed.'

'Why hadn't he told us before now?'

'He didn't want the theatre's reputation damaged any more than it has been already.'

'Shearman didn't tell us anything about the sacking either.'

'Well, he's been exploiting it, hasn't he?'

'How do you mean?'

'Encouraging Kate to think that by cosying up to him she'll get a reprieve. Small chance. Melmot runs the show and Shearman has hardly any influence with him at all.'

For Diamond, this was a new angle on the goings-on in wardrobe. 'So you think Kate is pulling him to save her job?'

'I'd put it another way. Shearman is cynically taking advantage.'

'I thought it was straightforward sex.'

'A typically male assumption, if I may say so.'

Sharp, he thought. He wouldn't get into a debate with Ingeborg about that. 'Nice work with Melmot, anyway. Things are making more sense. Are you working late?'

'That's what you asked us to do.' There was a definite note of dissent, unusual for Ingeborg. He expected it from the likes of Leaman and even Halliwell on occasions, but not Inge.

'I'll get back as soon as I can.' If Inge was unhappy, he could imagine there was serious murmuring in the ranks. He understood why. Most of the interviews had been got through and put on file by now. The team was marking time, waiting for fresh orders but knowing he was an hour's drive away. No doubt they were thinking of what they were missing on a Friday evening. He needed to convey his own belief that this was the calm before the storm.

Difficult, down the phone from Salisbury. When he'd started on this trip he'd expected to question Kate in Warminster and be back in Bath by early evening.

He pocketed the mobile and stepped up to the desk again and reminded them who he was and asked if he could see Kate now. He was told firmly to wait with everyone else. He asked how long that was likely to be and they said they weren't in a position to say.

More marking time. He wasn't good at it. Not that Friday-night clubbing held any appeal for a man his age; he just wanted to make better use of the time.

But an idea was coming to him. It wouldn't be the ideal solution. Better than sitting around here for a couple of hours.

When Rogers returned with the coffee and sandwiches, Diamond said, 'They're busy here. I've seen a couple of serious cases brought in while you were getting these.'

'It's Friday evening, guv. It's expected in casualty.'

'Could be a long one, I'm thinking.'

'Me, too.'

He took a sip of the coffee. 'This is welcome.'

'Good.'

'There's someone I wouldn't mind seeing while I'm over here. Lives at Wilton. That isn't far from Salisbury, is it?'

'Not far at all.' A twitch of Rogers' lips showed his immediate assumption: that Diamond had a woman friend.

'It's not police business,' Diamond said. 'I'd be leaving you in charge for an hour or so. Would you mind? You could phone me if there's a problem.'

'I'll still be here. I don't have my bike with me.'

CHAPTER TWENTY-ONE

'No violence,' Diamond kept repeating aloud while skirting Salisbury on the road to Wilton. The next hour would test him. The anger simmering for days was already threatening to boil over. He'd last felt pressure like this after Steph was murdered. Brute force had always lurked within him and he knew the signs, shallow breathing, gritted teeth, flexed muscles. Then the red mist came down and he was dangerous. No, he must keep reminding himself of the purpose of meeting Flakey White: to find out

347

for certain what had happened when he was a child. Only by getting to the truth of it could he hope to remove the block his brain had put up and give himself the possibility of closure.

This was it: truth time.

He'd thought about phoning White to let him know he was coming. In most situations it was the civilised way to behave. Turning up unannounced after dark wasn't a good start. But in this case, surprise was essential. If White were tipped off that someone he'd once abused was coming, he'd quit the house, or refuse to come to the door.

As it was, there was no guarantee he'd be at home and no certainty he'd be willing to say anything. He could clam up or deny all knowledge of the abuse. The meeting was one extremely demanding obstacle course.

But it had to be attempted.

Without Sergeant Rogers in the passenger seat, Diamond navigated for himself. Part of his brain, at least, was compelled to function normally. The map showed he didn't need to drive into the city centre and he was helped by Wilton appearing regularly on the signboards. At a roundabout he swung left and past the huge arched entrance gate to Wilton House, ancestral home of the Earls of Pembroke, not a bad neighbourhood for a jailbird to end up in.

Obliged to stop at some traffic lights where the road narrowed for the village, he studied the map again and worked out where White lived. A right turn brought him into North Street. Forest Close was off to the left.

The house was a squat, stone structure with the look of a converted farm building, single storeyed with a tiled roof much covered in moss. Crucially, the lights were on inside, behind Venetian blinds.

Determined to stay calm, he took a deep breath, rang the bell and waited. He was relieved to hear movements inside.

The door opened a short way, on a chain. He couldn't see much of the person inside.

'Mr White?'

'Yes.' The voice was tentative, unwelcoming.

'My name is Peter Diamond and you were once my art teacher.' He'd been debating with himself how to begin. This wasn't the moment to reveal he was a senior policeman.

'Oh.'

'It's late to be calling, I know.'

It must have taken several seconds for Diamond's first words to register. Without any more being said, White released the door chain and opened it fully. He was wearing a peaked eyeshade. White haired and thin-faced, he had worry lines etched deeply. He was shorter than Diamond remembered, dressed in a thin cardigan, corduroys and carpet slippers. His shoulders sagged. 'Do come in,' he said.

Then he held out his hand.

There is only so much you can anticipate. The handshake was a pitfall Diamond hadn't foreseen. Visiting the old paedophile was one thing. Touching his flesh was another. To refuse would expose the disgust Diamond was trying to conceal. He told himself it was only a formality, quickly over. How many hands have I shaken in my lifetime? How many of them were hands that had thieved, assaulted or even committed murder? A fair number.

349

He reached out and felt White's palm against his own, limp, bony, lukewarm. After drawing away he couldn't stop himself rubbing his hand against his hip to cleanse it of the contact.

White didn't appear to notice. 'I'll make some tea.'

'Please don't,' Diamond told him, civil to a fault. 'I had some not long ago. I was visiting the hospital. That's how I was in the area.'

The old man matched him for courtesy. 'Whatever the reason, it's an unexpected pleasure to meet a former pupil. Come through to the kitchen. I don't have a living room as such. I use that as my studio. Still doing art, you see.'

To reach the kitchen they took a few steps through the studio. A high stool was in front of a desk on which a drawing board rested, lit by a powerful anglepoise lamp. An ink drawing of a city street was in progress, drawn in the exaggerated perspective of the modern graphic style. Beyond question, it was the work of a skilful artist.

'I must have interrupted you.'

'No, no.' White pulled off the eyeshade. 'Don't be concerned about that. A visitor is a rare treat for me. I lead a hermit's life these days. I'm going to insist that you have a drink.'

'I'm driving. I won't.' The warmth of this welcome was disconcerting, the reverse of what he had expected.

In the small kitchen area, White fumbled between the fridge and the wall for a folding chair and tried to draw it open. He was not moving easily.

'May I?' Diamond offered.

'Please do, and then use it.'

'Where will you sit?'

He flapped his hand to dismiss the possibility. 'I could use my stool if I wanted, but I won't because it does me good to stand up. My back isn't the best these days. Occupational hazard, bending over one's work for many years. Draughtsman's back, I call it. What did you say your name is?'

Diamond repeated it. 'I was at Long Lane primary school.'

'I remember. The school, that is, not you. I only ever taught in two schools and that was the first. I don't remember the names of any of the scholars, I'm sorry to admit, and you'll have changed beyond recognition since your primary school days. Were you any good at art?'

'Useless.'

'More of a scientist, were you?'

'I wouldn't say that.'

'So what did you become eventually?'

He didn't want to say, and he didn't want White setting the agenda. 'Sport was my main interest. I played a lot of rugby.'

'As a professional?'

'No, no. Just amateur club stuff. I wonder if you can recall a school friend of mine called Michael Glazebrook.'

A shake of the head. 'I'm afraid I can't.'

'I saw him only the other day. He remembers you. In fact, it was through Mike that I managed to trace you.'

White blinked. The glaze over his pale blue eyes was probably cataract. 'How was that?'

'He saw your picture in a magazine.'

Some hesitation followed. He pulled the cardigan close across his chest and frowned a little.

351

'Recently?'

'Some while back, he told me.'

White began fastening the cardigan buttons. He was very uneasy.

Diamond said, 'It was a piece about book illustrators.'

The frown gave way to a look of relief, even mild amusement. 'Oh yes. I can recall being photographed for that. Such a performance it was, setting up an arc lamp and a camera on a tripod in my little studio. I have a copy somewhere. We artists don't often get that sort of attention, even if our work gets seen more widely.'

All this small talk had to end now, Diamond decided. 'Let me take you further back, a lot further. When you taught at my school you had some connection with a local drama group.'

'I did some scene-painting, yes, and I designed the tickets and programmes.' The enquiry hadn't fazed him. He smiled. 'Fancy you remembering that.'

'Mike Glazebrook and I took part in one of the shows, about Richard III.'

White raised both hands. 'Ah, you were the princes in the tower.' This was said with the pleasure of recognition, unqualified delight, it seemed. 'I recruited you, and very good you were, both of you. That's forty years ago, if not more. I'm so pleased you mentioned it, because I can place you now, both of you.'

I bet you can, you pervert, Diamond thought. 'It isn't a pleasing memory for me. I was put off theatres for ever.'

'Oh dear. That is a shame,' White said with what sounded genuine concern. 'On reflection it was a

352

gruesome story to be in, the murder of the young princes. At the time I expect we assumed you'd take it in your stride, two tough little suburban schoolboys.'

'It wasn't the play that affected me.'

'Stage fright, was it? You seemed very confident in front of an audience.'

'Come on, we both know it wasn't stage fright.' He was losing patience.

'You'd better enlighten me.'

'No, Mr White. I want you to enlighten me. I want to know what happened between you and me.'

The old man blinked and shook his head and talked on in the same urbane way. 'I'm sorry. I'm at a loss. As I recall it, I didn't force you to take part. I offered you the role and you were keen to take it up. I would have got your parents' permission, I'm certain. From what you say, something was amiss and I apologise for that. To the best of my recollection nothing "happened", as you put it.'

'Why did you choose me?'

'I expect because you were a confident child who wouldn't mind appearing on a stage. If you don't mind me saying so, you have quite a forceful presence as an adult.'

'I'm a police officer.'

The effect was dramatic. White's hand went protectively to his throat. His face drained of colour, his voice husky. 'I think I will sit down.'

Diamond got up from the chair and set it in the centre of the room. White was so shaken that he had to support himself briefly, holding on to the back before getting seated.

'I know about your prison term,' Diamond said.

Almost in a whisper, White said, 'That was a long time ago.'

'But it happened.'

'I served my sentence.'

'Early release after three years.'

'It was no picnic. They make sure everyone knows what you're in for and you get it tougher than anyone else. You're called a nonce and that's the lowest form of humanity inside. Sub-human, in fact.'

'You won't get sympathy from me.'

'I'm not asking for any. I deserved all I got. I did my time and I haven't offended since. You can check the records.'

'I have,' Diamond said. 'All it means is that you weren't caught again. People like you don't reform. The perversion is permanent.'

He didn't deny it. He nodded. 'In that way it's a unique crime. Other prisoners can wipe the slate clean. I'm a child molester, a paedophile, and that's how the world will always see me, even at my age. Is this about the sex offenders' register?'

'No. It's about you and me.'

As if he hadn't heard, White continued, 'All I can repeat to you is that I never worked in a school again. I was unemployed for a long time, incapable of getting my life back on track. When I did, it was my facility at drawing that was my salvation. I could have illustrated books for children. That's where most of the work is. I deliberately stayed out of that. Eventually I found a niche in graphic novels for adults. Why are you here, Mr Diamond?'

The anger was hard to hold down. 'Isn't that

bloody obvious? You say you changed your job and your style of life. At least you had the chance. It's not so easy for your victims, is it? They have to live with the trauma of what you did to them.'

White lowered his head. 'I'm aware of that. As a child I was abused myself. Many who commit these crimes had it happen to them. It's self-perpetuating. Please understand I'm not whingeing. I made these choices. I knew my conduct was wicked and unlawful. Believe me, after I came out of prison I stopped.'

Diamond still despised him. 'Mr White, I'm not interested in what happened after you came out or how you live now. I'm here because of what went on when I was a kid with a teacher I trusted, and who my parents trusted, apparently.'

He looked up wide-eyed and said, 'I didn't abuse you.'

Now he was denying it, the filthy creep.

The red mist descended. Diamond grasped him by the shoulders. 'What are you saying, you faggot, that it wasn't abuse?'

'I swear to God I didn't do anything to you.'

'Don't give me that. Think about someone else for a change instead of yourself.' Diamond hauled him out of the chair and held him up like an old suit. They were eye to eye. 'Each time I step inside a theatre something so foul is triggered in my brain that I want to throw up. I don't know exactly what. Mentally a shutter comes down. But I know precisely when all this started—during that weekend when I was in the play.'

White's face was contorted with terror. He tried to mouth some words and couldn't. All that came out was bad breath.

Diamond shoved him back into the chair so hard that it skidded across the floor, rocked back and almost overbalanced. He advanced on him, fists clenched. The impulse to hit him was huge.

White screamed. Blood oozed from the corner of his mouth.

'I didn't touch you,' Diamond said, disbelieving.

He was whimpering. When he opened his mouth it was obvious that he'd bitten his tongue.

The blood was White's salvation. The sight of it acted as a check on Diamond, reminding him of all the promises he'd made to himself about non-violence. It wouldn't take more than a few blows to kill this old perv, and what would that achieve?

'Admit it,' he said, panting for breath himself. 'You know what you did to me. I need to hear you say it.'

White simply shook his head.

This was not going as planned.

Diamond made a fist again and then unclenched it. He was making huge efforts to stay in control. He took a step back, grasping his own hands to stop them from lashing out. 'I didn't come here to beat you up. The least you can do is tell me the truth.'

White wiped some of the blood from his chin and succeeded in saying, spacing the words, 'I have never assaulted you in any way. Never touched you.'

'Bloody liar.'

'Really.'

'How can you say this? Come on, the truth.'

White raised a pacifying hand while he gasped for air. Finally, he spoke. 'Will you hear me out?' Breathing hard, pausing often, he said, 'You don't

356

know as much about me as you think. There are different sorts of child sex, Mr Diamond. I wasn't ever attracted to small boys. Yours was a primary school. My offences were all at Manningham Academy. That's a private school for girls aged eleven to eighteen. I took advantage of under-age girls of fourteen and fifteen. I'm a paedophile and ashamed of it, but I was never a pederast.'

Diamond heard the words and didn't at first believe them. He did a rapid rethink of how he'd learned about this. Mike Glazebrook had said his mother had read in the *News of the World* that White had been convicted of sex offences against minors at a private school in Hampshire. And Scotland Yard had later confirmed it was Manningham Academy. That much, at least, was fact.

Was the rest a misunderstanding? The way the newspapers reported such cases, the names of the victims protected by law, there was scope for uncertainty. Mrs Glazebrook had questioned Mike to find out if he'd been abused. She'd evidently assumed that the victims were young boys and this assumption had stuck with Glazebrook and been accepted unquestioningly by Diamond.

Big mistake, was it?

Apparently so. It would have been easy to find out what sort of school it was. He'd failed to make a basic check. How unprofessional was that? He knew why he hadn't looked at the newspaper files himself or tried to contact the school: because it was so personal. He'd backed off from the nauseating detail.

Yet the truth solved nothing. The facts still didn't add up. He could trace his theatre episodes

357

back to immediately after the Richard III play, when he'd gone on holiday with the family and refused to stay in the theatre at Llandudno.

'I'm certain something deeply upsetting happened to me over the weekend of the play,' he told White with a huge effort to sound reasonable. 'You knew the people involved. Was there anyone else who could have targeted an eight-year-old boy? The actor who played the king? He would have handled us.'

'Angus Coventry? I think not,' White said. 'He was having a passionate affair in real life with the actress playing Lady Anne. He wasn't interested in anyone else.'

'One of the others, then?'

'I doubt it. There wasn't the opportunity. It was a church-hall production, if you remember. The backstage area was minimal, and just about everything had to be done there, so it was always crowded with actors and scene-shifters and what have you.'

This chimed in with Diamond's memory. He was forced to conclude that he wasn't being duped.

White added, 'I remember a scene when you and the other prince were smothered. In the Shakespeare version the murders were done off stage, but this was very far from Shakespeare. Could that have been what upset you?'

'The smothering? I'm certain it wasn't.'

'I was thinking if Angus pressed too hard—'

'No,' Diamond said from direct memory. 'The pillow was placed lightly over my face and I had plenty of space to breathe. That wasn't the cause.'

'I can't think of anything else.'

'And neither can I.' To say that he was

358

disappointed was an understatement. He'd psyched himself up, confident of getting the truth, however painful. To be denied any explanation at all was so unexpected that he had difficulty dealing with it.

'What will you do about me?' White asked.

'You?'

'If it gets known locally what I am, people are going to feel threatened, concerned for their children.'

'Afraid of vigilantes, are you?'

'It's happened before. I've had to move out each time.'

'Why didn't you change your name?'

'Because when you get found out, as you will in time, you become an even more sinister figure, a pervert trying to pretend he's someone else, somebody normal.'

Diamond saw sense in that. 'This was a personal visit, nothing to do with my job. If someone in the police asks me if I know your whereabouts, I'll tell them. I know of no reason why they should.'

'What about the other man, Glazebrook?'

'He won't come near you.'

During the drive back to Salisbury District Hospital, Diamond reflected on his failure. The visit to Wilton had not been one of his more glorious hours. He'd messed up, big time. He could have killed that old man, and all through a mistaken assumption. He felt more shamed, more tarnished, than before he'd started. And he still didn't know how to deal with his private nightmare.

CHAPTER TWENTY-TWO

Lew Rogers was still in the Accident and Emergency waiting area.

'What's the latest?' Diamond asked.

'She's going to be okay. They're keeping her overnight as a precaution, but there's nothing seriously wrong.'

'Can we see her?'

'She's being moved to another ward as we speak, and we can talk to her there. Two of the local traffic guys are waiting to interview her as well.'

'Where are they?'

'Grabbing a coffee while they can.'

'Let's beat them to it.' He called to a nurse.

*　　　*　　　*

They found Kate in a room of her own in a white dressing gown seated in an armchair beside the bed. Her forehead was bruised and she had a bandaged arm. She produced a smile fit to fill the royal circle and said, 'Hi, darlings.'

'You're so lucky,' Diamond told her while Rogers was collecting chairs from the stack outside. 'We saw the state of your car.'

'Is it a write-off?'

'Total. Do you know what caused the accident?'

The smile surfaced again. 'I got into one almighty skid coming round a bend and hit a tree. Simple as that.'

'Going too fast, then?'

'Story of my life.'

'Was anyone else involved?'

'Did I hit anyone?' Her own words took a moment to sink in before the amusement stopped and she scratched her head. 'I'd have noticed, wouldn't I?'

'I meant were you trying to avoid another vehicle? Someone trying to overtake, perhaps?'

The giggle returned. She was in a strangely playful mood. 'Are you offering me an alibi, my love? I appreciate that. But I was a Girl Guide once and promised always to tell the truth. The crash was down to me entirely, driving too fast with my little mind on other things.'

'Like being sacked from the Theatre Royal?'

'God, no, that's water under the bridge. I was daydreaming about all the gorgeous fellows I'd like to sleep with.'

At this point, Rogers came in with two chairs, heard what was said, and dropped one of them. Diamond used the interruption to turn to him and mutter, 'Was she breathalysed?'

Rogers nodded. 'At the scene, I was told. Negative.'

Kate's light-minded talk had to be put down to shock, or a side-effect of medication.

She called out to Diamond, 'Were you asking if I was breathalysed? Christ, yes. They asked me to blow into something as soon as they dragged me out of the wreckage. I'm not stupid. I don't drink and drive.'

'That's all right, then,' Diamond said, finding it hard to believe.

'But they rescued my handbag as well, and luckily I keep a small pick-me-up for stressful situations.' She patted her hand against the pocket of the dressing gown and Diamond saw the glint of a silver flask.

'Do the hospital staff know you've got this?'

She winked. 'You bet they don't. No need to look so disapproving, ducky. It's brandy. It's medicinal.'

The good thing was that the drink hadn't taken over entirely. She was speaking coherently even if the delivery was overblown. Maybe a few extra truths would come out.

'So were you on your way home?'

'Be it ever so humble, there's no place like it, yes. What with this week's show closing, today was my last in the Theatre Royal. I collected my few possessions and walked.'

'Feeling depressed?'

'Positively murderous. Is that what you want to hear?'

'We want honest answers.'

'Well, you're getting them. There are sod-all wardrobe jobs in these parts.'

He took the chair Rogers had brought in and moved it so close he caught the brandy on her breath. 'Why did you let it happen, Kate? You were inviting trouble. You can't deny that the wardrobe room is in a mess. Even I can see it isn't meant to be like that.'

'It wasn't until lately. I ran it like Buckingham Palace for two years. No complaints and oceans of praise and I dressed some spectacular productions in that time, I can tell you, gents. Imagine all the costume changes in a musical, not just a handful of actors, but twenty or more dancers with about nine changes. Wardrobe has to run like mission control to stay on top.'

'What went wrong, then?'

'Sabotage by a certain member of my team.'

'Denise?'

She rolled her eyes upwards. 'I shouldn't speak ill of the dead, but I will. That bitch was out to get me. She'd worked in this theatre longer than anybody and wanted to queen it over us all backstage. She was only a dresser, bugger it, the senior dresser, I admit, but she was supposed to be under me. She saw I was running my wardrobe superbly and she hated it.'

'Jealous?'

'And some. Then things started going wrong. Clothes went missing mysteriously, the washing machine kept flooding, the irons overheated and scorched things. One morning I came in and found my button collection, thousands of them, all over the floor. You're thinking these are silly little glitches, but they ruined my system. Actors would come complaining about their costumes and I'd find the labels had been switched or seams had been loosely tacked and wouldn't stand any sort of use. I was forever trying to catch up. I stayed late, lost sleep, had to take tranquillisers. In the end, I thought what the hell and just did the minimum. I can't tell you the snide remarks and the gripes I endured from that woman on a daily basis. She could have run wardrobe so much better, in her opinion.'

'Had she put in for the job when you applied?'

'No—or she would have been handed it on a plate, according to her. She was one of those people—I expect you have them in the police—who won't take responsibility but are the first to slag off anyone who does.'

'I thought she held down some high-powered jobs before coming to Bath. You were telling me about them when we first spoke.'

'I wouldn't call putting cosmetics on corpses high-powered. I'm talking about heading a key department in a major theatre.'

'Didn't you say she ran a drama group in Manchester?'

'The prison. It wouldn't surprise me one bit if she was an inmate.'

'Manchester is men only.'

'Anyway, it must have been voluntary work, not professional. And when you say "ran" it, I'm sure the screws were there to make sure no one stepped out of line.'

Kate wasn't giving an inch in her demolition of Denise's CV.

'She also toured Bosnia, you said, with some theatre group. Presumably they were professional?'

'It was only a road show, darling. They all fitted into a minibus—cast, crew, costumes, scenery and all the props. That's not theatre. That's busking.'

'Did you ever accuse her of undermining you?'

'Frequently, and she laughed in my face and dared me to take it up with the management. She had a line into the board room, didn't she?'

'Francis Melmot?'

'Yes. Every time I had a crisis in wardrobe, his lordship would hear about it and come gunning for me. Bloody Denise was running a campaign to get me fired and eventually she succeeded.'

'Was she friendly with him?'

'You mean sleeping with the shitbag? I doubt it. She may have dangled the bait, but he's an odd fish, very odd. More like a jellyfish. And she was a stingray.' She giggled again. 'I shouldn't be talking like this. You'll be thinking I topped her. Actually I didn't. I wouldn't risk a life sentence for that creepy dame.'

'Was she telling tales about anyone else?'

'I couldn't tell you.' She smiled. 'Well, I expect she told Melmot about Hedley and me, just more proof that wardrobe had gone to the dogs.'

'How long have you and Hedley Shearman been . . . ?'

'Having it away? Not long. Hed's a serial flirt, I know, but he's sweet and does his best to fight my cause with Melmot.' She sighed. 'I don't think he has much influence really. He was outgunned when they hired Clarion to play Sally Bowles. What a disaster that was. I could have told them.'

'Did you?'

'No, but Hedley did, and they ignored him, poor lamb. They regret it now. The chickens came home to roost with a vengeance.'

'If Clarion was such a risk, I'm surprised they gave her the part.'

'It was the glamour thing, wasn't it? She was a sleb and Melmot was acting like a teenybopper. She stayed at his house. Men are so transparent, but I bet nothing happened. You can be sure his old mum was stalking the corridors all night. Have you met her?'

Diamond let it pass. There were more critical matters to explore while Kate was being so expansive. 'On the evening Clarion was killed, you and Hedley were together in the wardrobe department.'

'Having a five-star shag. You don't have to be

coy. Hed was over the moon because the theatre was saved. I was in a great mood, too, thinking I might get a reprieve and get my job back.'

'This was when he told you Clarion was actually in the theatre?'

'Bless her little cotton socks, yes.'

'Did anyone else backstage know that she was in the box?'

'Melmot, of course. And the security man.'

'Binns.'

'Yes, he's a waste of space, that one. I much prefer old Basil, our regular stage-door keeper. I hope they don't sack Baz.'

'Binns has the freedom to move around the theatre, doesn't he?'

'Part of his job. He should be the last to leave. He checks round and makes sure it's safe to close up at night.'

'Can the staff get in after hours? Say you left your handbag in wardrobe and needed it, could you go back and collect it?'

'No problem. I know the security codes. I could go back tonight if I want and burn the whole place down.'

'But you won't, because you'll be here.'

Her mouth curved upwards. 'Unless I discharge myself. I have a right, you know. I could bum a lift back to Bath with you.'

'No chance,' Diamond said at once. 'You've got an interview coming up with the accident investigation team. They have a lot to ask you about.'

On the way back to the car, Rogers said, 'You decided not to arrest her, then? Is she innocent?'

'That isn't the word I'd choose for Kate,'

366

Diamond said, 'but I doubt if she killed anyone.'

'She had motive, means *and* opportunity.'

'In spades, Lew, in spades. But there's a clear brain and cool planning behind these killings, someone confident enough to think ahead and pass off the murder as something it wasn't. Attention to detail, timing, method. Kate is capable of managing a wardrobe department if everything goes well, but under pressure she lost it. She was outfoxed by Denise. Her system collapsed into chaos. These killings aren't hot-headed crimes. They're planned and followed through with precision. We're not looking for someone who bonks the manager and runs her car into a tree and gets half-pissed in hospital.'

He grinned. 'Now you put it like that, guv, I've got to agree.'

*　　　*　　　*

CID wasn't exactly buzzing when he walked in about 9.30 p.m. Leaman had his feet up. Paul Gilbert had found a football match on the internet. Halliwell was eating a pasty. Ingeborg was texting.

'Okay, people,' Diamond said.

Order was restored. Paul Gilbert replaced the football with a screen saver. 'Hi, guv.'

'I thought you were out and about testing printers.'

'I've checked more than twenty. The theatre, of course, Melmot Hall, Shearman's flat, Binns's security firm, Titus O'Driscoll's house. I even went round all the city copying shops in case it was done there.'

'No joy, then?'

'None at all.'

'What about the actors—Barnes and the rest of them?'

'They're in digs. They don't have printers.'

'Their landladies do.'

He blushed.

'Tomorrow morning,' Diamond said.

Ingeborg, keen to show she, too, had not been idle, said, 'I checked with the lab and they've detected significant levels of Rohypnol in Denise's blood.'

'That ties in nicely. And are we any further on with our major suspects? Keith, you were marking Shearman's card.'

'He's a bundle of nerves, as you saw,' Halliwell said. 'I got a CV out of him. Bath was his first big job as theatre director. He's been through the hoops of assistant stage manager, front-of-house. Worked in any number of provincial theatres. Wants desperately to hang on to this job, so he kowtows to Melmot. If he planned these murders, I can't work out why. His reputation is in shreds.'

'And Melmot?'

'Inge did the digging on him, with some help from me,' Leaman said, feet now under the desk instead of on it. 'He's all front. Likes everyone to think he's the money behind the theatre, but in reality his only asset seems to be the house, and that's too expensive to keep up. I checked with the land registry and it's owned by his mother.'

'So he's not all he seems, but does that make him a murderer? What would he have gained from killing Denise and Clarion?'

'He'd be better off killing his mother,' Ingeborg said.

There were some smiles. Not from Diamond. 'Is that it? Is that where we are at the end of the week, reduced to making tasteless jokes about old ladies?'

Ingeborg turned scarlet.

'How about Binns?' Halliwell said, always the man to steer everyone into calmer waters. 'Fred Dawkins made some notes before he left for the *Sweeney Todd* walk-through.'

'Decent of him. Fancy going to all that trouble,' Diamond said with sarcasm even he regretted after speaking it. His mood was bleak. 'I was told his findings didn't amount to the proverbial hill of beans.'

'Those weren't my words,' Ingeborg said, still smarting from the putdown. She got up and handed him Dawkins' notes. 'Fred worked hard on this before he had to leave.'

He put up a hand in conciliation. 'I'm sorry, team. It's been a bloody long day. Let's draw a line under it. See you in the morning.'

They didn't need any persuading. Desks were cleared, computers put on standby. In two minutes only Ingeborg and Diamond remained.

'About Melmot's mother,' she said. 'I wish I hadn't said that. It was a cheap remark.'

'Forget it, Inge,' he told her. 'I've said plenty cheaper than that, as you well know. You caught me at a bad time.'

'This case must be the toughest ever,' she said.

'Yes, and I'm trying to deal with a personal issue as well. I thought I could settle it today and I didn't.'

'Anything I can help with?'

He shook his head. 'Like I said, it's personal.

You get home. I'll read these notes Fred made.'

After she'd left, he took the notes into his office, but he didn't read them. He closed the door and called Paloma.

'Are you still there at this hour?' she said.

'Winding down. It wasn't one of my better days.' He told her about his visit to Flakey White. 'I came away feeling a bully and an idiot. He appears to have led a blameless life since he got caught.'

'I wouldn't waste sympathy on him,' she said. 'Those under-age girls he had sex with won't have forgotten or forgiven.'

'I know, but it's different from abusing small boys. He never touched me.'

'Are you certain? Do you know about paedophiles? Do they make a distinction or do they just prey on children because they're vulnerable?'

'In this case I am certain. I saw the surprise in his eyes when he realised what I was on about. That was genuine.'

'So you're left in uncertainty again?'

'I asked him if any of the others might have touched me and he pretty well convinced me it didn't happen.'

'Something happened to you. Something deeply upsetting,' Paloma said. 'Let's get this clear. After the play finished you went directly on holiday at the farm in North Wales.'

Her desire to help was well meant. He suppressed the sigh that was coming and repeated the salient facts. 'Where my sister had her eleventh birthday and for a treat we were taken to the Arcadia Theatre at Llandudno and I refused to stay in there. I kicked up a fuss even before the

370

show started.'

'You were in your seat?'

'Yes.'

'So you hadn't objected to going into the theatre? Whatever this upset was, it happened when you were in there. Do you see what I'm saying, Peter? It wasn't the idea of going inside.'

'It is now. I damn near throw up when I approach the entrance.'

'But the first time it happened, you didn't. I was thinking this over last night. You told me your theatre phobia—you don't call it that, I know, but let's give it a name for clarity's sake—you said it didn't affect you some time later when you were taken to the Mermaid Theatre.'

'For *Treasure Island*. I was fine. Loved it. Can't tell you why.'

'Yet *Julius Caesar* at the Old Vic made you ill.'

'I walked out before it started. My teacher only found out later. Are you going to tell me the choice of play makes all the difference?'

'No, I'm not. It's obvious that the theatre does.'

He stared unseeing across the empty CID room. 'But why?' Paloma's reasoning seemed to be circular. He had no expectation of a breakthrough.

'Can you remember any other theatre where you weren't aware of the phobia and just enjoyed the show?'

He didn't have to dig deeply in his memory. His theatre-going didn't amount to much. 'Once when I was in Chichester with Steph we saw a comedy by some guy from somewhere up north, Scarborough, I think.'

'Ayckbourn.'

'Was it? You know better than me. Anyway,

371

there were no alarms for me. It was very funny.'

'Chichester,' Paloma said. 'Now that's interesting. Chichester has a thrust stage. It projects out into the audience, with the seating around it. And the Mermaid was open stage as well.'

'Does that make a difference?'

'You're the one who can answer that. There's no curtain in an open-stage theatre.'

'True.'

'No curtain, Peter, and no problems for you. Do you follow me?'

'Are you saying I have a fear of curtains? I'd never go anywhere if I did.'

'Theatre curtains. Bath has curtains. So does the Old Vic. And no doubt the Arcadia at Llandudno. As soon as your family were seated, you couldn't get out fast enough. Am I on to something?'

'Search me. Curtains.' But he tried to give it more serious thought. He couldn't deny that he'd gone to some lengths to avoid looking at the Theatre Royal curtain—the treasured house drapes donated by the Chaplin family. 'That would narrow it down for sure.'

'Did something unpleasant happen with the curtain in that play you were in as a child?'

'Nothing I can remember. I've no memory of the curtain. I suppose they had one. It was just a church hall.'

'They surely would. Give it some thought. It may yet come back to you.'

Enlightened? In truth, no. He'd said the right things to please her. She cared about him, and he appreciated that.

After putting down the phone he picked up the

372

notes Dawkins had made on Charlie Binns, the security man. As a piece of research, it was all he could have asked for. Fred was a pain in many ways, but give him a job like this and he was as reliable as anyone on the team. Binns, aged thirty-six, was a Londoner, born in Stepney to a couple who managed a dry-cleaning shop, a poor scholar who failed most of his GCSEs, joined the army as an apprentice and served until 1996, ending as a corporal. He'd had a series of jobs in the building trade, followed by two years as an assistant undertaker. He had then started in the security business as a part-time bouncer for various pubs and nightclubs. Twice divorced, he had a child by the first marriage and had defaulted a number of times on the maintenance payments. Over the last three years he'd held down a regular job with his current security firm and resumed the payments. He was living alone in a rented flat in Twerton, to the west of Bath. He belonged to a martial arts club and was a black belt in judo.

Below, Dawkins had written:

FOR FURTHER INVESTIGATION
Possible links to Denise
1. Army experience. Bosnian War? Check if his regiment was there when she was touring.
2. Employment in undertaker's. A long shot, but where did she work?
Possible links to Clarion
Bouncer at clubs. Pop concerts? Protection?

This was better than a solid piece of research, in Diamond's estimation. There was enough in the end notes alone to show Dawkins was thinking outside the box. Even if none of these potential links matched up, the analysis was intelligent and thorough.

Was Charlie Binns rising up the scale as a suspect? The motive wasn't clear, but there was enough to keep him in the frame. If he and Denise had crossed paths in Bosnia or even some funeral parlour, and got into a spat and then chance brought them together again at the theatre, maybe there was a motive. Old enmities could have triggered the violence.

He decided to take another look at Denise's original statement about the Clarion scarring episode. Fred Dawkins had put it on the computer, but Diamond liked reading things on paper and he'd got the printed version in a folder along with the pages of speed-writing from Dawn Reed's notebook. Did Denise mention the trip to Bosnia, or had that come up later? He thought he'd heard it first from Kate. And now, on checking, he confirmed he was right. Nothing about the previous work experience was there in Denise's words.

How reliable was Kate's memory?

A sound in the office outside disturbed him. He got up and opened the door. Fred Dawkins had walked in looking untypically svelte in his rehearsal gear of black top, trousers and black trainers.

'How did the walk-through go?' Diamond asked.

'You gave me a shock, guv,' he said, clapping a hand to his brow as if still in theatrical mode. 'I was starting to think CID had closed down, at least for tonight. The walk-through? Pedestrian, in more than one sense of the word. However, we'll persevere. I keep reminding myself that they are all amateurs, even the assistant chief constable. Do you mind if I check my voicemail? I'm hoping for an answer to an enquiry I made about Mr Binns.'

'Go ahead. I was trying to understand Dawn Reed's speed-reading. I'm getting good at it.' He returned to his desk. He hadn't been there long when Dawkins reappeared, as pleased as if he'd just hoofed the umbrella dance from *Singin' in the Rain*.

'A development, guv.'

'What's that?'

'I asked Alert Security, Binns's employers, how he came to be assigned to the Theatre Royal and they said he volunteered. They have the contract for the security system and he's been on duty in and around the theatre before. After all the publicity over the first night he pointed out that the stage door was the one weak point, relying on human control, rather than the digital locks everywhere else. He offered to man it and was accepted.'

Diamond nodded. 'So he volunteered. This is getting interesting.'

'There is more. I asked my contact at Alert about Binns's other duties in recent months and was informed that he is often on nightclub duty.'

'As a bouncer?'

'Indeed. I enquired what their duties consist of, and it seems they are there to deter undesirables, gatecrashers and any under the obvious influence of drink or drugs. In some cases they won't admit people unless they submit to a search.'

Diamond's patience was wearing thin. 'Fred, I know what a bouncer does.'

'Ah, but on a number of occasions they seize

375

drugs.'

He raised his thumb. 'Okay, I'm with you. I think I see where this is going.'

'I asked for chapter and verse and that was the voicemail I just got back. They confirm that on two occasions in the past six months Binns confiscated a quantity of Rohypnol.'

'Now you're talking.' And his own pulse was quickening. 'They should have handed the stuff to us.'

'I'm sure they did, or they wouldn't have told me,' Dawkins said. 'But it's not beyond the wit of a bent security man to pocket some pills himself and hand in a smaller quantity.'

Diamond nodded. 'Mr Charlie Binns has some questions to answer. Where would he be right now?'

Dawkins glanced at his watch. 'Normally, he'd still be at the theatre, but as the performances are cancelled I expect he's at home in Twerton.'

'A dawn raid might be timely.'

'I can lead it if you wish.'

'Thanks, but one of the older hands had better be in charge. Get a night's sleep.' He raised a finger. 'One thing before you go, Fred. You were there yesterday with Ingeborg when we found the suicide note on the stage. Have you mentioned it to anyone in the theatre?'

'No, guv. You asked us not to.'

'Good. The killer will be getting nervous about that note, not knowing it was found. He or she will think it's still tucked away in the German stove and doing no good there. In fact now that we're saying openly that Denise was murdered, it's a liability. The killer needs to go back and remove it before the set is broken up tomorrow. I've laid a trap in case this happens tonight.'

'May I help?'

Diamond smiled. 'Keeno, always volunteering. You'll learn. No, two officers are there already waiting to pounce. You know them both: Dawn Reed and George Pidgeon. Anyone gets inside the theatre, he's nicked.'

'If I may put it succinctly, guv, that's neat.'

'I wish you'd put it succinctly more often.'

After Dawkins left, Diamond remained in his office until after midnight dissecting the case, every statement, each report the investigation had prompted. This was a useful time to be at work, when the phones were silent, the press had gone away and he could deal with the information in his own way, circling, underlining and adding question marks, all on paper, rather than a screen.

Methodically he went through the process of sorting fact from mere suspicion. Between documents, he paused and stared at the wall, deep in thought. Until recently the killing of Denise had seemed like a direct consequence of Clarion's scarring. Now he was considering it in isolation.

He returned to the statement made by Denise about the scarring incident and read the opening words for the umpteenth time:

I've worked here six years and never experienced anything so awful as this.

Later developments had given this apparently innocuous document an importance he hadn't grasped until now. Thanks to Dawn Reed's speed-writing and Fred Dawkins' thoroughness it was a virtual transcript of the words Denise had used, ranging over her admission that she'd applied the make-up using her own kit, on the instructions of the director, Sandy Block-Swell, who had flown to America—which had led into a typical Dawkins red herring about double-barrelled names, leading on to a discussion about Clarion's stage name and other showbiz examples. Not all the conversational asides in the speed-written version were in the printed statement, but her testimony about the Clarion incident was entirely accurate.

'Bloody hell.'

He held the witness statement closer and stared at it. He had the answer in his hand. He reached for the fake suicide note and re-examined that.

He was stunned, but there was only one conclusion. Both documents had been printed on the same machine.

He knew what he must do. He went back to the computer and accessed the personal files of his own CID team. Then he turned to the brief notes he had on Denise's early career, the assortment of jobs she'd had, from undertaker's assistant to touring Bosnia.

Manchester Prison interested him most. He phoned there and asked for the duty governor. The man on the end of the line had obviously been asleep. He sounded peeved to get a call at this late hour, but he soon understood the urgency and promised to check for the information Diamond was requesting.

Meanwhile there was more to check. Flying in the face of his prejudice against the internet Diamond went online to search for names on the death registers. Next he phoned the National Identification Service at Scotland Yard and challenged another unfortunate on night duty to come up with information. He was getting close to a result and the indications couldn't have been worse. His reasoning was taking him into territory he hadn't visited until tonight, moving from disbelief to inescapable fact to near horror.

A mass of information was faxed from Manchester. He leafed through it rapidly and with a heavy heart.

Then his mobile rang. It came as a shock at this hour. He delved into his pocket for it. 'Yes?'

'Guv, this is Dawn Reed, in the theatre.'

'Speak up. It's a poor line.'

'Dawn Reed. I'm worried. Someone has got into the building. George and I heard noises. We separated, to cover both sides of the place. We arranged to stay in contact on our personal radios. Now his has gone silent. I can't raise him.'

'Where are you now?'

'The front stalls, crouching down between the seats.'

'Don't move from there, whatever happens, do you hear me? I'm coming at once.'

CHAPTER TWENTY-THREE

The timing had brought its own problems. The key members of Diamond's team were all off duty, settling into deep sleep by now. He could rouse them, tell them he needed them at the theatre in the shortest possible time, but for what? He didn't know yet, so there was no way of briefing them. They would come ready for action, expecting an emergency. Experience told him it was a huge error to go in with all guns blazing. Lives could be at stake here. Better, surely, for him to make a recce, assess the dangers, take the crucial decisions at the scene. But he would still need back-up.

All of this went through his head as he hurried downstairs. He paused at the front desk to tell a startled duty sergeant a major incident was taking place. Armed police were needed immediately at the Theatre Royal, enough to cover every exit. They were to stand guard outside the building pending further instructions. No one except himself was to be allowed in or out. Then he dashed to his car and headed for Saw Close.

He blamed himself for the cock-up. When he'd asked PCs Pidgeon and Reed to patrol the theatre at night it had seemed a smart idea, a baited trap. The killer would surely want to retrieve that so-called suicide note. Huge mistake. The note was not bait at all. What he'd done was set up the young officers as targets and now they were in danger of becoming the next victims.

They could be dead already.

He drove through the quiet streets at a speed that by his standards was death-defying, ignoring traffic lights, burning rubber at the turns.

The square three-storey façade with its balustrade skyline loomed over Saw Close, a sinister grey-black monolith deprived of any of the magic of theatre. All the lighting at the front of the old building was off at this hour. Diamond glimpsed the outline as he entered the forecourt from Upper Borough Walls and shuddered so strongly that it showed in the steering. He tightened his grip on the wheel, looked away from the theatre, brought the car to a screeching halt in

380

front of the entrance and resolved that this was no time to let his hang-ups get to him. He was going in, come what may.

He'd made good time. He stepped out and looked around. He could hear a siren wailing not far off, but no response cars had arrived.

This was it, then. He was going in, alone and in darkness.

A side entrance would be best. This side of the Garrick's Head in the paved alley were two doorways with the Victorian signs for 'Pit' and 'Gallery' still engraved above them. Hell or heaven? He chose hell. He fished in his pocket and—after a galling moment of doubt whether he'd brought it with him—took out the card with the door codes. He stepped back from the shadow to catch some faint illumination from the streetlamps in Saw Close. He could just read the combination.

The lock on the door was a bigger challenge. There wasn't enough light to make out the numbers. In the days of cigarette lighters, he'd have known what to do. After sinking to his knees for a closer look, he still couldn't see enough.

Smash the door down? He might have to. But he didn't want to announce his arrival in such an obvious way.

Resourceful as always in an emergency, he felt in his pocket for his mobile, opened it fully and the light was enough to see by. He stabbed in the code, pushed the door inwards and closed it behind him without a sound.

Total darkness. Good thing he knew he was in the corridor to the left of the auditorium. He'd be acting on memory from this point on. Maybe as his eyes adjusted he'd be able to make out a little more. Two tentative steps forward and he reached out and felt his palms against a cold, glassy surface that moved. He'd almost knocked a picture off the wall. He turned away and took a step left, a longer one than he intended. The floor was raked, like the auditorium.

By a series of shuffling steps he progressed down the slope as far as the door he remembered going through to enter the stall seating area. On reaching out, he found it was already ajar. Either the young officers or the killer must have come this way. The advantage was that he could pass through silently.

Dawn Reed had said on the phone that she was crouching between rows of seats, but where? He groped his way forward until he felt the padded arm of a seat and then grasped it while he listened for some sign of life.

Absolute silence.

He made a throat-clearing sound that wouldn't carry far at all. If she was close and heard him she might respond.

Nothing.

He looked around him. His eyes were adapting because he could make out the nearest row of seat backs, the vertical pillar of the proscenium structure and the curve of the royal circle. Yet he was getting a sense he was alone in this theatre, and with it came the suspicion that he was too late.

He could see enough now to move along the gangway to check whether Dawn Reed was still hiding between the rows of seats as he'd ordered. He would surely make out the dark form of someone crouching. She'd said the front stalls. He checked them all, going way past the front section, under the overhang of the royal circle and then across and down the other side.

She wasn't there.

Failure overwhelmed him. He'd obviously got here too late. Those hours in his office dissecting the statements had taken too long. Twenty minutes earlier and he'd have saved her.

Then he heard a small sound. Something had fallen and hit the floor not far away. In an old building like this it could have been boards contracting, or a fragment of plaster dropping off a damaged section of ceiling. A mouse could have dislodged something.

The sound had come from up on the stage. Up to now he'd avoided looking there. He turned.

His nightmare. The huge velvet curtains presented by the Chaplin family hung across the proscenium, thirty feet in length, crimson and gold when the lights were up, black as sin right now and he knew for certain that Paloma had been right about the fear he'd had since childhood. He was terrorised by curtains, drawn curtains hiding something unimaginably bad.

Pull them aside, Peter Diamond, and see what you get.

The shakes began. They started in his hands and spread rapidly through his entire body. Exceptional conditions, the dark, the solitude, the cold surroundings, his closeness to the curtains and the absolute necessity of seeing behind them, combined to make this experience more alarming than any of his previous panic attacks.

Get a grip, Diamond. This is your trauma. Engage with it. Analyse. Understand.

He stared at the place where the curtains met. His heart thumped against his ribcage. An image was forming in his brain.

As an eight-year-old he was back in the farmhouse his family had rented for their Welsh holiday. Night-time: his sleep disturbed by a strange sound between a bellow and a howl of pain, repeated several times over. Driven to discover more, he'd got out of bed and crept downstairs. The sound was close by, outside the house.

In the living room, a modern feature had been added, most likely as a selling point to visitors who rented the place, a floor-to-ceiling picture window that looked out across a field towards Snowdonia. A stunning view by day. By night long curtains were drawn across.

He had crossed the room and pulled the curtains aside.

He pictured what he'd suppressed all these years: the massive head of a beast with gaping, blood-red jaws and hairy lips drooling saliva in long threads. A huge pink lolling tongue. Manic staring white-edged eyes. And devilish horns.

He'd seen it as a child and never wanted a sight of it again.

Stay with it, Diamond.

He clung to the memory, hideous as it was. Part of his brain resisted, wanting to cut the scene. He refused. He had to know the truth. By force of will he succeeded. Out of the horror came an explanation. After all the years, he recognised the monster for what it was: a cow. His sister had told him on the phone about the distressed cow parted from its calf and keeping the family awake with its

384

heart-rending sounds of distress. The poor beast was in the field behind the farmhouse. It had come close to the house, right up to the window, to make its protest. Man had taken away its calf. Man lived in the house. Man should hear its calls.

To a young boy unused to the country, the sudden close-up of the cow's head at a level with his own had been horrific, enough to traumatise him. From that night on, drawn curtains would induce this petrified reaction while the censor in his brain would dumb down the real cause, refusing to revisit the image. He'd experienced the first such crisis the same week in the theatre at Llandudno. He'd panicked. He'd been incapable of explaining why. The effect had repeated itself each time he saw long curtains. Even the prospect of going into a theatre became an ordeal because of what was inside.

Was the fear conquered? Knowledge is strength. To understand is to overcome, he told himself.

Dawn Reed wasn't where she'd said she would be. She was in danger of being murdered. It was essential to look behind those curtains.

He reached up to the stage. The level was higher than he expected and he was no athlete, but the strength returned to his limbs.

He hauled himself up, thrust his arms between the heavy drapes and parted them.

CHAPTER TWENTY-FOUR

Some lights were on, not powerful, but dazzling to Diamond's eyes. The set of Christopher

Isherwood's Berlin flat was still in place as he'd instructed, the three walls lined with the solid-looking furniture dominated by the stove. On the sofa at centre stage lay PC George Pidgeon, bound hand and foot with duct tape. A strip of it was across his mouth. His eyes were open, but not moving.

Dead?

Diamond pushed the curtain aside and crossed the stage.

The eyes slid to the right and fixed on him. George Pidgeon was alive. He braced his body and struggled.

Diamond leaned over the young man and started easing the gag from his cheek, but Pidgeon jerked his face away, the tape ripped from his skin and he yelled, 'Behind you!'

In the microsecond before the shout, Diamond had seen Pidgeon's eyes widen in alarm. He flung himself across the constable's body and the blow intended for his skull caught his shoulder instead. It was a glancing hit rather than full impact because it slid down his ribs, but it still felt as if it had splintered his shoulder blade. All he could do for protection from another blow was make a piston movement with his arm. His elbow struck something solid. There was a grunt from behind.

Pidgeon yelled, 'Guv!'

He rolled left. The weapon whizzed past his ear, struck the upholstery and ripped a gash in the fabric. It was a claw hammer.

Diamond's reflex action brought him crashing to the stage floor. All he could do from here was make a grab for his attacker's legs. He got a hand on one leg, but the other kicked his arm away.

Even so, he'd done enough to unsettle his assailant. He watched the legs step away, turn and run off the stage.

Now it was down to priorities: go in pursuit, or release Pidgeon? His right arm felt numb after the hammer blow. He was going to need assistance. Besides, he had to find out what he was dealing with. He got to his feet and worked at the tape around Pidgeon's wrists.

'Guv, you won't believe who did this,' Pidgeon started to say.

'I don't need telling,' Diamond said. 'Where's Dawn?'

'I can't tell you.'

'When did you last see her?'

'I don't know how long I've been here. He grabbed me from behind and put something over my face. I think it was chloroform. When I came to, I was lying here, trussed up.' The last of the tape parted from his arms. 'I can untie my feet.'

'She phoned me,' Diamond told him. 'Said she was hiding somewhere between the seats, but she's not there any more. He means to kill her if he hasn't already.'

'Dawn? Why?'

'There isn't time to explain. He must have got her backstage.'

'He could have left the building.'

'No chance. All the exits are covered. He's in here somewhere. We need the house lights on. There must be a control room.'

'Back there.' Pidgeon pointed towards the auditorium. 'I'll see what I can do.' He finished freeing his legs.

'Right. I'll check behind the scenes.'

'You're not armed. D'you want my baton?'

'Keep it. After that whack on the shoulder I couldn't lift it.' He crossed to the prompt side, glanced up in the wings to make sure no one was in the DSM's position, and moved along the passage towards the three main dressing rooms. He located a light switch and was relieved when it worked. On trying each of the doors, he found them locked. What next, then? He could dash upstairs to four, five, six and seven, but would a killer on the run risk being trapped up a staircase that led nowhere else? Anyone so familiar with the layout would surely have taken a route with more chances of escape.

He moved on to the fly floor. Faint beams of light leaking from the other side of the scenery allowed him to see his way at ground level but the vast space above his head could have been the inside of a coffin. For a moment he stopped and listened. There was no sound. It was wise to remember that if the killer was lurking here he, too, had just enough light to see. He edged forward with caution, primed for another hammer attack.

He'd just crossed to stage right when he was stopped in his tracks by a voice speaking his name immediately above his head.

Impossible. Nobody was there.

He heard the hiss of static. He squinted in the poor light and found himself looking at a loudspeaker.

The speaker boomed again. 'You can stop charging around like a demented elephant. She's been dead twenty minutes.'

'You bloody maniac. Where is she?' he shouted

back, and got no reply except the click of a disconnection. 'You gain nothing by killing her. You're finished.'

The last word echoed back to him from the fly tower.

He turned and ran back towards the opposite side, thinking that the DSM's console must be the source, but nobody was there. Obviously there were other points in the building linked to the loudspeaker system.

Dead twenty minutes: callous words spoken with the disregard he expected of this killer. If true, this was the worst outcome imaginable. Dawn Reed was young, inexperienced, brave. The killing of any police officer on duty is rightly treated as the ultimate crime. She'd been here obeying orders, his orders, his alone. He should never have sent her in.

He shuddered, more in horror than fear. Urging himself to concentrate on what he had to do, he accepted that some, at least, of the killer's words couldn't be denied. This was, indeed, a pointless pursuit. The building was too large for two men to search. Soon there would be reinforcements he could call on. The arrest would follow. The real urgency had been to save Dawn's life. How much reliance could he place on the words of a murderer on the run?

In this case, enough for huge concern. This man picked his words with care.

The tannoy crackled again. This time the voice was Pidgeon's. 'House lights are on, guv.'

'Okay, I'm coming,' he said. His words weren't going to be heard. He spoke them to release some tension. He moved fast around the outside of the set, pushed open the scenic double doors and crossed the stage. The curtain held none of those childhood fears now.

He parted the heavy lengths of velvet and stepped forward, and the horseshoe auditorium was before him in all its magnificence, the best view of the house you would get, every light now glowing, including the central chandelier. The great actors of seven generations had stood on this spot and delivered curtain speeches. But the significance was lost on Diamond. He was watching for a movement, and there was nothing. No one was in sight.

The sound of a handclap began, a slow, ironic slapping of palms. One pair of unseen hands was mocking his appearance in front of the curtain. He couldn't tell where it was from, except that it seemed close, not the back of the theatre or the upper tiers. Presently it died away.

If nothing else, he knew for certain that the killer was out front and could see him. Some kind of resolution was imminent.

He decided to remain where he was. This was as good a vantage point as any. Staring out at the rows of empty seats, he tried to picture the sequence of events. Dawn had been out of sight crouching down in the stalls. Presumably she'd been discovered, attacked and taken somewhere nearby. Moving her upstairs would have been impractical.

A voice surprisingly close called out, 'Do you want a prop? A skull would do nicely.'

He knew who it was. As ever, the words were spoken with deliberation and wrapped in some allusion he didn't understand. 'What did you say?'

'What are you up to, standing centre stage? Is this an audition? You'll never make a Hamlet, but you might get by as one of the gravediggers.'

He glanced right and left. No one was in front of the curtain with him and the voice hadn't come from behind. It wasn't amplified.

'That's a clue for you, the *Hamlet* reference. They always use the trap for the graveyard scene. Her body is below where you are standing, in the understage,' the voice continued, relishing its advantage. 'I don't suppose you knew there was anything down there. You get to it through the band room. No need to hurry, however. You're too late to make any difference.'

Now he could see the speaker—in the lower of the two boxes to his right: the Agatha Christie, a fitting place for a murderer's last stand.

Fred Dawkins.

The traitor had been speaking just out of Diamond's sight-line, masked by the near side of the box. Now he had stepped into view, close enough to shake hands if Diamond were to move along the front edge of the stage.

A handshake was not in the plans of either.

'Keep your distance. I'm still holding the hammer,' Dawkins warned. 'I'll pay you a compliment, Superintendent. I was streets ahead of you before tonight. Now I'm a mere half dozen yards away and I don't flatter myself that I'll walk out of this theatre a free man. So let's exchange some home truths. What changed your mind? You weren't planning to come here when we last spoke.'

Centre stage was new territory for Peter Diamond. He wasn't comfortable in this position, being invited to lay out his case, yet he couldn't risk walking off when he had the man in sight. The sensible response was to engage with Dawkins for as long as possible in the hope that George Pidgeon would see what was going on and come to his aid. So he started to voice some of the things that properly should have been spoken under caution in an interview room with a tape running. 'I got your number, quite literally,' he told Dawkins. 'Five-one-eight-nine, on a seven-year rap in Manchester Prison, Strangeways as it was known then, 1983 to 1990, for fraud, embezzlement, false pretences, depriving old ladies of their life's savings. I spoke to the deputy governor this evening. You're a con man, known at that time as Hector Dacreman.'

'Quite a leap from Strangeways to sergeant of police,' Dawkins said, unimpressed, as if there was room for doubt.

'Yes, but you're good at what you do. I asked for the names of prisoners active in the drama group that flourished then, the group Denise Pearsall supervised as a visiting tutor, and I was told convict Dacreman, 5189, was one of the leads in the 1988 production of *Waiting for Godot*. There is even a photo from the prison magazine, scanned and e-mailed to me. The likeness satisfies me. It would satisfy anyone.'

'It's of Estragon, presumably.'

'Dacreman, I said. That was the name you were known by.'

'Is the actor wearing make-up? Is it really me, do you think? They say everyone has a double somewhere in the world.'

'You kept the same initials, too. Hector

Dacreman. Horatio Dawkins.'

He gave a sarcastic laugh. 'Nothing gets past you.'

'They're sending your fingerprints.'

'One way or another, you seem to think you have snared me.'

'You snared yourself,' Diamond said, 'the first day you worked in CID.'

A slight frown. 'How was that?'

'Your version of the interview with Denise in the case file. I asked you to type up all the witness statements. When I compared the printout with the notes Dawn Reed made with her speed-writing, I noticed you left off the first words Denise spoke when she saw you: "Have we met before?"'

'Small talk,' Dawkins said. 'You don't put small talk in a witness statement.'

'Not small in this case. It came as a huge shock for you that Denise thought she recognised you. You quickly glossed over that by saying she must have seen you patrolling the streets of Bath and she seems to have accepted that. She wouldn't have expected one of her former convict actors to reinvent himself as a police officer.'

Dawkins smirked in self-congratulation.

'In your prison days she wouldn't even have known you were a con artist,' Diamond continued. 'It's not the thing for visiting tutors to ask the inmates about their crimes.'

'Please go on. I'm learning volumes.'

'So the moment you met again at the theatre and she thought she knew you, she was at risk of being murdered. You're a vastly ambitious man. Conning your way into the police after serving a prison term was a triumph, difficult and

393

dangerous, but you managed it, a massive investment of time and deception. I've seen your record, the lies, the forged references that got you into Hendon as a recruit.'

'And if you've seen my file you'll know Horatio Dawkins was the star of his year at Hendon.'

'Amazingly, yes. Praised for supporting the young recruits straight out of school and improving morale. Eighteen weeks of training and then a job in the Met, and within four years a sergeant's stripes and the move to Bath Central. Not enough. You set your sights on a transfer to CID. And what an opportunity arrived when the assistant chief constable joined the BLOGs group you were choreographing.'

He smiled again. 'There is a saying: he dances well to whom fortune pipes.' His ego couldn't resist these asides, regardless that they were confirming Diamond's case.

'And yet Denise had the knowledge to destroy all you'd achieved. She had to be eliminated. You thought of a way of killing her that would be passed off as suicide. You set an elaborate trap. First you armed yourself with Rohypnol. As a sergeant from uniform you'd had ample opportunities to acquire the drug, confiscating it from night-clubbers. An opportunist like you isn't going to surrender all the drugs he snatches.'

'Speculation.'

'We found traces in dressing room eleven.'

'I know that, but you can't link it with me.'

'Forensics will. Let's stay with the trap you set for Denise. You sent her some kind of message to lure her into the theatre on Tuesday night after everyone else had left. My guess is that you offered to tell her the true explanation for Clarion's accident. Poor woman, she was distraught about it, half fearing she'd made some terrible mistake with the make-up, so the chance of redemption was sure to reel her in. She was to meet you in dressing room eleven. You're familiar with the layout of the theatre, having choreographed several BLOGs productions. Knowing the door codes, as you did, you could come and go at will. You met Denise, slipped Rohypnol into her drink, took her on to the riggers' platform in the fly tower and pushed her off. It was meant to be interpreted as suicide.'

'And does that complete the case for the prosecution?' Dawkins asked in a measured voice as if he was a judge, not the accused.

'No. There's more. It became increasingly clear to me that someone on our side of the investigation was bent. The murderer was getting inside information.'

'Such as?'

'The call that came in from Bristol police about Clarion discharging herself from hospital. You put it on computer instead of telling me directly.'

'I acted properly, filing the call. As a newcomer I wasn't to know you need telling everything by word of mouth.'

'That wasn't the reason. You were alarmed. Clarion was a loose cannon. None of us knew what she'd been thinking while she was stuck in hospital or what she intended to do next. You could see the suicide theory being blown out of the water.'

'Immaterial,' Dawkins said. 'You insisted on keeping an open mind about Denise's suicide.'

'Which was precisely why you decided the time had come to remove all doubt.'

'You can't believe the suicide note was *my* doing.'

'Oh, but I do. I know. It was deviously planned, I give you that. You came up with the suggestion that an extra powder box spiked with caustic soda was hidden somewhere backstage. I sent you and Ingeborg to search for it. You had the fake note ready in your pocket. While you were making the search, you planted the note in the German oven and of course it was discovered after I arrived. Neat. But there was a flaw.'

'The famous specks of ink?' Dawkins said, still unruffled.

'Yes. I had Paul Gilbert checking everyone's printer and he couldn't find the right one. The reason is that it was in our own CID room. Tonight after everyone had gone I examined the statements you typed and I looked at Denise Pearsall's and saw the telltale specks in exactly the formation we found on the suicide note. It was bloody obvious that it had been printed in our own office and we had a killer on the team.'

'No prizes for guessing who you thought of first.'

'I had to be certain. I wanted to know precisely who Horatio Dawkins was and how he came to join the police service. I had a hunch that you used the old trick of stealing a dead man's identity, so I looked in the death registers for someone called Dawkins of about your age who fell off the perch between 1990 and 1994. I found him, got his date and place of birth and matched them to the details on your file.'

'Admirable,' Dawkins said in a flat voice. It may have been meant as sarcastic, but it sounded like defeat.

'Getting back to Clarion,' Diamond said, 'Bristol police told you the hotel she was staying in.'

'The Cedar of Lebanon. Nothing secret about that.'

'Except that you decided to drive over there last night and find out what was going on. You called on her at the hotel, didn't you?'

'What makes you think I did?'

'It's the logical explanation. Clarion wanted to talk. She had a bad conscience about what she'd done on the first night, the caustic soda she'd smeared on her own face without fully realising how damaging it was. Denise was dead and the theatre faced a commercial disaster. She wanted to make amends, give money to the theatre. But the danger for you was that she was about to destroy the theory of Denise's suicide you'd painstakingly built up. Denise didn't use the caustic soda. Clarion did. Clarion was a chronic self-harmer. You learned that she was about to confess everything to the theatre management.'

'What am I supposed to have done about it?'

'You must have thought about murdering her in the hotel. It would have been simpler, but I guess something went wrong. Maybe you were seen on a security camera. Whatever it was, you could afford to wait for the next opportunity. You got back in your car and followed her limo to the theatre and murdered her there. Nobody suspected you because nobody knew you were in the building that night. You let yourself in through the side entrance while the first half was in progress, waited for the interval, entered the box and suffocated her with a plastic bag. You were out of there and away without anyone seeing you.'

'Leaving no traces.'

'I wouldn't count on that. The scene of crime people have been through. As you and I know, DNA is a marvellous aid to detection, but getting a result takes time. The men in white coats can't keep up with the pace in a fast-moving case like this one.'

'So it's down to you and me to sort things out,' Dawkins said.

'You, me and the armed police waiting at every exit. Waiting for Godot.'

'Estragon, to be precise,' Dawkins said. 'I played Estragon.'

'That's good, because the only thing I know about the play is that Godot never arrived.' Diamond paused. 'Where are you?'

Dawkins had vanished.

Simple, of course, to do a disappearing act when all it needs is a step backwards into the box. And Diamond had no way of stopping him. The mobile would have been useful at this point, but he'd forgotten it existed.

With all exits sealed, Dawkins could hide, but he wouldn't escape. Diamond's mind was on a more disturbing duty.

He stepped to the front of the stage and let himself down to floor level, the orchestra pit. He tried the door to the understage area normally used by the musicians and found that it opened. There were steps down into the band room. The light from the auditorium allowed him to see a little way ahead and he found a light switch.

He discovered Dawn Reed lying on the floor towards the back. She was bound and gagged with duct tape, as George Pidgeon had been. Like him,

398

she was still alive. Dawkins had conned and lied to the last.

Peter Diamond wasn't a religious man, but he thanked God, just the same.

CHAPTER TWENTY-FIVE

The final-night party for *Sweeney Todd* was held in September that year in the Garrick's Head. No question: the show had been a resounding success. Every performance had sold out and the reviews were better than anyone could remember for a BLOG production. If some of the choreography had looked a little under-rehearsed, not one of the critics mentioned it. Allowance was made for the loss of the movement director before the rehearsals really got serious.

Georgina was triumphant. She'd reserved a whole row in the stalls for her colleagues in the police and they didn't let her down. Paloma was there in her own right as costume consultant and she insisted that Diamond was present the same evening.

'A good show?' Paloma asked him after he'd downed a large beer.

'Very good. Pretty graphic, I have to say, some of the throat-cutting.'

'Don't throw a wobbly, whatever you do. You're over all that, I thought.'

'Happily, yes.'

'And the case? Is that all wrapped up now?'

'It is.'

'Georgina was telling everyone at the bar about

young PC Pidgeon making the arrest on the staircase behind the boxes. Apparently he did a brilliant job, got an armlock on the guilty man and delivered him to the police van. He and Dawn Reed are both being recommended for promotion.'

'So I heard.'

'Well, the armed police weren't needed after all.'

'Right,' he said. 'Georgina is pissed off about the cost of the operation. It was all double-time, being at night, and we're way over budget. I told her if she hadn't insisted on Dawkins joining CID, none of this would have happened.'

'You won't get a commendation for tact.'

'It was the truth.'

'Are you certain of that?'

'Well, I guess he would still have done the murders as a uniformed sergeant, but it would have been more difficult covering them up.'

'When will the case go to trial?'

'Not this year. The law works slowly.'

'And then he'll get life?'

'That's automatic, but don't waste any sympathy on him. I feel sorry for the prison governor who gets him.'

Titus O'Driscoll joined them, a glass of wine in his hand. 'Do you mind if I butt in? There's something I'm anxious to know.'

'What's that?' Briefly, Diamond wondered if it was about his relationship with Paloma, but it was not.

'When you and I went backstage and looked at the number one dressing room, we found a tortoiseshell butterfly, dead, and to my

400

embarrassment I passed out.'

'I remember.'

'Furthermore, I was informed that when you searched the box where Clarion was murdered, you found a second butterfly caught in a cobweb.'

'That's right.'

'My question is this: did the murderer have anything to do with the butterflies?'

'You mean did he place them there himself?' Diamond paused for thought. 'It's one question he wasn't asked. You're thinking about the superstition, aren't you? If you want my opinion, Titus, they found their own way there. It was a natural occurrence, or supernatural, depending on your point of view, and I think I know what yours is.'

Titus smiled.